NOAH

a supernatural eco-thriller

Patricia L. Meek

*To my parents, A. J. and Belinda Meek,
for their unconditional love and support.*

And, for the animals.

*Special thanks to the following people whose gift of time, talent,
and energy made this project possible.*

James Gordon Bennett   *Dorothy S Shawhan*
Jeane Cooper   *Caroline Johnson*
Maureen Joyce   *A. H. Hofer*
Rhonda Mouser   *Erika Johnson*
Laura Alford   *Seren Morris*
Lorrie Ogren   *Marika Richards*
James Lengerich   *Alex Cross*

Chapter 1

Noah Noland heard the faucet dripping long before he was ready to open his eyes and face the 180th day of his fifty-sixth year. If he kept his eyes closed, he didn't have to face reality. The reality being he was fifty-six and the slumbering form, curves warmly pressed to the flesh of his back, was twenty-nine. If that wasn't bad enough, her name was Bambi. He had to remind himself every morning that he wasn't a cliché. He wasn't having a mid-life crisis. He wasn't every man's fantasy, although every man he knew wanted to know how he managed to do it, and *do it* was always hushed and vague. Noah reminded himself that he wasn't misogynistic. *Stop the shame…stop the shame…stop the shame.* He repeated the mantra the way Bambi had coached him. She was a psychotherapy graduate student, and so knew many affirming mantras. And if he *was* all of those things, she taught him how to sit with the discomfort.

" Noah," she'd say, "it's just your conditioning. Nobody's going to live your life for you. This is between you, me, and God." Not only was Bambi Bambi, she was Southern … Georgian … very Southern.

She was good for him and he liked to believe he was good for her. They seemed good for each other, and she was so understanding about everything. She didn't complain when he complained about how often he felt tired, aging-carpenter tired. "It's a noble profession," she'd insisted when she'd first met him. Nobody had ever made him feel that good about himself for things he did naturally. She often told him how she loved his hands, how they spoke the rawness of creation. They didn't live together yet, but she had the top drawer of his dresser and half the closet. She also had a toothbrush in the bathroom, which for Noah was about as good a commitment as any. When he came home at night, she smudged him with mountain sage and had a hot bath waiting for him. "Who does this for each other anymore," he would ask.

She would laugh. "We do." She scented the Epsom salts. He discovered that he favored peppermint, and that it did make him feel better. His muscles were less sore. The guys on the site, who were cynics, said, "You'd better enjoy it while it lasts. This time next year …." They would shake their heads. However, they had been together for over a year and it was only getting better. Noah figured this was as close to true love as it was going to get, and he was grateful. For his part, he was willing to do whatever it took not to lose her. She was his greatest gift. He would do *whatever* it took not to lose her.

Her breath was now rising and falling in the rhythm of the dripping faucet. Drip, drip, she breathed in and it was life affirming. Drip, drip from the faucet, and it reminded him how close the world was to dying in this land without rain. They lived outside of Santa Fe, in the desert, and each drip added up. He had to fix that drip today. That was enough to get him out of bed. He gave Bambi a quick kiss. She stirred, but did not wake. Noah went into the bathroom, relieved himself, and then shut the water off from underneath the sink. In the silence, he went about his morning routine: made coffee, fed the dogs, washed out his favorite mug, poured his coffee, and then sipped it while staring out the window in the direction of the arroyo where he would take the dogs for their morning run once he was awake enough to lace up his boots.

He had a modest adobe ranch, straw-bale. It suited his needs, which were quite simple. He had constructed his home, and his was a pride beyond ownership that many men would never know. Because he had built it, there wasn't much room. He didn't need much room: living room, bedroom, kitchen, and bathroom. It was solar. It was uncomplicated and efficient. It taught him how to live like the snake — how to shed what no longer suited him. When there was no more room, he pitched or gave his things away. It was a constant cycle and, as a result, he had minimal material possessions, and the space that opened up for him was as expansive as the desert sky.

Noah finished his coffee. He pulled on his jeans, jersey shirt, laced up his dusty boots, and strapped on his daypack. It was late August, almost September, and it was cooling at night, but it would be several months before the first snow came. Ginger Bear and Red Girl were already at the fence line, wagging, leaping, and wiggling. He gave each of his girls a dog biscuit, opened the gate, and away they went down the trail. The dogs went on ahead, dashed back to check on him, and ran off again, kicking up dust. The morning sun blazed across the desert that was like a dry ocean bottom. The sterile white light brought the rock faces to life in chiaroscuro. Noah called these rocks the sleepers because everywhere he looked another face was revealed. Most of the faces looked as if they were in various poses of repose, and if he stared at them long enough it seemed to him that the entire planet was breathing. They seemed alive, so alive that in one mighty shake the entire field of stone could suddenly wake, stand, and be unearthed. In the desert, he reminded himself, he was never alone. Not only was he not alone, his aliveness was insignificant to that of these rocks. They knew too much. They would always know too much.

The dogs sniffed out the trailhead, and Noah lagged behind. The trail sharply curved then dropped like a gulf shelf, seemingly to disappear into the arroyo's dry river bottom. It had been a couple years since he'd last seen water pool between the cisterns and rocks. The earth was as dry underneath his feet as moon terrain. Rock formations towered above him, adding to the sense of being on a foreign planet.

Noah scaled up the side of the biggest rock he could find. The dogs followed and stood by his side panting. He lifted up his arms like a primitive man and with a mighty yelp celebrated his aliveness, as insignificant as that might be. "God! I am your divine creation. Behold me. I am Noah!" He howled and the dogs joined in. He stood on the rock and slowly turned to face the four directions, offering each direction a Native American prayer. For each prayer, he saw what the world was becoming: global dimming, the gradual reduction of surface irradiation which meant that the planet's life force was slowly being snuffed out. There were melting ice caps, increasingly ever more powerful gulf storms, drought, famine, killer earthquakes, war. From where Noah stood, planet prognosis wasn't so good for the human species—or any species, for that matter. Noah wasn't so crazy about the human race as a whole. He liked individuals fine—there were some amazing people in his life, and, by all indication, there were amazing people everywhere. But by and large, it seemed that the whole rat race had really messed things up. From where Noah stood there was nothing but sand, rock, and some stubby shrubs. It was hard to believe that there had been an ocean here at one time. It was so dry that it was becoming harder and harder to remember that there had been any water anywhere. Recent news reports tried to say that this was a natural desert cycle. Perhaps it was. Perhaps the magnetic poles were shifting; perhaps this was the onset of another glacial ice age. Either way, it was difficult to witness such planetary distress. Although Noah was prone to fleeting moments of hysteria—on most days he was numb—he wasn't convinced that this was the end times, but he wasn't convinced that they weren't, either. Like a lot of folks, he just wasn't sure.

It was easy to remain disconnected in a culture of comfortable distraction because to feel otherwise was to be gripped by an anxiety and depression difficult to pull out of, and Noah had battled with his acute sensitivity most of his adult life. The only way he knew how to cope with such grief was to stop choking on materialism, to simply stop buying. It had been radical in the early 1980's, but now there was an entire green movement. Bambi called the grief *Eco Depression*. For the first time, Noah knew what to call it and, because there was a name for his over identification with the dying natural world, he felt less alone. As far as his numbness, he was working on that, too, by allowing himself to feel it all, including the helpless feeling of falling in love with a woman who could have been the age of his daughter if he'd had one. She also encouraged him to go into the depression and dare to experience that fine line between the living and the dying. That was what Noah was doing in the present moment. What was that story about the apocalypse? The horsemen? And if this was the end times, Noah thought it was not really any of his business, given there was not a lot that could be done.

Noah climbed down and continued to follow the dry river bottom. As the dogs clicked back and forth over the red and black rock face, he kept a keen observation out for interesting trash. Illegal dumps were common in these arroyos. Getting the necessary dumping permits was difficult, and they cost money. For many, it was easier to throw stuff out when nobody was looking—let Mother Nature break it down. The desert was so unforgiving that there wasn't much that couldn't be broken down. Discarded objects were transmuted by the wind and the heat and the relentless sun, and transformed into found art objects. A lot of metal that Noah picked up was riddled with bullet holes. Anything material was fair game for the shooters: abandoned cars, cribs, refrigerators, TVs, stoves. Noah had a collection of pieces he'd brought home. Sometimes he painted on the rusted metal; sometimes he built birdhouses, or crafted funky sculptures. Sometimes he left the artwork raw. Bambi had several necklaces Noah had made for her from the smaller pieces of found art. Some pieces she'd actually worn more than once. Noah didn't really know what her giggling meant, but he thought she liked them well enough.

Noah knew the area well enough to remember the landscape of trash and treasure. So far today, it looked as if there weren't much new or interesting. He walked up to one of the bigger illegal trash piles where four-by-four tracks led over the mesa, and noticed that the dogs were hot. They looked up at him, tongues hanging jellyroll low, so he stopped to fish out his water bottle and the collapsible bowl from his daypack.

Noah was suddenly overcome with fatigue as the dogs lapped up the water. He walked over to the nearby floral couch. It was brown with a daisy print riddled with bullet holes; he'd set it upright on a previous jaunt. Much of the stuffing was gone, but there was enough of the couch left for a man to comfortably sit. As was routine, Noah checked the crevices for snakes and scorpions, and sat only when he was satisfied that it was safe. There was a TV nearby, intact, looked to be a Sony 24 incher, though the S had been scratched off, so it read Ony. The darkened screen was like a hole in the desert, like sucking space, a one-eyed monster watching him. Noah thought this domestic scene set out in the middle of nowhere was comically absurd. The humming in his head intensified. He closed his eyes, and listened to the happy sounds of his dogs. Other than their noises, it was so quiet that the silence had a presence. Noah listened until the gentle hum in his head took him deeper into a world of his dreams, boyhood memories of safety and comfort.

He wasn't sure, but when he opened his eyes again, he guessed that he had been asleep. He felt as if some force had simply put him down like a baby. Noah was slightly disoriented as he looked around. He squinted. There was something different. He wasn't sure what. After several minutes of rapid blinking, he realized that he was staring at the screen of the Ony with great expectancy—later this expectancy would strike him as odd. There was a light there. It was barely perceptible, but he had a feeling that something was coming in at a rapid rate. He looked away and then back over at the screen. The Ony was glowing with a golden light and there—or rather almost there—stood a child within five points of light. "The rebellion is coming!" the child giggled and then disappeared as mysteriously as it had appeared. The vision was so dreamlike in quality that Noah assumed that he was still asleep, except that he was staring at the impossible: the iridescent screen glowing in the middle of nowhere.

It took him a moment, but when he realized that there really was a light and that it was growing in its brightness, Noah jumped to his feet. The instant he realized that he was about to receive a vision was the instant that he actually received a deep knowing that God was speaking, or, rather, the voice of the radiance was inside his head and in his heart.

When Noah would later recount his story, he told it this way: *Yeah...I was sitting on this old, abandoned couch in the middle of the desert and—I know it sounds crazy—but this abandoned Ony—I mean it was supposed to be a Sony but the S was missing—began glowing, and then I was told that I was being called into service. It was kinda like my whole body knew it, not just my brain.*

What is it that you want me to do? I asked.

Build a vessel.

What kind of vessel? Do you want something ceramic?

Noah! The voice spoke again, stop asking so many questions and believe. Build a vessel worthy of a birth.

And when I looked again there was this child standing in the center of five points of light. I couldn't tell if it was a boy or a girl. It was both, and it smiled at me.

My being trembled, and I said in a whimper, okay.

What do you think that means?

When the light was finished with Noah, he sat back down on the couch and cried. He wasn't crying because God had just spoken to him and he had to explain that to Bambi. He was crying because he had been seen. He was crying because he had been picked. He was crying because he could no longer remain invisible, and that meant he was responsible to do something. But to do what? He felt very much like a boy, confused, and quite certain that he was insufficient to carry out any divine plan. Build a vessel worthy for a birth? What did that mean?

"Could you be more vague?" he cried out. He then got angry. He got really angry, and he began trashing the trash, throwing tin cans, an old tennis shoe, and rocks as hard as he could against the rock walls until all of his fear and anger was spent.

"Does this mean," he shouted to the sky and to himself, "that I have to become a Christian? Because I really don't want to do that." His question was met with silence. "Come on! Are you sure you have the right Noah?" He hollered at the TV. He waited and waited, but his question was again met with silence. There was no more response from either God or the Ony.

Chapter 2

"Do you believe in God?"

"What?"

"Do you believe in God?" Noah repeated to Bambi, who was distracted with a crossword puzzle. She sat cross-legged on the couch in her *Strawberry Shortcake* cotton pajamas. Her shoulder length blonde bob was pulled back into a ponytail. She looked so young it made Noah feel strangely guilty. She barely looked up.

"Noah, we've had this conversation many times. You know how I feel."

"Tell me again."

"I'm working on this puzzle."

"I'm serious, Bambi."

"Well, I am, too," she sighed. "Have you ever heard of Pascal's wager?"

"I think so."

"Pascal's wager," she looked up over the rim of her glasses, "is Pascal's argument to the existence of God. Basically, he maintains that there is no way to prove the existence of God, and since there is an infinite set of possibilities, it is best to wager for the possibility of God. Suppose you have two possible actions, action one and action two—"

"I get the idea."

"I see." She looked back down at her crossword.

"I didn't mean to cut you off. Well, maybe I did, but I'm working on that. Sometimes, when you bring in the academics, my attention drifts."

"When you're bored?"

"I wouldn't say bored. It has to do with focus."

"Like I said. Bored."

"More like ADHD."

"You don't have ADHD, Noah."

"Yes, I do. I'm distracted by the honey-curve of your lip."

She continued to ignore him and he smiled lovingly at her.

"Come here." She finally patted the cushion next to her. "You are impossible."

He sat next to her, fully aroused. "I'm sorry." He pulled her close, kissed her on the back of the neck and behind the ear.

"Noah, I was in the middle of something here." She held up the paper.

"Eight down spells 'please'."

"That's not going to get you anywhere." She laughed and swatted him with the rolled up paper.

"Okay, I can respect that." He got up.

She grabbed his wrist. "I didn't say that I wanted you to go. I wanted you to ask."

"I said 'please.'"

She rolled her eyes, but she was kissing him back. He returned his attention to the back of her neck. She purred. He loosened her hair. She began to work her hand against his thigh while he traced the contours of her face and slid his hand down the length of her body. "Whatcha got in that little shortcake for me?"

She giggled, nipped him on the back of his arm. "I guess you're going to have to go on in and find out."

He pushed the corner of her panty to the side. He was patient. He teased her and felt her heat begin to rise. She began to writhe. Still he was patient and in his own time slid his finger deep inside. She took in a sudden, short breath, and as she exhaled her scent flowered into musk.

Wildness from deep inside took him over. With constrained roughness, he pulled off her clothes—his, too—and mounted her until their hips found the living rhythm of universal procreation. In their unison, her shortness of breath was punctuated by throaty moans. He pushed into her until her moans turned into welcoming ecstatic screams. He could have fucked her for the rest of the morning, were it not for the sensation of losing control that all men suffer when they feel the urgency of dying upon them. He slowed just to keep her satisfaction going, and in that way allowed his maturity to mask what he physically had difficulty sustaining. He knew that there was no race to win, only her pleasure for as long as she would have him.

When she finally came, Noah was relieved. He sped up, let himself go, and then collapsed on the couch.

"God, that was great." She looked over at him. "You wanna go again?"

Noah didn't answer. Already his eyes were closing. "Noah. Noah. Are you all right? Good Lord, did I kill you?"

"No, baby. I've just got to rest a bit. Give me a second." He closed his eyes.

Noah woke up to the sounds of his as perfect-as-it-gets life. Bambi was off somewhere in the next room banging on a pipe and being loud in her aliveness. God bless her. He had waited a long time to feel this good about life. Then he remembered his morning encounter and felt a twinge. He tried to keep the memory at bay. He knew that whatever it was that had gotten a hold of him out in the desert wasn't going to let go. If that presence had found him way out in the middle of nowhere, it was likely to find him anywhere. Noah figured that he was going to have to deal with it sooner or later. But the first thing that he had to discover was how

Bambi was going to react.

"Hey, Bambi, would you mind coming in here?"

"Hold on a minute. I'm trying to take care of this leak."

"I'm going to fix it, don't worry."

"I'm not worried."

"I'll look at it. I need to talk with you more about God."

"Noah, what has gotten into you?"

"Tell you the truth, I'm not totally sure."

Bambi bounded into the room. She gave him a smack squarely on top of his head.

"So what is it about *God* that you want to tell me?" She sat next to him. "You've been hinting at it all morning. Ever since you got back from that hike. Did something happen?"

"What would you do if a client came in to see you and claimed to hear God talking?"

"Has God been talking to you?"

"Now, wait a minute, I didn't say that it was *me*. Strictly hypothetical."

"Well, it all depends on how they make the claim. I'd have to distinguish between a transrational experience, which is similar to what indigenous cultures accommodate as normal and reasonable—it's the shamanic experience, earth based religions, et cetera—or a psychotic break, which is pathology, signs of a diseased mind."

"How do you know the difference?"

"It has a lot to do with how a person is able to integrate an experience in the psyche. If they never question the validity of the experience, nor seem to recognize that there's incongruence to the realities that they're reporting on, then there's usually a problem. A crazy person never believes they're crazy."

Noah was relieved. He knew he was crazy.

"Now, are you going to tell me what this is *really about?*"

"I saw God on TV this morning when I took Red Girl and Ginger Bear to the arroyo."

Bambi didn't flinch. She didn't even blink.

She's good at this, Noah thought. Bambi held the space for a long while. In the silence, Noah heard the ticking of a clock.

"What?" Bambi finally spoke.

"When I took Red Girl and Ginger Bear—"

"Yeah, I got that part. Tell me about the other part."

"I fell asleep on that brown floral couch that's dumped out there." Noah waved in the general direction of the desert.

"I know the one."

"I fell asleep, and when I woke up the TV was glowing."

"A TV?"

"Someone dumped a TV. A Sony."

"It was glowing?"

"It was glowing, and then I heard—can't say it was a voice; more like a profound knowing of truth. I was told that I was being called into service to build a vessel worthy of a birth."

"What the hell does that mean?"

"I don't know. I was going to ask you."

"Called to service? I don't think this is very funny."

Noah felt sad. This wasn't going well. His worst fear was that she would eventually find a diagnosis for him in the DSM. "Let's not talk about it anymore."

"Noah, I'm not trying to discount your experience. It's just different when it's you and not some random aborigine. I don't understand. How do you know it wasn't an elaborate prank?"

"It's a feeling. I can't explain."

"Why didn't you tell the voice 'no'?"

"The experience was powerful and the presence was big...and you know the stories. Resistance is futile. Besides, there's more."

"What do you mean there's more?"

Noah didn't want to tell her the rest of the experience. He didn't even want to admit to himself that he'd seen a child standing in the center of a bright light. A star. That was the only word to describe the illumined being. "There was this star child who said a rebellion was coming."

"Star child?"

"Yes, a child standing in five points of light."

Bambi's eyes widened and began to well up. "I don't really want to know about this right now."

"Are you overwhelmed?"

"So what if I am!"

"Only asking."

Noah knew better than to push her. He could tell she was in a state of agitation and fear. Best to let her settle into the idea. He hoped that eventually she'd be okay with everything so that he could be okay, and that together they would remain okay.

"I have to have some time to digest what you are saying to me. Do you understand?"

Noah nodded. "What do you need me to do?"

"Let's just stop talking and sit here for a while. Is that okay?"

Noah exhaled very slowly. He would do whatever she needed. He was not willing to rock the boat. He hoped that the whole matter would simply blow over. Although he knew that his life was forever altered, Noah kept his thoughts to himself and focused on breathing in and out.

As long as there was silence, there was hope that all would remain the same.

Chapter 3

Someone pulled the blindfold off. Jonas, dressed in a white robe that was embroidered on the breast in golden thread, "POA," stood before a golden altar. Seven of the most powerful men in the world stood behind the altar on an elevated stage. They were similarly dressed but hooded, so Jonas couldn't make out their features. He had a good idea who they all were. He was aware that they were calm, even complacent. Behind them were the seven golden horsemen of the Apocalypse. The statues stood twenty feet high. He had only heard about them whispered in certain gentlemen's clubs where the power deals were made, and he couldn't help but stare. The light from the torches dappled the gold so that each horseman had a mercurial quality. Jonas could almost hear the mighty power of their hooves descending upon the earth to right the wrongs, to keep the power on the side of good. The protectors. Each of these men represented one of them. They were the protectors of the Apocalypse, the chosen members of God's justice on Earth. Now that the world's population had reached a critical mass and the oil reserves had long passed peak production, it was becoming chancier to control through the usual means. They couldn't risk that genie getting out of the bottle. Just as prophecy had deemed it was time to break the seals. Andburg and his cold fusion idealism had forced their hand.

Jonas reverently lowered his eyes, trying not to stare. He was grateful to be on the side of justice. He had worked hard all of his life to do the right thing, to prove himself worthy, and they had noticed. This was the most sacred moment of his life, and he could not believe that out of all of the best and the brightest they had chosen him. This night was equivalent to a coronation.

"Jonas, please kneel."

Jonas knelt.

Someone appeared from the shadow with a red Bible on a gold-corded purple pillow.

"Swear on this Bible."

Jonas placed his right hand on the bound leather. The red stone in the protector's gold ring seemed to blaze up for a moment. He wore the same ring that every man in this cavern wore, and Jonas would get a ring just like it before evening's end.

"Do you swear this night forward to uphold the law?"

"I do."

"Do you swear to be a protector of the rights of man?"

"I do."

"Do you give your allegiance to the POA as the one and rightful truth?"

"I do."

"Please take the Bible. Keep it safe, for it is very important for the success of this final mission. More will be revealed."

Jonas took the Bible and held it next to his heart. It seemed to him that it had a heartbeat and that reassured him.

"Is there anything that you wish to say?"

Jonas smiled. "Yes. I accept this honor in the name of my Lord and Savior, and for my mother, Mona, who was a just and decent woman who fell to the spirit of lust. I strive to correct the past."

"Very good, son. Now bow your head as you are knighted."

The one who held the Bible unsheathed a silver Daisho, the ceremonial blade of the Samurai warrior. Jonas flinched when he heard that blade sing; he knew it was sharp and deadly.

Jonas bowed his head and the blade lightly touched each shoulder.

"Rise and accept your first commission."

Jonas dutifully stood.

The Bible was taken from Jonas' hand for the time being and he was offered the sword. "This sword and Bible are yours to keep in exchange for your allegiance to the Cartel. Now for your first exam."

Jonas gripped the handle and guard of the Daisho and stepped into the warrior posture of the Samari as he readied himself.

"There is a traitor among us, a whistle blower, one who would have the law unraveled."

A young man near Jonas' age was shackled and forcibly led front and center by two amazingly strong men. He wore a hood, but Jonas could tell by the plaid short sleeves and the aviator watch that he was a science nerd, maybe even someone Jonas had been in the lab with.

"Please separate the head of the serpent."

The hood was roughly removed and the young man was forced to kneel before Jonas. He had black hair and squinted, for his glasses had been taken from him. He was pale and beads of sweat glistened on his brow. Oddly enough, he did not plead. He said a prayer and then, almost disbelieving, "I have a wife, Martha, and a child. Please let them know what happened to me."

Jonas drew back the sword and swung. The blade went cleanly though the neck just under the right ear. As the head rolled forward, blood splattered on Jonas' white robe. He stared at the red blossom against the white and had the strangest sensation that he was no longer a virgin. Two men approached Jonas. They both bowed. One man removed the Daisho and the other led him off the altar.

"Very good, sir, if I might say so." He helped Jonas off with the robe and handed it to a very compliant subordinate. "I see that you have a spot there."

Jonas looked down and saw that there was a spot of the man's blood on his chambray shirt.

"Well, we'll get you cleaned up before the feast. Before we dine, we have some paperwork to go over. I'll need your signature. We're prepared to offer you a percentage of the world's wealth through oil and gas receipts. Although you are a junior partner, I think you will be very pleased. Your first mission has been assigned. I think you will be pleased about that as well, as the Arctic is your specialty."

Jonas grinned inside, though he was mindful to control his emotions as he had been trained to do. He knew what the offer meant. They stopped just before they left the giant, cavernous room. "We've been watching you for a very long time, and we are pleased with your progress and your lineage. We have a very important role for you, very important role. Shall we go? It is a spectacular evening and I hear the kitchen is preparing duck tonight. Do you like duck?"

Jonas nodded.

"Very good, sir."

They exited through a mighty door into one of the well-lit tunnels. Jonas knew that after the feast he would a get full view and debriefing of this underground system that linked the power nodes of the world with the most powerful men of the world. He would also get his directives. The time was fast approaching when everything they had worked for would come into play. Jonas was a now a major player; he had his mother and Andburg to thank for that. Redemption was a great motivator.

Chapter 4

Three days later, Bambi suddenly asked to see the TV. Noah promptly laced up his boots and whistled for the dogs, and they all marched out into the desert. Noah knew the hike well. It didn't take them long to rediscover the couch, but they did not find the abandoned Sony right away. Noah gave up the search rather quickly, and sat back on the couch and watched as Bambi carefully picked around the trash pile.

"Are you *sure* it was a TV?"

Noah grinned. "Baby, it's hard to get an old TV confused with anything else."

She sighed with exasperation. "It just seems that if it had been here, it should still be here. Nobody's coming back for it."

"You can tell me that you don't believe me. You won't hurt my feelings."

"I believe you. I do." She kept hunting for the television.

"Look under that juniper." Noah pointed over to the nearby tree. It wasn't where he'd seen the TV last, but he had a hunch. Bambi lifted up one of the dying branches. "Noah," she gasped, "I found it. It's here. It's here." She pulled the 24 inch from underneath the branch and, with some struggle and much triumph, brought the set over, placed it half teetering on top of a flat, red boulder.

"Now plug it in."

"Noah, don't be silly," she laughed.

"Do be careful with it. I'd hate to see the tube implode if that set should fall on the ground."

"It's fine." She rocked it back and forth to make sure. "See. Now what?" She walked over and sat down on the couch next to him.

"I don't know."

"I guess it's a lot to ask for lightning to strike twice and with a witness."

"Yes, it does seem to work that way. Why does God have to so often speak when there is no corroboration?"

Bambi playfully pinched him.

Noah shrugged.

Together they sat and waited. In Noah's imagination, they struck a very odd picture: A couple sitting on an old couch, staring at a dark screen as if the desert were their living room.

Nothing happened. Noah finally got up and examined the set more closely.

On first inspection, it seemed that the box was intact, but when he peered into the slatted back, he could see that there were no electronic guts—no electronic cards, no electronic Cathode Ray tubes. Technically, it was impossible for this TV to have any life of its own, not to mention there was no electricity. Somehow, that seemed fitting. God had breathed life into it—even if were plastic, metal, and glass, nothing more than a shell.

"Hey, Bambi, didn't this set seem extraordinarily light to you when you lifted it?"

"No, it seemed like a normal television."

Noah rocked the box. There was resistance; it felt heavy enough. "Hmm. That's odd." Noah looked down at his hands. He began to doubt the reality of his senses. For a moment, he thought that he would literally go mad—if it weren't for Bambi being here with him. At least it was a shared experience. "Come here. I want to show you something."

Bambi got up and looked where Noah was pointing. "Wow." She whistled. "There's nothing in there."

"Strange, huh?"

"Yeah, heavy for being so empty."

"Someone went to great lengths to gut this set."

"I see your point." She looked at him, shrugged. "What can we do?"

"I don't know. Don't think I have any answers anymore."

Bambi nodded her approval and seemed a bit relieved. Noah couldn't help wonder what she was really thinking. He wanted to ask her if she believed him now, but found himself frozen despite their shared experience. He was still afraid of what she might say. "Do you want to keep walking, or do you want to go home," he asked instead.

"We can walk a bit longer. Maybe we should go to the dump and see Andrea."

"That's fine, but let's not tell her about this."

"Okay. That's probably a good idea. I mean, we don't know what really happened to you yet."

Noah was quiet. He wasn't sure what to make of her response. She seemed supportive enough, but he couldn't quite tell. They continued to walk toward the dump where they would find their friend, the dump manager, who had always supported his work by leaving some of the best trash for him.

Andrea was the manager of the legal dump, which meant a permit and a small fee was required. Noah called it the magic dump because Andrea redistributed the wealth, and this being America, and close to Santa Fe, the trash disposed spoke of a spoiled and restless class, one in search of constant material change. Unlike the city dumps that worried about liability, she allowed scavenging. For many, what was found on the trash heaps was truly a treasure. Noah had found books, records, clothing; it never ceased to amaze him what people threw out. Often

Andrea pulled out the most salvageable items, and what she didn't designate for Noah she left for easy access by the side of the road when she closed the gates at the end of the day.

It took them about twenty minutes, following the arroyo, to get to the boulder landmarks that indicated where they could climb over the two hills, the last one crested above the dump. It took another fifteen minutes, huffing upwards, before they could clearly see sudden civilization below. From where they stood they could see Andrea maneuvering the backhoe. She handled the heavy machine like a man. In fact, Andrea looked like a seasoned cattlewoman, a step out of time. She appeared to be the last of a true grit breed with her broad, weathered face, man-sized hands, toothy-gap grin, dirty dungarees, and wide brimmed straw hat slung behind her back.

She waved when she saw them approach the recyclables, large metal dumpsters where refuse was divided into paper and glass. Noah and Bambi waited patiently for Andrea to get a moment to pause.

She parked the backhoe next to her dump truck—she was very proud that she owned her own dump truck—cut off the motor and stiffly stepped down from her seat. "How you folks doing?"

"Just *fine*." Bambi's slow Southern drawl was always more pronounced in social situations.

"How's that artwork of yours coming?" She turned to Noah.

"I haven't done a whole lot with it lately—been busy with the new well."

"You digging it?"

"Got help. I want to go 500 feet. Hope to land in that aquifer."

"Good luck with that. It's getting harder to hit the liquid gold these-a-days. I hear Canada is going to be the richest country because of their water source. Not that I plan on leaving any time soon. I'd rather become an incinerated old prune then leave the desert." She turned her focus onto Bambi, changing the subject. "I have a few choice items set aside, remnants from an estate sale if you want to take a look." She waved to her manager's station where there was a collection of salvaged items and thriving plants that she lovingly brought back from the twigs people had discarded. "There is a pretty lacquered jewelry box—only thing missing is a back hinge. She smiled broadly. "I'm sure Noah could fix it right up for you."

"Let's take a look." She strummed Noah on the back of the arm. They began to head in the direction of the junk when Andrea stopped them.

"Did you hear about that girl outside of Albuquerque who found the image of Christ on an ironing board? Her family erected a tent over it, and it has become an instant shrine for pilgrims. I'm thinking about going myself." She laughed so loud it startled Noah. "I've never been one for those kinds of things, but these are odd times. I mean…we never know when we'll suddenly be a voice for God."

Noah looked quickly at Bambi. She looked as puzzled as he felt. Suddenly a pack of stray dogs came sniffing up from the road and began to run aggressively toward Red Girl, who immediately rolled on her back. Andrea spun around and stared hard at the alpha dog. It unexpectedly stopped in its tracks, stared back at her, and then backed away. The pack followed. They returned to the road and then disappeared.

Noah was aware that he must have had his mouth agape because he closed it. "How did you do that?"

"It's a gift," she said vaguely and then quickly directed the conversation back on topic. "I got a bike over there for a little girl in my neighborhood. Her family can't afford her one. Right now she runs alongside her friends, seems to have fun enough." For a brief moment, Noah saw pain on her face that she quickly masked. "Anyway, I'm fixing it up and delivering it to her today. Take anything you want over there, but not that."

"You're an angel," said Bambi.

"I'm no angel, but I know how to see treasure in trash."

"Like Noah."

She smiled. "Like Noah." There was a slight pause, and then she tactfully dismissed herself. "Excuse me, but I've got to get back to my sorting." She was already walking off. "Recycling about twenty tons a year now."

"Thank you," Bambi called out.

"Was she messing with my mind?" Noah whispered.

"I don't know. It's probably synchronicity. Listen, people have visions out here all the time. It's New Mexico. You know they say the veil is thin here between the worlds. I'm sure it was a coincidence. Try not to get too paranoid. Let's look at this box and go home."

"And did you see the way those dogs reacted to her?"

"Yes."

"Have you ever seen anything like that?"

"No, but she said she had a gift. Maybe she's an animal communicator."

"An animal communicator?"

"Someone who talks to animals."

"I know, but that's weird."

"Hey, who's the guy who just heard God's voice on a broken Sony?"

"Okay, point taken from the woman who accepts thin veils but has difficulty believing me." Noah saw the box on top of a three-legged stool. He picked it up and lifted the lid. There was a tiny ballerina leaning toward a cracked mirror. "Do you want it?"

"No," Bambi sighed. "It smells musty. Some old lady had memories in that box and she's dead now. I don't want it. I don't want to carry the weight of the dead. But I'd like to bring this home." She held up one of the little plants that Andrea had brought back to life.

"That's a rugged little bugger. I like it. Let's go home and practice the weight of the living." Noah whispered something into her ear about being sorry he had hurt her feelings and all the ways he would like to atone for such transgression. She blushed. "Maybe," she replied, but held his arm tightly all the way home, the dogs trailing behind and a tiny fragile plant in her hand.

Chapter 5

Noah's Daemon, Dan, and his personal Demon, Charlie, were in the middle of a chess game and drinking beer that wasn't really beer. They had been playing for a long while: several million years, but this recent assignment had been only fifty-six human years to be exact. So far, it was an evenly matched game because Noah was perfectly balanced between the darkness and light, although he was nowhere close to being aware of his integration process, nor of his unique role in the tipping point of the planet. Noah would have confused his Daemon with his Demon if he'd been aware of their existence; they, along with his ancestors, his spirit-guides, his angels, and his fantasies made for a full house in his psyche's interior. That's why their intrusion into his life thus far had been subtle at best. This was about to change.

It was important that Noah confuse the two. His Daemon was there to bribe, cajole, entice, seduce, and/or annoy Noah to do the right thing in his life. True, he was a holdover from a Hellenistic belief system and had been considered a lowly order of spiritual being, a go-between for mortals, but Dan was rather proud of his lineage. He liked to see himself as a motivating spirit, a guardian, and a protector. Noah's Demon, on the other hand, was there simply to make Noah's life miserable in any given opportunity. His job, in that respect, was profoundly easy.

"How's this game going to play out," Dan asked. He knew that Charlie believed that the statistical odds were in his favor, and perhaps they were.

"I don't know," replied Charlie. He never looked up from the board.

"You could make eye contact," Dan noted.

"Why should I?"

They often played this quarrel. Dan thought Charlie could get away with a lot more impolite behavior because of the role he'd been cast. "Thought you might make an effort."

"You always think that."

They both returned their gaze to the board.

"So how's this thing going to play out?" Charlie parroted Dan.

"I just asked you that."

Charlie grinned in a way that only demons can. "I think we are going to have to manifest ourselves down there. See what happens."

Dan nodded. "I was thinking the same. I'd like a head start."

"Are you saying I'm too powerful?"

Dan was going to say no, but when he saw Charlie's claw click against the marble edge of the game piece, he wavered.

"Okay, then," Charlie said. "You got three human months. By that time, he's got to pass three tests. Accept the commission, overcome the illusion that his ego is separated from his loving, and then the biggest test of all." Charlie moved a game piece. "Knight to Bishop's Two."

"Ohh." Dan looked mildly surprised. "What's the third test?"

"The illusion of death. Take your time. You've got three months."

"Whose death?"

"Love's fickle," Charlie cast off an easy statement.

"Not the girl."

"It's always the girl." Charlie chuckled.

"I don't like the death thing."

"You don't like the death thing? You don't like the death thing?" Charlie stood up. "The death thing is coming, Dan."

"It might not happen."

"It always happens. This is the *flood*, Dan. This is *it*. This is the *ultimate melt down of the polar ice caps*." Charlie sat back down and cracked his wicked knuckles. "Plus there will be the endless rain, plus all of the pipes breaking—*everywhere*. Plumbers are going to make a killing on this one." He laughed.

"I don't find that funny."

"Come on, Dan. Don't take everything so seriously. It's just life—human life at that. It's not like we don't know the story. The story keeps on repeating and repeating. God, I wish there were a different plot line already."

"Are you saying, Charlie, that you don't believe in the Mystery?"

"Are you saying, Charlie, that you don't believe in the Mystery," Charlie mimicked.

"They'll blame it on you."

"Yeah. It's fun thinking about all that attention. Poor bastards! All that suffering. They brought it on themselves."

"What about the part you play?"

"The part I play? I don't exist if they don't want me to. None of us do. They created me from their endless fear and their attachment to pain. They get addicted to it. Can't get enough. They want their share, and then they want to share it. *All you need is love....*" Charlie hummed a familiar tune. "They have the technology to save their entire race, but they won't until they're forced to change the rules? You know that friend of Noah's? What's his name? Andburg? He's close to beneficially changing the world, but he's set up to fail. A good cleanin' is a comin'—water, no soap. There will be survivors, of course. A few rats always get away, though personally I dig rats. I hope the experiment keeps up because I get a lot of perks with this planetary game."

"It's not like anyone can stay whole down there. It gets confusing, and easy to get lost. I know. I've been there before. You'll see."

"Sounds like a party to me." Charlie moved another game piece. "You should be paying better attention, Dan. Queen to King's Eight. Checkmate."

Dan shut up. He could see where this was going. Besides, he had to focus on the game plan. What or who was he to become when he materialized into form for that blink of an earth eye? How was he going to get Noah to build an ark and survive the other two tests that Charlie had in store for him? Dan wasn't sure, but he knew that he didn't have a whole lot of time. He had three months—but knowing Charlie, he knew it would be three weeks at best. He decided it was time to get going. "Thanks for the game, Charlie. Meet you on the other side."

Chapter 6

When they got back to the house, Noah heard the dripping faucet. He had to fix it. Bambi had wanted him to process further, but he couldn't fully explain how exposed he felt, so he became frustrated and then just shut down. He felt that putting his attention onto an immediate house project would get him off the hook from having to *investigate* his feelings. All he needed was a drip to fix.

It was breaking the communication rules to walk away from an active discussion. He did it anyway. He went to retrieve his toolbox from the shed where he had all his tools, nuts, bolts, and washers neatly organized.

He walked back into the house. There was only one thing on his mind: the drip.

"Noah, I recognize that you have a lot on your mind." Bambi had her car keys in her hand and a duffle bag slung across her shoulder.

"Are you leaving me?" Noah regretted those words as soon as he said them. He hated to verbalize his insecurities. "No, silly. Gym bag." She looked down at his toolbox. "Fix what you need to fix. I'm going to get some things done. I've been neglecting myself lately." She tried to smile, but only managed a look of concern. She was damned good at that. "Before I go, though, I need to hear from you that we will be able to further discuss this."

Noah went over and gently hugged her, then kissed her on the check. "I am so grateful for you. There is nothing to worry about, except that drip, and I'm going to take care of that."

"Okay, but can we talk later?"

"Of course."

She smiled and slung her bag over her shoulder. "I'll be home before dinner. Unless I change my mind about leaving you." She winked.

"That's not funny."

"I know." Then she was gone, and he turned his focus onto the immediate problem at hand. Armed with a wrench, he opened the cabinet doors, removed the few under-sink products, and knelt down to get a closer look at the elbow joint.

He had just replaced the washer and tightened up the joints, when he heard a loud knock at the door. At first he thought it was Bambi locking herself out of the house, but he remembered she had a set of house keys on that enormous key chain of hers. Janitors and therapists, he laughed. He got up and walked over to the door. From the window, he saw the dark green Hummer. Andburg. Who used to be one of his closest friends. They'd partied a lot in college, but now that Noah had sobered up they weren't as bonded. Besides, Andburg was involved in some high security government project. Noah didn't know much about it other than it involved NASA and a renewable energy source. When Andburg spoke about it, he always spoke in code, in hushed whispers, and seemed completely obsessed. According to Andburg, this discovery was not only going to revolutionize fuel resources as the world knew it, but it was very likely to save the planet. Noah also suspected that the project involved the military since Andburg had worked up in Los Alamos for all those years.

They made for strange bedfellows. Noah had never felt completely comfortable in Andburg's company—he seemed to turn everything into a competition—but they did have a long history and Noah was loyal. It didn't really matter, though, as Andburg's visits were becoming more infrequent.

Noah had long ago realized that there was no competing with Andburg. He was charmed in sort of a God-like way, though he was all too human. He was brilliant. He was also a highly functioning alcoholic and an addict. No one on the streets—except his dealer—would have guessed. Andburg had long since traded in his Birkenstocks for a spit-shine polish and impeccable grooming. His beard was neatly trimmed, and he looked more like a banker though he still attended *Brews and Blues* festival in Colorado on a regular basis. It was there that he said he felt most like himself—away from the crushing pressures of launching a successful enterprise. He could wear his T-shirts and shorts, put on dark shades and a wide brimmed hat, get stoned and dance; be silly and get lost in the throb of the crowd. He often confessed that if he hadn't wanted to save the world from its addiction to fossil fuels, he would have become a kick-ass banjo player.

Andburg got high the moment he got out of bed, claiming that the herb brought him closer to God, his creativity, and his authentic feelings. He worked hard, played hard, invested in expensive toys, and as soon as he was off duty, he partied. Too much brilliance, too much pressure, too much acceptance in *that's the way things work* among the highly motivated. Without drugs and alcohol, how would the high-power deals be made? What would he be without the image and experience of invincibility that the high brought? How would he be able to stop thinking?

Noah was one of the few who knew about Andburg's addictions and the way he drove off every woman who wanted to share his life with him. He was charismatic, one of the good guys, a super hero, but his personality easily shifted to one of harsh judgment and criticism. None of the women he ever dated remained good enough. If they were too nice, too loving, they became too safe and he got bored. He hadn't yet learned this about himself. All he knew was that he found fault with each and every one of them, except for Tracy, who was a narcissist and so didn't care what Andburg thought. For him, that was exciting. He hated her, but found her so alluring, unpredictable, and exciting, that he couldn't stay away. If truth were known, it was Tracy who was the primary addiction. Everything else was a symptom. They had great sex, verged on violence; it was the way that they made up that kept them believing that life wasn't worth living without each other. Tracy was a high-powered attorney. She made his life hell. In turn, he made her miserable as well. He wanted her to know about all of the fabulous women he could get at any time. Sometimes, he would bring the other women to places that held Tracy memories. He secretly hoped that she would be there to see him and the newest her. Sometimes she was. She dashed off hateful emails and slandered his name around town. Together, they believed that they owned each other for life, and a great many hearts that had gotten in the way of their mutual damage had been broken.

Noah knew all of this, but he was a loyal friend. For Noah, Andburg was humanity. He was both the best and the worst of what it meant to be human. Noah also knew about his childhood: the way he had never measured up to his father—his father who was a renowned scientist, who had climbed Kilimanjaro, and who had once beaten Andburg with a two-by-four that he was using to build his own sailboat. Andburg wasn't sure what he'd done, but he was certain that he had deserved it. It was his father who had beaten the drive right into his flesh. Andburg was complex, fascinating, and generous to his friends, but there was good reason that he self-medicated.

It was good to be Andburg's friend. He was a hobbyist archeologist. He knew where to go for the best off-the-grid camping. He made great drinks, and threw lavish parties. When he held a party, it was a great concern of his that everyone was excited. He wanted people to be happy and made sure they had a great time when they were in his company. For this reason a great many people wanted to be around him; few suspected how dark he could become. Few were trusted to be that close. Noah was tolerated because he had become a confidant. Noah knew where the bodies were buried, so to speak, as each broken heart was rationalized into a general category of incompatibility. Although new lovers had become less frequent, Noah did his best to hint to each one. It was always the same. They were so smitten with Andburg's persona that they justified any contradiction to that impression. Andburg was golden, and there was a part of Noah that wished he had an ounce of that charm, just an ounce. That desire was changing, however, the more his love for Bambi deepened.

The knock sounded again, more urgent. "Noah, come on. I know you're home."

"Andburg! Buddy! Come on in."

"Thanks. I was in the area and wanted to stop in, say hello."

"Come in. Have a seat. Can I get you something to drink?"

"Sure, man. That'd be great. If it's not too much trouble."

"No trouble."

Noah brought Andburg the last of the Pale Ale that Bambi occasionally drank. Andburg relaxed. "Thanks." He tipped the bottle, a mock toast. "What you been up to? Still with that same girl?"

"To my good fortune, yes."

"Commitment. That's good. That's good. How's work?"

"My contracts are backed up and on my days off I am an at-home-projects man. I'm digging a well, and there's this devil of a leak under the sink." Noah pointed toward the bathroom. "Just finished tightening it up."

"You sound busy." Andburg seemed distracted and not that interested. "Hey, I'm having a little get together in two weeks. I'd love to have you and Bambi come to the party. Don't worry about bringing anything. Tracy's having it catered. She wants an Arctic theme that includes circus-size tents. It's costing me a fortune. But, there's going to be a fantastic local band called Jamaican Snow. They play a Reggae and Blues fusion. Very happy music."

"Tracy? I thought you two were over."

Andburg rolled his eyes. "I know. I think I'm cursed, or it's some sort of karma. I can't seem to shake her, and she's ruining my life. She's been firing off a rash of emails again. She tells me I'm an asshole, and no woman is ever going to love me. I'm sick of it. I really think I turned a corner, though. I'm done dealing."

"You've been done dealing for over a year."

"I know, but like I said, it must be karma. Besides, it's just a party and she does a good job handling the caterers. She's got something going on with tents. I don't know," he sighed. "It's going to be expensive."

"Karma? You believe in that stuff?"

"There has to be some explanation for her. I want to quit her for good, but something always happens to pull me back in again. I want to have a normal life. I want to stop hurting people. I want to stop being hurt." Andburg stared off into space. "Sometimes I think it wouldn't be such a bad idea to dry out. I got bigger problems, though." He looked around. "Are we alone?"

"Yes."

"I'm working in some deep government shit," Andburg spoke in a near whisper. "You got another beer?"

"There might be one more."

"Do you mind?"

Noah got the last beer in the fridge. It was a Coors and it was probably a year old. He popped the lid, handed it to Andburg, and sat back down.

"You can't tell anybody, not even your girlfriend. These are the kinds of secrets that could get you killed."

"Why do you want to tell me then?"

"I need to. I don't know why. Have to tell someone. My team and I are really close in duplicating the McGuffee and Sands theory at our labs on each of the poles that a low temperature nuclear reaction can be achieved. If we can sustain the quantum electrodynamics for one more trial run we are going to have full control over cold fusion. They said that it couldn't be done, but we've got it. Damn it to hell, we're going to pull this thing off. If we can create a cheap and renewable energy source then we can use that energy to melt a controlled portion of both the Arctic and Antarctic ice and create the first hydro-harvesting system. The world will never know hunger again. Isn't that cool?"

"Hydro-harvesting. I don't understand."

"Geologists have known for a long time that there was a series of mega floods during the last ice age. They've gathered enough evidence from the erosion patterns of the channeled scablands of the Pacific Northwest that 500 cubic miles were affected in the compromise of glacier ice dams. This sudden cataclysmic flooding happened over and over. They believed that if they could duplicate the natural process, and control the amount of release, then they'd have enough energy and water for the entire planet and at a fraction of the cost of ocean desalination. A good idea. For once they were thinking about alternative sources besides oil and gas. The potential for harvesting water is *huge*! Big profits, and we could save the planet. No more droughts. More food—full bellies in Africa. You know, get Greenpeace off our backs. It was supposed to be, excuse the pun, the wave of the future. In fact, that's what we called it: Operation Future Wave. It was our team, Noah! We were on the cutting edge of it *all*. Do you know how exciting that was for me?"

"What do you mean *was*?"

"For you to understand you need more of a context. It's complex. The harvesting system is difficult to explain in laymen's terms, but I'll try."

"Keep it real."

"At a certain temperature—way below freezing—water remains a liquid. It's beyond dry ice. This ultra cold liquid can be channeled through our reactors to cut upwards toward the ice flow. At that temperature, the water functions like a laser. Because the nuclear reactor can produce enough energy to not only melt but to quickly refreeze, we can control the amount of polar ice cap we cut into. It's like having a giant knife of water that can also melt and refreeze ice flow, so we never have to worry about losing mass. Our intention was to harvest manageable hydro quadrants and use the byproduct, which was mostly water, to refreeze."

"In theory, by stabilizing cold fusion and creating a hydro-harvesting system, we were creating an endless hydro-energy resource."

"However, I didn't have the cold fusion stabilized, and I was worried that the military was about to pull funding. I gave a premature go ahead to test at our northern lab. We didn't have the nuclear *knife* really under our control yet, and our most recent readings present that there's been a lateral breach in the glacial matrix system. It looks like a branching root that's compromising the ice shelf. What that means is that the polar caps could melt from the heat and friction of those spreading cracks. This cold water is exactly what undermined the ice flow naturally fifteen hundred thousand years ago."

"Can't you fix it?"

"The only person capable of revising the miscalculation is missing. I think he might be dead. And other team members are disappearing. I believe there's an assassin on the team, but I can't put the pieces together to know for certain. There's a high probability. Someone is targeting me. I know that for a fact. At first I thought it was Tracy trying to do away with me, because she's that cold-blooded, but she's not that sophisticated. She doesn't know anything about disabling brakes, and if she *had* hired a hit man, I'd have a bullet right here by now." Andburg pointed to his temple. "Honestly, I'm nervous. I've reduced my travel time, but this project is going to blow. I have to get to the Arctic. We have a crisis on our hands that I don't know how to fix, and now I can't even trust my team."

"What are you saying?"

Andburg gazed doggedly inward as if desperate to solve an elusive problem. "Any land mass not already under water, and not above ten thousand feet, will be flooded within four to six weeks."

"The only lands that will be left are mountain tops?"

The silence was uncomfortable.

"I'm just a carpenter, Andburg," Noah finally managed to say.

"Actually, we don't really know what to expect. We never encountered an issue with these global ramifications. I don't expect anything from you." Andburg's abrupt laugh sounded like nervous tick. "You're my best friend. Thought I ought to tell you."

The end of the world? What does a man do with such information? Had he been a good man? Had he loved well? What had he really wanted to do? What was left undone? All he could picture was curling into the sweet comfort of Bambi until the waters washed over both of them.

Then he thought about building a vessel. A ship was a vessel. The ark was a ship. Was he supposed to build an ark? He struggled within himself whether to tell Andburg about his vision. He had an overwhelming need to assure both of them. But what was he going to say to this scientist, to this friend who was ill and out of control? Not to worry? God was acting in the world. That there was a plan, though none of it had been revealed. Noah knew that a vision was a slippery slope. Religiosity had created so many problems in the world over the centuries—how could any one man's account of the divine be the only way out of doom? There was no such thing as one person saving the world—that was just as silly as Andburg being the one person to destroy it. Noah knew that in the end the collective journey was the most important. In the end, Noah had nothing to say. "I wish I knew what to tell you. I don't," was all the profundity he was able to come up with.

"That's okay, man. I'll figure it out. I always do." He gave Noah a bleak smile, stood up. "Please come to the party."

"You got it. Andburg?"

"Yep."

"It's going to be okay."

"I know." Then he was out the door, leaving a hot pool of shame and defeat. Noah could feel it. He wished there were something he could do to help. Andburg was his friend, no matter what. A man who believed he was responsible for the fate of the entire planet; how alone he must feel.

Noah sank into the couch and stared out the window. Red Girl snapped her tail against the floor, crawled over to Noah's hand, but he didn't feel her cold comforting nose. He continued to stare out the window and wonder what was coming next. What could possibly top Andburg's confession?

It was the one thought Noah could hold onto as he drifted off into oceanic mind. A geologic timeline of dinosaurs, Dodo birds, mammals, and humans flashed on his mental screen: all extinct. Would it be a new era of fish and whales, or something else? When the water receded, would the ants emerge to claim the landmass? He'd seen a sci-fi movie about that once. Nuclear radiation, genetic mutation, giant ants taking over the world. The unfolding events were surreal.

He thought about the Ony. Was his vision linked to Andburg's confession?

"This is karma," he whispered to Red Girl. She wagged her tail. "Do you think it's too late to change my name?" He thought he might settle on something ordinary like Bob or Frank or Harry. He practiced what he'd tell Bambi. He had no idea how much he'd be able to tell her. Did he need to protect her? Would she look to him to save them both? If it *were* the end of the world, what could he say? Nothing Noah had in his mind was adequate, so he remained silent and thought where the answers might come from.

Chapter 7

The owl fluttered from the roof and settled on the railing, startling Andrea. She jumped back, swore, and instinctively reached for the broom. That reaction was not what Dan expected. Briefly, he questioned if this bird manifestation was the best choice for his purposes. Returning to the physical plane as a bird had been more whim than practicality, but he'd been drawn to the metaphoric significance of the owl: prophecy, wisdom, the magic inner light, and, yes, a portent of death. Charlie was right: *death was coming*.

Dan glided across the length of the porch. Andrea swung hard again, and Dan's left wing was nearly clocked. Dan knew that if Andrea didn't break him with her broom—or her gun, which was loaded and propped behind the door—he could form an alliance with her. Although Andrea was one of those humans who could see and *hear* animals, she was clearly not listening now. If she would befriend him, there would be no limit to her influence on Noah and Bambi, especially Noah, who needed to pass his first test: Accept the spiritual commission and believe in the impossible.

Dan let out a screech and settled precariously back down on the railing. Andrea was clearly nervous. Dan glided over to the nearest tree and watched her.

"What do you want?" She scolded him with a hiss. "I ain't ready to die, so you best be getting on with yourself."

She was superstitious. Dan knew that he had to find a better way to communicate with her or he'd be sitting up in the tree for a long time. Dreamtime was an easy and portable way to move information, but it was unreliable. There was no telling if she'd remember or even act on the information. If humans weren't so influenced by the pack, he would have worked with Noah's dreams, too, but Noah was already resisting everything not in consensus reality. He needed Andrea on his side to influence Noah to accept and then act on the commission.

Andrea watched Dan for half an hour before she went inside her trailer. He waited. Stillness settled into his bird bones; it was as if he were part of the tree and the night air. After an hour or two, the small light from within the trailer went out. He waited for another twenty minutes, closed his eyes and, without moving a feather, took flight on invisible psychic cords that linked him with the sleeper. He could see her curled on a bunk with a thin blanket pulled over her. The plants she'd rescued thrived in the trailer, as well—so thick, they threatened to take over the tiny space. She had two cats amidst the jungle, tucked in the crevices like dream catchers. Their eyes glowed with a mysterious golden light, illuminated by the starlight and Dan's inner essence, the part of him that was not mutable. The cats were curious but did not disturb the silence.

Dan's essences thinned close to Andrea's nose and, like particle adrift, he surrendered to her inhale. Almost instantly, he was in an unconscious space with her. Her own dreamway was unfolding, though it was very dark and difficult to get a true reading on the randomly forming pictures.

Dan stepped up to a rapidly changing shadow. He caught it, breathed his own breath of light and—like a projector—illuminated the apocalyptic horrors that were coming. Andrea's sleeping body grew restless. She began to perspire but did not awake. Dan continued with the projection. He downloaded images of Noah and blueprints of the ark. He gave her an emotional impression of Charlie because Charlie was coming as well, and she should know how to fear him. He showed her the flood. He showed her the ark's blueprints, and the life codes that would become a matrix in the fifth dimension. They'd be returned one day, completing an evolutionary process. Utopia was possible if she would work with him. Dan wasn't sure how Andrea would interpret this information, but he exited her breath knowing he would have to be patient, wait, and observe. He drifted under the door and reconstituted himself as an owl peering down at a trailer somewhere in the middle of nowhere.

Although Dan didn't know how the plan would go down, he was painfully aware that everything would soon drastically change. In the blink of an eye, the ocean that had become a desert would return to an ocean. There would be suffering. That could not be avoided. There would be a return to the source, and life would be given a chance to incarnate again. The Mother Earth was awake and sentient and she was in need of deep purification of the poisons. The planet would have her moment of rest, of healing. The world would start again fresh as long as the genetic material could be saved.

Dan didn't presume to understand the great Mystery the way Charlie did. Dan didn't know what would happen to the genetic material that Noah was commanded to collect. He was prepared, however, to do his small part. He was grateful that Charlie was not there to mock him. Charlie was bored with the story—he was ready for the final showdown, a sure win one way or another. Dan preferred balance. He liked the story. He didn't mind it being played out again.

Dan settled into his bird body. He marveled at the species—the exactness of sensory sight and hearing, a sharp, perceptive bio-machine. Dan swiveled his head, tracked the nuance of a mouse sound. He squelched the urge to kill. He wondered if that urge to kill was the power Charlie had to control every moment of his life. No surprise he was ill humored so often. Dan waited for the sun to rise, the exact moment of complete balance between the dark and the light, barely perceptible. The

Hindus called it Narvessawn. At that exact moment anything could happen. Dan decided that he'd better start talking to Noah, even if he wasn't sure that communication would work. Better than getting swung at again by Andrea. Besides, time was of the essence.

Chapter 8

Noah was in the same spot on the couch when Bambi finally breezed through the door. He'd lost track of how long he'd been staring at nothing. He looked up at her. She was so beautiful fiercely standing in her worry, a tender and awful moment.

"What is it?" She set her bags down on the floor at her feet as her gaze locked on his face.

He didn't know how to respond. "Come here." She went to him and sat down. He held her until some of the tension eased. "Andburg came by."

She looked at him quizzically.

"He wants us to go to a party."

"Is that it? Is that what's got you unnerved?"

Noah lost his train of thought. "Life has gotten so strange that I'm not sure what's real. How can I tell you?"

She touched Noah on the curve of his cheek. "Close your eyes and tell me the first thing that comes to mind."

"Disaster." Noah finally spoke.

"Disaster?"

"Andburg says that he's been contracted by the government to melt the polar ice caps and that something's gone wrong. It's no longer under his team's control. There will be massive flooding."

"Oh." Bambi's face went completely blank. "How can our government simply melt the ice caps? Doesn't that have to pass Congress?"

"I don't know. He spoke in code—I'm not sure I can adequately explain. Sounds like they came up with a way to cut into the ice by using nuclear fusion."

"Nuclear fusion?"

Noah nodded. "Cold fusion."

"That's impossible."

"Is it?"

"It's a hoax. All the papers reported so about ten years ago. Don't you remember the cover of *Time*?"

Noah shook his head. "I've known Andburg a long time. Despite his flaws, he's brilliant. If he says he did it, I believe him."

"Noah, there's a very thin line between creativity and madness. All of those good old boys have some sort of God complex. Why is it so easy for you to believe him?"

"Come on, Bambi! My vision makes more sense after his explanation." He gave her a look and her face softened, but Noah could see that she didn't completely agree with him.

"What are we going to do?"

"I have no clue. I guess I'm going to build a ship."

"Something's got to be done," she said, suddenly standing up.

"What are you going to do?"

"I don't know. I'm going to fix that drip." She laughed. "I'm going to do something normal."

"I fixed it."

"Well, it's dripping again." She picked up the toolbox from the hallway and went into the bathroom, locking the door behind her. Noah could hear a tremendous amount of banging, and he was concerned that she was tearing the room apart. He decided to let her bang away if that's what she needed to do. She could shred the entire house if she needed to.

She continued to pound. He was certain that he had fixed that drip. He didn't know what to make of her behavior, but decided that it was the least of his worries. He put on his boots and whistled the dogs over. He needed movement.

"Babe," he hollered over the clanging. "I'm going for a hike with the dogs. Would you like to come?"

"No," she whispered through the door. "I want to fix this once and for all."

"Okay, but don't hurt yourself."

"Fuck you!"

"Bambi, what's happening to you?"

"I'm scared." He heard her mutter from the other side of the door.

"I love you." Noah retreated from the door, and the banging resumed louder than before. He was convinced that indeed she was tearing the room apart from brick to foundation. He sighed. The dogs followed him from the house, away from the frustration, the terror, the surrealism, and the confusion. He took comfort in their companionship. They were in the moment, and there was no other place that he would rather be. Out the gate, on the trail, toward the arroyo that led to the Ony.

Chapter 9

Noah took his time with his walk. His dogs trailed behind. There was no reason to hurry. He wanted to capture the desert nuances in his memory as if he were a living camera. A part of him felt sad holding onto these memories as if he would never again see the pale and vibrant southwestern colors. The browns only vivified life's fragility. Noah concentrated on one foot in front of the other, and before he knew it he stood before the Ony still sitting undisturbed on the rock.

The humming in his head was gentle. He smiled. He knew. His commission was to build the ark. He closed his eyes. In that moment, he was grateful. His heart was completely open, and he was willing to accept anything. Deeply, internally, he said *yes*. Although Noah had never built a ship, he affirmed his *yes* again. He believed that plans would come to him. Pleasant warmth ran down his body; his heart was flooded with love for the whole world. When he opened his eyes, he was a little disappointed that the Ony was not glowing.

Worrying about Bambi compelled Noah to head back. He wondered how much of the bathroom was still intact. He was halfway up the trail when a rather large bird began to slowly circle overhead. This was the desert; it wasn't unusual for large birds, especially vultures, to circle, slow and low. Noah stopped and studied the wings. The dogs stopped and barked. He shushed them and they responded to his command. He could see that it wasn't a vulture at all, but rather an unusually large owl. He stared at it a long time before he understood that what he was looking at was a Great Gray.

"Ah-ho," he greeted it. His hand shaded his eyes from the intense sunlight. "You belong in Canada, friend."

A fast, smooth swoop, and Noah ducked. "Damn! What are you trying to do?" The owl suddenly swooped again, aggressively close to the top of Noah's head. He ducked again, and when he stood up he began chucking rocks. The dogs ran off in the direction of home. The third time the owl swooped, Noah ran. He ran until he got to the nearest tree, protected by the branches. The owl glided in, barely disturbing the branch above Noah's head.

"Okay, who are you?"

"Whoo-ooo-ooo-ooo," came the soft low-pitched call until Noah was able to understand a type of human name like a bad voice-over translation. "I'm Dan."

"Okay, Dan. How are we communicating?"

"The veil is thin."

"What do you mean the veil is thin?"

"Your psyche is willing to understand. You can hear me right now because you choose to, so we are communicating. And you've been meditating on the love you have for your girlfriend, so you are vibrating at a higher frequency."

I bet, thought Noah. "Okay, so who are you?"

"I'm your Daemon."

"A demon! What's that supposed to mean?"

"No, you have one of those. His name is Charlie."

"I have a demon named Charlie?"

"Yes. That's what I said."

Noah looked cautiously around.

"No, no. He's not here. I really don't want talk about Charlie, if you don't mind. We don't have a whole lot of time."

"Okay, so tell me *what* are *you* again?"

Dan shook his head and his feathers ruffled. "A Daemon is a half divine being. The other half I'm not sure. Human thought, I guess. I'm here to keep you on your destined path, a go-between, so to speak, between you and the Mystery. Haven't you read Plato?"

"Who are you? English-lit Nazi?" Noah was defensive partly because he had read Plato, but he couldn't remember any of it. "The Mystery? What's that?"

"Oh, it doesn't matter if you read Plato." Dan sighed. "The Source, and since the Source remains constant but the manifestation of source is ever changing, we all call it The Mystery. Humans named the source God because you still want all things solved. God is a little word. It goes down easily, like a pill."

Noah wasn't sure, but he thought Dan might be making fun of him. He'd done his share of pills, but that was a long time ago. In some ways, he wished that he still did them because then he'd have at least some form of explanation. "If my commission is destined, then why do I need you?"

"There's still always choice. The Mystery is a paradox and…there is Charlie, you know."

"No, I don't *know*, frankly."

"Congratulations!" Dan stated. "That's exactly where we begin: with the not knowing. Not to change the subject, but there's not a lot of time. You accepted your commission to build an ark. I thought that was going to be a tough one for you, but you sailed right through." Dan fluttered his massive wings in excitement. "That saves us both time."

"How do you know that?"

"According to Einstein, time is—"

"No, I meant how do you know I accepted this commission?"

"To build a vessel worthy of a birth?" Dan closed his eyes. "I told you. I'm your Daemon. It's my job to know."

Noah tried not to show his surprise. Mind reading was still a little shocking, especially from a talking owl. "So tell me, is it the end of the world?"

"I don't know. What I do know is that life is always changing. There is always a new chapter. With every new chapter, there was a chapter that came before and ended."

"I don't want a new chapter. I like this chapter."

"Come on. Aren't you curious? Just a bit?"

"Building an ark. Is that the new chapter?"

"Mostly."

"Mostly? Do I have to trap animals?"

"You have to gather their DNA."

"How do I do that? Break into an animal testing lab?"

"You could do that, but what we have in mind is that you collect scat. I think a zoo would be a good start."

"I have to get *shit*!" Noah began marching home, waved his hand behind him as if to shoo the bird away. "I'd rather drown."

Dan circled. "Look. It's not that bad." He swooped down. "Most of it will eventually be dry. Besides, the poop has all of the informational coding for the entire planet—everything that was consumed. It is the most efficient way. And if you don't...."

Noah didn't slow down.

"Bambi will die for sure."

"That is manipulation and that is not fair!" Noah paused. "Look me up next week. I'll give you my answer then. Remember, I do have free will. I'm going to hold you to it. I don't mind building you guys an ark, but I don't know about gathering poop."

"We don't have a week."

"Then give me three days and leave me alone."

"Okay. Three days. But if I were you, I'd start the blueprints."

"What blueprints?"

"They're coming." Then Dan vanished, gray phantom fleck into the brassy sky.

Chapter 10

Noah charged through the door, still upset at what he'd just been told, and entered into absolute silence. He went to the bathroom and cautiously peered in, expecting the worst. To his great relief, the bathroom was very much intact. It looked as if it had been, in fact, cleaned. He turned on the faucet full blast, quickly off again. There was no drip. Somehow, Bambi had managed to fix it.

He found Bambi standing in front of the bedroom mirror pulling her hair back into a ponytail. Her eyes were puffy and her nose was red, but she bravely smiled. He held her tightly and kissed her. "No matter what, it's going to be okay."

"There's someone here to see you," she whispered and pointed toward the living room.

"Andburg?"

"No, Andrea."

"Hmm." Noah loosened his embrace. He walked back to the bedroom door and peeked. Sure enough, Andrea was sitting on the couch, elbows propped on her knees, looking down at her boots. She held a poster tube in her calloused hand and looked extremely uncomfortable. He wondered how he'd missed her when he'd come in. The dogs sat by her feet and looked up at her worshipfully.

"How long has she been here?"

"She arrived shortly after you left. She helped me fix the leak."

"Do you know what she wants?"

"Sort of, but I think you need to talk with her. It's confusing. Noah?" Bambi held his elbow and slightly tugged on him. "You were gone a long time."

"I'll tell you about that later."

"I thought you weren't coming back."

"Bambi, *please.*"

Andrea stood up as he approached. Her hands visibly shook as she looked at him with a probing gaze and held out the tube.

Noah dumped out the contents and unrolled them, and saw the complete plans for a ship. "It's the ark!"

Andrea stared at him. She looked very serious. "I knew I had to get this to you. I hope you know something about this because it seems *big.*"

"Where did these plans come from?"

Andrea grinned, showing her horse-like teeth. Noah found her smile reassuring and infectious. For the first time that day, he felt his tension dissolve into the up-turn of his returned smile.

"I dreamed it!"

"You dreamed it." Noah repeated. "That's impressive."

Andrea nodded her head. "Ain't it something? I dreamed it and when I woke, I penciled these plans. I took some art classes before, but nothing like this."

"What do you think we should do with this?"

"We should build it. I bet between us we can find everything we need. We can start framing this puppy at the dump—there's plenty of flat concrete space, and the metal structures are already in place in the sorting hanger. I bet those solid steel rafters will be strong enough to hinge the cradle. All we need is money to buy the material. I thought one of us could apply for a credit card. One of those platinum cards. I always wanted one of them. Visa, it's everywhere you want to be." Andrea laughed. "Actually, it's easy for me to get an extended line of credit because of my sanitary landfill."

From the corner of his eye, Noah could see Bambi standing in the doorway, arms crossed. He knew she was having a difficult time with the unfolding events, so he wasn't surprised to hear her voice her disapproval.

"Noah, I don't know what to think about all of this. A credit card? You don't even believe in credit cards. I'm not even sure if any of this is real. We could be caught up in some sort of mass hysteria. Remember the Salem witch trials?"

"I don't remember the Salem witch trials. Unlike some of your friends."

"That's not fair." Bambi fell quiet. "Noah, a ship?"

"It's a leap of faith. A ship is perhaps too grandiose. Let's just call it a boat for now. If that's too much to handle, let's just say we are going to build something boat-ish."

Bambi turned her back and stared out the window.

"Maybe I should get going." Andrea looked uncomfortable. "I'll get the credit card, don't worry."

"Do you have a number where we can reach you?"

"Naw, just come by the dump. I'm always there."

"Thanks for bringing these to me." Noah rolled up the prints and slid them into the tube. "We'll all figure it out." He looked lovingly at Bambi who continued to stare out the window.

"I don't think there's much to figure out. This is bigger than all of us." Andrea gave a quick polite nod. "Come by when you're ready to build." And then she left.

"Baby, is it possible that you're just scared?"

"Do you blame me? I mean, you're about to build a ship in the middle of the desert. God's been talking to you on an abandoned TV. Andburg says it's the end of the world, and it's his fault. Andrea's here with

46

apocalyptic dreams and blueprints. I'm trained to spot psychotic episodes, and I can't even tell what's real any more. Of course I'm scared."

Noah put the palm of his hand against her back.

She leaned into him. They moved together toward the bedroom, neither of them saying a word, and made love in silence until tears welled up for both of them. She was so beautiful in her vulnerability, and Noah felt powerless to make her feel safer. They held onto each other, adrift in a timeless current of human chaos, taking each other to the center of the moment where there was peace in having to do nothing but love each other completely.

Through the climax and return to separation, Bambi stared out the window. She didn't move a muscle, and Noah stared at her, not wishing to disturb. He suddenly felt powerfully alone and was worried that she would disappear into her numbness.

"Bambi, sweetheart, what do you need?"

She turned her head and continued to stare at him as if he were the window. "A drink." She finally spoke. "I think I left a bottle here."

"Andburg drank it."

"He drank it?"

"The rest of the beer."

Bambi began to laugh. "Beer? I'm not talking about beer, Noah. There's a bottle of Tequila in the cabinet over the refrigerator."

"Oh, I forgot about that."

"Bring it."

"Are you sure?"

"Bring it."

He got out of bed and padded into the kitchen where he found the dusty bottle exactly where she said it would be. He brought it into the bedroom with some trepidation because Bambi rarely drank. It wasn't in her nature to distract from problems. Bambi sat up, the sheet draped over her body. She drew her knees up and cupped her hands. She took the bottle and tipped it back. Noah felt uneasy, but he didn't say a word. On the fifth swig, she looked over at him and grinned, but there was something in her face that had become hard. "Don't worry. I won't stay drunk until the end of the world." She took another swig. "Though who would blame me? You know what, Noah? I was just thinking that every age has its fanatics and freaks predicting the end of the world, and the planet keeps on rotating. We keep on living." She took another long drink. The color of her eyes began to darken. "How do I know you're not becoming like that?"

Noah felt a pang of betrayal. "You don't."

She waved the bottle. "How come you've been given so much

responsibility?" Her gaze drifted. "I think you're pretty special, but I don't think you're that unique to have God personally speak to you. I mean, why you? So the planet is 'perhaps' dying, but what does that have to do with us? The entire collective should be held responsible and not one man who happens to be you. Dogmatic, patriarchal, and creepy." She took another gulp and her body began to sway. "I just can't believe it's the end of us. Of course there were the dinosaurs. They died out." She took another tip from the bottle, and wiped her mouth with the back of her hand. "But I thought we were better than that!"

"I don't have any of the answers. I only know the experiences I feel are real to me. I just had a conversation with an owl. Hell, I hope I *am* delusional."

"Would you be willing to go to a psychiatrist? A cognitive-behaviorist?"

"Bambi, that's not fair. You wouldn't even go to cognitive-behaviorist. What about Andburg and Andrea?"

"They can come, too. Maybe we could get a group together. Have some meditation, do some art."

"Group therapy?"

"Sure, group therapy. Something."

"Bambi, I love you. You don't have to believe me. I don't know if I even believe me. You can leave anytime if you think this is crazy. Besides, I don't feel comfortable discussing this when you have a bottle of Cuervo Gold hanging between your legs."

She looked down. "Oh," she giggled. "I guess you have a point." She suddenly dropped back against the pillow. "I need to sleep, Noah. I'll decide in the morning."

Noah drew the sheet up over her body, gave her a kiss. She was a lightweight. It didn't take much for her body to react. He watched her for a moment, made sure her breathing was regular, and when he felt reassured that she was resting peacefully, he got dressed and paced while he tried to determine the best course of action. He stared at the plans that Andrea had left. Everything was surprisingly clear to him. He knew the basics of shipbuilding from a college course he had taken a number of years ago—before he had moved to the desert. The boat resembled a barge, with lapstrake construction—a design first used by the Vikings. This meant there was a slight overlap to the beveled planks. It would be a little more difficult, but the vessel would be flood-worthy. He'd need lumber—lots of it, as well as glue, epoxy—hardens like steel, sands like wood—nails, screws, jigsaw, table saw. Noah began to outline a list and an order of operations. He was confident he could begin construction.

As he developed his plan, he began to feel more in control. Finally, there was an activity toward action. He felt like a man again—doing something, determined to fix the problem at hand. He wondered how many generations this feeling went back to. Was it genetic? He decided that it probably was, and he was grateful for his direct bloodline of industry. He was grateful for the side of him that was capable. But was he capable enough? That was yet to be seen.

He calculated the amount of wood that he needed: 200 linear feet to start. He decided to bring Andrea to Home Depot. *You can build it; we can help*. Their motto made him laugh. They'd ask him what he was building. What was he going to tell them? I'm planning for a flood. I need to build a ship. He'd let Andrea do the talking. She had a way of confusing people without letting them know they were confused. They'd get the lumber and set up shop; they could figure out how to build a ship that would not sink.

He knew that a project this size could take up to five years. He didn't know how he was going to accomplish such an undertaking. He could hear Bambi in his head, asking him why he was so special. He didn't have an answer. He didn't feel powerful at all. He felt confused. How come God didn't just present him with a prefab ship from eBay? Why reinvent the wheel? Wasn't the Navy auctioning off sea carriers? Why did he have to build something from scratch? Why a ship at all? How much room did shit need, anyway?

Noah sighed, frustrated. Then he felt angry. He was going to have to talk to that bird—what did it call itself? Dan? How was Dan going to answer all of his questions? He reminded himself that he had to take it one step at a time, nothing more, nothing less. Maybe he should go talk with Andrea. Perhaps they could begin preparing the building site. He needed to do something to expend his nervous energy.

He left a note for Bambi. He knew she'd probably wake up to a hangover. She so seldom drank that her system didn't have high tolerance. Her behavior of late was unpredictable. She wasn't taking this crisis as well as he'd hoped, although he didn't know what he had expected. How could he fault her for reacting the way she was? It was an honest reaction. He hoped she would remain sleeping until he returned home. However, he couldn't stay and wait for her to wake up. He hoped that she didn't wake up feeling abandoned, but there was too much to do. If he was going to build this thing, he reckoned he'd better get started. He drew a big heart on the outside of the note and left it on the countertop.

As he started up his old truck, he prayed for a miracle. He hoped that the platinum credit card would arrive soon and that he would find a bargain on wood.

Chapter 11

Bambi woke up fitfully wrapped in the sheets. She called out to Noah. When he didn't respond, she became angry. She had a headache, and she was alone. She let out one long wail that trailed off into a whimper. "Motherfucker!" She wasn't sure if she was yelling at Noah or something else. She was scared.

She kicked herself loose from the sheet, hurriedly put on her clothes. She got to the kitchen, saw the note, and calmed down. He did think of her. She tore it open, the love note. As soon as she saw his awkward heart and his handwriting, she reminded herself how much she loved him. It didn't matter if he was crazy. She was feeling crazy, too. She loved him anyway.

She looked pensively around. She didn't want to be alone. She saw the phone lying on the counter like a lifeline. She needed to talk with someone, someone in whom she could trust. Since she was in school to become a therapist, she had many friends who fit the bill; they were, after all, practicing confidentiality. However, there was the Tarasaf. She was pretty sure that having knowledge of end of the world events fit into *duty to warn*. But who would believe her? Would calls go out to a supervisor? Would there be a knock on the door? Police officers? Hospitalization for Noah? Heavy sedation? She didn't want that. There was no telling how far this could go.

She heard Ione's voice before she fully realized that she had dialed. "Ione, you're home!" She scrambled to say something that sounded neutral. Ione, who had already been in practice for fifteen years as an intuitive healer, had returned to school to be credentialed for insurance purposes.

"I'm home. A client cancelled. What can I do for you, honey?"

Ione was a voluptuous woman with a spring load of golden-red curls that had begun to gray. Thick hands, feet, and belly, she wasn't afraid to move herself through the world. She was a belly dancer. She was the mother earth. She was thirty years older than Bambi, but it was difficult to pinpoint her age because she looked much younger than her years. She made Bambi feel very safe. She once told Bambi that she had been named after the Greek verb "to be." Ione had long ago decided to put into principle her name.

Ione believed in the transformative forces of unity and the powers of a single life to light the dark the way a candle burned in the night. At the same time, she didn't discount the dark forces of life because they, too, were integral to living and growth. Her ideal was to integrate the two through meditation, which made her an excellent healer, and, though she was still in school, she had a long list of clients. She had learned much about integral psychology having studied Andrajana, the whispered lineage, in Tibet before the monks were burned. It was an esoteric practice, a Buddhist fast track to enlightenment that had only been opened to westerners in the last forty years to insure survivability of the knowledge. The Chinese government still believed, as did many governments, that they could control dissention by killing the dissenter. Andrajana was intended to integrate everyday life with a spiraling movement upwards toward God. It meant that kitchen cooks were waking up as fast as monks, and thus the government viewed this as a threat to the order that they controlled. And they were right. Since Ione had been practicing Andrajana, she had become a clearer channel and was able to disseminate the channeled information she was given through her healing. It was one of the many spiritual gifts that she'd brought back from the East, but she was always careful not to share too much. *A person should never know more than their readiness.* She was a careful advisor, and Bambi trusted her.

"Honey, are you okay?"

"I'm trying to be."

"What's going on?"

"Noah's building an ark!"

"Hmm. How interesting."

"Don't you think that sounds crazy?"

"I can't answer that. I don't have enough information to make an assessment. However, it does seem like you think so. May I assume that you'd like to come over?"

"Could I?"

"Come. I'm trying a new apple-flax scone recipe. It's healthful and sinful all at the same time."

"Give me about an hour."

"Take your time."

A tremendous wave of relief filled Bambi's body. She no longer held a secret, and by letting go she no longer felt so alone. Secrets were no good. It felt much better to get her needs met, to find comfort with her friends. She reminded herself that the source of her pain and discomfort could not be the source of her comfort. She had to get away from Noah for a little while. Bambi moved through the house collecting her purse, shoes, and keys. She got into her car and sped down the dirt road, taking the ruts and potholes without hesitation. The quicker she got to Ione's, the quicker she'd feel grounded. Bambi made the forty-five-minute trip in just over a half hour.

Ione lived in a small adobe duplex owned by an elderly woman who had sold her Manhattan flat to be in the desert where the low humidity and heat soothed the pain that had long settled into her bones. Ione had shared all of this and more. Mrs. Zucker was a good landlady; she needed companionship more than she needed the money. Ione had created a nice relationship with her, the type of relationship that Mrs. Zucker often lamented that she hadn't developed with her own children. "My worst fear is to die alone," she had told Ione. "Looks as if I am living out my worst fear. Not as bad as I thought it would be."

Ione was taking out the first batch of scones when Bambi sprung through the kitchen door into the oleander-colored kitchen. "Oh." She started a bit. "It didn't take you any time at all." She placed the cookie sheet down on the table and then opened her arms and gave Bambi a most nurturing hug. Open kitchen, open arms. "It's going to be okay, honey."

"You're right. Everything is going to be all right." Bambi picked at the corner of a hot scone. Ione smiled and handed her a plate.

They sat in the tiny living room, sipped brewed tea—mint and lemon—and ate hot, fresh scones. Bambi had memories of being with her grandmother. It was the feeling of safety that she most craved. Ione didn't say a word, but kept her soft, loving gaze on Bambi. Bambi knew she only had to speak when she was ready and comfortable.

Bambi self-consciously laughed. "If I tell the whole nightmare, I'm afraid it'll become real."

"There are many realities. Why are you defining the experience as a nightmare?"

"Ione, if this flood thing is going to happen, think of the suffering! How many will die? It makes me sick to think that everything on this planet that I love will be washed away. Doesn't that thought frighten you just a bit?" Bambi felt indignant and a little angry.

Ione continued to remain calm, her countenance, serene. She made no effort to reply.

"And if it's not going to *really* happen," Bambi continued, compulsively filling in the silence, "then I have to face the fact that the man I love is psychotic. Maybe just manic-depressive with psychotic features. Could be schizophrenia? I'll have to review the DSM later. Do you have one?"

After a moment, Ione spoke. "Let's stick to the now. Tell me what's been happening."

"He says he heard God and he's building a ship."

"He's building a ship. That's the now. Anything else is out of your control. Your brain wants to solve this to keep you safe. That's what brains do, but there is no way to solve it. Thus anxiety and disease come in. The only thing possible is to become friends with the discomfort."

"I know that. I remind Noah all the time to do that. But for myself, how do I do that?"

"You have to figure that out, sweetie. It's practice. It's doing the next right thing. Diagnosing Noah is probably not it." Ione's voice was gentle, and Bambi did feel much calmer just listening to her. "You have to learn how to witness the fear and understand that fear is a construct of the mind. If there is a true evil in the world, its greatest weapon is fear. Fear keeps us all imprisoned."

"How did you break free?"

"Practice, the same as you."

"But you began your practice in Tibet studying with a master teacher. Noting like that has ever happened to me."

"The way to truth happens each and every moment. You don't have to go to Tibet."

"It would be nice, but since I can't go today tell me the story again. It gives me comfort."

Ione smiled and nodded her consent. "I had searched all summer for someone to teach me Andrajana, which is that esoteric form of Buddhism I told you about. They acknowledge that one doesn't have to become a nun in order to reach enlightenment, and so it was the perfect path for me. However, I could not find my teacher."

"I had given up and was in a teahouse on the last day of my trip. This kind, older man came in to buy a newspaper. He sat down next to me, smiled, and we began to talk. He asked me what I was doing in Tibet, and I told him I had come to find my teacher. He asked me what kind of teacher I was looking for, and when I told him, he smiled and said, 'I am your teacher.' As it turned out, he was one of the few master teachers of Andrajana still living. He found me when I had given up all hope of finding him."

"I spent the next eighteen months in an ashram sitting on a zafu until I thought my knees and spine would never recover. I had to break through the pain and the impermanence of the body. I was told many times that the pain would not last. When the pain did crack open, I experienced rage so intense that I thought I could murder somebody. This rage was soon followed by love. I was so flooded, complete and whole, that I never experienced another sore back, and I was granted many spiritual gifts. The most enduring has been the gift of compassion and a deep understanding that all suffering is illusion of separation, including death itself. In Western terms, going into the Christ wound until one becomes unified with pure love. Fear cannot touch love. It dissolves into light. I think it will happen like that for you. I want to show you something."

Bambi followed Ione to the back of the house where she'd set up a cozy office space. Pictures of all the spiritual masters were framed and hanging on the wall. Jesus, Yoganadi, and Krishna, all compassionately gazed down into the study. On her bookshelves, she had stacks of books, papers, and journals, most of the titles relating to the esoteric knowledge of the mystics and the Gnostics—inner knowing, the spiritual interface between the material and the divine. Bambi knew because she'd borrowed many of Ione's books.

It was not the books that Ione wished to show her now; it was the window that looked onto the courtyard to the right of her own back window. "Have you ever seen Brighton's window?"

Bambi gazed into the yard where Ione had created a rock garden and hung bird feeders. Brighton was Ione's reclusive neighbor. "Yes, once. He was standing in the shadow by his window holding a cat. He had environmental depression? I was telling Noah about it."

"Environmental depression is—at least not yet commonly identified—a disconnect that has developed in the inexorable connection between the environment and our psyches. The most sensitive humans are unconsciously aware that the planet is dying, and many of them are profoundly depressed. Some are self-destructing, but professionals can't identify the root. The phenomenon occurs with beached whales and other groups of animals dying in mass."

"Is he okay?"

"Brighton hung himself in his closet two weeks ago."

"Oh, my God. That's awful! He was so young."

"He was twenty-nine. He'd been a senior at NYU film school when he got sick and had to come home."

Bambi didn't know what to say. She continued to stare at Brighton's window and tried not to imagine the horrific scene.

"My teacher demonstrated how to contact those passing. Sometimes they need assistance, especially those stuck in the transition of dying. Deep suffering sometimes strongly attaches to the environment. Brighton doesn't want to move on."

"He's still here?"

"When a person forces himself out of this reality, it creates a tremendous psychic explosion in the fabric of space, like a bomb affecting everyone in the vicinity. I think that's why one suicide often stimulates the impulse in others."

"If he's still here," Bambi crossed her arms, "the idea of ghosts and spirits unnerve me. I feel as if I should explain them away."

"The way you want to explain away Noah's experience?"

Bambi nodded.

"The way you'd like your experience explained away, too?"

Bambi was quiet. "But what about Brighton? Isn't there a way we can help him?"

"Hold his suffering as your suffering?"

They walked back into the living room. The tea was already cool. Bambi's mind reeled. "Why are you telling me all of this?"

"I was going to illustrate a truth about the nature of dying. A point that all great spiritual masters teach. Brighton refuses to go the eternal source, and by refusing to do so he will haunt these grounds because ghosts have no reference to self or time. It's a tragedy, but one day I know he will be healed, as all of us will. Even the most stubborn karmically learn the benefits of non-attachment. Once he stepped away from his body, I had hoped that he'd have had the realization that he was not suffering. He stood there and saw himself—or what he used to be—and realized he was not his body. He could let go of his body, but he could not let go of this space, which for him is the shell that makes him feel safe. The day he lets go of his attachment to his suffering, to his failure, is the day he'll pass into a column of light, and begin to heal."

"The moment I knew how to let go of my attachment to pain was the moment I became free. As you will, too. As will the planet and all life as we know it. This is a transition. The only thing we can control is how we react, even while facing our most overwhelming fears. We can't avoid suffering. We can only ride it out and go through the storm. We can only do the best we can. We are only human, after all. However, the longer we remain attached to the pain, the longer we remain as ghosts."

"Ione," Bambi whispered, "I don't want to die."

"Nobody does, Bambi. You might as well get on the metaphoric boat."

She nodded. "I guess I could be more supportive of Noah and less worried about the state of his mind."

"It's best to enjoy the lilies of the valley while they're in full bloom."

Bambi smiled. "Thank you for talking with me. I am grateful for the teaching."

"We're all teachers in some way to someone. Now, let's go pull up some carrots. I have to attend to my garden and would like the company."

***

Bambi stayed with Ione for most of the afternoon. They gathered fresh vegetables in the nearby community garden. They didn't speak much, but there was a lot of laughter when they mid-wifed some very stubborn carrots. It felt good to have garden dirt between her toes and to be with a woman who felt like a mother. Bambi stood up, stretched her lower back, and dusted her hands against the fabric of her dress where it lay across the lines of her hips. She looked for a very long moment, fully absorbed in beauty. A storm was blowing in. Half of the sky was deep purple, turbulent, tattered clouds of indigo, while the other half was filled with glorious light, like crowning jewels. There was a sundog—the paintbrush tip of a rainbow ring around the sun. It was only the second time in her life that she had seen such a phenomenon. There were birds swimming in upstroke and bees buzzing in low drone. There were flowers and life and abundance. Life didn't get any fuller than this.

"I love my life," Bambi said out loud. "I love every second of this life. I love living on this planet. I don't want it to end."

"Value every second," Ione reiterated. "Stay present, even to the despair, even to the darkness, and remember that life itself has a powerful drive to live, even after the flood, even after the fire. Clearing. It's all clearing for new growth, new levels of being. We never really die; we just change form. Be grateful for the now."

Bambi let out a tremendous sigh and inhaled love until she thought her heart would break. She pulled another baby carrot roughly out of the dirt and ate it raw. Tears of great joy and great grief streamed down her face. She smiled, and whispered to herself, "Yes." She was willing to try.

Chapter 12

Noah and Andrea pulled into the Home Depot parking lot in an empty dump truck. Noah carried with him the newly issued credit card — Visa Platinum Plus. There was no limit. Andrea said it had been easy to get, and she had put his name on it, too. She'd paid off the only credit card she'd ever owned and so her rating was very high, and, of course, she had the dump as collateral. The creditors were anxious to get her hooked once more, and extended to her the ultimate credit line, which should be enough to build two ships at a nine percent interest rate until June when the rate would jump to 21 percent. If the flood came, they wouldn't have to pay it back. If no flood came, they could always figure something out. Perhaps, they would sell the ark on eBay.

As Noah walked across the parking lot, he felt a sudden wetness seep into the neckline of his shirt. He touched cooling slime. "Yuck, pigeon shit!"

"Need this?" She held out a wrinkled Kleenex. "It's clean."

"Thanks." He carefully wiped the poo, folded the tissue, walked back to the truck, and put it on the dashboard to dry.

"Don't you want to throw that out?" Andrea sounded disgusted when he returned.

"Naw, I need to save it. For the DNA."

"You're collecting…that *stuff*?"

"Dan told me to."

"Who's Dan?"

"My guardian owl."

"I think I know that owl! Showed up last week, nearly scared me to death. Tried to bang him with the broom. Didn't realize he was a friend of yours. Might have been kinder. Then again, he never said anything."

"Well, he had a lot to say to me. He told me I had some tests to complete."

Andrea grimaced. "Like saving shit?"

"For the DNA."

"If it's just shit that we must collect, why the ark?"

"Don't know. Andrea…can you really talk to animals?"

"Yes, but I don't like people to know that. Once folks know, they want to know what their lap dogs really think of them. Too much pressure."

"I understand."

They exchanged a knowing smile and then got two large carts. Noah pulled out his list and they moved down the wide aisles dumping in anything that they might need, as well as a few impulse buys.

Andrea tried on a pair of safety goggles. "We need these."

"What for?"

"The primates have good aim."

Noah sighed. "Put them in the cart."

"Naw. I think I'll just wear them, get used to them."

Noah was a little embarrassed, but he did enjoy her sense of play. His motto had always been live and let live. They continued to shop. Andrea wore the safety goggles until she got bored and tossed them in the cart. They bought a stack of disposable jumpers, the kind painters wear. Noah bought a lot of new tools. He hadn't bought tools in a great number of years, and the Platinum Plus temptation was too hard to resist. It didn't take long before both carts were completely filled.

When it was time to order the lumber, they were helped by a big, friendly guy wearing a lumbar brace under his orange vest. "Hi there. Welcome to Home Depot: You can build it. We can help. What can we do for you today?" He pulled an order form from underneath the counter and uncapped his ballpoint.

"I need four hundred linear square feet of wood."

"Will that be board feet, linear feet, or 1X6?"

"Didn't I say linear?"

"What are you building?"

"A ship."

"What kind of ship?"

"Actually, I'm building an ark."

"So will that be teak or cedar?"

"What's the difference?"

"Both are seafaring. Teak is slightly more buoyant. More expensive, though."

"That's not a problem."

"Teak is endangered," Andrea whispered.

"I really don't think that's an issue anymore," Noah hissed.

Mr. Home Depot did some calculations on his computer screen. "$147.00 a foot times four hundred feet. That will be $69,000, but keep in mind that's just for the order; there's tax and delivery. You bought a consultant? It will take seven to ten business days to get that order in." He handed Noah the paperwork to fill out. Noah wrote his name, address, and directions to the dump, where the lumber was to be delivered, and handed the paperwork back. "Can I interest you in our Home Depot low-interest credit line?"

"We have unlimited credit." Noah put his card down on the counter.

The man quickly glanced at the name. "Noah? As in Noah's Ark? Are you really building an ark?"

"Yeah."

"Trying to live up to your name, huh?"

"Yeah."

"Your total is $110,910.00. That does include all of the building materials and incidentals. Would there be anything else I can do for you today?"

Noah shook his head.

"If I were you, I'd try to get God to pay for some of this." Mr. Home Depot slid the card through and handed him the receipt for his signature.

Noah signed without blinking. "I'm sure somewhere he is."

"Tell him that I've got bills, too," he said, laughing. "Noah's Ark. That's funny. You made my day, sir."

Noah smiled. "I'm glad."

He and Andrea left the store with twenty-six plastic bags of starter stuff, an order form, and a guaranteed delivery in ten days.

"He was a nice guy," Andrea said, unlocking the truck. "Do you think we should tell him about the flood?"

Noah looked back. "Naw. If he'd wanted to know he would have asked."

"Is that going to be our rule of thumb? Don't ask, don't tell?"

Noah felt overwhelmed and unsure of himself. He looked hard at her and then shrugged. "Do you have any better ideas?"

She remained silent, and Noah took this for a *no*. They loaded the truck and headed back to the dump. Their biggest shopping day was over, yet there was a solemn silence about the implications of their secret. The hard part was still ahead, more than they could imagine. In the meantime, they had enough to get started before that bird showed up again, and for that Noah was thankful. He wasn't sure, but thought that perhaps he had passed his first test. Even so, Andrea's question struck him with sharp pangs of guilt and uncertainty. This discomfort was fortunately relieved with the knowledge that the project was underway. There was nothing left to do for the day but the next thing, and as far as Noah knew the next thing was to unload the truck before dark.

Chapter 13

Dan felt Charlie's presence break through the material world. It was an odd sensation knowing he was around though he couldn't see him, and not knowing what form he would take or by what name he would call himself. As he glided overhead, Dan wondered how he was going to convey the stepped-up urgency to Noah.

He found Noah and Andrea unloading a dump truck and setting up tools. The dogs were resting in the shade. Dan lit on top of a nearby juniper. The branch gave to his weight like a trampoline. He fluttered, hooted, and then settled. He hadn't completely mastered gracefulness. He watched as they struggled to unload a table saw, a job meant for four men. Andrea was strong enough for two, but Noah was on the puny side. Dan looked again; he was stronger than he seemed. Andrea backed the metal leg against Noah's shin and he cursed like a sailor. Dan shook his head. The way they worked together, it was a miracle anything got accomplished. Still, he had to admit, they had done remarkably well. They had managed to secure a cradle. It hooked from the open-air sorting hanger's overhead support joints. There was some stacked lumber, enough to begin cutting out the transverse frames, and a large table where there were professionally drawn plans neatly rolled. They even had a water cooler. Dan was impressed. Not bad for human resolve.

He flew in closer, perched on a beam and enjoyed his bird's eye view.

***

Andrea saw him first. She nearly dropped the saw, which gave Noah cause to grunt.

"Sorry. But that owl is back."

This time Noah nearly lost his grip.

"Don't let go. We almost got it."

They got the table saw in place. Noah had no intention of ever moving it again. "Where is the bird?"

Andrea pointed to the metal crossbeam. Dan was stationary like a carving.

"Come to pay us a visit? Well, I have a whole lot of questions for you."

Dan remained silent.

"I know you can communicate. You did that mind-meld on me last time."

Dan remained uncommunicative.

"What do you want, then? I've been doing what you asked of me. I've got pigeon crap, does that count?"

Dan tucked his head in and stared, and then he nodded.

"That's good, then. I'm doing some things right. So does Andburg have anything to do with this flood?"

"I don't know," Dan hooted.

"Why does the ark have to be so big?"

"I don't know. You are the co-creator."

"How much time do we have?"

"I'm afraid I don't know that, either."

"What do you know?"

"I know that your demon is here, and it's going to get more difficult for all of us."

"I don't know how it could get any more difficult. I'm just supposed to do what I'm told without much direction? Is this how it works?"

"You have direction. All you have to do is get quiet within yourself." Noah turned away. Dan could see Noah didn't believe that would be enough.

"So Charlie is here? Will I meet him?"

"He will find you."

"Who's Charlie?"

"He's my personal demon," Noah said sheepishly to Andrea.

"You got a demon? Oh, yuck." She inspected him as if he had told her that he had a skin disease.

"Everyone has one. At least one," Dan assured her.

"What am I supposed to do?" Noah demanded.

"You have to get into alignment with the Mystery. Your demon doesn't have any more of the answers than we do, but he will be persuasive. Be on guard. Listen to only the voice of love and light. That which brings you peace is your friend."

"Anything else?"

Dan whistled once, *believe in yourself,* and then he was gone.

Only then did the dogs begin to bark.

***

As Dan flew off he knew deep down that he needed to negotiate with Charlie if these humans were going to have a surviving chance. He would try, but he knew he'd better take his own advice about alignment with the Mystery. He needed to find a place to sit where he could remain undisturbed so that he might find his own center. The next few days, he knew, would be brutal.

Chapter 14

Charlie buttoned his orange vest and gave it a firm yank. He wanted to look spiffy when he met his man. He combed the cowlick of the thinning brown hair over his part line. He liked the way that looked. He lifted his arms up and pinched. He didn't have a lot of muscle tone, but he'd make do. He could feel the Quarter Pounder unsettled in his stomach. He unhooked the plastic badge and peered curiously at the name, George Greer. He flicked off a speck of dry blood. George Greer, retired Coast Guard, member of the SCA—Shipbuilder Council of America —and Shipwrights Association. He'd been a tugboat captain on the Mississippi. Divorced twice, three grown kids, and a swallowed pride to work for corporate. Charlie admired corporate—suck the life, diminish the soul, to hell with long term. It was a very efficient structure, luring the desperate and the frightened. What could George have done? He was passionate about shipbuilding, and because of his kids and custody he was trapped in the desert. This had been the best gig around; at least he could build stuff. When he had gotten an order to build a ship, he had been so excited. It had been the first order like that in ten years, and he'd been sent to Pasadena. Prior to that day, George had stuck his badge on his vest every day, took it like a man. He had a job to do.

Charlie reached over to the fish tank and removed George's face skin. This was Charlie's least favorite part. It always took a moment to adjust to the bio chill of flesh struggling to breathe fresh capillaries. There were other ways to set this thing up, but he hated having to put on the whole suit—he'd rather the mask—and a few visible parts. He struck a pose in the mirror. He thought he brought a renewed virility to his human costume. He touched the name again; it disappeared into the fogged plastic and then the name Charlie reappeared.

Charlie practiced his voice. He had to make sure to avoid split tones. He did not want to freak anyone out. He had to be careful with that because it was sometimes difficult to judge. He looked at his watch. He was ahead of schedule by ten weeks. Charlie snickered. *Poor Dan. Why is he so stupid?* Charlie shook his head—a little too violently. He quickly had to readjust to the limited mobility of human flesh. Charlie inspected his new skin in the bathroom mirror. He did not wish to make any necessary repairs so soon. Everything was fine, no tears. He returned to the living room. He opened his briefcase and pulled out his case notes and photographs. *Ahhh, Bambi.* He held up her photograph.

The glossy photo finish caught the overhead light. She was like the original fallen angel, keeper of light, a Siren that stirred in men something so primal that they had no choice but to turn to the forces that had constructed Charlie as a means to control that which they most craved—unless they were queer. Then it was only a slightly different game, one with even more drama. Charlie touched the photograph and made it come to life like an iPad movie. It was a self-indulgent trick that he'd developed, a keeping up with the times. He could stage scenarios before he made up his mind how he wanted any given scene to play out. He used a fantasy file ranked by the nature of the evil. He was in the mood for something racy.

Bambi sat on a rock waving to Noah, who held a camera. She smiled broadly; her eyes shone like first love diamonds, like trust before the betrayal. She wore shorts—her gazelle-like legs were tanned and strong from hiking—Charlie liked that. She wore a simple halter-top and a choker Noah had made from carpenter nails hammered flat. She was fresh and she was young, and Charlie knew all about the soft underbelly in Noah's psyche.

Bambi was totally unaware of the power of her sexuality. She was the girl next door. That was the best kind, the most fun to corrupt. With her long slender legs, a handful of tits, and body hair like the first feathers of a gosling, she was going to be a treat.

Charlie froze the frame. He changed Bambi's costume. She now wore a corset. The delicate pink of her areole edged the leather lining. Charlie put her into leather shorts. Kinky. He put her into thigh high boots instead of tennis shoes. He arched her back against the rock. He placed Andburg in the frame. Andburg, the one man Noah secretly envied, who in turn secretly envied Noah. They had unwittingly formed a brotherhood of secret agenda. Charlie then unfroze the frame. She writhed with sexual expectancy. She unbuttoned her shorts and began to masturbate. Noah was forced to watch. Charlie could feel the magnitude of Noah's heart, the beating, the uncertainty, the need to protect his angel.

"You are way too old for this one," Charlie whispered into Noah's ear. "What Bambi needs is a good fuck."

"I always wanted her for myself," Andburg said without apology. "Now I'm going to get me some of that."

Charlie could make Noah feel things. He could make him believe that she had a burning desire for Andburg, that she had secretly craved him for years.

"Are you coming up here or not?"

Andburg stepped up onto the flat altar of rock. He pulled Bambi up, bent her over, pulled her shorts down, and began to ride her as she clawed at the rock with the intensity of someone unable to get enough, someone willing to be split wide open.

Noah turned away in agony, but Charlie patiently held his chin so he could not look away. His heart blistered with the betrayal and then began to bleed. He began to wither inside as a murderous impulse arose. He wanted the pain to go away. He cried and both Bambi and Andburg looked at him and laughed. "Honey, I really don't want you to internalize this. It's not you. It's me," she moaned. "Ohh, this is so easy," Charlie said as he flicked off the image. Only the ascendant masters had learned how to transcend the experience of that kind of pain by never stepping out of the center of pure loving. Only a Noah, willing to love Bambi despite the illusion of betrayal, would be able to free human consciousness in the next dimension. If Noah was successful, he and Bambi would enter a time porthole, and their child, a product of their pure loving, part human, part star being, would one day return. This divine teacher would illuminate a life of unified duality. Noah could become the father of a golden age. This was unlikely, given the insurmountable challenges that he had to face. And if for some reason he did manage to escape the traps, then the sight of her dead body would shred anything left into a mush of insanity. He crossed himself, and addressed God. "You could have brought me a greater challenge. Really, what's so special about this guy?"

Charlie looked around the apartment once more. He inhaled the isolation, the loneliness. For a moment he sympathized with these humans. He couldn't understand why they even wanted to keep the whole experiment going. In terms of evolution, they still needed to learn to love that which they most hated within themselves. If they could accomplish that, they'd understand that Jesus was not the only one who could perform miracles. If they could do that, there would never again be an Armageddon. There would be no evil to project onto the world.

He put the photograph away and locked the briefcase which held a photo stack of other important players, some very powerful on the world stage. Charlie hoped to pay some of them a visit if he had a chance, check in on them again and find out some of the details of the sabotaging plans.

He practiced his voice once more, and then teleported to the building site where all the materials had miraculously been delivered. Charlie was going to build the ark. It wouldn't take long at all. It could be instant if he so wished, but he needed enough time to befriend Noah, enough time to sow the seeds of doubt, to corrupt Noah's mind against the person he loved most.

He didn't know how many chances he'd get to do all of that. After all, Dan was right about the Mystery. The Mystery was the only thing that Charlie really couldn't control, a cosmic force, one in which even he had to obey the laws of engagement. In the Mystery, there was a point of singularity and pure unadulterated love where there was no dualism— no good, no evil, only divinity. Not even Charlie could bend that force to his will. If he ever reached that moment in time and space, would he suffer an identity crisis, or would he experience the bliss of being a prodigal angel? He'd heard that had happened to some of the fallen ones.

Charlie sighed, picked up a hammer and a saw, stepped forward and stopped in his tracks. He was impressed by what was before him—the ribs of a boat—like Adam's ribs—freshly cut and stacked under the sorting hanger. "Very industrious," Charlie said out loud. He was impressed with the human drive to do the next right thing and to survive. He could tell, however, that they were doing it all wrong. The lumber they were using was too heavy, and they should never have begun constructing it on this low ground. They didn't understand that it was going to rain. "Over there," Charlie commanded, and the entire ship reappeared on the higher ground, supported by a wood cradle. "That's better. Now, let's get on with it."

Chapter 15

Dan found Charlie sitting on a park bench in the long shadow of the Cathedral Basilica of St. Francis of Assisi off of the Santa Fe Plaza, staring blankly at the flagstone labyrinth and the dull shine of his black loafer shoes. It was the last place Dan would have figured to catch Charlie, but that's where his intuition had led him.

It was the instant shiver that led Dan to the man dressed in shades of gray, trench coat, nondescript, his legs stretched out in front of him so that it appeared he slightly slumped. There was no other significant indication of demon, just that deep shiver that pierced the hollow of his bones. Dan glided a few low circles before landing in a nearby tree. There was a light drizzle. The sun was beginning to set; shadows were dissolving the clarity of the physical world. From where Charlie sat, the main entrance was offset, and directly above the massive cathedral doors were the stained-glass mandalas, the smaller one illuminating a bursting dove, Holy Ghost, like a full moon.

This was one of Dan's all time favorite cathedrals. He wasn't sure why he liked it so much, there were so many in the world more grand, but when he looked at it he saw a column of pure light running through the center, as if the structure had been built upon a geyser of energy. Four hundred years of spiritual practice had fortified the place, and it had grown stronger in intensity despite the bloodshed—priest and Indian alike—that had crescendoed in the Pueblo Uprising of 1680.

Soon Charlie flicked his gaze toward Dan. Other than that, he didn't move, not even a twitch. Dan flew to the St. Francis of Assisi Dancing on Water fountain, and perched on top of the bronze tonsure. Charlie finally looked over.

"You lied," Dan said smartly. "You arrived early."

"I do that from time to time."

"I thought this game was pretty easy for you."

"Terribly so. Always has been."

"Then why cheat?"

"I'm bored."

"All I'm asking is that you not kill them. Would you be willing to do that?"

"I don't need to kill them."

"So we have an agreement?"

"If that makes you feel better."

Dan let out a long sigh of relief.

"What will I get out of it?"

"My suffering?"

"I already have that. I have all the suffering I can stand."

"You created it."

"If you believe that then you really don't understand the game."

"What do you want?"

"Your unconditional love."

"You have that, too." Dan didn't sound so convincing.

"Do I really? You're afraid of me. With fear there can be no love."

"But you are prone to cruelty and rage."

"I want your access to divine light, and to do that I need unconditional love."

"I can't give that light to you. You have to claim it for yourself."

"I will, through your compassion." Charlie looked over at Dan and began to laugh. "See. It's easy to talk the talk, but to walk the walk, now, that's a whole other ballgame."

"That's not amusing."

"Amusing? Okay, Dan, I thought you'd gotten to know me better over these last several centuries. I'll cut you some slack because I'm in a rather good mood. You can hang around and watch as much as you wish, but you can't directly interfere. If you can manage to do that, I won't harm a hair on any of your friends' heads."

"Okay, okay." Dan stared at Charlie. "Your face. Where did you get it?"

"My face? You like it?"

"You look unremarkable, yet creepy."

"Thank you. I was going for this look. Camouflage. I wouldn't ask too many questions, however. Trade secrets." Charlie winked.

Dan swiveled his head to look at the cathedral fully lit with the outdoor lighting, preparing for the onset of night. "Why here?"

"I like this cathedral."

"I do, too. It is a magnetic place, a thin place, a very holy place."

"I like this cathedral because I've been assigned here before." Charlie stood up. "Death comes for the Archbishop." He laughed. It was the exact moment that darkness swallowed the last remaining vestiges of day. Then, like a sorcerer, he disappeared.

"Charlie? Charlie? Where did you go?" Dan used the full capacity of his razor-sharp vision, but there was nothing to detect. He steeled his nerves. He didn't know if he had made the best deal; perhaps no deal should have been made. But it had been done. What could he do now but face the consequences? It was hard stuff to watch loved ones suffer. Noah, Bambi, and Andrea had become family. He'd think of something. There was always a loophole. Charlie had taught him that. There was something about being aligned with the light, with the singularity of holiness, wholeness, that Charlie didn't count on: it healed. If miracles happened, they didn't have to do with Dan. They had to do with the Mystery. Technically, he could not intervene anyway. Dan felt like the Indians who swapped Manhattan for glass beads from Dutch traders because it was still true—nobody could really *own* land—just as no one could own a miracle, or prevent one. The Divine Mystery didn't give a fig for deeds, land grants, or contracts. "To hell with you, Charlie," Dan said under his breath. "You make it difficult to love you, my brother."

Chapter 16

It was almost noon when Andrea picked Noah and the two dogs up in the dump truck, and they headed out past Airport Road, toward La Cienega, where they would cut across the ranch lands on a dirt road that led to the dump. They'd managed to do what they could to get building under way. By the end of the week, they were pleased with their progress. They had finally set up the saws, gotten most of the equipment organized, had even begun to cut and stack some of the wood. The full order of lumber, of course, had not come in, but the delivery date was approaching. Noah rubbed his shoulders, thinking about the weight and the fate of the world. He wondered how men in power did it. He suddenly felt a lot of compassion for Andburg. For Noah the difference between him and Andburg was that, unlike his friend, Noah couldn't make it alone. His thoughts shifted to Bambi.

She seemed to be accepting the situation better. She didn't really want to discuss anything ark related, choosing to focus on her studies, for she was approaching midterm exams. If she was worried about anything, she wasn't showing it. The only thing that she had told Noah was that she was spending a lot of time *processing*. He wasn't sure what she meant, but as long as she wasn't drinking too much, or running away, he figured processing was a good thing. He was proud of her. And if not for the undeniable reality that he was spending his days building a ship out in the desert, their days had returned to what appeared, on the surface, routine.

Andburg's party was also coming up, and he was looking forward to taking her to an event. They both needed a diversion, a place to rejuvenate in the joy of simply being alive. Bambi was always beautiful, but when she dressed up for engagements, she looked like a Hollywood star. She was so stunning that both men and women turned their heads when she glided by with the ease and grace of a natural beauty. He loved her for many reasons. Her beauty was one of the attributes he treasured because she shone with an inner radiance, and an undercurrent of playful goofiness.

The sun blazed directly above; not even the shade could hide. Noah rested his elbow out the open window, right next to Red Girl's nose. Even in October, he could feel the heat reddening his skin, but he didn't care. He didn't even care about the beads of sweat that evaporated into a dusting of salt. It was impossible to escape dust, just as it was impossible to escape the white light of desert glare. As they cut across the dirt road, a great cloud of more dust billowed up and lingered over the long red dirt road that cut directly into what would otherwise be unblemished ranch land. There were cows. There were coyotes. There were lizards, birds, and snakes. This was high desert, and it hummed with the life capable of survival. It seemed to Noah that many Americans had long grown disconnected from that parallel reality—survival of the fittest. There was a middle class assumption of convenience, an avoidance of suffering that was understandable, though it was held above accountability, and that's where cataclysmic events seemed to be catching up to shatter the illusion of safety. Noah didn't believe that anyone deserved such rude awakening, that no one people or place deserved it above another, but he understood that the waking planetary consciousness was not so concerned with the individual. The planet's cleansing forces were capable of leveling everyone equally.

As they turned toward the locked gate, Andrea pulled over, put the truck into neutral, got out, and unlocked the padlock. There was a sign: Dump closed for renovations until further notice. Noah wondered how a dump could be renovated. Didn't they just move locations once landfills became full? But if it kept people away from the ark, he wasn't going to argue. Obviously, someone had not liked the sign. They had scrawled a response, *fuck you,* in red marker. Five large garbage bags had been tossed out, blocking the gate. Several had been split open, probably by those same roving dogs that they'd seen earlier. Scattered about were Miller Light cans, stained meat Styrofoam trays, diet Coke bottles, and a diaper. Andrea had to kick the stuff out of the way before she swung the gate open.

"Bastards," she said, grinning when she repositioned herself behind the steering column. "They don't like change. It's going to be a big mess if I don't open that gate soon." She drove the truck in low gear up the steep gravel hill that led to the weighing station. Noah was about to return to his point about whether dumps could be renovated when she whistled. "You see that?"

"See what?"

She abruptly applied the brakes, stopping short. When his head stopped spinning from the jolt, he saw exactly what she had whistled about. Not only had the entire shipment of wood been delivered, but the entire transverse frame, the ship's ribs, had been perfectly cut and laid along the inside of the cradle. It was several weeks' worth of work done right away, and done very, very well. Someone obviously knew what he or she was doing. The thing Noah couldn't get his head around was how the entire ship had been moved to higher ground. He kept staring at the basic rib line of the ark about 500 feet further back from where they had left it. Noah turned to Andrea in disbelief. "Did you do all of that?"

She took off her straw hat, smoothed her unruly hair back toward her gray braid, and shook her head. "Are you kidding?"

They stepped down from the cab, the dogs sliding out behind them, and walked up to the building site. Noah felt so giddy looking into the belly of his whale that he didn't notice that both dogs were barking. "Shush!" he finally commanded. They stopped barking, but continued to pace, clearly nervous.

"They don't like it," said Andrea, speaking to what Noah thought was the obvious. She rubbed her leathery hand across the teak. The wood was gorgeous in its depth of burnished brown. "Who could have done all this?"

"The Home Depot consultant? He's supposed to be a retired shipbuilder, but I had no idea that he would actually build."

"Noah, nobody could have done this without divine providence. Besides, with Home Depot, wouldn't you have had to sign for the delivery?"

"I don't know. Maybe I did sign already. There were so many papers. Besides, let's not look a gift horse—I mean, look at this ship! We should have built it here to begin with. Someone knows what he's doing."

Andrea didn't say a word. She surveyed what needed to be done, nodded, picked up an uncut board and began to measure for the double bottom. Noah stepped up to help her. Although he hadn't planned on it, they began to slowly pick up where the Mystery had left off.

They had been into the project for a steady two hours, and in that time, despite his usual competency with wood, Noah had banged his thumb with the hammer, scraped his knuckles fitting butt joints, and regained all of his capacity for swearing. They took a water break. Noah dumped a full cup of water over his head, enjoyed the two minutes of fresh chill. He wiped his eyes and saw a dusty cloud on the horizon.

"I hope that's no dump delivery. I forgot to lock that gate." Andrea sounded alarmed.

Five minutes later, Bambi pulled up. She waved as she shut the car door, the dogs galloping up to greet her. She petted them both. She wore an above-the-knee dusty-rose dress and white mules with a low heal. She carried a wicker basket. "Thought you two might be getting hungry."

Andrea stopped and wiped her hands across her jeans. "Oh, boy. Who brings picnic baskets anymore?"

"Well, I do from time to time." Bambi was already clearing off a section of the workbench. "I've not been so supportive lately. I wanted to make up for that. Here you go, Captain." She held out a tempi sandwich with organic sprouts for Noah and a carefully wrapped roast beef sandwich for Andrea. He and Bambi had given up most of their meat consumption after attending one of Andburg's safari-kill barbeques. He took the sandwich with a quiet thank you and blushed because her Southern belle charm still worked on him. He didn't want to admit to the power of that stereotype.

"Bambi, I can't figure you out." He took a hefty bite out of his sandwich.

She blinked, and Noah immediately knew he'd said the wrong thing. "I've just been feeling a little insecure lately," she whispered. "I plan on helping you with this thing, or at least trying to do better." She looked over at the cradle. "You two have made soooo much progress. I'm shocked. Truly."

"Me, too," said Andrea, mouth full of beef.

"At this rate, you might be done in a month or two. Seems like someone here has built a ship before." She beamed a prideful smile toward Noah.

"They have. We ain't met 'em yet," Andrea said, swallowing hard.

"What do you mean?"

"Some gift horse did all of this before we arrived today."

"And you don't know who it was?" She shot Noah a look.

"Come on, baby. Just because we're building what we're building doesn't mean we have to stop accepting help when it comes our way."

"You *are* confusing. If we can trust outsiders, then why can't I tell people about what's going on?"

"I don't want to have a crowd of folks out here, that's all."

"Noah," Bambi nearly snapped. "If this thing is real, how are you going to keep it a secret?"

"Honey, listen, calm down—"

"Ooh, don't tell her that." Andrea sat down on a crate, amused. "I would never tell an angry woman to calm down. That just makes them nuts."

"Andrea is correct, Noah," said an unidentified male voice. "Why would you want to silence such a beautiful emotion from such a beautiful woman?" The voice took everyone by surprise. All three jumped. Charlie seemed to materialize out of nowhere wearing his orange vest, carpenter khakis, and black loafers.

"Where did you come from?"

Charlie laughed. "Now *that* is a long story. My name is Charlie, and I've been assigned to your project." He held out his hand.

Noah shook it. Charlie. That name set off an alarm in his head. Wasn't that the name of his personal demon that Dan had warned him about? "Noah. This is Andrea, and my girlfriend, Bambi."

Charlie nodded at both of them. It was just an instant, but Noah caught something in Charlie's gaze, and he noticed how Bambi self-consciously crossed her arms. That was very unlike her; usually she was warm and welcoming. She said a quick hello and then busied herself with unpacking the rest of the basket: cheese, grapes, and almond cookies.

"I didn't mean to intrude." Charlie seemed to have caught Bambi's briskness as well, for he addressed his comment to her.

"No, it's fine," Noah said. He looked back at the wooden skeletal system of his ship and knew that he had to make up his mind right then what he was going to do about Charlie. Noah felt stuck. He knew that if he wanted to get this thing built, he'd need the kind of help that Charlie was capable of providing. However, if he were a demon…Noah inspected Charlie. He looked pretty normal. "We were wondering who did all of this?"

"Yes, that was me. No surprises, I'm sure."

"Thought it was odd that we didn't have to sign papers first," Andrea said.

Charlie turned to Andrea. "I know that I didn't follow protocol. But I don't get many orders for shipbuilding, and it's my passion. Sometimes a person doesn't follow the limitations of rules. I do have all the paperwork right here, ready to be signed." He handed over a stack of papers in triplicate. "Your signature, sir."

"Thank you." Noah took the paperwork and began to flip through.

"I guess I can understand." Andrea squinted at Noah. "I'm not much of a rule follower myself."

"I can see that, and it is a noble quality. Patriotic in that early American sort of way."

"You've done an amazing job here." Noah returned the signed paperwork to Charlie. "How did you do it so quickly?"

"I've built a lot of ships. I've even built an ark before."

"How did you know it was an ark?" Bambi said, startled.

"I know every ship plan ever built. That's my job," Charlie reassured her.

She stared at him. He was an incredibly average looking man in his fifties, looked much older than Noah, but there was something about him that she couldn't put her finger on. She couldn't decide if he repulsed her or if she found him irresistible, in a Jack Nicholson sort of way. She hadn't considered another man since she had fallen in love with Noah. She had looked, of course, but this was very different. All of a sudden she felt very tempted.

"I have to go," she said. "There's plenty of food." She shot a bashful glance at Charlie and pecked Noah on the cheek. "No reason for anyone to go hungry."

"Bye, sweetheart. Thank you for the picnic. It was an amazing surprise."

"I'll bring the dogs home with me. They looked tired." She whistled and both dogs reluctantly got up and followed closely by her heels, their tails between their legs. She waved and then got into her car.

If Noah had been more observant, he would have seen Charlie jab a fingernail into his own flesh so as to resist making a rude comment about Bambi's ass. "Would you like a sandwich? She made enough for all of us."

"No. I've already eaten. Besides, I have a stage to build today, but I appreciate the offer. Shall we meet back here tomorrow, say eight a.m.?"

"That sounds great."

"Work for you?" Charlie turned to Andrea.

"Yes."

"Then tomorrow. And try not to mess up my work," he growled. He turned and walked across the lot and into the sage dotted landscape. Noah and Andrea watched as he slipped further away until he dissolved into the distortion of the desert light.

"Where's he going?"

"I see a truck out there." Noah pointed.

"I don't see a truck."

"There's likely a truck." He couldn't take his eyes off the ship's bones. "What good fortune," said Noah. He was thinking that having a personal demon wasn't so bad. Besides, if it were something that really shouldn't happen, he would expect Dan to say something. After all, Dan's job was to keep him on the right track. Noah sighed. "You know I'm supposed to be collecting—"

"Shit? Yes, I know. Still got that napkin drying on the dash board."

"Technically, scat. Do you think that would be something you might help me with?"

"Sure, I ain't got a problem with that. I can start with my kitty's litter box."

Noah groaned.

"Life does take some turns, doesn't it?"

Noah shrugged and began picking up tools. "Stinky turns."

"I got a friend who's the director of the Albuquerque Zoo. I could call him tonight. Make our job much easier."

"That's a great idea. What are you going to tell him?"

"I could say that you're working on the Space Port project, and that you'd like to do some experiments on animal organics in space."

"That's brilliant, Andrea. Sometimes I think you're a genius."

"I am. Haven't I told you that before?"

Noah gazed at her. He couldn't read her. Perhaps she wasn't kidding. "Keep coming up with ideas like that and I'll be sold."

"I wouldn't mind selling you on calling it a day. I bet you and Bambi have a lot to talk over. She didn't seem to like this Home Depot guy all that much, and I can't say that I blame her. A real creepy vibe."

"Yes, that might be true, but from where I'm standing," Noah looked over at the ship's progress, "he makes the most sense."

"That sure was nice of her." Andrea polished off the last almond cookie. "Not politically correct to say it, but she'd make a good wife. I'd have already done married her."

Noah smiled. "You're right. Time to call it a day."

They did one last check before walking back to the dump truck. Andrea dropped Noah off and continued on toward her trailer. Noah headed to the hearth where Bambi was waiting with a host of personal opinions about Charlie The Home Depot man.

Chapter 17

Andburg was naked in the dark. Heavy drapes were pulled across every window in his master bedroom. Another team member had disappeared, and last night he had tried to forget about that. Tracy was somewhere in the bed near him. Although he couldn't feel her, he knew she was still passed out from the night before. It comforted him knowing that there was a body there, someone familiar. Oddly enough, he felt safe in the insanity that they shared like twin stars. He *knew* her. She *knew* him. That was the way it was. That was the way it had always been. And though he half-heartedly wished that it were different, it was the way it would always, always be. They could not escape each other. Andburg was tired of trying. At this point in the morning—was it morning?—all he wanted to do was to spoon and take tender comfort there. Of course, he knew better than to ask her for that. That kind of emotional safety with Tracy would forever be a wish unfulfilled.

Their relapse into coupling had started off as a Neighborhood Crawl. Members of his team not in the Arctic each volunteered their home for one of the courses of a seven course meal. As it happened, they all lived fairly close to one another in a luxury development of sand colored adobes called Las Campanas, which boasted two Jack Nicklaus signature golf courses. Andburg felt a little bad about the golf courses because of the water shortage in the desert, but he appreciated the security, and he lived a comfortable distance from his team members. They playfully called it the White Rez.

After each course, the merry party became merrier as they banded to another house. Somehow, Tracy had managed an invitation and was waiting for him by the second course in her high fashion, which leant a stark contrast to the outback inspired gear: Bundu—African for bush—multi-pocket shirts, Zambezi hats, and why bother Bermudas that team members liked to wear not only for comfort, but to also be hip in the way of people who jetted off to exotic destinations, or could if they wanted, to discover treasures that most of the world would never see, much less understand.

It was all a bit elitist, Andburg was the first to admit, but it came with being a full contributor to the understanding of the planet and of global issues. Had they not all paid their dues? The years of studying? The years of training? The years of being beat up to do better, to *be* better? Either by Dad or by the competition. So what if there was some after hours partying, some letting down the hair sort of thing? Who did it hurt? They deserved their rewards. They worked very hard, very intensely, put in long hours to make sure that everything that needed detail got full attention. It was 110 percent. They knew the stats. Drugs and alcohol burned brain cells, of course, but they had crunched the numbers; they all had cells to burn and still be part of the top 1 percent. Their parties by no means ever got in the way of work. His little problem in the Arctic was already under control. He was scheduled to fly to both labs, pole to pole, right after the party next week, but until then he wasn't worried. Although he didn't really trust anyone, he trusted his team, or he had until recently. They were all mini-reflections of him. After all, he had hired each one of them. The one person he relied on now was Dr. Smart. Dr. Smart was sending him daily updates. Two days ago, he emailed the good news that he'd addressed the miscalculation and the most recent seismographic data no longer indicated a breach. Their project was still very much a go, although he was still trying to identify the source of the original problem of what he could only now guess had been a quake.

Andburg could no longer say for sure which course it had been when he saw Tracy, her legs neatly crossed, sitting on a massive leather sofa. There had been good food along the way, French cuisine: pan-garlic shrimp, heart-shaped caviar canapés, and lemon crème brûlée tarts. He wondered if the same chef had been hired for the entire crawl. Didn't anyone cook anymore? It didn't matter, because the food was secondary to the flow of expensive wine, cocaine, Ecstasy, pot, and, in one home, a crystal bowl centerpiece filled with hallucinogenic mushrooms, which party goers chucked back like trail mix.

Andburg really loved mushrooms, but he only indulged in them once a year. This was the night. It seemed to Andburg that he'd had a strange trip that he was just beginning to recall as he sat up. He remembered a bathroom; the tiles had spun, free-floating mandalas. Then God pried open the roofline and peered down. "Do you want to live? Or do you want to die?"

The funny thing was, Andburg wasn't sure. "You choose," he finally said and promptly threw up. He vaguely remembered cleaning the closed lid of the toilet, and then finding his way into the hazy lights of the party where he found Tracy and begged her to bring him home.

Andburg slowly moved his hand around, feeling for her. He wanted to be reassured that he was alive. Disheveled sheets and a wadded comforter were the only forms that he could detect. Just as he was going to call out her name and tell her that he loved her, the bedroom door swung open, spilling blinding light that made Andburg double over, scrambling for a sheet to cover his nakedness.

"What is your problem, you freak," Tracy bitterly chastised.

"You startled me. I thought you were next to me."

"You don't expect me to stay dead in the bed with you?"

Andburg looked around confused. "What time is it?"

"Should ask what day is it."

"Day?"

"That's right, dufus."

"Why are you so pissed?"

Tracy stepped across the bedroom, kissed Andburg on the lips. "I'm pissed for the last time you fell in love with someone else." She stood up. "Oh, that's right, you were never in love with her. You just gave her a ring and lived with her, made wedding plans. Poor bitch didn't realize someone else owned you. But I know your secret."

He looked at her standing in the grayish bedroom light. Her collarbone protruded sharply against her skin. He'd never realized how thin she had become. For a split second, it occurred to him that she was back because she needed to feed. "What's my secret, then?"

"You rather like being owned."

Andburg didn't say a word.

She stared at him for a long moment. Andburg didn't know if she was going to pounce on him and make love or kick him in the head. "Whatever," she finally spit out. "I'm glad you decided to wake up. Some Home Depot guy is here for you. He's building the stage. Get your lazy ass out of bed and take care of it. He gives me the creeps, but he's kinda cool. I invited him to the party."

"Fine, I'll take care of it. Would you mind leaving me alone now?"

"You're such an asshole!" Tracy turned on her heel and stalked out of the room.

Andburg could feel his rage percolate. He knew he had violent tendencies. It was in his blood with the richness of his Welch/German rip-your-head-open-like-a-grape ancestry. Such frenetic energy was present now and it ran the length of his spine to the impulse of his knuckles. In some ways, that was why he drank every night, to tamp down impossible urges. He knew he had the ability to go berserk in the same way the word was derived: Icelandic tribal warriors who grew their thumbnails out like knives so when they dug into a man's chest it was easier to pry apart the breast cavity to pull out the heart. Andburg knew what it was like to have his heart pulled out. It had happened so many times he had grown accustomed to ignoring the pain that was always there. Even now, he could feel the bloodline of his father and his grandfather and beyond, all those men who had used fear, intimidation, and control to claw their way to the top. He hated that he was so much like his father; he could never escape the man from whom he used to hide. He hated knowing his father that well, that intimately, now, when he was never allowed to do so as a boy. His worst fear was that he was doomed to become his father. His second worst fear was that Tracy was right: he liked being owned.

Andburg got out of bed, stood and squared his shoulders. He was ready for this day's curve ball. He didn't understand why the Home Depot man was such a big deal. Andburg found some clothes neatly folded on the chair in his room, took them into the bathroom where he quickly showered. The spray from the showerhead not only cleaned him, but he felt cleansed. He decided that he wouldn't kill Tracy today, but he would do his best to ignore her. He shaved, put on cologne, dressed. Then he went outside to see the work in progress.

Across the landscaped flagstone, Andburg saw that the wood stage was erected, nearly finished. From what he could see, the stage was being done right, professional, especially once the lighting people arrived. It would be one less thing that he had to oversee. If he wanted to, he could bring in the fucking Rolling Stones. *Let It Bleed.*

He approached and was surprised to see one man slinging a hammer with rhythmic precision. He seemed a bit older, and Andburg was amazed that he was working alone. Why he hadn't hired some Mexicans for the labor? Even without help, construction was being done quickly. Andburg decided that the man must have been out here slinging for days while he had recovered from the crawl. *I can't lose that much time again,* Andburg told himself. He looked down at his watch, but realized he hadn't worn it. It was unlike him to neglect a detail like that, even if he was attending to his own garden party.

"How long have you been at this?" Andburg gestured in a lazy way at the near-completed stage.

The guy stopped hammering and looked up. He didn't appear as old as he'd seemed from a distance. There was timelessness about him, a quality that Andburg had encountered in a handful of spiritual gurus. There was something else as well. Andburg wasn't sure what it was until the man spoke, and then he connected his voice—much later, of course— with the realization that, except for the face, this man was his father.

"Since ten a.m., sir."

"Call me Andburg."

"Andburg, the stage should be done within the hour. I believe you will find it to your liking. I have some papers for you to sign. I would have had you sign earlier, but I guess you weren't up."

Shame spiked a hot flash across Andburg's face for the first time in twenty years. He squelched his urge to reply with a "yes, sir," or to defend himself. "The stage looks good." Andburg walked the length of it, inspecting.

"It's perfect," Charlie retorted. "So who's going to be up there?" Charlie nodded toward his construction.

"Jamaican Snow. Local," Andburg replied. "Friends of mine who play electric Reggae Blues fusion."

"This is a mighty fine stage to be building for friends. You should get the Stones in here."

Andburg stared at him for a moment. That's odd, he thought. "Friends are everything to me. I'll get the Stones in next year."

"That woman I met, Tracy? She's your wife?"

Andburg shook his head. "No, not my wife."

"If I might be so bold," Charlie stopped short in mid thought and fished from his pocket what looked to be a very stylish Blackberry. "Excuse me for a moment." Charlie took the stylus and typed in "freeze" and then "History File."

For a brief second, time stopped and perspective shifted. Andburg stood frozen with a slightly sarcastic expression, like he was going to have to explain his love hate relationship. Tracy. Charlie had a hunch. He'd met her before, but where? It took him a moment to place her. When he saw who she really was, he caught himself from howling with wicked mirth. "You've got yourself a live-wire, son." Charlie smiled at the images of her throughout history. A Desert Jinn, a goat-like huntress who demanded blood sacrifices from the Israelites. They served her for centuries in fear and awe, but it had been a long time since she'd wielded such power. She was still pissed about the Inquisition, one of the rare instances in which the clergy had been right when they'd set a blaze under that morsel of a woman that they called Nightshade. Charlie almost felt sorry for Andburg. Almost. Andburg, however, had a choice with this dame. She wasn't powerful enough to be there without consent. He chose not to be free. It wasn't his loving that kept him miserable; it was his wedded addiction to pain.

Charlie looked deeply at Andburg. He saw right away that there was an angry sixteen-year-old housed in Andburg's heart. The teen that Andburg had once been, the teen who had prayed nightly for his father's death, the teen who began to abuse alcohol in the family garage while he lifted weights like a prisoner doing time, the teen who hid from the world because he believed that he was worthless, all the while driven to accomplish greater heights to prove otherwise. No matter how much he succeeded, it was never enough. He couldn't get far enough away from the pain packed tightly in his inner core. Why would his father do those things to him? His father had died of lung cancer, a death that was both too soon and too late. There could never be any forgiveness, closure, or peace. There would never be any "I'm sorry, son. Forgive me. I knew not what I had done." There was only revenge of the tumor and that wasn't enough.

Charlie had seen enough. He unfroze time and perspective returned to linear.

"We can't always choose who we love." Andburg looked down at his feet; really he was looking at the dirt around his shoes. He wanted to be anywhere other than having this intimate conversation with a stranger who somehow felt oddly familiar. "That's what I've told myself. I try not to allow her to ruin my life, but I'm not doing such a good job. She has a hold on me. It almost feels supernatural, not that I really believe in all of that."

"Good for you. The supernatural is over rated."

"Stage looks great." Andburg scanned the work one more time, confused by the conversation. "Let me know if you need anything. Have a beer with me when you get finished."

Charlie stood taller in a menacing sort of way. Andburg shrunk just a bit. "I plan on drinking with you, buddy," Charlie said. "If you don't think that's inappropriate."

Andburg hesitated briefly, but only a moment. "We all need a drink now and then." He nodded. "You're doing a great job here. You deserve a beer."

Good boy, Charlie thought a thought that went directly into Andburg's subconsciousness. *Stay drunk. It's easier. You don't have to feel and you will believe that you are closer to your authentic self. Stay drunk, Andburg. Stay drunk. The end of the world depends on you.* "As do you," Charlie flatly stated.

Andburg looked distracted when he slowly headed toward the house. He also looked defeated; the reality of his internal enemies weighed heavily on his mind.

***

Andburg was stone cold sober when he got the nerve to return to the finished stage. It was late afternoon and he was bringing the promised beer. He was strangely reserved around Charlie. He still couldn't say why. He had spent the day catching up. He had business to complete. There was a trip to the Falklands, and another to the Arctic that needed to be booked, not to mention the Antarctic. Because of his unique military clearance, he had to do this work himself, and it took bureaucratic legwork. But it was done, and Andburg felt that he was once again in control. He would be in even more control once he could get to the substation and look around first hand at his project.

He checked his cell phone. Tracy had called five times, leaving messages that she had made the final arrangements with the caterers. If everything went as planned, he would have a blowout weekend before he left town, not that he deserved it. A part of him wished Tracy hadn't gotten involved in planning what was fast becoming an event, but she was good with themes. She had rattled off something about fake snow.

Fake snow? Whatever, Andburg thought. He didn't really care. She was already being difficult. She was threatening not to come. He knew that if he ignored her, she would show up and make a spectacular scene. If he reassured her, there was a fifty-fifty chance she'd leave him with a modicum of peace. What did he care if they had fake snow or not? He made a quick call and left her a message and told her to stop being difficult, of course he needed her there, and fake snow was brilliant.

Charlie was calmly sitting on a stone bench near a juniper on the edge of the patio when Andburg approached, carrying two pint-sized glasses of Amber.

"Thank you," he said as he accepted the communion of hops. "What should we toast to?"

"Here's to the stage."

Charlie lifted his glass. "To the stage … and to pretty women." Charlie enjoyed the beer's honey-nut flavor, but alcohol itself had no effect on him. He watched as Andburg pulled up a lawn chair, and drank the first beer. "Would you like another?"

"No. I've got enough, thank you."

Andburg got up and went in to the house only to return with a refill. "It's been a long week."

"No reason to explain," Charlie smiled like a diplomat; he could be a disarming demon. "We have an acquaintance in common."

"Who's that?"

"I met Noah and Bambi. Aren't they friends of yours?"

Andburg smiled. "Noah's like my brother."

"Good thing he's not."

"What do you mean?"

"That girlfriend of his. Bambi. I wouldn't want to have such distracting thoughts about my sister-in-law."

Andburg was quiet as he stared into the depth of his glass. "I'd ask you not to speak rudely of a friend of mine."

"Sure, didn't mean any harm. It's just that as a man of your stature, it must be torture on some level to be around a woman like that who's out of reach. I'm sure you're used to getting any woman that you want, except one. Your brother's wife."

"I'd rather not talk about this." Andburg's voice rose perceptibly. "In fact, after you finish your beer, I think you should go." Andburg reached for his wallet and pulled out a hundred dollar tip. "Thank you for your services. You did a most excellent job on building the stage."

Charlie smiled and stood up. He had known all along how simple it would be to crack open Andburg. Human weaknesses were too easy. "You must be a very successful man. Your father must be very proud of you." He began to walk away, then paused. "I didn't mean to offend you.

But I do understand the slow death of unfilled desire. If you'd ever like to talk, I might be of use to you." Charlie produced a card from seemingly up his sleeve. "I'm glad you like my work. Call me."

Andburg didn't look up. He stood up, put the card in his wallet, and walked back into the house, feeling exposed. He could sense Charlie looking deeply into the fire of his soul. He knew that such thoughts were crazy but it seemed that Charlie had inhaled a part of his soul, savoring the flavor of misery. Andburg gazed back over the patio. Charlie was gone, but he left behind a faint, faint smell of sulphur.

Chapter 18

Bambi was too keyed up to sleep. She slipped out of Noah's embrace and sat on the sofa, staring out the window at the stark white beauty of the moon. Her experience with Charlie had left her feeling uneasy, and she couldn't shake it. Her instinct was to run, but she couldn't imagine where she'd go. She looked up into vastness of the night sky and wanted to be embraced by the moon, but its coldness offered no such comfort.

She couldn't say for sure why Charlie made her feel corrupt. Perhaps it was the way he looked at her with an undercurrent of raw sexuality. It left her with feelings of unbridled possibility and ultimate freedom. She knew that she could tap into her most primal self with that raw and unapologetic energy. She liked how that power felt. Once, when she had been a teenager—budding sexuality—a boy named Hunter had pulled her down onto his lap in homeroom. He'd had an erection. At the time, she wasn't even sure what to call the bulge in his jeans, but she knew that she liked it. She bolted from him. She knew, though, he would follow her and he did.

For several weeks, she allowed him to catch her in the empty halls of lockers and, without speaking, press himself against her. She was afraid. She was curious. They never went further than immature exploration, but they might have if Fanny Jones hadn't caught them, hall pass in her hand like a paddle. Fanny Jones, whose mother was the math teacher and who wore smock dresses and white patent leather shoes that matched her white leather handbag. Her gasp said it all. Then the gossip started. For the entire school year, Bambi's reputation as a slut echoed behind open milk cartons and steamed soggy vegetables destined to be scraped away into garbage pails. Bambi had been shamed. When more boys began to come around, she felt hunted, and took refuge in the library. No one would pay attention to her hiding behind the knowledge of everything worldly. After a year, and after Percy Spears had become mysteriously pregnant, no one seemed to care.

Charlie's gaze made her feel naughty, seen, appreciated, desired, and hunted all at the same time, made her feel like a teenager again. Charlie wasn't what he seemed. She knew that. She'd caught a glimpse of something else. She wasn't sure if she'd imagined it, but for a split second something had been revealed when she looked at him with a sidelong glance. He had, of course, been looking at her, and something in his face slipped. It was as if he wore a mask, a face that didn't quite fit. It chilled her.

Bambi checked in with herself to make sure that her perceptions were true. She couldn't tell and that frightened her because it had been a long time since she couldn't trust herself. She'd sat through the night tracking the nearly imperceptible arc of the moon, arms wrapped around her knees for warmth. She was trying to figure out what she had seen. Her imagination made it ten times worse. She was frozen within her perception. She thought many times that she should wake Noah, but she never did. When he finally emerged from the bedroom, his unruly hair in his face, the dawn was in checkmate with the moon. Bambi felt oddly comforted by that moment; like the moon, she could simply stop her internal struggle and surrender to change: dark to light, light to dark, dark to light.

Noah was boyishly cute, not quite awake. It was a quality that he'd retained even as he aged, and was one of the things that had attracted her. He stood six feet tall, lanky, especially in his long johns, longish hair, and bare feet. This image of him made her smile. She loved his creativity and his loyalty. No one else she'd met in her life could match his steadiness. Most of all, she knew the value of a man who was centered within himself, and led from his heart. Such a gift was more precious than anything material—gold, cars, diamonds, and a big house with a wraparound porch. Bambi was grateful that she'd been ready for such a love. He didn't mirror her physical beauty in the ways that the boys whom she'd given her heart in her youth had. But what had they done with that love? What did they know about such a gift? They mistook love for weakness. They erroneously believed that there would be an endless supply of women. For a great part of their life, because they were handsome, they were probably right. It was after all, a consumption culture.

"How long have you been up, sweetheart?" Noah said as he sat next to her on the couch and held her tight. Together, they were warm in the early morning chill.

Bambi rested her head against his shoulder. "I don't know. Two? Maybe three?"

"Why didn't you wake me?"

"I don't know. I didn't want to."

"Do you want to talk?"

Bambi buried her face in his chest and moaned. "I don't even know what to say. Things aren't right. I want the world to stop changing. I want everything to be the way it's supposed to be. The way it was."

Noah held her for a long moment. "I don't know what to say to make you feel better. Life is always changing. You know that."

"This is different. Don't you think?"

"I try not to think." Noah exhaled heavily. "How can I help you?"

Bambi got up from the couch and began to walk back and forth the length of the room like a caged cat. "I have anxiety. I want to escape, but there's nowhere to go that feels safe. I want to be held, but I feel inconsolable. I feel like I'm living between two contradictory poles and I'm being pulled apart. It's like a river of time, and the current is speeding up, and I'm trying to hold onto the bank. I don't want to die, but I want to get it over with because the waiting is worse. It's difficult to trust anyone right now." She stopped pacing and looked at him. "Even you." She saw Noah flinch, but his gaze never left hers. "It's hard for me to say that, but you asked. I'm trapped." There was more, but how much could she risk revealing? Should she tell him about the paradoxical experiences around Charlie? In that moment, she realized that it wasn't Noah whom she couldn't trust, it was herself. She was trapped because she couldn't escape herself.

"You feel trapped?" He sounded utterly helpless.

She couldn't help herself; her heart melted and she walked over and gave him a kiss.

"That's it? You're feeling better?" Noah sounded confused.

"No. I can't imagine feeling better anytime soon. But what can I do?" She sat back down on the couch and once again buried herself next to him. He smelled good, a hint of man sweat and sleepy boy. "I don't think you should let Charlie help you with the ship any more. He gives me the creeps."

"We talked about this the other day. We all think Charlie is a little odd, but at this stage I'm grateful for his help."

"There's something not right."

"There's no reason why you need to be there when he's around. Besides, I'm not going to let anything happen to you." He kissed her on top of the head. "Just avoid him."

She smiled, but she didn't believe him. What power did Noah have if anything went down? What power did any of them have? If the world turned into fire and ice and then melted again, what was he supposed to do? No wonder she didn't trust him; he trusted too much—a voice from a broken TV, a man who could build a ship at a superhuman pace. Bambi couldn't help but wonder, what next? Who else was Noah going to trust? I won't let anything happen to you. He really believed that? She could have laughed out loud. Human life was fragile. She was learning just how fragile it was, and her instinct was to bolt, to keep moving so whatever this shadow of change was upon them all, it could not find her. She could only hope that perhaps Noah would go with her.

"Noah, do you think we could just leave?"

"Where would we go?"

"I don't know for sure. The mountains. I know a man who owns land in the Sangre de Cristos. Maybe we can join a commune. Eat roots and potatoes until this storm blows over."

"Bambi, I know about wanting to run. A part of me would like to do that, to forget all this happened, but I took on a commitment to complete this project. I don't know what I'm doing, but for better or worse, I plan to follow through. I have to believe that all of this is for a higher purpose. It's not about me anymore."

Bambi sat up. She was angry. "I can understand your need to follow through and to honor your intuition. But you're sounding like a religious nut. I can probably tolerate that, but it would really help if you didn't make promises that you can't keep."

"What do you mean?"

Bambi began to cry. "Don't promise me that everything is going to be fine and that you're not going to let anything bad happen. You don't have the power to promise me that."

"Bambi, I know that I can't control much, but I will do my best to protect us both."

"But you won't go with me."

Noah didn't respond. He became stolid, uncharacteristically so. She had only seen this side of him one other time. She couldn't remember the reason. It was early on in their relationship when she was still trying to decide if she loved him. Seeing him like this now—stony quiet like all the books she had read about men—she was conflicted. Part of her felt abandoned. He didn't choose her. The other part of her admired his stoicism. It was a complex combination, but Bambi knew that they were at an impasse. She knew not to beg the issue or push any further. She grew sullen. He drew her close. Language had failed them. They waited as the full morning light teased awake all of the living sounds Bambi was flushed from lack of sleep, but she didn't care. Then the phone rang and everything became something else. Noah stood up and walked over to answer it. Andrea's voice came through the line, loud and excited. Noah wrote something down on a notepad.

When Noah finished the conversation, he turned to Bambi. "Would you like to go to the zoo today?"

"The zoo?"

"Andrea contacted the director of the Albuquerque Zoo. He's a friend of hers. I don't know what she told him, but we have permission to collect excretion samples."

The part of Bambi that loved Noah was excited. The part of her who was hurt and abandoned was disgusted and embarrassed. "How are you going to get it home?" was all she could manage to say.

"That's a good question." Noah became lost in thought.

Bambi sighed. "Ziplocs come in all sizes. Bring plastic gloves and face masks."

"And we have those jumpsuits. I have to figure out a way to dry the stuff."

"Drying racks and this desert sun."

"But won't there be a risk of contamination?"

"I don't know. How *do* you keep that dust out? Microbes? Maybe God won't mind contamination." He was already gathering his things. He had on a baseball cap and a sweatshirt and old beat-up jeans.

"I'm not going." Bambi was abrupt.

His face fell, though he tried to cover his disappointment. "Are you sure?"

"I'd rather not, if you don't mind. I'll wait and see how this trip goes."

"Are you going to be all right?"

"Of course. Haven't I been so far?"

He looked puzzled.

She offered her cheek, and then pushed him toward the door. "Don't forget the sunscreen."

"I've got some in the truck."

"Don't forget to label the bags. I'd also do an index of what the animals have been fed to cross reference the genetic material."

"That's another great idea, Bambi."

"Don't forget to call me after you get back and clean up some."

"Okay."

"Oh, and Noah?"

"Yes, baby."

"Don't forget the prairie dogs."

"I won't."

Then he was gone, and she was left to struggle with her insecurities, fears, and anxieties. She stood up, determined to do something productive, anything to keep her mind off the reality of their unfolding story. The last time she felt this way, she'd gone over to Ione's. She remembered something Ione had told her. *I go on silent retreats when I need to center.* Bambi mulled it over. She had a place in mind. A safe place near Abiquiu. *That's what I'm going to do. After all, I'm spending so much time alone, anyway.* She robotically walked to her car, and started off into the world of the unfamiliar. She had great conviction and she wanted to honor that. First, though, she had some things that she had to take care of. She had an exam to take and then she planned to drop in to see her friend, to check in and find some temporary comfort.

Chapter 19

It couldn't have been a more beautiful day to go to the zoo. Only in the vast west, where the atmosphere was a bit thinner, did the sky deepen to the color of cobalt. Noah sometimes felt turned upside down, like the sky meeting earth was a shoreline, and he was looking into the calm breath of deep ocean, a kingdom of air. The interstate landscape to Albuquerque became even sparser as they headed across the valley toward the Sandias. It was here, across this valley, where once a year hundreds of hot air balloon aficionados fired up their burners and lifted off into the air like so many Christmas tree ornaments, many of them in the shapes of animals Noah would encounter at the zoo. He couldn't remember the last time he had been to a zoo. He loved zoos, and he hated them. He had long ago lost interest in them, and without children, there never seemed to be an excuse to go. Noah still didn't like seeing animals penned up. All his life, he had been very sensitive to animal consciousness. To him they were as self-aware as human beings, though not split from the nature within. Even as a child, he had known that their freedom was exchanged for a life less lived, but a life lived nonetheless. Many of them were rescued from the blade of extinction, but who could say they didn't want to go from this planet being systematically destroyed one habitat at a time? His excitement as a child had always turned into heartfelt tears for the ones who suffered. Not all of the wild ones could take the trapping without losing their minds.

As they drove, neither spoke. Andrea was pensive, nearing on sullen, which was uncharacteristic of her. Noah settled into the silence, and didn't ask her what was on her mind. He figured that if there were something she wanted to share, she'd speak.

They were nearly to the zoo when she turned to him. "Doesn't it bother you that the animals we see today might drown in some near future?"

Noah was silent. He tried not to think too much on the dying. He didn't want to shut down.

"Don't you think we ought to tell folks? Set a plan for saving our furry friends?"

"I'm not even sure we can save ourselves. How many animals can we bring aboard without sinking?"

"I'm not sure it's the animals we have to worry about. Animals are pretty smart. They can always find higher ground." She fell quiet.

"It feels too big." Noah finally filled the silence. "People won't believe us, and even if they do, what's accomplished by spreading fear? I have to believe that in some small way I'm doing my part to save the genetic code of their species, and to give them a chance to return to a world that won't keep them locked up. To a world that remembers mutual cooperation between all the brothers and sisters of the planet. To a humankind that is once again ready to be in balance with life itself."

"That sounds noble. But who of us is ready? How do we get to decide that? I keep seeing all of the faces of people I pass on the street, and I keep wondering what's so special about me? How come I've been given an exit plan and they're going on with their lives as if there's no other way out?"

"I don't know. I wish I did. What do you propose that we do?" Noah turned to her for the answer. Andrea's body tightened. He could see that her jaw line was set and determined.

"I thought that we could just set them free. I mean the animals, not the people."

"Today?"

"No. Not today." She cracked a stiff smile.

Noah sighed and shook his head. "I don't want to know about it." He knew any attempt to control the behavior of his accomplice would be futile. He decided that he wouldn't worry, couldn't worry.

By the time they pulled into the Albuquerque Zoo parking lot, the gates were open and already there was a sparse scattering of cars. Noah had a good idea how they should work. They should group the samples based on animal size, and sweep the compound from back to front. They'd begin with the elephants because their exhibit was in the very back and would provide the largest sample. Andrea agreed; she usually agreed on everything. Once they got out of the truck, they put on their jumpsuits, gathered their backpacks, each packed with Ziploc bags and sealed containers. They had a couple of saw-toothed spades, water bottles, hats, glasses, and nose plugs—just in case. Andrea had a bag of apples. Except for the polar bears and the lions, she was pretty sure that she could make friends offering apples. Fully geared, they transformed into a clean-up team, looking much like those who tagged behind in the circus parade. The image made him laugh.

They marched through the parking lot to the entrance, and walked up to first ticket window without a line. Andrea gave her name and stated through the round slotted window that they were guests of Dr. Richard Roach. The middle-aged woman, pasty, trapped, and resigned, took out a list. "ID, please."

Andrea and Noah took out their driver's licenses and slipped them through the slot. The attendant made a quick cross-reference to her computer screen.

"Thank you." She returned the identification and looked at them for a long hard moment. "Go through Gate B." She loosely gestured in the general direction of right. "Dr. Roach's office is behind the Magic Garden Pavilion." She slid a thin paper map through the slot. "His office is 36B West Pavilion. He'll have badges for you that you must have on before you enter any of the exhibits. And you must be escorted at all times."

"Thank you," Andrea replied. She turned around, disoriented. Noah beckoned. They went through the clack of the turnstile and, as instructed, headed in the general direction of right turns until they found themselves in the Magic Garden. Several children stared at them, confounded by the sight of the two adults in their outrageous get ups.

The Magic Garden was amazing, not like anything zoo-ish Noah remembered. There were giant mushrooms, dragons, ants, and bees, images influenced by Lewis Carroll's *Alice in Wonderland,* sized for a dirt-level perspective. Noah was impressed by the innovation and creativity. He tapped on a mushroom stem, a polymorphous concoction like the stuff used to fill cracks on the space shuttle. He still hadn't figured out what the high-tech substance was when they went down the rabbit hole and looked up at the root system of carrots.

It took some time to get out of the Magic Garden and more time to find the pavilion where Dr. Roach had his space, tucked away from the crowds, down a long hall of painted white cinder blocks. One knock, a greeting, and then they were in Dr. Roach's office.

Dr. Roach had a desk job belly, thinning hair, and wore glasses. His plaid shirt had a starched creased pocket. He looked like a run of the mill dad. The only thing that distinguished him from the average administrator was that he wore blue jeans, not faded, very blue, and very new. Overall, he was dressed neatly, pressed, but seemed appropriately ready for the as-needed rough-and-tumble work of zoo life.

Dr. Roach's handshake was firm. He smelled faintly of peanuts. He smiled at Andrea, but his eyes revealed a shadow of confusion when he offered them a seat on the two hardback chairs in his office. "Good to see you, Andrea."

"Well, it's good to be here, Richard. Thank you for letting us collect the raw data."

"No problem. I know how challenging research can be, especially getting a NASA proposal ready."

"NASA?" Noah shot a probing look at Andrea's leathery, poker face. Andrea shot him a warning look.

"How do you two know each other?" Noah said.

"High school chemistry." Andrea's reply was curt. Noah picked up on the cue not to ask too many questions.

"I'm indebted to this woman. She single handedly got me through Ms. Hernandez's class. If I hadn't gotten through AP, I would never have come this far. I always said if there was ever a favor…I just never expected to see Andrea again after all these years. And from what she's told me," Dr. Roach smiled, "she's been a very busy woman."

Andrea blushed.

"This project sounds," Dr. Roach searched for the right word, "fascinating. You will have to explain more about your proposal, if that's not a breach. I know how the government can be."

"A DNA catalogue. That's what I like to think we're creating. But we should keep the details under wrap."

"Of course. NASA." Dr. Roach shifted in his chair. "Did you say you were up in Los Alamos?"

"No, the Space Port down around Truth or Consequences."

He leaned in a little closer. "Is NASA in the military's back pocket, as well? If that's private funding, do you mean NASA has a hand in it, too?"

Both Noah and Andrea sat stone-faced.

She leaned back in her chair and coolly gazed at him. "Will you be coming along?" She redirected him into not pursuing his questions.

There was a long pause. He looked nervous. "Unfortunately, I have to get ready for a staff meeting. I must finish budget plans. There's a sick elephant, and a zoology conference in March. I am presenting." Dr. Roach looked pleased. "You'll be in good hands, however, if you should need anything," he continued. "I've alerted the staff to the nature of your field research. I do ask that you enter the thirty-pound plus carnivore exhibits with an escort—liability issues." He slid across the desk a stack of papers. "Release forms. Please sign. That includes all primates, bears, big cats, and so forth. And, the elephants. They can become agitated. All other installations, small mammals, marsupials, non-poisonous snakes, insects, et cetera, you can enter at your own discretion because you have such a high government clearance."

"What about the aquarium?"

"That's a separate addition, and if this goes well, I'll make the arrangements, but I'm afraid that you won't be able to access everything today. Our zoo is too big and shoveling waste is hard work."

"I guess we can't expect to get all our shit done at once," Andrea said with a wry smile.

He pointed at her, chuckled, then reached into his desk and got them each their ID badge and a walkie-talkie. "Wear these at all times, and staff will unlock the cages as needed. Here are walkie-talkies; call if there's a question or you have any difficulties." They all stood. "Good luck," he said as he walked them to the door.

"Thank you," Noah replied, and shook the man's hand with firm earnestness. "We're grateful for your help."

"No problem, son." Dr. Roach patted them both on the back.

"You're an ace!" Andrea was stuck in exuberant mode as he opened the door.

"Good luck," he said one more time as he gently guided them back into the hall.

They returned the way they had come, down the long white hall toward the sounds, smells, colors, and general activity of the zoo. They were the clean team. They were the *Ghost Busters* of poop. They were cleared, tagged, and ready to scoop.

They decided that the zoo train would be the quickest route to the elephants, and stood in line with the children. One kid, mistaking them for janitors, threw his soda pop can down near Andrea's feet. It rattled a few rolling inches before it lay inert. Noah stared at the metal top glistening in the sun until the next train pulled in. The conductor disembarked and directed them to the open cars, each brightly painted as a favorite zoo animal. The children rushed forward toward the elephant and the lion. Andrea and Noah stepped into the second car before the caboose, which was brightly painted like a parrot. Once the rush of children settled in like landing birds, the conductor went over instructions: keep arms, elbows, hands, beaks, wings, and heads inside the window if they wanted to keep them attached to their bodies. The children giggled. Then he made a hand signal, and the tiny train lurched forward. Slowly, slowly they moved through the zoo at a pace only slightly faster than a quick stroll; fast enough, however, to keep the kids happy as they saw all the animals from behind the scenes: feed troughs, butts, poop and all. Noah noticed that many of the animals were being fed breakfast and he figured that by the time they returned there would be plenty of fresh samples. They got off soon after the second stop. The train was traveling so slow they simply stepped off, and went straight for the pachyderms, who were well on their way to excreting the large amount of sweet hay they had been fed only hours before.

Chapter 20

The elephants were bored. Noah could tell because they were staring at the back of each other's knees. There were two cows and a calf. Andrea was already at the back gate, wildly waving at the keeper and holding up her badge. She grinned from ear to ear.

The keeper nodded, set down his wheelbarrow of hay, and walked over to the gate. The elephants all turned to look at the intruders, and began to side step, swinging their trunks in agitation.

"Make sure that you move slowly," the keeper stated when he unlocked the outer gate, one of a two gate system, and swung it open for Noah and Andrea to pass through. "The elephants get grumpy before ten in the morning, and they've been even more wound up as of late. I don't know why. Maybe that's why they've been getting sick. I'm changing out the hay today."

Noah could feel his heart pounding. He knew that animals were aware of seismic activity even from hundreds of miles away. He wished they could talk. He wasn't sure if he was more excited or intimidated by the 15,000 pounds of potential destructive energy.

"Don't make sudden moves, and keep your eyes averted. There's a fresh patty near the southwest corner."

Andrea gripped her spade a little tighter. To Noah, she seemed to be a bit over zealous. The keeper unlocked the next gate, and then they were inside the compound. "Don't worry, you'll be fine." Then Andrea and Noah were left to their daunting task.

It wasn't difficult to find the elephant scat. The elephants didn't care where they pooped, and they did it everywhere, more than enough to keep their keepers busy. Much of the keeper's job was loading hay and shoveling shit. Just as he'd said, there was a particularly fresh pile in the southwest corner of the grassy compound, near the water source. Since it was Noah's first sample, he approached it cautiously, not exactly sure what to do. How much should he take? How much shit did God require to recreate an ecosystem?

Andrea kept an eye on the elephants that watched with much curiosity. They didn't seem agitated at all. In fact, the way Andrea was focused on them, they seemed to be entranced. Andrea, the animal whisperer. He knelt before the pile. It measured about sixteen inches in diameter—an entire foot of poop plus some. It had an interesting texture, pieces of undigested hay sticking up like straw men. Noah poked with the tip of his spade. It was nearly the consistency of clay with adhesive properties, almost like a straw bale brick. He saw right away how the dung could be used as a building material in Africa. It was actually a smart idea. Once it dried, the musty oak smell would diminish and it would make a fine wall. Noah took off his backpack, unzipped it, and pulled out one of the large bags. He opened it, scooped up a generous corner of the sample with his spade, and sort of plopped it in like cookie dough.

"Congratulations," Andrea nodded in support.

Noah labeled the bag, double sealed it, and carefully packed it. "Where to now?" He looked up at Andrea who was holding the map.

"Are we ready for primates?"

Noah sighed. "Might as well."

"How about the gorillas?" she suggested.

"If the gorillas are aggressive..." Noah wrestled with a twinge of nervous tension. "I'm not sure what to do."

"Pretend to be Jane Goodall." Andrea suggested.

Noah wasn't sure what pretending to be Jane Goodall meant, but if something crossed his mind he would try it.

They both gestured to the keeper who was filling up the water troughs. He nodded, turned off the water, and headed toward the gate with his keys.

"Did you get what you came for?"

"Yes," Noah said a bit sheepishly.

"Good. You should come back every morning. There's plenty more where that came from." He laughed. "These elephants can provide a thousand pounds a year. There are some hazards to this job." He grinned.

"Like what?"

"There was an Australian zoo keeper who gave his constipated elephant an enema."

"What happened?"

"The force of the release knocked him to the ground, and he suffocated before anyone discovered him."

"Is that true?" Noah sounded doubtful.

"Where you headed next?"

"Primates," Andrea chimed.

"Say hello to Randy. I think he's got the gorillas this week. He's my poker buddy."

"We will," said Noah, who was very happy to step out from behind the gate.

"You don't think that story is true?" Andrea said when they got a little further away.

"Sounds like an urban legend."

"Well, I bet it happened, but I don't think it was an accident. You know, those elephants think he's an idiot." She pointed to the keeper who was now spraying down one of the females. "That one gal talked to me.

She said she felt nervous."

"She talked to you! Why didn't you tell me? I had questions to ask."

"It doesn't work that way. They have statements to make. They don't want to answer our questions. They've been fed up with our arrogance for a long time. She wanted her voice, and what she had to tell me was that there wasn't enough room to roam. She felt like roaming, but didn't know how. She wanted me to find her a *Roaming*."

"What's a Roaming?"

"I don't know. A place large enough to roam?"

"What did you tell her?"

"What could I say? It's sad. Their loving for the planet is huge. It's like their entire purpose for being has been robbed, and now the places that they used to keep alive with their loving are dying. There is not enough room to roam."

"I'm sorry, Andrea. I bet all the animals have a lot to say. Maybe your ability to hear them gives them a little relief."

Andrea tried to smile. "Thank you. I hope it helps some, because it's painful not to be able to help alleviate the suffering. If the primates tell me anything important, I'll let you know. Oh, one more thing. She told me to tell you that it's a conspiracy."

"What's a conspiracy?"

"I'm not sure. I guess this end of the world problem."

"Too bad you're not an elephant. They remember for a thousand years."

"I've heard. They somehow pass down information like migratory passages."

"Yes, but the old elephants are poached for their ivory tusks. And because the young elephants don't know the way to escape, they're dying from drought."

"That sucks. Let's go find the gorillas and not get lost in elephant memory. It's too painful, like you said. We still have so much work ahead. Besides, I wonder how an elephant knows about conspiracy or even understands the concept."

"I wish we could ask her, but she's no longer open to talking."

"Gorillas."

"Yep, gorillas."

***

The primates were chewing bubble gum and flinging grapes at the crowd. The fruit never made it past the retaining wall, but the children laughed with glee at the sport. Noah didn't see the keeper at first, but as they stood there and watched the crowd watching the primates, and the primates watching the crowd; it was difficult to say who was the exhibit. Adding to the drama, there were two babies somersaulting off a broken tree limb onto the soft bed of dirt below. The four hundred pound silverback squatted in the shaded corner biting off bitterroot and glaring at the crowd. The male gorilla's instinct was to protect babies from the mass of human eyes, but its instinct to kill was curbed by the limitations of incarceration. There was a circus-like chaos, and Noah knew that collecting the sample was going to be difficult.

Noah walked down the concrete embankment to the lower level where the back door was locked. He hollered and, when no one responded, unhooked his walkie-talkie and pressed the talk button. A garbled voice crackled on the line. Noah had no idea what was said, but he leaned in closer and spoke into the speaker. "I need Randy to let me in."

There was more static and then the noise went silent. Noah waited. Noah waited nearly fifteen minutes before a long haired kid who looked a bit stoned appeared at the gate.

"Are you here for the shit?"

Noah nodded.

"Dude, you should have been here first thing while they were drowsy. They get attached to their crap. You'll probably get some flung on you."

"Are you going in there with me?"

Randy shifted his gaze. "No way, dude. Don't stay long, either. And do not, I mean, do not, catch the big hairy one's gaze. He'll rip your head off and try to throw it across the retaining wall at those kids there."

This statement did nothing for Noah's nerves.

"In you go," was all Randy said.

Noah looked at Andrea. She pointed up. "I'll be more effective up there."

Noah wasn't sure how that was going to be the case, but he wasn't going to stand around and debate it. He just shrugged and steeled his nerves.

In the end, it was the smell that almost knocked him out. "What do you guys eat?" Noah dug in his front pocket for the nose plugs. He put them on and looked desperately around for shit. He couldn't see anything but garbage and gorilla eyes. The primates began dancing, at least that's how Noah interpreted their primitive gestures, grunts, and jerky movements. Whatever they were doing, it made him extremely uncomfortable, which made his job that much more difficult. Noah felt a piece of chewed up fruit hit his chest. He could have fallen over right there, pretended dead, but just then he saw two balls of poop on top of crisscrossing of banana leaves. Noah took off his pack, bent down before the pile, and proceeded with operations. He moved quickly, all the while keeping one eye on the babies who were quite capable of stealing his pack and everything in it. To add to his tension, the silverback male was up from his crouch.

Noah scooped into his plastic bag a sizable ball of dung just as the silverback leapt past to the retaining wall where Andrea was doing just what she wasn't supposed to be doing. She was holding the gorilla's gaze. The gorilla was obviously agitated. Noah hurried to finish, in case the male became inflamed. He still held the image of his head bouncing of the retaining wall. He involuntarily shivered and sealed up the bag. Noah slowly stood up and Randy escorted him quickly out. As Noah exited the gate, something squishy landed between his shoulder blades.

"Dude, he got you good." Randy wiped him off with the terry towel. "I've got some wet ones. Ocean Breeze."

"No. I'll be all right. I can change if it gets too intolerable."

"Suit yourself."

"I appreciate your help. I'm going to find my partner."

"Call me if you need anything else. I'll be around." Randy headed slowly back to wherever he'd come from. Noah figured he was off for another toke and to tell his tale of poop and danger.

When he caught up with Andrea, her eyes glistened with excitement. "Noah, did you see that?"

"I was sort of there."

"He spoke, he spoke. The silverback spoke, and I was able to keep him off you."

"Thank you. Well?"

"Okay. Let me get this right. He said. No, rather he announced: 'Under no circumstance am I willing to accept that you rodents are decedents of our noble lineage. The animals all know exactly what you humans are.' Isn't that cool?"

"What did you say?"

"I reminded him that we invented bubble gum."

"That's all you could come up with?"

"I believe that's when he nailed you, so I couldn't get much more in. Did you get it?"

Noah patted his pack. "Got it."

Andrea circled Noah and pointed to the stain on his back. "I see that you did."

"Yeah, I got that, too." Noah was flooded with relief and began to laugh uncontrollably. Somehow, he had mastered his fear, and was now on the other side where he could still laugh. In fact, he was downright giddy. "Where to next?" he choked out between snorts.

"Your call."

"Let's find the prairie dogs and make Bambi happy. She adores prairie dogs. She loves their pear-shaped tushes."

Chapter 21

Tell me again, Dad, about the town from where our ancestors came.

In 1910, a huge metropolitan area was discovered on the high plains of Texas—our mother city. It was our cultural and spiritual center, our Machu Picchu, our New York, our memory. Four hundred million of us lived there. Four hundred million other prairie dogs lived in the most sophisticated colony ever created on this planet.

What happened next, Dad?

The bulldozers came.

The oil drills came.

We were relocated to the zoos—the few of us left.

Is the zoo bad?

No, son, not anymore. It's our home.

The colony was maintained at fifty. It was big enough to have several coteries. Prairie dog males had several of the reproductive partners that humans call wives. It was a complex system governed by an even more complex communications network on par with the dolphins, who weren't even originally from the planet. The prairie dogs were given enough space to dig every day, but not enough to create an empire, and in that way they were kept poor in spirit—never able to live up to their full potential, never able to conquer the known world. Only a few of their sages knew this; only a few of the wise ones knew what the zoo really was. The rest were content to be fed every day, to lie under the desert sun, to wiggle in the fine imported dusty dirt to keep clean, and to play. In many ways it was such an easy life—no threats, only meals. It was so easy that they now had to make the effort to stand on their hind legs like the prairie dogs that they were. They did this from a deep sense of tribal duty. It was part of their communication system, so not to stand was consent to be mute. It was a distant cultural throwback, a compulsion. Besides, it kept the human children happy like the Queen's changing of the guard. *Look, Mummy. They stand so still like wooden solders. Are they stuffed, Mummy?*

They, the prairie dog collective, liked the human children who barked like prairie dogs only louder. It was the human children who had the carrots. It had been one of those days, nothing much to do, until one little girl showed up with her father and a big bag of carrots. There were two others, dressed in white jump suits, odd, not like the rest. They were assessed as not a danger; likely zookeepers, new. Anyway, it was all about that bag, that big bright bag of orange carrots. At first, as the carrots were distributed, one shaved, smooth carrot at a time, a rumor quickly spread throughout the ranks that there would not be enough.

Lack was simultaneously communicated through a series of quick snorts and a bark as if it were one voice. They all agreed there would not be enough. *Did you know that there is a shortage of carrots?* The clicks and barks bounced off the rounded walls. A small dog was handed a juicy gem, and as she sunk her teeth into it she sighed with delight. It was suddenly ripped from her clutches and she screeched. She in turn turned around and stole a carrot from yet a smaller, junior member, who also screeched. The little girl laughed and clapped her hands. "Look, Dad, they don't think there's enough." She handed out another small carrot and stood back as the prairie dogs became thick in numbers.

"Well, give them the carrots, then."

The little girl looked for a moment and then dumped the entire bag into the pen. Very soon every single prairie dog had its own carrot and the entire colony was humming in satisfactory harmony and bliss.

"Look, Daddy, there is enough. They all have their own carrot."

"Yes, honey, they all have their own carrot, and they seem very happy."

The prairie dogs were so happy that they hardly noticed when the two humans dressed in white jumpsuits gingerly stepped over the barrier and carefully picked up some of their waste pellets, placed them in a plastic bags, double sealed, and snuck back over the wall. It was odd at the time, but who really cared. Every prairie dog had its own carrot, and all was well in the world.

Chapter 22

"He's at the zoo. Andrea's there, too."

Ione didn't say a word. She was in deep listening mode, and she was driving toward the dump. Bambi had said the same phrase from the moment she'd stepped through the door. That was okay. Ione didn't mind. She knew that the human mind often had to repeat loops in order to get used to an idea.

"He's going to bring poop home. Is that unreal, or what?"

"Sounds like you're having a difficult time with it."

Bambi stared out the window. "I couldn't go with him. Truth. I'm embarrassed. I'm ashamed. I don't really know what to believe, but you have got to see this ship to fully understand what I've been going through."

"We're heading there right now," Ione said, her voice modulated in neutrality.

"Have you ever been in a situation like this?"

"No. No, not like this."

"What should I do?"

Ione understood that what Bambi was really asking her was to tell her what to think. Ione recognized that if Bambi could hook into someone else's cognition, then she could momentarily feel safe and forgo the struggle of responsibility and free will that led to complete surrender into spirit. Ultimately, no human ever knew a damned thing. That was because the Mystery forever changed. The Mystery itself was alive. Ione could never ever tell another being what to think, because every thought was changed by the uniqueness of human perception. Each individual held in the back of their brain a camera of the mind that absorbed all, but focused on what was already familiar and known to select as reality. Ione couldn't help Bambi because Ione was no longer addicted to the illusion of safety. It made perfect sense that a flood was coming and that Noah was down at the Albuquerque Zoo gathering DNA samples for God. It was possible that the ark of Biblical lore was the ark of the present moment. It was possible that arks and angels, devils and floods existed on a parallel track and every so often interrupted the course of commerce by crashing through and upsetting the collective notion of consistency. If so, then time was fluid, multi-dimensional, and could flood the levees of the material world. Maybe this flood that was coming wasn't water, perhaps—and Ione nearly trilled out loud with the thought—it was a flood of time and space.

Ione believed in everything and accepted nothing, not even her own ideas and musings, beloved creations of thought. It was in this way she had negotiated the trials and tribulations of wisdom by the ancient teachings of non-attachment. She was able to take her elaborate schema, dance with it, and then put it away. She felt no need to bother Bambi—upset her further—with such sudden ideas. She would have expressed her thoughts if she believed that the notions would bring Bambi comfort. However, in this moment, they would more likely create confusion. Ione quickly glanced at Bambi. She looked thinner, pale, fragile. She was a flower bloom in a dusting of snow, and she sat in the passenger seat nearly crumpled up against the window.

Ione felt maternal toward her friend who was a candlelight of sweetness, but, like all mothers, she didn't know how to help in order to make everything completely better. She tried, so when Bambi showed up and wanted to go to the dump to see the ark, Ione agreed without reservation.

They continued driving past the relief route, past the small airfield, the waste treatment plant. Further out still, there were cow pastures, and then a couple of houses followed by nothing but fences. Somewhere out there, across the terrain on the mesas above, there were petroglyphs. Ione had hiked out to them many times before. The ancient human recording of what was once present and important—animals, time, and spirit—the ancient human recording of the planet breathing. Ione turned right on an unmarked dirt road that nobody-not-from-here would know where it led, and cut across a swatch of land that was still being used as ranch land, although developers had been working for years on the old man to sell. Someday, five hundred new homes would be built there, despite the cry against urban sprawl and the need for water conservation.

A few minutes later, Ione drove up into the dump and parked the car. She sat and stared for a long time. She could see the bones—like whale ribs—before she got out of the car. It was one thing to be told that the ark existed; it was another to see it folded up toward heaven.

"He's worked on it," Bambi said, mouth slack with disbelief, "a lot!"

Ione knew right away that she was referring to Charlie. Ione said a quick prayer for light and protection before she stepped out of the car, joined by Bambi who held on to the door handle for a moment.

"Ione, you should have seen it just a few days ago. It was mostly planks laid out, and they were over there." She pointed somewhere closer to the car.

"Mr. Charlie is a little something out of this world," Ione said.

"Maybe he had help. A crew or something."

"Perhaps." Ione knew that Bambi didn't really believe that, either.

Ione began walking up the hill toward the construction site. Bambi followed. "It is beautiful craftsmanship," Ione said when she reached the stern and stretched her tentative hand out, touching the wood for the first time. "It's powerful. I can feel it."

"You think so? Strong enough to survive a storm?"

"Yes, and you are, too."

Ione caught a glimpse of Bambi's face. She was smiling.

The two women circled the ark several times before sitting on two large rocks nearby. "What should we do now," Bambi asked.

"I have no idea, dear. What should we do?"

"I want to run away."

"So what's keeping you?"

"Noah. I don't want to disappoint him, but I've been thinking about what you said, that harmony is achieved in the silence."

"Did I say that?"

"More or less. Anyway, I've decided on a little monastery near Ghost Ranch in the Rio Chama River Valley called Christ in the Desert. I made arrangements today."

"I know that monastery. There is no electricity, and anyone who visits has to maintain a vow of silence."

"Yes, that's right. It is a magical, healing place, and the rooms are very inexpensive."

"Are you going to tell Noah?"

"I don't know yet. I mean, of course I'll tell him, but perhaps not until after I leave. I don't want to lose my courage to go. I wanted to tell someone, though, where I was going."

"That's a good idea, Bambi. I'm glad you told me."

"So you think it's a good idea?"

"I think it's a wonderful idea, and I'm sure you need the rest."

The women sat there for a long time and watched the shadows from the ark form sharp angles across the rocks. A hawk circled low and caught a mouse. The wind blew, but not too hard. It was a beautiful day.

"Do you think he'll show?" Bambi was referring to Charlie.

"Are we waiting for him?"

"I was hoping that you'd meet him and get a read."

"There's no better person to read him, Bambi, than you. You should listen to your own intuition."

"I know, but I wanted a confirming opinion."

Ione smiled as she turned her gaze inward. "He's like a storm, but for now he's helping Noah. Try to trust, but be careful. I feel that he is treacherous."

"Thank you." Bambi gave Ione a hug.

" Shall we go, then?"

They got up and mutely returned to the car.

***

As the women drove away, becoming a mere dot on the landscape, Charlie watched them from a mesa top with his demonic laser vision. Very little escaped his attention if he really wanted to see. Right now, he didn't want to see Ione. He knew she would see too much. The women stood in very clear light, and that's why he'd chosen not to show himself, though he knew it was he whom they'd come to see. Ione's wings were unfolding in the material world, and thus she was more trouble than she was worth to Charlie. He didn't mind time alone with Bambi, but he'd have to catch her on another day. Charlie was confident that he wouldn't have to wait all that long. Besides, Charlie made it his habit to choose the moment. He didn't just show up on demand. Not even for Bambi.

Chapter 23

When Bambi returned to the house the first thing she heard was the drip. This alone was enough to send her over the edge. The second and final straw was that the entire house, with the exception of the bathroom and the bedroom, had been turned into one giant lab—heavy clear plastic sheets were taped up on the ceiling and hung down, creating make shift rooms. In these plastic rooms were drying racks of animal waste. The whole house smelled like a barn. Andrea, dressed in overalls, carefully loaded up a screen with what looked to Bambi like mud pies. Andrea half stood up, trowel in hand, and exuberantly waved to Bambi when she entered the room. Her lips were pursed, ready to tell her all about it. Bambi didn't want to hear anything about whatever it was. It must have showed in her face because Andrea hesitated, grinned, and then returned to work. Noah didn't look up at all, and that hurt. Bambi slipped into the bathroom. There was no one there to comfort her as her heart broke wide open into a flood of tears. Like a wounded animal, she balled up on the bathroom floor and cried and cried and cried—sometimes silently, often in low sobs.

When Andrea knocked on the door, she told her she was all right. When Noah knocked on the door she told him to go away. She knew she'd be fine, but it was going to take some time. They left her alone, though she could feel the worry from both of them, which somehow made it all worse. The only thing that really distracted her was the sound of the drip. It was rhythmic, constant, and soothing. Oddly enough, Bambi realized, she had grown accustomed to its predictability. It was the one thing that seemed to remain stubbornly the same. No matter what, Bambi could count on the faucet to leak. After a while, her sobs were intermittent and seemed to fall within the hollow spaces of the drips. Bambi almost laughed at the whimsical and bizarre harmony that the water and her hiccups of grief made. It didn't take long before she was lulled into sleep, right on the bathroom floor.

***

Bambi finally woke and went to bed. She slipped under the covers next to Noah. He smelled musky, not offensive, but in a mannish I've been working and my girlfriend was sleeping on the bathroom floor so I couldn't shower sort of way. She was thankful, though, that he'd given her space. She curled around him, nuzzled the back of his neck, and very softly asked him how his day went. She had to repeat her question several times before he woke up.

"Hey, what time is it?"

"I don't know."

"I guess it doesn't matter. How are you feeling?"

Bambi was quiet as she checked in with herself. "I think I'm doing okay."

"What happened?" Noah rolled over and held her. She was grateful for the comfort.

"I saw the ark."

"How does it look?" Noah's voice was dreamy and soft.

"It's nearly finished."

Noah bolted up. "What!"

Bambi looked at him and saw the disbelief that she knew all too well. Noah began to get up. "Where are you going?" Her hand was on his arm.

"I have to see it!"

"Please don't. I need you."

He looked at her for a long time, their eyes connecting in the dark. Her heart sank when he didn't automatically respond. She felt him leaving. "Please. You've never made me beg before." She rolled over in stony silence, a brief streak of shame and anger coloring her checks.

"Honey, I'm sorry." Noah scooped her up and held her. For Bambi, the tears began again. There was nothing she could do to stop them, so she just let them flow.

"It's supposed to be my project, and I don't even know what's going on."

"It's real, Noah," was all she could say. She was exhausted. She decided suddenly that she would have to confront Charlie, find out who he really was. It was the one courageous act she could think of. She tried to ignore the core of her shame, that annoying attraction. She was leaving in the morning, anyway. She intended to tell Noah, but the words never came. She meant to tell him that the leak was back, and she wondered if he might not try fixing it again. That was one more thing that would have to wait for the morning. She let it all go. Then she slipped under the weight of sleep and it was welcoming.

Chapter 24

Charlie was full of surprises and Dan had little to do but watch the unfolding. He'd been there the entire time the ark was under construction, made sure the ship was not booby-trapped. Dan did his job well. He watched. He did not blink, not once. He did not see one missed nail. There were no apparent spells, no mutterings, and no calling on anything unholy. Just Charlie, his tool belt, his electric saw, his nail gun, and his demonic speed. Dan grew confident that the ship was just a ship and of sound construction. It would not sink. It was truly amazing and nearly a miracle that Charlie was working so hard for anyone other than himself. Dan wasn't sure what the catch was, though he was certain that there was one; it just hadn't yet been revealed.

Dan waited and, like clockwork, Charlie showed up, tool belt hanging low, whistling annoying little tunes from the Cartoon Network. He sounded a little like one of Snow White's little dwarfs only more menacing, especially when he wasn't putting energy into maintaining his human mask. The sun was just beginning to crest the mountains.

"Good morning, little bird. Hope *you* didn't poop on anything." Charlie smirked. "What do you think? It's a fine ship. Bet you couldn't find one thing wrong." He turned one red-rimmed golden eye toward Dan and winked. "Goes to show there's absolutely no reason for your existence other than being my chess partner. You remind me of one of those pathetic old ladies who have no life of their own and so spy on the neighbors and gossip as if what they have to say is of importance. You think you're a player in this saga? Do I really have to be the one to tell you you're not?"

Dan had gotten used to ignoring Charlie's comments, but this morning more than a feather was ruffled. Charlie was a bit too close to the truth of Dan's self doubt. Dan was beginning to wonder what his purpose was. Was it enough to simply watch?

"Oh, by the way, Bambi's coming over." Charlie didn't even attempt to hide his glee. "We're going to play, and don't get in my way if you want those kids live to see another day." Charlie picked up a hammer gun and began firing away.

Dan was worried. He wasn't sure what Charlie was orchestrating, but he felt he should get ready for a battle just in case that pretty little girl was in trouble, though he had not forgotten the bargain. He really hoped she'd stay away, but as soon as he formed the thought, he saw on the morning horizon an etching of car dust. His bird heart sank. He knew that Charlie was telling the truth. A few moments later, Bambi pulled up in her old car and cautiously walked over to the building site. Charlie smiled but didn't turn around. He knew women well enough to know to ignore her just enough. He'd make her work for his attention.

"Who are you? Really?" Bambi finally called out. She seemed angry, tempered by a high degree of nervousness.

Charlie made her call to him twice more before he put his nail gun down and slowly turned to her. "Who do you think I am?"

"I can't say for sure, but I'm pretty sure you're not a Home Depot man."

Charlie grinned. "What gives you that idea?"

As if to present the obvious, Bambi stretched out her palm toward the ark. "No human could do that!"

"I do my job well."

Bambi lowered her arm, and stood there, unnerved, feeling very much alone. Charlie dismissively turned around and resumed work. He was good at manipulation. "The problem with women like you, you think truth is based on any silly feeling that you get. Just because I make you nervous, and," Charlie peeked over his shoulder and looked at her directly, "I do make you nervous, it doesn't mean I'm not capable of doing the impossible."

Bambi's face deepened in color.

"I know you don't like me."

"I never said that I didn't like you," Bambi stammered. "I don't even know you."

"Bambi," Charlie said her name in almost a growl, "you're no less beautiful when you lie."

"Okay. You're right." She stood taller in her truth. "I don't like you, and you do make me nervous. I've seen something in your face that scares me, but then you're doing this amazing thing for Noah."

"I'm not building this for Noah." Charlie once again set down the hammer gun, and turned around to fully face her. "I'm building this for you." He bowed his head.

This comment stopped her in mid-gesticulation. She was frozen. In the next instant, it appeared to Dan that Bambi got weak in the knees. Oh, you're good, Dan thought as he saw her swoon. The nerves in his wings twitched as if he might step out of his skin to keep her from dropping to the ground. There was an involuntary flutter, but he couldn't move. He was quite aware of how ineffectual he really was. He couldn't just fly her out to safety. In that regard, Charlie was right, Dan was completely impotent.

It was Charlie who caught the falling woman and drew her close. Dan, riveted to the horror, thought for sure Charlie was looking up at the hanger, grinning as if to say, "See?"

He remained perched, watching and waiting. Dan, like any creature bound to the laws of the Universe, could not save anybody. Dan knew he could not do God's job. It was up to individuals to save themselves by calling on the power of the Creator that resides within. He hoped Bambi already knew that, but he also knew that humans were always slow with that lesson because it meant that they had to still their restless minds.

Charlie drew closer to Bambi, who quivered in his embrace but remained defiantly still. He was very close to her lips and Dan could see his nostrils flare, like an animal. Dan knew he was smelling her, inhaling her, tasting her. She struggled and he turned her loose. She turned to leave, but he caught her gently by the arm. "I know you love Noah and you would never do anything to intentionally harm him, but what I see in you, what I know you crave, is to be free in all that is animal, all that is natural, all that is both creation and destruction. You are Kali, the great Goddess force of the universe. I can help you access her, to become her. Don't you wish to become undone?" Charlie tenderly kissed her on the neck and grazed her nipple with his finger over her shirt.

Dan saw that she no longer struggled and there was something hard in her features. He drew one wing across his eyes, but continued to peak through it, unable to resist.

"To become all that is powerful," he heard Charlie. "Men forever have feared you. Men forever will fear you. The earth force itself will be under your spell. Come dance for me the Dance of the Seven Veils and I shall give you the kingdom of my heart, and anything you ask. I could, you know, stop this flood."

She swelled. Dan turned away and cried. This wasn't fair. No human could ever resist that temptation. She pushed his hand away from her belly. "Yes, you are right. I feel something from you that I like and you bring that out in me, but I don't want it this way. I don't wish to feel disgusted about myself."

Charlie laughed and patted her on the buttocks. "Come, my little angel. Let me show you the ship I've built you so that you will remain safe from danger and dry as a bone." He took her by the hand and led her to the parts of the ship he wished her to appreciate.

From where Dan was perched he could still see them. The changes in her features spoke of channeling higher forces that brought into the material world greater possibilities. He could see that she was becoming the great Hindu goddess, Kali, just as Charlie had promised. There was a belt around her waist from which hung a hundred severed heads. Spontaneously, a hundred arms grew from her torso, and in each hand she gripped a saber.

Charlie helped Bambi up to the deck planks. She stood tall, proud as a queen. She was feeling her power, Dan could tell. Charlie looked up at her in amazement. Dan had never seen Charlie so speechless. "My God,

Patricia L. Meek

you are Kali," the demon whispered. Dan turned his head, unable to watch.

When Dan looked again, the transformation was complete. She had become the Mother Goddess, the source of life and fertility, the all-creating and all consuming feminine principle. Dan realized suddenly that Charlie had intentionally invoked that particular archetype for the challenge of it. Charlie was going to try to seduce the most powerful feminine force ever known.

Kali began to laugh, deep throaty. "I will dance for you, Mr. Charlie. I will dance for you this one time. I will give you audience and if I don't kill you before the end of this rhythm, I will hold you to our bargain. One dance, I will claim the kingdom of your heart or anything that I ask. Right now, I command that once the flood comes and this ship sets sail that your interference will cease and that you will allow us to sail in peace."

Dan let out an involuntary snort when he heard Charlie agree to the terms. It was the first time Charlie had given up some of his power, and for Charlie time went back a long way. The old adage is right, Dan thought, as Charlie shot him a hateful glance, there is a first time for everything.

"Remember, you set the conditions." It was the last human thing that the feminine form said before it set into dance a whirling dervish. The dance of Kali began in a rhythm that even oceanic currents had to obey. Charlie stumbled backwards and sat down hard on a sawhorse. Long strands of blonde hair undulated with movements Dan had never seen before and knew he'd never see again. She used the ship's mast as a pole for a teasing, playful bump and grind, removing her clothing one button at a time. She leapt on top of the ark's rail and did some impressive gymnastics that made Dan contort his head to keep up with her moves. She unrolled her tongue, which seemed to make Charlie very excited.

When she tired of pleasing Charlie, she leapt from the plank's edge, landing on the ground with the grace of a leopard. The dance resumed, but took on a serious note as the earth began to shake. A stream of blood began to flow from beneath her bare feet, and she wielded her sword high above her head and swung it low, very close to Charlie's groin. Dan chuckled as the demon crossed his legs. When she spun around again, Charlie calmly stood up and moved out of the way. The blade went clean through the sawhorse and came up again. Kali reset her gaze on Charlie, grinned, and moved toward him, the white of her bare breast flashing in the sun. Charlie began to run. She gave chase and ended the game.

Dan could see nothing but small trees growing in the puddles of blood that had been Kali's footprints. The silence was profound. As soon as he got over his shock, he began to titter. The titter turned into belly hoots, and he launched himself into the air in a leap of joy. "I guess she

118

showed you, Charlie, old man. Need you? I don't think so." Dan knew that he no longer needed to be so vigilant. The playing field had just gotten a lot more level.

Chapter 25

Noah's heart was heavy as he pulled up to the dump. He was determined to complete the arduous task of putting his blood, sweat, and tears into finishing the ark. Bambi was gone. He found her note on the night table, explaining that she needed to time to reflect. She was going out into the desert to a silent retreat. He'd gotten out of bed, gotten dressed, gathered his tools, and slowly packed the truck. He'd fed the dogs and gave each of them a chewy. The weight in his heart slowed him down, but he eventually began the drive out to the ark.

It was unclear to Noah what his role was now that the ship was nearly complete. He couldn't pretend he was in charge of this project. His ego was bruised because a usurper had taken over his task, but at the same time he was truly grateful that something no less than a miracle had taken place.

Although he was troubled by Bambi's reaction to Charlie, Noah wasn't sure he believed that Charlie was his demon. Surely a demon wouldn't help him with the largest undertaking of his life. To Noah, Charlie was more like some sort of angel. Why wouldn't he believe that he'd been sent divine forces to help him complete an impossible task? He practiced letting go of his insecurities by reminding himself that building the ark wasn't really about him. It was about getting a ship built for the highest good of all, and who was he to determine the best way that was to be done? Noah conceded to himself that he didn't know God's plan.

Noah decided that he needed to relax and take things as they came, which meant allowing Bambi to run off to the desert with as little upset in his heart as possible. Though, if he thought about it too much, there was a spark of anger. He felt abandoned. Not just by Bambi, but by that owl, as well. He couldn't remember the last time he'd seen his daemon, who, as it turned out, hadn't been much help at all.

He pulled into the drive and sat in the truck. He barely remembered driving, so tuned in was he to his own interior drama. Finally, he looked up toward the crest of the hill and, in the open space just beyond, the ark was cradled like a baby. When Noah saw it, he fell in love. The ship was beautiful, and it was born into reality, as real as anything he'd ever seen. It was made of dark, well-seasoned wood, and there were carvings on the sides, though from where Noah sat he couldn't make out any details. As a carpenter, Noah had a deep appreciation for the craftsmanship. Hats off to Charlie, who obviously knew what he was doing and was doing it extraordinarily well.

Not only was Noah grateful to Charlie, he also suddenly felt vindicated. Every self doubt and insecurity regarding the soundness of his sanity slipped away as he beheld the proof that he was doing what he was supposed to do. Seeing the ark, Noah's purpose was strengthened.

Noah stepped out of the truck and climbed the rocky path. As he got closer, he saw something that stopped him, mid-stride. Lining one side of the ark and trailing off toward the horizon were small, mysterious fruit trees that were only slightly taller than bushes. Thin in girth, they had waxy leaves like a magnolia tree, but were trees like none other. They bore a strange fruit—blue in the stark mid-morning light. Noah approached and, as he gently held cupped one in the palm of his hand, the stem hooked to the leaf like an umbilical cord, he decided that it could have been a plum if not for its iridescence. If he'd been a braver man, he would have tasted it, but it was too foreign, and it frightened him a bit. Noah let loose the plum-ish fruit. He gazed at the line of trees that stretched as far as he could see, and took them as an affirmation that the divine universe was supporting him in his task.

Noah circled the ark. He had to admit that it would have taken him a couple of years to get to this stage of construction. Up close, the tiny carved details popped out, and Noah plainly saw the history of man, both the good and the bad. There was the plague. Tiny rats danced on medieval bodies in an old Londontowne street. There were men on horseback, heads of infidels dangling from their saddles. Noah thought that scene might be the Crusades.

His scalp tingled when he saw the mushroom cloud near the bow. He decided to try and pick out only positive images. He focused on some of the cathedrals. He managed to find the printing press. There was a fingernail-sized rocket to the moon. There was the Buddha under the Bodhi tree. There was a unicorn. Noah tried to keep a running tally in his head, but he had to give up. He felt a bit uncomfortable, just for an instant, as if something crucial was being held in balance. He didn't want to set sail with the weight of that evidence.

Noah shook off the unsettled feeling and got to work. He tentatively picked up a nail gun and climbed aboard the vessel. It felt strange, almost as if he was trespassing. Most of the deck had been done, but he found the last seam that Charlie had nailed together, aimed and fired. The nail went firmly in. He could not resist. He fired another and then another; there was no stopping. Noah was firmly in the rhythm of building when he heard the low rumble of Charlie's voice, which startled him like a sudden storm. Noah jumped back.

"You should have asked me, Noah. If you don't know what you're doing, we'll have to undo all of this." Charlie bent down, pulled out a nail with his finger and thumb and flicked it with disgust overboard. "Not in alignment!"

Noah heard the tiny ping of nail bouncing off rock. He gingerly put the nail gun down. "Hey, man, I meant no harm." Noah stood up, hands tucked in his back pockets. "You're probably right, but I didn't see a problem. Forgive me, I should have asked first, but this is my project."

Charlie glowered. "Your project?"

For the first time since he had met Charlie, Noah was rattled in his bones.

Charlie took a big breath—he was winded—and smoothed down his hair. He looked like he'd been running. He muttered, "What a mess," and something else about women that Noah couldn't quite make out. Charlie shook his head, looked around at the deck. "It's okay. Don't worry about it." He spit. "I'm here to serve you, anyway. What would you like *me* to do, *Captain*?"

Noah was startled and uneasy. The sarcasm in Charlie's voice left Noah at a loss for a response. "Ahh-ahh-ahh," he stammered.

Charlie shook his head again. "Come on, pick up that nail gun again and I'll show you what I've done."

Noah did as he was instructed and went into a near trance as Charlie spoke in intimate detail the construction of the ship, as if he were caressing the curves of a woman. "Unlike most girls," Charlie finished his explanation, "this one will not fail you! I personally guarantee she will not sink. I should know; I've been a riverboat captain for thirty-nine years. Up and down the Mississippi River between St. Louis and New Orleans."

"That would make you nearly seventy," was all Noah managed to say. Charlie didn't look at all like a seventy-year old retired riverboat captain. He was in great shape for seventy; he looked fifty-five at best.

"I hide my age well." Charlie shrugged. "What can I say? Good genes."

Noah looked again. It was possible for a man to look twenty years younger than he was. Noah knew that he didn't look his age, either. At that moment, he was fooled; he believed Charlie to be mortal. "Since you're working on this deck," Noah said, regaining his confidence because he needed to, "I reckon we should finish this last groove cut, and finishing nailing this line of planks."

Charlie flashed a wicked smiled. "Right away, sir."

They began, for the first time, to work on the ark together. Never before had any human witnessed Charlie work. Charlie created an optical trick, an illusion that he was hammering away at human speed though much, much more was occurring between eye blinks. The only one who could really see it was Dan, who was still watching—and laughing. Of course, Charlie was the only one who could hear him. His nemesis' laughter irritated Charlie, and if he weren't playing such a crucial role, he would have snapped the little birdman right off the metal beam. Charlie closed his eyes and concentrated on ignoring the annoying twitters.

For the first time in a long time, Charlie actually suffered, and it had to do with an impossible female who had chased *him* into the desert until she tired of the game and left him on his own. It had taken him the rest of the morning to find his way back, just in time to get rid of her car before anyone else showed up. It had been a bad morning, but Charlie bit his demon tongue and kept to the task at hand, for he had more destruction to look forward to. He glanced at Noah, who was wonderfully oblivious, naive, and charmed by the mastery of the ship. It was all good, and it would make his real work that much easier.

Chapter 26

Noah was incredibly thirsty. He stopped to take a break and took several long gulps from the water jug. His thoughts turned to Bambi. He hoped she was all right. He put the jug back and climbed down the rope ladder, headed to his truck to check his cell phone. He had left his phone in the truck in an attempt to not obsess. His heart sank when he flipped it open. There was no message. He bowed up, refused to worry one more second about her. She was quite capable of being where she needed to be without his protection. He refused to be hurt. He had a job to do, and he couldn't afford to be undermined with personal strife and obsessive thoughts. He dared not anger Charlie again. He put the phone down and cleared his mind.

He returned to the ship, got back to work in concert with Charlie, whose skill was uncanny. He never paused nor undid a single mistake. There were no mistakes. He was truly a shipbuilding master, and Noah wondered how he'd learned the craft. He tried not to watch him work, taking only sidelong glances, but the rhythm of the work told him the speed of production. It was as if the ship was being built by the wind. "How's that girlfriend of yours?" was the first thing Charlie said in a number of hours.

It took Noah a moment to respond, so unsuccessful had he been putting Bambi out of his mind. "Fine." He knew enough not to reveal too much.

Charlie continued to work, sliding planks together. It took him a long time to ask another question. "You know, a woman can process twenty thousand words per day while men can only handle about seven."

Noah began to chuckle. "Your point?"

"You could give me more to go on than *fine.*"

"Conserving my word quota." Noah measured the same cut twice; he was self-conscious and his heart hurt.

"She's too beautiful not to be a pain in the ass." Charlie's rhythm seemed to slow. "Don't worry. They come back. They always come back, if for no other reason than to hear the other ten thousand words for *I'm sorry.* Of course, it's been my experience that when they do come back it's only to do more damage."

Noah tried to ignore Charlie, but his gut hardened and he felt a sudden cold chill. Charlie's voice was getting in and it was poisonous.

"Hand me that tape measure?"

Noah tossed it to Charlie, who plucked it out of the air with great speed. "Thanks. If someone knew something about Bambi, would you want him to tell you?"

"Of course. Do you know something about Bambi?"

"I'm going to do you a favor, then, but you don't have to believe me. Oh, never mind. It'll probably upset you"

Noah suddenly felt desperate. "What," he commanded.

"Okay, I shouldn't be telling you this, but ..."

"But what?"

"Andburg's fucking your girlfriend."

"What? What? That's absurd. She doesn't even know him. He's only met her a handful of times."

"You only met her handful of times *once*, too."

"How do you know this?"

"Andburg's having a huge party, right."

Noah's face went pale. "Right," he stuttered. "How do you know that?"

"Buddy, who do you think built the stage? I saw them together."

Noah's knees buckled. He sat down, stunned.

"You saw them together?"

"Why would I torture you?"

Noah stared at nothing.

"Does she know that Andburg's responsible for this flood? I mean, if I was her, I wouldn't leave you for him."

Noah's mouth dropped. "How do you know that? I mean about the ice caps?"

"I'm building an ark. It's my business to know stuff." Charlie's voice began to rise.

Noah didn't want Charlie angry. "Yes, she knows that. I told her." His voice was faint.

"Maybe she digs it, then. She might feel safe with him. Is she home now?"

"No."

"Do you know where she is for sure?"

"No, not really. She said something about going out into to the desert to be with the monks."

"And you believe her? Did you know she came to see me this morning before you were even awake? She wasn't dressed like she was about to visit monks." Charlie began to laugh. He couldn't stop. "Monks? Hahahahaahhahahah. Ladies and gentleman," Charlie cried into the seamless landscape of desert and light, "the verdict has been read. Guilty! Guilty!" His voice was so deep and great in its condemnation that he flushed a flock of desert blue birds roosting in the brush. Startled, they lifted into the air and flew away like a disappearing line of shimmering blue.

Noah felt completely flat. "I have to go now."

"Okay, but when you get tired of staring at the walls and think you might go crazy waiting for her, remember that I'll be here hammering away, getting a job done."

Noah wasn't sure that he was completely in his body. He wasn't even sure where he was going to go. Would he drive blindly and madly out into the desert, or would he show up drunk and angry at Andburg's? Perhaps he would just go home until he knew.

Charlie peered over the side of the ship. "I'm sorry, Noah. I had to tell you. You're too good a man to be treated that way. I'll help you fix it. I promise. All you have to do is ask. I know how to fix it. Trust me."

Noah looked up and he thought he caught his reflection in Charlie's pupil. It was impossible, but he saw his shadow cast in flame. Embers of hate and revenge, buried deep in his heart, suddenly flared savagely. He wasn't sure how Charlie could help him, but he wasn't going to say no.

Charlie grinned. "You can trust me I know the pain of an unfaithful woman." Charlie smiled, bowed his head. "I'll see you in the morning, hopefully. Don't do anything that I'd do."

"Thank you for telling me."

"It's the least I can do. And, Noah?"

"Yep."

"You're a fine carpenter. It's an honor to work with you."

Noah wasn't sure if Charlie was making fun of him or was sincere.

"I mean that, son. I really do."

"Thank you." Like a zombie, he returned to his truck. He unlocked the door, but before he could step in and close the door, he felt thin air ripple the hair on his head like a whizzing bullet. Noah hit the ground flat. He hadn't known he could react that fast. He lifted his head from the dirt and looked up just in time to see the owl loop around and take another dive at him.

"Leave me alone!" Noah spit out just before he had to duck again. "I'm not in the mood for this," he said as he dove across the bucket seat of his truck, a wounded man trying to get away from the winged messenger.

Noah cranked the ignition, popped the truck into reverse, peppering rock against the oil pan. He heard something. Was it a hoot? Was it a voice? He didn't care. The last time he listened, he was set on a course of action that likely had cost him Bambi. The only thing he was focused on was finding out the truth. Were they lovers? Noah was suddenly insane with jealousy. He decided that if that bird got in his way again, he'd simply run over it. He sped down the road at a pace the truck hadn't handled in a long time. Noah looked only once in his rear-view mirror. He saw a winged speck falling further behind in a cloud of dust, but never slowed down.

Chapter 27

Bambi was curled under the wool blankets of a twin bed. The sound of vespers came in through the open window just as the angles of light shifted into prisms of soft gold. She looked around, confused. How had she gotten into this room? She searched her memory, but could recall nothing. She'd once read that losing memory was an odd experience, with an awareness of absence, a feeling that something was supposed to be there—a missing slide from a slide show—but the mind can't retrieve the image. Bambi felt that awareness of absence as she lay in a strange bed staring at light that looked incredibly pure and peaceful. She knew something was missing—how she got to where she was—but she couldn't pull it out of her mind. She wasn't even sure the last time she'd blinked, so transfixed was she on the deepening lucidity of amber light. She was relieved when her eyelids closed for a moment; she'd been worried that she'd lost her mind.

Bambi raised her head. The room was small, neat, stripped of worldly excess. A simple wooden crucifix hung on the wall behind her bed. A crude pinewood table holding a tallow candle sat next to her. She looked around for a light switch, but realized there was no electricity when she saw neither light fixture nor outlets.

Bambi folded back the thick wool blanket and got out of bed. She was stiff. She tried to remember what she had been doing. Was it yoga? Yoga had never made her feel stiff before. She found a pair of sandals at the door. She slipped them on, her attention focused on the sounds of evening prayers. She was curious about where the sounds were coming from.

The interior door led to an exterior courtyard, and the cooling air pulled up goose pimples on her exposed skin. She crossed her arms for warmth, still confused as to where she was and why she had no coat. New Mexico in the evening was always chilly, no matter the month. She knew that she would never have forgotten her coat, or a sweater, or some type of wrap. The sun was nearly down, but there was enough light for her to make her way around the adobe wall and up a gravel drive that led to what was obviously a chapel. Like many churches in the area, it was made from adobe brick, with a cross erected on top of the a-line roof. A famous Japanese architect had designed this sanctuary, she knew, and she could see the Asian influence with the jointed doors called *artsugi*. Bambi couldn't remember how she knew that. The information seemed to surface from nowhere; she hoped more of her memory would follow suit. The sanctuary was so beautiful, she reflected. Vertical lines of windows followed the church face up to the roofline. They glowed from inside.

Bambi, drawn to the warmth, crept to the rustic door that stood slightly ajar. She peered in. It was a modest space: simple wood benches, candles everywhere. The monks, dressed in white robes, were preparing to take their sacraments. Bambi did not want to be seen. She felt self-conscious as she stood in the shadows of the doorway. She listened to the angelic chanting, singing that she knew was prayer, but oddly foreign to her ears. She couldn't make out most of the words, but the ones she did hear were lovely.

Rejoice, Daughter of Zion.
Glory to the Father, and to the Son, and to the Holy Spirit.
Rejoice.

Bambi was quiet, lost in the moment. The more they chanted, the more she was able to let go. She experienced what she would later define as a total immersion in the prayer. It was as if it were being sung just for her, as if they'd known all along that she would be there. She let the sounds lift her up, up, up until she felt as though she was disembodied. She beheld for one instant the world as it was—all of it, shadow and light—in singularity, as the monks offered the harmony of divine intention in their devotion. When she couldn't be lifted up any further, her heart broke open, and she wept with uncontrollable passion. In this way, Bambi claimed for herself her own painfully beautiful vision. She saw everything in one divine moment: the totality of light and dark, and the totality of life. In that one divine instant, Bambi knew herself as the creative forces of the universe.

She saw a canopy of sacred and holy woods.

A fly on the rim of a honey jar.

A flower bloomed in snow.

Oh Creator of the stars of night.
Your people's everlasting light.

She heard the cries of birth and the moans of death.

A soldier was shot. The sniper's bullet went into his eyeglass lens, piercing his right eye. His brain exploded at the very moment he realized that he would never get a chance to surf the killer waves of Hawaii.

His brain was shattered.

A bomb went off. For thirty seconds,

there was absolute silence.

Knees bend.
Hearts must bow.
Heal a wounded race.

A whale gave birth deep in the ocean,

the amniotic flood curled once like a red ribbon

before it dissipated into the Aleutian current.

She saw the Kobe tribe, high in the Andes. They were dreaming, and in their dreams they sat before a loom. They were brown and naked; their bodies were painted in bright parrot colors. They wove silver cords into a silver web, desperate to pull together widening tears. They wove swiftly and with strong arms, trying to repair the rips in humanity. But no sooner did they fix one hole than another rent appeared.

Redeemer, save us all.
Heal a wounded race.
As it was in the beginning, is now, and forever will be.
Amen.

As the chant ended, Bambi crashed back into her body, her heart pierced by the magnitude of which she saw. She continued to weep, her tears holy. She knew something she hadn't before. She had had found her way into the Christ Consciousness, a current that cut a deep and loving channel right through the suffering of human experience. She now knew how to drink from it. She knew that God, The All, whatever name was applied, was a living substance buried deep within her soul. This living substance was accessible to anyone who allowed themselves passage through the growing pains of self-discovery. It was in a hidden cavern few people discovered, because it was within the last place most would look: inside their own heart.

In Bambi's heart, she no longer struggled to understand Noah's mission. Her understanding no longer mattered to her. She had given up her struggle to understand her God.

She was about to turn and leave when a young monk approached her and smiled. "Hello."

She returned his smile. "Where am I?"

He put his finger up to his mouth, a silencing gesture, and beckoned for her to follow him the few short steps to an adjoining building, where quietly unlocked the door, and led her inside a darkened room. He turned on a light and shut the door. The electric light was slightly unexpected. She looked around and realized they stood in a gift shop, filled with hand-carved wooden statues of St. Francis, a table stacked with books, cards, and journals. A rack of clerical wear held cassocks, capes, and brightly colored throws filled the remaining floor space. Rosaries hung from the wall.

"This is the only place where we can speak. Sound travels easily here, and I didn't wish to interrupt sacrament." He smiled, and his smile was unhurried and soothing. "I'm Brother Benjamin. And what is your name?"

Bambi formed the words to tell him, but nothing came out. She tried one more time and stuttered. "I'm so embarrassed, but I don't know."

The monk looked troubled, but only for a moment. He returned her gaze with the uncomplicated serenity of one who completely trusts God's plan. "Perhaps a good night's sleep will help you remember."

"Where am I?"

"Monastery of Christ in the Desert, in the Chama River Canyon."

She had a vague recollection that she had intended to come here, but the details still escaped her. "How did I get here?"

"We don't know. You showed up this morning, delirious, and without shoes."

She looked down at her sandals.

"Those belong to Brother Jonathan. He has rather small feet. I see that you don't have proper clothing to keep warm." The monk went over to the rack of hand-sewn robes and drew a long tunic-robe and a cape off the hanger for her. "Put these on. You're not supposed to wear this, but, under the circumstances, I'm not sure what else to do."

Bambi excitedly slipped on the robe, not because she would be warmer—and she was—but because she was now cloaked in belonging. She looked down at the form of the fabric, how it draped her body and allowed it to disappear into the freedom of space. She saw that the hem nearly covered her toes. She lifted her arm and spun around giggling. "I feel like an angel."

"Perhaps you are," the monk said, smiling. Love radiated from his eyes.

"This is the first time I've felt safe in a long time."

"Good. I think you will find the energy here healing. Is there anything else that you need for the evening?"

Bambi shook her head. She couldn't think of anything.

"We retire soon after vespers, and are up at dawn for morning prayers. We stay in separate quarters. This is a working monastery, and the monks have taken a vow of silence."

Bambi continued to nod. She felt so happy; it wouldn't have mattered what he told her.

"We ask that you observe silence unless in this building. Two other guests are staying in your compound: a retired professor from Pennsylvania and a divinity student from Albuquerque. We charge twenty dollars a night, but make some exceptions when a traveler is in need."

"Thank you."

"If you require anything else, return here. There will be someone who can reach me." He bowed his head. She awkwardly bowed in return and followed him out. He disappeared into the night, and she headed back to her room, feeling both safe and lost at the same time. She wondered why her amnesia wasn't bothering her as much as she thought it should. Perhaps it was because she felt peace in a way she was certain she hadn't felt in quite a long time.

Back in her room, she carefully removed her priestly robe, folded it and laid it on a wooden chair. She got back into bed and went immediately to sleep, holding on to her feeling of peace until dreams brought the image of a Hindu deity. Was that Kali? It was some form of the divine feminine with thousands of arms and hands. Arms and hands used for every imaginable purpose. Arms and hands to hug with. Arms and hands to cradle with. Arms and hands that moved pots and pans around fire pits and stoves. Arms and hands that reached to clean. Arms and hands that tenderly stroked skin. Arms and hands used to smack hard. Even arms and hands that were capable of cleaving and killing.

Bambi became that deity, and she felt very powerful, but she also felt a bit like a centipede. She had little use for so many arms and hands.

Then she found herself on an ark, cutting through large piles of poop. "My name is Bambi," she murmured to herself. Then she remembered the ark, and a man she loved named Noah. The more poop he drug aboard, the faster she was able to cut through it. Even in her dream, Bambi thought, how odd. Her sleep deepened, until it was beyond memory itself.

Chapter 28

Noah went to bed wrestling his personal demons rather than killing Andburg. He must have slept; he wasn't sure. What he experienced could have been a dream—it had the qualities of one—or a portent of a future reality.

Noah had assumed command of the ark. It was raining. Not a heavy rain, but a steady, methodical drip. Although Noah had never navigated a ship before, he intuitively knew what to do, mostly. Star charts were posted above the helm, and when he gazed at them they blazed with clarity. He didn't have to plot a course; it was given to him, and Noah knew the sailing would be smooth if he could get out of his own way. He was aware that he wasn't alone, but wasn't sure if he had charges aboard. He imagined not an entire cargo of animals, but enough that the ark felt full. As the drip turned into a steady rain and then into a deluge, Noah wondered where Bambi was. He envisioned her asleep in her berth. The window in his deep psyche opened onto her room. He was reassured to see her so peaceful. He knew then all was well. When he looked again, he saw Charlie sitting placidly near her bed, reading scriptures. He looked up and smiled. Noah was filled with dread.

He wanted to wake up from his lucid dream—the dreamer watching the dream—but was unable. His attention was diverted, as the water grew rough. He had to be careful. There was a lot at stake.

He returned his focus toward Bambi just as the door to her room opened and Andburg slipped in. Charlie greeted him and shifted his weight in the chair so that Andburg would have more room to get by and to access the tiny bed where Bambi was tucked in. Charlie continued to read. Bambi opened her eyes and smiled. She sat up and greeted Andburg as if she'd been expecting him. She held open her arms and hugged his neck when he lowered his body down next to her. Charlie looked up at Noah, who looked through this open window of the vision with horror. Charlie grinned and shrugged. *What did I tell you?*

A wave crashed into the ark and Noah was knocked off center. He tried to hold on and navigate, but his compulsion was to stare at the scene below deck. *Maybe you should stand this one down*, Noah heard Charlie say. His voice sounded as if they were in the same room. It was then Noah realized that he had abandoned the helm and was now below deck. He stood behind Andburg who taking comfort in the arms of his beloved. *You've risked everything for her. You do realize that?*

Noah ignored Charlie. He bear-hugged Andburg from behind and lifted him from the bed with a strength that he didn't realize he had. He knew then how easy it would be to break his best friend's back. They began to wrestle. Andburg broke the grip and lunged into a counter attack, the two forms locked in a death embrace. Sometimes Noah felt his own life slipping away and other times he could feel Andburg dying. Noah lost track of how long the physical engagement lasted, but it felt like hours. Meanwhile, the ark listed terribly low.

It might have continued into disaster but for Dan's intervention. The owl swooped in and began to tear at Noah's face, talons shredding away the illusion. When Noah looked again, he plainly saw that he was struggling with his own form. He was trying to destroy his own face, gouge out his own eyes. By the time he recognized the trap, the ship was taking in water, and Noah knew all was lost. Charlie continued to read, but now he was reading the Last Rites for the entire human race. Noah looked once more into the depth of his own eyes. He saw an angel there, and before he let go, he silently commanded, *Bless me.*

Noah never knew how the dream ended. There was a knock at the door, then another. Noah realized that the sound was real, and got out of bed to answer. Andrea stood outside, grinning as always, dressed in overalls and ready for work. Noah left the door open for her as he shuffled back into the room and landed lethargically on the couch.

"Are you okay?" She followed him over to the couch.

"I'm fine. Just woke up from a crazy dream."

"Me, too. I mean, I've been having crazy dreams lately." She sat beside him. "What was yours about?"

It took Noah a moment before he could respond. "Bambi."

"Where is she, by the way?"

"I don't know. She needed some space. Last I heard she was thinking about going to a monastery in the desert."

"Are you okay?"

"I guess. I've been working on the ark with Charlie. He told me that Andburg and Bambi are having an affair."

"Oh, come on," Andrea guffawed. "That's impossible. I've seen how she looks at you. She loves you. Does she even know Andburg?"

"Yes, they've met. And Charlie says he's seen them together."

"You're not going to believe that old reprobate? My motto's to believe only half of what you see and none of what you hear."

"I'm not sure I can be like that. I felt it in my core when he told me. Then she mysteriously took off. Just like that," he snapped his fingers, "she was gone."

"I guess you have to be patient, wait for her to come home, and then hear her side of the story."

"I'm not very good with patience, especially when it comes to love."

"What are you going to do?"

"I don't know yet." He said again under his breath. "I don't know."

Andrea started to say something and paused. She tilted her head, listening intently. "What is that? I hear a drip. Do you have a leak?"

Noah turned red. "I know. I've been working on that. Can't seem to fix it."

"Well, maybe we can look at it together."

"No." Noah was adamant. "I don't want to."

Andrea wasn't sure how to read her friend. "I think we should work on the ark today, then, if you don't want to deal with the leak. Idle hands are the devil's workshop."

Noah stared at her. "Not sure I can. If Charlie says one more thing about Andburg and Bambi …."

"Let's go, Buddy. I don't want this wound to fester. If it doesn't work out, then we can go do something else." Andrea pulled on his hand, and after some more cajoling, Noah got off the couch and consented to follow her to the truck and make the familiar trek back to the dump where the world's most significant project was still a secret, but not for long.

Chapter 29

Bambi was awake before dawn and quickly got up before she got sleepy again. She had been in retreat for three days, and still no memory. The monks had been patient with her, allowing her to stay for free with the expectation that if she got well she might send in a donation. She thought that was more than fair. Every morning she asked her waking mind, *Who are you?* It seemed to her that at night she knew, but by the time she woke up again she'd forgotten. She had to concede that perhaps she didn't want to know.

She went to the bathroom, washed her face in cold water in the basin, then gave the rest of her body a chilly sponge bath. When she felt refreshed, she slipped the robe back on. It made her feel safe; she wasn't sure she ever wanted to take it off again. She smoothed out the folds with her hands and looked closely at the detail of the threads on the edge of the sleeve. It was a tight weave. The cotton seemed extra white. The robe seemed somehow familiar to her, and if she had lived a multitude of lives, she was certain that she had been monastic. Religious practice felt known to her, and if not for the dogma…she listened to the quiet. The monks would be getting ready for morning prayers, and Bambi decided to join them. She left her hermit's retreat and returned to the dark desert morning where she could see the edge of the Milky Way, smell the sweet scent of desert sage, and hear the early morning sounds of coyote hunting jackrabbits defended by speed.

Bambi felt the delicate pull of anticipation as she neared the sanctuary. The night before, she hadn't been able to bring herself to cross the threshold, but this morning she could do it with ease. She sat in the back on a simple wooden bench. The room was small. The walls were smooth; a diamond gray plaster covered the adobe. One or two very simple crosses adorned the walls, but there wasn't much else, except a clear window behind the altar that spanned floor to eaves. She looked upon the early morning sky in its massive deep purple before dawn. There was a mountain face. Bambi couldn't make it out, but she was aware of its form. Several brothers dotted the sanctuary, heads bowed in prayer, rosaries hung loosely from their hands like running water. They were so dedicated to their meditations that they didn't open their eyes to Bambi's presence. She felt very held by them none the less. Bambi bowed her head and said a humble prayer of gratitude, and then asked that she might remember who she was. For some strange reason, not knowing didn't bother her, but she thought that it eventually would, and she ought to know before someone asked her again. *Dear, Lord. Please remind me who I am.*

More monks streamed in and filled the space. She wanted to be one of them, and her heart hurt just a bit knowing that she was not allowed to take sacraments. She knew, too, that it hadn't always been that way. Bambi closed her heart to the pain. Soon she was able to settle back into the silent space deepened with the power of prayer—hers and theirs. Bambi decided she no longer needed the Eucharist to feel as if she, too, were in the body and blood of the living and holy substance that they called Jesus—the Christ.

The deep purple faded into the wash of dawn: pale blues, pinks, grays, rose, striated and backlit by diffused light. As if on cue, the fireball of morning sun crested over the large cliff face, and Bambi saw what she had only guessed. The cliff face, adorned with petroglyphs and carved by wind, shone through the large sanctuary window. It was one of the most intense and singular moments of Bambi's experience. There was no separation between the interior of spirit and the external manifestation. It was nothing less than spectacular and glorious. It was the most sacred spot Bambi had ever seen, and her eyes widened with amazement.

Bambi stood up, book clamoring to the floor, at the exact moment the monks, with a unified *Ahhh To Glory,* began their morning chant, breath, prayers and all, and Bambi's heart cracked open, and it seemed to her that she was suddenly surrounded by a thousand tiny points of light. If she hadn't known better, she would have thought them to be fairies buzzing around her head, though they looked like tiny stars. It seemed to her—much later—that they went into her body, because her insides became warm as if she had been sipping brandy on a cold night. If her conversion the night before had made her weep, her unity in the singular being known as God dropped her to her knees. She closed her eyes and felt herself completely dissolve. This must be what it feels like to die, she thought. Then she thought no more. She sang, even though she knew not the words, because there was no other way to express the love other than open her mouth. She did, and then she opened her eyes again and, because the way light played on the plastered walls, she saw a cast shadow of face and form. It looked familiar, but when she looked dead on, it disappeared into gray. She knew that the monks in their faith had manifested the face of the one they called Christ. Bambi intuitively understood that she had been initiated into their holy order, because those who could see could *see,* and she could see. She could see so well, she knew that Noah who had already surrendered to such a sacrifice of love. Once she knew that, she knew who she was again. Her name was Bambi, but she was Bambi transformed.

She had entered the tension point of the wounded world, the dense, material world, the world of chaotic mess. It was messy to be human, but it wasn't her fault. She understood that in a different way, and so she could forgive herself her imperfections. She suddenly let go of something she hadn't realized she'd been carrying. The struggle of heart and ego had opened her up, and she was forever changed. It didn't matter what the DSM said about Noah and delusional mania, or what it would say about her experience. To experience was to know, and that knowledge was beyond textbooks written by the sons and daughters of humankind. It didn't matter if she hadn't felt safe or that she, like millions of others, needed to control in the temperament of absolutes. She felt safe in the now moment, right here, right now, and that's all anyone got. Time only expanded in the present moment. Nothing else mattered.

Bambi decided she could return and support Noah unconditionally, taking such baby steps in the present. She no longer needed from him what she'd thought she needed. Noah wasn't big enough for that. Bambi committed herself fully to herself in spirit. It was cool. It made everything easy. Bambi had caught the big fish, and the big fish caught her. She consented to do the next right thing and stick to the holy moment when she could. It no longer mattered that a flood was coming; it only mattered that every single breath counted.

As the monks went one by one to the altar and knelt for the Holy Sacrament, Bambi stood up and followed suit because she had the self-proclaimed right to do so. She had simply changed her mind about consenting to be separate. She would settle for nothing less than complete unification. She would take the sacraments. Who was going to stop her now? She behaved as if it were so, and no one said a word. No one dared to tell her no. Brother Benjamin offered her the wine and another monk provided the bread. She dipped bread into chalice, looked up into their deep, mindful eyes and it was true: she was home. No matter where she went now, she was home. Nobody would ever be able to take that away from her again. Bambi had returned to the true nature of her own heart.

Chapter 30

Noah had just handed Andrea the hammer, a level, and a sack of nails when he heard the first rumble of distant thunder. At first, he thought it was Charlie somewhere down below growling up at him again. They had been working on this ship for three days with no sign of him. Noah thought it odd, and felt a bit abandoned. Learning his lesson from before, he would never have gotten on the ship and proceeded to work without Charlie if Andrea hadn't talked him into it. No matter what, Andrea never seemed bothered. She was always in a good mood and took life strictly as it came. She admired the ship, but she didn't seem to be impressed with Charlie. "There's nothing Charlie can do that we can't do. It just might take us a bit longer," she'd stated confidently.

Hearing her say it bolstered his own confidence. He also remembered the compliment Charlie had given him, and he worked with ease and power. Unfortunately, part of his mind remained obsessed with Bambi and Andburg. His thoughts tore him up from the inside, grinding away at his compassion and his ability to reason. Noah had a vague understanding that he was obsessing, but he was powerless to break the cognitive loop. So tortured and poisoned had he become in his mind, he was relieved to hear the thunder because it meant he could stop for a moment and change his focus.

"I have a bad feeling about this, boss." Andrea stood up and stretched.

"It's just a thunderstorm. It'll pass in a few minutes."

Andrea shook her head and gathered some of the tools. "I guess we got to break, but I got a bad feeling about this storm."

"Andrea, it's New Mexico! If you don't like the weather, wait five minutes." Noah couldn't tell if he felt grumpy because of Andrea's sudden uneasiness—she was never concerned about anything, why this? —or his daydreams of betrayal and revenge.

Noah gathered a few things from off the deck, and together they climbed single file down the rope ladder. They made it to the hanger where they had first begun their project before Charlie moved the construction site just as the first giant drops hit the ground and splashed up reddish dirt. They settled on a wooden sawhorse as the sky turned black and completely opened up. The temperature suddenly dropped. There was nothing but sheets of a cold, hard-driven rain. He folded his arms and sank into his chest. He watched the front pass and thought about the sea-worthiness of the ship. There was so much yet to do. It wasn't sealed, but it might actually stay afloat even now. Noah hoped that they wouldn't have to find out. Noah hoped this storm would pass because he didn't want to have to work on the ark in the rain. That would make a most difficult task seem impossible.

They watched the storm for close to an hour. To Noah's great relief, however, the worst of it passed and, though there remained a steady rain, it wasn't violent with lightening strikes. The storm clouds were still full and low to the ground, but the sun managed to come out, and when Noah looked over toward the east, he saw a sundog. A sundog, it had been explained to him once, was a phenomenon unique to the western states, a ring of color, a rainbow fully wrapped around the sun. The native peoples of the southwest believed that sundogs would appear with greater frequency in the time of the White Buffalo, which signaled the end of one time and the beginning of the next. It was the time when the sacred teachings would be shared with all races. The rainbow ring was a promise of peace and hope through the dying times.

It was beautiful, but Noah couldn't stare at it too long. It was like looking at an eclipse, and Noah didn't want to be reminded that all cultures had their prophecy.

He pointed it out to Andrea, whose lips were pursed, and she smiled as she gazed upon it. "The storm passed," Noah said, trying to reassure her.

She nodded and smiled, but didn't say a word.

Noah stood up and stretched. His lower back had cramped from sitting on that strip of wood. "I think I have rainbows figured out," Noah said, jumping up with a big and mighty yelp, exhaling breath that had been filled with tension.

"What did you figure?"

"Rainbows are the invisible made visible. That's why it's a promise that everything is okay."

"What do you mean?"

"The color refractions are always present as frequency, but we only see them under certain conditions, the invisible made visible."

"Kind of like faith."

"Yes, kind of like faith."

"What do you think God meant when he promised to never destroy the world again by flood?" It sounded like she had been thinking about that for a good while.

"It's a mystery. All I know is that once I figure anything out, everything changes. Perhaps it won't flood. Andburg seems to think it's going to be fire and ice. He's working with nuclear fusion—does it matter if it's cold or not? Maybe it's not a God thing anyway. Perhaps it's a human thing."

Andrea nodded like she got it. "Robert Frost, right?"

"That's right."

"Perhaps we're all being too literal with our notions of creation and destruction. What if it's all the same?" Then she became quiet, thoughtful, and with the deepest sincerity said, "I know you're mad at Andburg right now, but, remember, you don't know anything for certain. I wouldn't trust Charlie. He's a bit slippery. He might be a sociopath, you never know."

Just the sound of Andburg's name brought forth death-wish fantasies. "You think?" Noah said, keeping a tight rein on his anger. He didn't want to think of Charlie that way. He wanted to think of Charlie as his friend, someone who would look out for him and tell him what others probably saw but kept secret. Noah could feel that he was infected. Perhaps it was Charlie's doing. "There's a party coming up next weekend. I'm not sure if Bambi will come back, but if she does and we go, I'll know more. I'll watch them."

Andrea shook her head. "I wish you luck with this." She wasn't saying everything that she wanted to say.

Noah turned to look behind him and so happened to see a couple walking down the road. He touched Andrea on the back and gestured. She turned to look.

"I guess the word's got out," she stated matter-of-factly.

As they approached, the guy waved and hollered a warm hello. He was an average sort, tall and lanky. He was scraggly and wet, and covered in mud. He wore jeans, motorcycle boots, a T-shirt, and a woven Peruvian vest in rainbow striped colors. The young woman at his side was heavier set, with long black hair tied back, and a darker complexion. She looked perhaps Spanish or Native American. Noah couldn't quite tell. She was dressed similarly in jeans but wore a black frayed coat and tennis shoes. She seemed to be holding something under her coat.

When they got a little closer, the man introduced himself. "My name is Tabani and this is Ma Shepard. We're friends of Ione."

"Welcome," Andrea said. "Who's Ione?"

"She's a friend of Bambi's," Noah whispered.

The pair looked at each other. "She's our friend," Tabani repeated.

"Have you heard from Bambi?"

"Who's Bambi?"

"Never mind." Noah didn't even know where to begin with *who's Bambi*.

"We come here to bless the boat. Should have been saged in the beginning." Tabani pulled from an inner pocket of his vest a carefully wrapped medicine bundle. He removed a red cotton swath of material. Inside were fresh sage and a beaded leather pouch, a Cantojuha, a *container of heart*. It held the bowl and stem of a ceremonial pipe. "Do you mind?" Tabani asked.

Noah shook his head no. He had learned long ago never to turn down a blessing. Noah had been to enough Native American pipe ceremonies to know that the tobacco Tabani was offering was sacred, always grown with prayer—never fertilizer—and the seeds passed down from generations of shamans. That kind of tobacco carried with it a lineage of original intent. Noah had heard the legend of the tobacco plant. A great and powerful being came to the ancient healers and offered itself. Tobacco, the grandfather spirit, claimed the miracle of life, but came with a warning: *if you ever use me outside of prayer, I will kill the people.* Medicine healers had been reputed to bring back those on the brink of death by blowing ceremonial smoke deep into their lungs. As with many things sacred, greed interfered, and the healing ways were lost to the people. The prophecy had come true. The grandfather, misused by mass production and addiction, had killed the people by the millions.

Ma Shepard didn't say a word as she removed a gray wool blanket from her unbuttoned coat. The rain suddenly stopped. In the abrupt silence, Noah realized that she hadn't said a word since she'd first walked up. She knelt down and spread the wool blanket near Noah's feet.

"This is my sister. She's a seer, so chooses not to use her voice. I have become her voice." He knelt beside her, already loading the red soapstone bowl, the feminine principle in the ceremony, representing the earth. He held it in his right hand. With his left hand, he held the wooden stem, the male principle. It represented all of the things that grew on the earth.

Noah knew that when Tabani joined the male and female principles, together the pipe would be as alive as the great mystery of creation itself. That was how it worked: man imitating the creative forces of the universe to give back to the Principle that which had created them.

Wakan Tanka, Great Spirit, Creator of us all, Creator of the four directions, Creator of our Mother Earth and Father Sky, and all related things, We offer this pipe.

Tabani joined the pipe. He pointed the stem to the East. *Grandmother and Grandfather of the East. The seat of red. The seat of passion, thank you for our blood the life force of our life. Bring us a new day and another chance to learn. We thank the Great Spirit for each day we are allowed to live upon Mother Earth under Father Sky, Tunkashila. We pray for Knowledge, for from Knowledge comes Peace.*

Tabani faced the South and loaded the pipe again. A prayer followed. He reloaded the pipe for each direction, and for each direction spoke a prayer for the ancestors and animals that lived in that corner of the medicine wheel.

Tabani lightly touched the ground with the pipe and then lifted it toward the sky when all the directions were complete and finished with: *To all the animals, rock, tree, to all that which flies and crawls and swims. To all my relations, Aho.*

Tabani passed the pipe around, and everyone touched it to their hearts and prayed. No one inhaled, but rather released the smoke toward the heavens, ensuring that all the prayers would go up into the sky and be received by the messenger winds to the great creator. Noah held the pipe close to his heart, and he let the message within feed the pipe. He was careful to concentrate on only the most pure intentions.

When the pipe was once again in the hands of Tabani, Ma Shepard stood up and looked deeply into her brother's eyes. They broke the gaze and Tabani addressed Noah. "We would like to offer the prayers on the vessel. We will remain in prayer until told otherwise by spirit."

Noah turned red. "Do you mean the ark?"

Ma Shepard nodded. Her dark eyes glistened.

"How long will you be there?"

"Can't say. The energy around this ship is out of balance. There is too much darkness. Without balance, the ship will sink. Our prayers will integrate the light and dark forces."

Noah thought about the carvings. He thought about Charlie. He thought about Andburg and Bambi. Balance was probably a good idea. "That will be fine."

Tabani nodded. Together he and his sister folded the blanket. Tabani turned and looked at Noah. "There's a bad storm coming. You must go home. Your woman will be there." Ma Shepard touched Tabani on the sleeve. He turned to look at her and then back at Noah. "She says that you must look at her through your heart and not your eyes."

They watched as the strange and shadowy figures strode out to the ark and climbed up the rope ladder with agility. "Wow," Andrea said. "That was heavy."

They stood out there for some time before Noah turned to Andrea. "Let's go. You heard what they said. Bambi is home."

"Hubba-hubba." Andrea gave him a goofy smile and patted him on the back. "All's well that is well," she badly quoted Shakespeare.

Noah didn't entertain her with a response, though it was funny. He suspected she'd done it intentionally, for an easy laugh, but he couldn't laugh right now. There was too much hardness in his heart. She had no idea how stirred up and scared he was. Still, he couldn't help himself and grinned broadly. For a moment, he forgot that he was angry. Truth be told, he was grateful that Bambi was back. A raindrop fell on his nose and punctuated his relief. By the time they reached the truck, the rain had returned. Rain was a blessing in the desert. Perhaps Andburg's party would prove that Andrea was right. *All's well that is well.* He imagined

Bambi, beautiful in a way that only she was beautiful. Maybe it would be clear that Charlie's tale was a lie. He was filled with hope. The party was a week away and then it would be "all's well that ends well." He had to believe that. It was all he had for now.

Chapter 31

Bambi was glad to be home, though it had been raining since one of the monks had dropped her off hours before. She wasn't really feeling well. She'd been having waves of nausea. She was grateful for the rain; it made her think of something else beside her cramping and sudden appetite. Everyone she knew was talking about the rain. Some said that it was a return to old weather patterns, that it had always rained a lot through the fall season as winter approached. It was the desert monsoon. Others claimed that it was a sign of global warming and an extreme weather pattern shifting further north. The skiers thought it was a sign for a healthy snow pack, and skiing would be most excellent. Everyone said that it was a blessing.

Some complained about the mud. Mud was everywhere, and Noah had taken to getting rides from Andrea in the dump truck out to work on the ark so he didn't risk getting stuck on what once had been a dirt road. He and Andrea continued to work in the rain, although progress had, of course, slowed.

There had been no sign of Charlie in over a week. They were speculating as to where he'd gone, but not talking about it. As long as Charlie was away, there was some peace—especially for Bambi.

When Noah returned in the late afternoon, he was wet, achy, and sore. Bambi hadn't met the mystic twins, but Noah had told her all about the brother and sister, Tabani and Ma Shepard, who had taken up residency on the ark, living in tents and tarps. There wasn't much else to tell her, other than that they mostly prayed.

The combination of incessant rain, mud, no Charlie, and new boarders on the ark made Noah grumpy. Noah was grumpy a lot lately. Bambi thought maybe it was because he couldn't forgive her for running off into the desert. He also couldn't seem to grasp that she had no recollection of doing so.

Bambi looked out the window at the water rivulet coming down from the corner eave. She'd always loved rainy days. They were the best days to dream. They were the best days to curl up like an animal in its nest and read and be. But since Bambi had accepted the ark as reality, she could no longer appreciate the rain in the same way. Every drop seemed to be a reminder of the end times. In addition to the rain, the faucet continued to drip. She had resigned herself to the idea that it could not be fixed. She looked at the dogs curled together in their dog bed and was grateful for them. I am grateful for my life, she thought. She missed the monastery, the one place she had felt peace. The silence had been liberating. Not knowing who she was had been liberating. She knew being present in the moment was important. Ione had tried to tell her that, but putting it into practice was hard. I'm glad to be here, she told herself again. There's no place like home. However, home was different, in an indefinable way.

At first it had been wonderful to see Noah. He was a handsome man, and Bambi got to see that as if with new eyes when she returned from the desert. He'd been working outdoors; his body was strong and fit. He was tall and looked young for his age. His long hair, which he pulled back, made him look like a white Indian—still wild and almost forbidden. He was beautiful and God-like, and she loved him. The morning she'd returned, he and Andrea had showed up almost on cue. He'd been encouraged by their progress, filled with the breath of outdoor life, and happy to see her. He'd been boyish—vulnerable, excited—as he looked at her standing in the kitchen with wide-eyed honesty. *Welcome back, baby. I missed you.*

After the kisses, after Andrea went home, and after a day passed, Noah began to shift. It was subtle at first: his jaw-line hardened and he withdrew. It was as if he became another person. Even his face seemed the face of a stranger. He stopped touching her and seemed to watch her more—in a way that he never had. It was bizarre at best and made her feel very uncomfortable. She could tell that he'd been worried, because he kept asking her questions, especially when he found out that she had gotten a ride back to town with one of the monks. They were odd questions for Noah. *What was the monk's name? How old was he? How long has he been a monk? Where did he drop you off? Did you come straight home?*

Bambi had answered all of his questions with a lot of patience, but couldn't ignore the nagging internal voice that kept telling her something was different about Noah. Bambi wasn't sure what. It was as if his mind had been poisoned against her. Had he changed while she was gone, or had she? Had he always been that way, and she was just now noticing it? Bambi didn't know. She felt as if she'd been gone for a long time.

Bambi knew she was different, but couldn't say how. In between the rainstorms, when the sun struggled to keep above the clouds, she appreciated the nuances. Light faded, but while it lingered it was sublime. In the morning, the wall glowed like pools of water teased by breeze, and in the evening delicate pinks and gold banded along its length like a cinemascope. She took comfort in knowing that light still existed, but it seemed increasingly rare. She felt as if the world were slowly dimming.

Tonight's the party, Bambi reminded herself as she stirred from her trance It was important to Noah that they go. Bambi didn't really want to go. She didn't have the energy, it was raining, and she didn't have anything to wear. *I don't have anything to wear.* She repeated the thought. It was the first time in a long time she's wondered what she'd wear to a party. She went to the closet and pulled from hangers the best of her wardrobe. She tried a few things on, but nothing felt right. She hadn't bought much in several years. She'd been frugal since she'd been in school. Noah had also modeled a material free life. He didn't seem to need much, and his attitude had influenced hers. She would have been happy with the monk's robe if they'd allowed her to take it home. Noah did want her to look nice. He had said so, and had even given her the credit card. This wasn't just a party; it was perhaps the last party she would experience. The more she thought about it, the more she realized that she, too, wanted to be in style. Maybe it would distract her. She wanted her fifteen minutes of glamour. What she spent didn't matter; that was the best part about the world ending. She wasn't sure what she'd bring to wear on the ark, but she was guessing it wouldn't be chiffon.

Bambi put the credit card in her purse. She slipped out to her car, not minding a bit that it was wet outside. She knew just where she'd go. She was heading to Heaven, a dress store in Madrid, New Mexico. Heaven was a boutique with one-of-a-kind dresses—all designer—and was geared toward the big city transplants. The prices were logged into a ledger; only those with a large disposable income could afford them. Bambi had only been in the shop to look, twice. The second time she'd browsed was the first time she'd seen the most beautiful dress ever made. Created by a Russian designer, the dress that Bambi had admired was a chocolate-mint silk with French lace and an Empire waist. Bambi was exhilarated as she merged onto the interstate, hoping that she'd find that dress again. She'd always promised herself one of these gowns if she ever had a special enough occasion. Bambi decided that this was it: the possibility of having a last party was special enough, and she hoped to get Noah's attention once again. Bambi had designs to become so transformed in her beauty that Noah couldn't possibly ignore her one second longer.

Chapter 32

Tracy was in Heaven buying a dress. What else could she do? It was raining, and had been for days. The party was that night, and Tracy was stressed. She was certain the party would be ruined. Not only was it raining, but Andburg hadn't listened to her. If he'd only put up the tents sooner. She'd hoped for an icy, Arctic theme to celebrate his upcoming trip. She couldn't remember now which outpost he was heading to; either way, he was heading to one of the snowy poles. He'd been mortified at the thought of artificial snow. What did he know? Why worry about water conservation when it snowed all the time, everywhere, somewhere. Tracy decided he didn't have vision. She'd hired a company anyway to theatrically design a grand effect. Tents were the least of her worries now. At midnight, there would be black lights and snow. She would have her snow!

She was so excited by her surprise that she decided to let the disagreement go. They'd been fighting for weeks, or at least she was fighting and he was ignoring her, which she hated. How could she stay angry when she was treating herself to retail therapy?

Heaven was one of the best-kept secrets. She had everything to wear and nothing she wanted to wear. Her mood was always changing, and it was no telling what kind of an entrance she wished to make at the party. She wondered if Marie Antoinette had had this problem. *Probably not,* she decided, *she would've had a dresser.* For a moment, Tracy felt a bit out of time and disappointed.

Heaven was the only place close that she could buy a gown that didn't look so…*New Mexican.* Turquoise and silver had its place, but not at her party where making a statement was essential.

Tracy was lovingly touching raw silk when a pretty blonde walked into the store. She was tall, thin, and had a tidy a-line haircut that bounced just above her shoulder. At first, Tracy thought she knew her, but when the woman seemed lost in the store, tentative in trying on dresses, Tracy decided that she didn't know her at all. The girl started to go through a pile that Tracy had left off hangers on a nearby table like some bargain sale. Tracy thought that was funny for some reason. They were just the dresses she didn't want.

Easily distracted, Tracy's returned to the glittering frocks she hadn't yet inspected. She found a pretty chocolate-mint gown—silk and lace, empire waist. It was a Russian design, patterned after vintage, perhaps nineteenth century royalty: classic and romantic. Right beside it was a pink Chanel with tiny budded roses. *Perhaps too spring, although roses in snow, now that could have a lovely effect.*

Finding such high-end fashion so near to home was a little like falling in love, fleeting perhaps, but heady for the moment. She was nearly flying when she stepped out of the dressing room wearing the chocolate-mint, the other beautiful gown draped over her arm like a prized skin. She expected immediate attention from the clerk; after all, she was about to spend a fortune. The clerk was helping the pretty blonde, and Tracy felt her blood rise. She took a deep breath and managed to curb her ire. The young woman turned and stared at the dress she was wearing. Tracy flushed. Right away, she knew. The woman had come in for *this* dress. She hadn't seriously considered the dress before then. It probably *would* look better on this woman, but how could she resist taking it for herself?

"Do you have more like that?" The woman asked the clerk.

"I'm sorry." The clerk shook her head.

"These dresses, my dear, are all one of a kind, thank God." Tracy said what the clerk had not. "Try on this." She reached over to one of her discarded silks.

The young woman looked disappointed, but smiled. She glanced around the room. "They're all so beautiful. I'm feeling a little awkward. I'm going to a party tonight." She took the silk. "My boyfriend will like this, don't you think?"

"As long as you like it, he'll like it. Who is your boyfriend?"

"Noah Noland."

"Yes, I know Noah. He's a friend of my fiancé, Andburg. You're going to our party."

"Incredible." She nervously laughed.

"Bambi." She awkwardly held out her hand with the silk tucked under her arm. Tracy had to resist the urge to rescue it from potential pit stains.

Tracy smiled coldly and obliged the handshake. "I'm Tracy."

"You think this dress will look good?"

"It's a Chanel. It would make a hag look sexy as long as the hag could afford it."

Bambi stiffened some.

"Try it on, see how it feels."

"Thank you, I will. What time should we get there?"

"Eight or nine. The party is going to be a blowout for Andburg's departure to the Arctic."

Bambi didn't blink, and Tracy couldn't help but wonder if Bambi wasn't one of Andburg's conquests. "Have you been to the Arctic before?"

"It's way too cold for me."

"What about the Antarctic?"

"Not sure it's a place I've ever considered going."

"It's going to be an Arctic night—at least by midnight—a surprise for Andburg."

"Perhaps I should buy a Polypro-lined dress."

Tracy didn't laugh. "This dress is charming. Trust me."

"Yes, I think you have an eye. I'll see you tonight, perhaps in this dress."

"So it seems." Tracy returned to the dressing room. After changing, she went to pay.

She drew her finger along the neckline. It was a beautiful dress. Not for her, but she enjoyed the power of buying someone else's happiness. Tracy signed her name and took the garment bag, her mood greatly improved.

Chapter 33

"Is this iron?" Dan said to Charlie, ticking his talon against the hard, darkish blue cornerstone that had fallen over into the green grass. It had been part of the first Christian church in Greenland, called Brattahlid. Dan and Charlie were sitting on the fallen stone, watching whales in the Baffin Bay surface and spout, killing time until Andburg's party.

Charlie knew he'd set up the party dynamics so well he really didn't need to go. He'd seen the same fight for centuries—after Cleopatra and Anthony, all other lover's quarrels paled. Of course, Salome serving up John the Baptist's head on a silver platter was pretty good, too. That serving plate had been one of his better ideas. There had been others, but that one stood out in his memory. The way the candlelight reflected from the rim and caught the nuances of red was a dramatic focal point, and he didn't mind taking credit.

Noah's suffering was contemporary, in many ways more subtle, but Charlie's plans for Noah would be no less dramatic. He would count on Bambi for that. Though it lacked the silver platter, he was proud of his staging. He'd likely go to the party, he knew, just to satisfy himself that he was, indeed, the genius he knew he was. He didn't really care if Dan went or not, although something about Dan's personality put a damper on the fun.

Charlie looked over through a half-slit eye. "Iron? Yes. What you're sitting on used to be the bottom of the first-ever ocean. Scientists have discovered that it's sedimentary and not igneous. It is actual ocean bottom. That rock pushes back the earth's biological clock to 3.85 billion years. Four and a half billion years ago there was a nuclear fusion of a gas cloud. They call it the Hadean period—you know, like Hades." Charlie grinned. He pulled a cigarette from midair and lit it with his thumbnail. "Breathing is so automatic. Oxygen used to be a poisonous gas to the first bacteria that struggled to live here."

Dan scratched the stone. He marveled at the living history.

"You're scratching at Eutraryotes, the first bacteria to take a breath and not die. No human would have evolved without them. Oxygen continues to decays tissue."

"The very thing that sustains life decays it."

"Exactly!" Charlie blew a smoke ring.

A whale surfaced and blew a geyser of water. Waves lapped against the shore, and Dan clearly heard the cracking of ice somewhere. To Dan, in that moment, the entire planet was swelling with its inhale. If humans had remained aware that the planet itself was alive, would they have been better stewards? He wondered if the next generation of survivors would do a better job. He wondered what Noah and Bambi's lineage would do. Were they even destined to remain on the planet or would the human experiment be pulled into another dimension? He wondered if duality could be transcended. Charlie had always tried to tell him that there was no difference between good and evil. On some level, dualism was unified. The great avatars, those great spiritual beings who deliberately incarnated to the lower spiritual realms of humanity to be of service to this planet, knew this. Was it selfish to want to transcend good and evil? Right now the cycle never ended. No wonder Charlie was bored with the Mystery. Was it really a mystery? Dan suddenly felt very depressed. A daemon was supposed to know its purpose in divine light. Maybe Charlie was right. Maybe he was an ineffectual being. Dan stuffed his feelings down. Charlie could smell weakness. Fear was in the sweat.

Charlie was getting bored. "Where to now, Danny Boy?"

Dan shrugged a wing. "I kind of like watching the whales."

"The whale is the one species on the planet that I have a soft spot for." Charlie looked out across the bay. "They won't be able to stay here much longer. The water's too warm."

"At least they'll be fine in the flood," Dan said hopefully, still looking at the whales.

"You think so, huh? What about all the toxic spills?"

Dan remained quiet. He didn't really like sharing his innermost thoughts with Charlie.

"Do you know why I'm important, Dan?" Charlie asked but didn't wait for a response. "I facilitate destruction, and without destruction there would be no growth."

"Not meaning to demean you, but I've always thought of you as temptation and suffering, the ego's shadow, wouldn't you say?" As soon as Dan spoke, he regretted it. He'd forgotten how difficult it was to stand within one's own truth around Charlie.

Charlie began to swell with venom. "Many turn to the light only when they are suffering," Charlie hissed.

"Are you telling me that you're responsible for saving souls?"

"I don't like labels." Charlie stiffened. "Besides, I don't really have anything to do with the ego directly. It's too small for me. The ego is the hook on my fishing line, that's all." Charlie turned around and singed the tail of a rabbit. The rabbit ran. Dan let out a sigh, knowing it could have easily been him. Charlie showed some impulse control. That was surprising.

Time to change the subject, Dan decided. "Why did you allow Kali to make that deal with you?"

"It's an easy bet to make because that ship will never sail." Suddenly, the bay disappeared and Dan was sitting on an iceberg. There were hundreds of penguins huddled together. The wind was blowing very hard and frozen air went right through his feathers to his goose pimply bird flesh. "You could have warned me."

"Sorry."

Dan knew Charlie wasn't really sorry.

"Where are we?"

"South Pole."

"The Antarctic? That's the other side of the globe."

"Very good, Einstein."

"Could you hook me up with a coat?" Dan asked, ignoring the insult.

"We won't be here long." Easy for Charlie to say; he was melting the ice he stood on.

"I'm cold."

Charlie thought before replying, "I could roast you like a duck."

"But you won't."

"I'm checking on something; won't be but a second. Now I want to show you something."

The ice storm cleared enough to reveal a dodecahedron-shaped building on giant skis for easy portability. Built from state of the art materials, it was white, and nearly disappeared into the landscape. Ten-sided, it was a very sturdy construction. They were looking at the first station Andburg had created.

"That's one of Andburg's labs," Charlie explained. "Have you ever heard of cold fusion?"

"No."

"Man's attempt to recreate the sun's nuclear core in a bottle. A successful little discovery that could mean unlimited power. Instead of splitting the atom, they've learned to compress them. And they can do it at lower temperatures. They believe that it's safer, more cost-effective, and *less dangerous*."

"Well, this is a lower a temperature," Dan said, but he didn't like how Charlie had over emphasized *less dangerous*.

"Over there, deep under the ice, are several nuclear bombs ready for detonation."

"Why?"

"Security purposes," Charlie smiled.

"Are you sure that they're there?"

Charlie chuckled. "No worries. What you can't see won't harm you. There are two stations. One right here; the sister station is on the polar ice cap in the Arctic Circle. Hidden bombs are there, too, but don't tell Andburg. He doesn't know yet, and we don't want to ruin the surprise. Well, even if you tried to tell him, he wouldn't be able to do much about it, and he wouldn't believe you anyway. You see, Andburg has a son who has come back to seek revenge. Some men don't learn from their Shakespeare, Andburg obviously is one. His abandoned tyke is impressive, a world-class psychopath. Come on, let's take a closer look before we head to the Arctic. That other station is malfunctioning."

"Andburg has a son?" Dan was hesitant as *malfunctioning* echoed in his mind. "What's wrong with the station?" He wanted to know what he was getting into, but the scene changed too quickly for a protest, and they were standing in front of a donut-shaped containment vessel hovering above men in protective suits. Here in this gleaming nuclear cauldron, deuterium gas was being energized with seven million amperes and heated to 300 million degrees Celsius, more than ten times hotter than the center of the sun. The atomic nuclei were agitated, colliding.

"This is the genie in the bottle," Charlie said with great enthusiasm. He was truly excited. There was a part of him that admired the human experiment for its ability to get so out of control and unleashed. He related. Sometimes he just had too much energy to contain, like standing before Prometheus' marble table where the centerpiece was the fire pit of glory, where the first fire embers were being carefully attended to, kept alive. This was fire, but fire of a different kind, fire with the potential of melting the entire planet. Fire in the hands of the well meaning but misguided Andburg, who was being undermined by a group whose intentions made Charlie look like a saint.

There was life inside this substation. A team of internationally known men and women, who had been living this undertaking in secret, were walking around checking monitors and writing down data. They looked like astronauts.

"This station is operational," Charlie whispered. "But we could change that." He thumbed his finger across the seal of a not so obvious T-joint.

"Don't," Dan squawked.

Charlie turned and looked at Dan with disgust. "Why should I listen to you? Oh, never mind. Let's go."

The next station they stood in was empty except for the ice particles flowering up the side of the walls. It was very cold inside, and looked like the inside of an icebox, except for the eerie red light flashing like a heartbeat, casting an eerie and hellish pall over the tiny substation. Dan's instinct was to escape. There was no sign of life; the place reminded him of a morgue.

"They were all so excited about this technology, and, I have to admit, it's impressive," Charlie flatly stated. "Andburg met Billy Bolin in Santa Fe."

"Who is Billy Bolin?"

"He's the retired scientist who worked at the Los Alamos lab with Andburg on nuclear motors for space vehicles. He was one of the first to build the fusion reactor and prove that it worked. The government spent billions on it since the 1950's, but Bolin did it for less than $50,000 because he didn't want to be beholden to "backers." His lab consisted of surplus supplies and an aging Macintosh computer. He was sort of a thrifty guy. Liked to make do because it made experimentation more interesting, though he was a meticulous double blind kind of guy. He'd never make a claim unless he knew for certain. Then his findings became the revolutionary cornerstone for a couple of scientist slicks: Clyde McGuffee and Winston "Wanna Be" Sands, who suddenly announced their discovery of "cold fusion." They tried to steal the findings right out from under Dr. Bolin, which was a bad idea considering he hadn't revealed all of his secrets. What a splash. Wow, for a while their mugs were everywhere. They were on the cover of *Newsweek* and *People*. There were rumors of the Nobel Peace Prize. It was the most heavily hyped science story of the decade. Then an independent commission came sniffing around looking for the reports. The findings looked good—they were close—close enough to believe it themselves, but, like I said, they couldn't back all the data because they were relying on Bolin, and he withheld key pieces of information. So the excitement turned to accusations of fraud and incompetence."

"What a story," said Dan. "What happened to them?"

"They're dead, but that's not important. They were small fish. What's important is the back story."

"What's the back story? Does that have to do with the bombs?"

"Very good, Dan. You're getting smarter. The reason the idea had been discredited to begin with didn't have much to do with scientists. It had to do with the Corporate Cartel."

"The Corporate Cartel?" Dan looked up at Charlie. "Are you kidding me? Sounds like a bad movie. Can't be real."

"Focus, Dan! Where do you think movies come from?"

Dan could tell Charlie was enjoying dragging out the intrigue. "Okay, what happened?"

"The entire idea had been discredited partly because the U.S. government had its own agenda. I mean the U.S. government as it is "influenced" by key players of this Corporate Cartel that have no allegiance to nation states. In fact, there are no nation states, no USA, no Russia. There's been a corporate merger, democracy and free trade, illusions that power is balanced. Nationalism, a mechanism for control. The Cartel is a power merger that ended the need for centralized government decades ago though they do manipulate esprit de corps of

Nationalism as they wish. They have global interests in both the Antarctic and the Arctic and wanted the story buried."

"I thought that the Antarctic was under international jurisdiction."

"It is," Charlie stated, and the way he grinned made Dan uncomfortable. "Dan, do you think you can keep up with me here?"

"Okay, go on. Global interests, global interests. What global interests?"

"The largest oil-rich fields still left on the planet are right under where we stand." Dan compulsively looked down. "Not only do they plan to protect their oil interests, but they intend to control global population—sort of killing two birds with one stone. They recruited Andburg because he had been a friend of Bolin. They knew that if anyone could get the missing keys, Andburg could. He's just smart enough to get the job done and just drunk enough not to ask too many questions. They gave him the proper military approval and helped him set up stations on both poles so he could experiment with technology that was never supposed to work. In addition to that, there was an inner circle within this inner circle that called themselves the POA, Protectors of the Apocalypse. They saw Andburg as the messenger of the seal. They saw Andburg as the signal to set in motion prophecy."

Dan peeked around. He was feeling unsettled and he knew that what Charlie was revealing to him was just the tip of the iceberg, literally and figuratively. Dan couldn't see much from where he was standing, so he hopped over a few yards and turned around. He looked for an open door or window, any reason why the snow was drifting in. An igloo would have been warmer. Dan saw the kitchen area and made his way there, partly because the red light cast a pretty pink glow. Underneath the drop-down counter table of the kitchenette, he thought he saw the dark side of the full moon resting on the ice-covered linoleum. Dan stared, transfixed. The moon didn't move. It was inert and polished with frost, and gave Dan the chills.

Charlie stepped up behind Dan, but didn't say a word.

Dan hopped closer. The face of the moon had a visor. "What is this?"

Charlie stepped over, put his hand on the moon to melt it some, and lifted up the visor. "Meet Samuel Smart, the project manager. Of course, he's not so smart anymore."

Dan screamed in a very bird-like way that embarrassed him.

"Come on, Dan, don't lose it on me. You'll just make me dislike you more. It's just a corpse. Everyone is one sooner or later."

Dan ignored Charlie. He was focused on the frozen face in the visor. The horror. Everything visible was wide open and blue: his eyes, mouth, even his nostrils flared in an instant flash of frozen human emotion. The man's mustache riveted Dan. It was perfectly intact, each hair encrusted with an ice particle. "I told you a long time ago, Charlie, that I didn't like the death thing," Dan managed to say with great sadness.

"Word of advice, Dan. You'd better make friends with it or it'll eat you alive."

"What do you know about this fellow?"

"Those are MIT brains—frozen. Those are 150,000 dollar brains right there. Too bad the planet won't survive long enough for people to play out their cryogenics project." Charlie laughed at his own wit. "Don't worry about him. He's just a scientist, suckered in by a dream and betrayed by folly. He tried to save this station. Looks like he went down with the ship. Funny thing, Andburg believes he's still here and it's all still under control."

"What do you mean?"

"Do I have to explain everything to you, little man? How do you expect to help Noah if you can't think your way out of a paper bag?"

"That's uncalled for, Charlie. I have faith in the revelation of the next right thing. You don't have to continually malign me."

"I'm a demon, Dan. It's my duty."

"I think you are the Devil."

"Ouch. Bambi rather enjoys the dark edge, and would understand me if she were here, but she's going to that soiree tonight. I bet she's going to look hot, too. She has nice tits. Don't you think she has nice tits?"

Dan remained silent, embarrassed.

"Haven't you noticed?" Charlie looked at Dan a long hard moment, and sighed. "I suppose you haven't. Anyway, she would say that my maligning you was merely a projection of my own wounding. If I malign you, imagine what I must do to myself on a daily basis. Don't you feel sorry for me?"

Dan looked at Charlie, who was doing his best to look pitiful. "No."

"Good, not as sensitive as you seem. Not everyone is invested in saving the planet. The Corporate Cartel isn't interested in anything other than making money. They're invested in turning global tragedy into a win-win situation for themselves. As I was telling you before, if the ice caps melt it will be God's way of providing them with access to the oil. They have faith, too. The POA believe they're the chosen ones and if the planet is purged, they'll have more opportunity to own the whole damn thing. Bring on global warming, more land to reclaim for themselves. Right now, they're working on ways to privatize the waterways, which includes the ocean."

"That's horrible."

"That's adaptation. That's industry. That's Manifest Destiny. If this cold fusion had worked, it would have been the end of global warming. The entire energy infrastructure of the world would have been retooled.

There would have been millions of new jobs, more leisure time. With a cheap source of energy the oceans could have been desalinated. Imagine, paradise on earth, the deserts would have been in bloom. The POA has no use for happy Africans."

"They don't want that?"

"What they don't want, what they didn't count on, was that their drunken fool came very close to pulling it off. They wanted complete control. They didn't have complete control, so they sabotaged the project. Andburg doesn't even know how close he was."

"Was?"

Charlie smiled. "Key players began to *mysteriously* disappear." Charlie emphasized the word hand-gestured quotation marks. "Andburg, truth to tell, was scared and stayed away from the lab. He believed he could control the operations via satellite. And he did, for a while. A mole had infiltrated the project; Sam Smart was in the middle of a text message relaying suspicion and the possible identity when he and the rest of team were brutally murdered."

Dan wondered how much Charlie embellished. No matter, dead was dead, and Mr. Smart was proof that something had gone terribly wrong here.

"The mole is still in operation, firing off dummy satellite images to Andburg, which is why he believes everything is fine. Andburg needs to believe. It's a control issue for him. That's why he drinks. That's the only way he can let go and feel more like himself—or the self he would most like to be."

Quite unexpectedly, the sound of the dead scientist's recorded voice came over the wireless PA system, startling them both. The interview was from the height of his career. Dan thought it was sad. Charlie rolled his eyes: glory was fleeting. He of all beings knew that. His best work had been drawn from the disarming lights of fame. Charlie wasn't impressed with this particular parlor trick. The man's monotone and neutral voice echoed from the frozen walls.

"Dr. Smart, can you explain in layman's terms what cold fusion is?"

"Cold fusion is the fusion of two heavy hydrogen nuclei to form a helium nucleus at near room temperature. Cold fusion happens when we take heavy hydrogen and we load it into a metal such as palladium, much as water is loaded into a sponge. When the hydrogen loading reaches a certain sufficient threshold level, then all of the sites in the metal lattice that are available become filled. If we keep pushing harder, then the lattice continues to fill, and if we continued to push in a sufficient amount, then eventually, if the conditions are correct and if we actually have prepared the metal a little bit, then we know that there are certain sites in the loaded metal where these desired reactions occur.

Cold fusion then does occur. Under the appropriate conditions, some of these pieces of palladium appear to generate reactions that involve heat directly from the new generation of helium-4."

"Is it true that you are looking at the poles for the most likely source of hydrogen?"

"Yes, that is where the most abundant and natural supply lies. It's endless, quite frankly. We are currently looking for backers, but preliminary calculations have already been made. It's a green light and very exciting. It's very exciting. It's very exciting. It's very exciting...."

The recording got stuck in an endless loop. "How did they sabotage the project?" Dan asked over the recorded hype.

"They went conventional," Charlie ambiguously replied.

"What do you mean?"

Charlie turned to Dan. Charlie looked purely evil. His eyes were flat and lifeless—like a shark's—and yet as vast and deep as a black hole. Charlie had never revealed that side of himself to Dan before. Dan waited for the answer, but he cautiously moved one feather inside the coat to make sure he hadn't turned to stone. "They buried seven nuclear bombs under the ice right from the beginning," Charlie said without emotion. "Four are at the South Pole and three are here. A backup plan, so to speak, a way to terminate the experiment if things weren't handled according to internal mission. That countdown has begun."

Dan was silent. Nuclear bombs under the most vulnerable places on the planet. It was tantamount to global homicide.

"What we're standing on will sink into the water in a fortnight or so as the polar shelf cracks from the bottom up. I'm not going to share much more with you. You figure out the rest. Good luck, little birdman." With that last confession, Charlie was gone, leaving Dan stuck and confused in the substation with a crew of corpses. "Damn you, Charlie. You can stay in hell."

Chapter 34

"Truffle?" Ione handed her guests a plate of very fine chocolate truffles.

"Is this from Kakawa?"

Ione nodded to the little red-haired girl who sat cross-legged and damp on her living room floor. She thought the spunky curly haired one had said her name was Heartsong, that's my real name. There were six of them. She'd counted them as they came through the door. Two from St. John's College, one from UNM, and three others from Southwestern College. Somehow word of the ark had gotten out to the world. Ione wasn't sure how. The Prophet Twins had already been to see her; she somehow knew that they would, and she had directed them to the ark, but these six college students were a different matter.

This group had showed up that morning in the rain in two unfamiliar cars, where they sat for a good forty minutes before ringing her doorbell. Ione later concluded it took that long for someone to get the courage to approach. One of them—she couldn't remember which one—said they'd had a dream and that was how they knew to come. They'd been following the details of that dream.

"Excuse me, I know this sounds crazy, but are you the one called To Be?"

At first, Ione wasn't sure what he meant, but then she thought of the ontological meaning behind her name. Of course! "Yes," she'd said. "My name is Ione, which means *To Be*. Come on in." The kids remained hesitant. They weren't sure they had the right house, but Ione assured them they probably did. They filled her small living room with their exuberance for adventure.

Ione thought that following a dream to reality was pretty good. She'd had plenty of fortuitous and prophetic dreams but had never followed up one herself. She felt respect for this younger generation of seekers. They seemed more evolved and natural with their gifts of perception. She reflected that the Socratic rational mind paradigm had privileged a masculine lineage of thought for so long it had leached civilization for centuries of its creative potential and its ability to live within wholeness for self and others. Native Americans knew that everything a person needed for health was within arm's reach, unless it was a miracle cure— then a healer might have to walk the day to find a specimen. A lot of that knowledge was now gone, although Ione also realized that although humans could be killed, the message never was. Like water to the sea, new pathways were created. It just took longer. However, it hadn't helped *anyone* that many indigenous people who had been keepers of the collective dream had been systematically eradicated, taking with them their vast knowledge and wisdom. She knew that Gaia had always been conscious, breathing, co-creating, but the thought struck her that now she was birthing a new creation in her attempt to detoxify from the last litter of ungrateful children. She wouldn't kill all—just a good clean sweep. There'd be no judgment, no separating sinners from saints, no sifting the chafe from wheat, no discrimination, nothing personal; just more room, just survival. This newest generation was hip and they were in the throes of environmental angst—a deep alignment with the plight of the Mother and a deep understanding that life was dying and that something had to be done—a new type of urgent activism. It was about remembering indigenous wisdom. Ione personally thought activism was futile since it brought the seeker out of the now and into fear and conflict, but she would never questions another's path. Besides, she thought it was endearing that these young visionaries wanted to try. It was right and good that they should want to try.

She had sat and listened to them as they'd carried on with much enthusiasm their plans to create a better world, sharing their hopes and dreams.

It was the dawning of a new age and it wasn't *Aquarius.* Shifts were happening so fast in planetary pockets that some believed it to be the end times. Despite more massive destruction, there was a greater awakening to higher consciousness for those willing to stretch beyond the material notions of what was real. Ione decided she wouldn't tell the kids that. No reason to raise anxiety—they probably already knew anyway, and it would waste too many words.

Now that the room had settled, it was time to enjoy the world's most specialized and brilliant chocolates ever made. Ione would serve the cacao elixir as the Mayans intended, a ceremonial offering to bitter water, life itself, and the Chocolate Goddess who brought to earth the first cacao tree in a beam of light.

Ione was doing her best through prayer and song for these beautiful children. She hoped that the chocolate ritual she was about to perform, using unadulterated chocolate elixir made of Criollo beans, pure as the Mayans had originally created for ceremonial purposes, would offer them peace and serenity as purported.

She went to the kitchen to attend to the thick ceremonial chocolate, brownish and tinted red like raw earth. She whisked it into froth, and poured it into a delicate robin's egg blue cream pitcher and placed it on a lacquer tray already filled with an odd assortment of demitasse cups, ceramic sake cups, and an orchid centerpiece, fine white petals with a deep purple beard. She carefully carried the tray back into the room where the chattering suddenly turned into sober silence. Her guests crawled about to form a circle, leaving a spot open for Ione. She set the tray down centered in the circle before lowering her own body to the floor. Youthful faces lit up as the thick, dark drink was served.

"Mortals died for this?"

Ione nodded, couldn't speak, already overcome with the fragrance. "Like Aztec priests."

Someone handed her a silver sage bundle and a feather fan. Ione lit the sage and in loving silence smudged the space, clearing it of negative energy. She then called in the keepers of love and light and said a prayer to Xochiquetzal, offered a blessing and petition that the heart, as the center of knowing, would be opened. She asked them each to say out loud an intention for the future. In a harmony of hushed voices each person spoke a heartfelt intention.

I will teach my children to be light bearers.

How to be good stewards of the planet.

And to do no harm.

As she passed the cups around, the silence held. One of the boys refused to partake, and, though there was nothing obviously wrong with him, he had a stubbornness that chilled Ione. She wasn't sure why he was there. The group referred to him as Icepick. She took this information in and then released it. Then she directed them to drink. The silence was broken when one of the girls started crying and ran from the room. The others looked at each other, stunned. Ione alone knew what had likely happened. The girl's heart had opened into the collective pain body.

The girl's tears reminded Ione of her own and she guessed that this girl was very gifted in her sensitivity. Ione got up with a little less grace and a lot more stiffness and walked to the bathroom door. With the gentle hand of a mother's knock, she asked the young woman if she was all right and would she mind letting her in. After several minutes, the door cracked open a bit to reveal dark haired girl with pale skin and panda-brown eyes — big like she'd come to the planet prepared to absorb every ounce of the entire experience, both the joy and the sorrow. "May I come in?"

She lowered her eyes and Ione stepped in and sat on the toilet while the girl sat on the edge of the tub and continued to cry into a hand towel.

"Tears. They are highest form of prayer."

The girl looked up. "It's so painful." Her voice was soft like a muted bell and Ione could barely understand her.

"I know. It's a powerful experience when the heart cracks open."

"I feel too much."

"You do have some control over this, you know."

She looked at Ione with her big, wide-staring eyes.

"Sometimes what spirit brings in for us to learn is too much. You can ask for the experience to be more gentle."

The girl looked more hopeful. She laughed self-consciously. "I think I might sit in here and cry a bit longer." She sounded grateful. Tearful, but grateful.

"Would you like some privacy?"

"Would you stay with me a little longer? It's something I never got from my own mother."

"She never listened to you?"

"She was frightened of me."

"You two are probably resolving some old karmic baggage."

"What do you mean?"

"They say that we incarnate as light beings into family systems that are in need of healing and emotional evolution."

"Is that why my mother continues to send me spiral cut honey-baked hams even though I'm vegan?"

Ione tried not to laugh. "Perhaps she's just worried about your diet." She leaned forward and gently rubbed the girl's back. "It's okay to cry. You cry for all of us. Remember, you are not personally responsible for the entire planet. It only feels that way." She sat back and the Panda Girl lowered her arms. Her eyes were red rimmed and puffy.

"I can't stand the suffering. It makes no sense to me. I think we are responsible! Who else is clear-cutting the rain forest? Who else is killing the animals? I went to rural Louisiana once with my parents to visit my aging aunt at Christmas. It was a beautiful time with beautiful people. Then it was time to go home, and we packed the car and started on our return trip. As we reached the outskirts of town, I saw that one after another raccoon lay dead on the shoulder. After the eighth raccoon and empty beer bottle, I realized that someone had made it a sport to kill as many coons as he could. I had to witness that, and I could do nothing but cry out in my heart an apology for the human race. That's when I decided not to eat animal flesh anymore. I just couldn't."

"There doesn't need to be more light," Ione whispered. "There just needs to be enough. Those who consent to keep their hearts open despite the pain are Light Bearers. And as a Light Bearer that's all you need to do: stay in your loving and your gratitude no matter how the chaos appears."

The young girl stopped crying and became very still. She eventually smiled and though her eyes glistened with tears it seemed to Ione that the worst of the emotional storms had cleared. "I'm going to check in on the ceremony," Ione said. "Would you like to stay here or come back with me?"

"I'm ready." She stood up lifted by the glow of grace. She took a bold step to the door and turned to look at Ione. "Are you coming? We saved you one of those truffles that you love. You can sing out in ecstasy. You don't have to hold anything back on our account."

Ione let out a belly laugh. "Certainly."

They returned to sounds of giggling and play. The chocolate goddess had left her effervescent gift of happiness. One of the curly haired boys softly strummed a guitar. She hadn't seen when he'd brought it in. Everyone smiled and welcomed Panda Girl back into the circle. Before too long she was smiling—brimming with love—and giggling, too.

They remained in each other's company for a while longer, enjoying the sounds of the rain and the music in the warm friendly buzz of the chocolate. Ione was so filled with agape that she saw in each of these children the golden face of divinity. They were all so sweet that she sincerely believed that there was enough light to keep the darkness at bay. In that moment, the world was already saved.

Ione stood up. She knew instinctively what to do, what seemed to be the next right thing. "How do you feel about camping in the rain?"

No one responded.

"How do you feel about camping in the rain?" she said louder and with more authority.

Someone finally said, "Who likes to camp in the rain?"

Ione shook her head. "If you were standing in your conviction, would you do it then?"

"Yes, if there was a greater purpose."

"What if you believed that you were saving the planet?"

"I'd camp through a flood," the curly haired boy firmly stated, putting down the guitar. Ione had begun to refer to him as the Dreamer because he was weaving a dream in the melody of his artistry.

"I have something magnificent to show you, and I hope you'll come with me. I'm going to help my friends complete an ark." She turned and began to busy herself with the preparation.

"That was what the dream was about," one of the girls said. The young people stood up, one by one. None of them seemed sure of what they should do. "We don't have any camping equipment," someone stated.

Ione paused and looked at them. "We are going to make do and trust that we already have everything that we need." She went to her closet, opened the door and instructed them to begin going through certain boxes that she had sworn she'd never go through again in her lifetime because she had gotten much too old. Ione laughed at herself. That's what she got for thinking such things and forgetting that the Universe indeed had a sense of humor.

Chapter 35

When Bambi stepped through the bedroom door, Noah wasn't prepared for her great beauty. He had been prepared to ignore her. In one stunning moment, he was struck down in his pride. She, above all other women, had the power to completely crush him. Any attempt for him to make her believe that he was defended and fortified from being hurt by her was stripped away by the sight of her. Bambi was golden, from her blonde hair swept up into a French roll to the golden silk that draped her body like honey to where it abruptly stopped at her thigh. The soft fuzz on her arms glistened with golden dust—something she must have sprayed on. More importantly, she radiated from the inside out. There was something goddess-like and pure that he had never noticed so potently before. Noah imagined himself touching her, and his heart broke. He cried on the inside at defiling such beauty with a single wicked thought. Although he knew that the power of love was magnificent only when it was freely given, the thought of himself losing the expansive golden light that graced his impure heart crippled him. Her beauty—like the very Light itself—couldn't be owned. He knew that. He knew that. He knew that he could only appreciate her this deeply in this one single moment. She was like the mountains that take one's breath away. Such majesty remains stationary even as another human breath is taken in and another day goes by until even the mountains disappear within mundane existence because eventually all human beings returned to sleepwalking. Noah didn't want to sleepwalk through this. He wanted to stay awake. This one moment was singularly his, no matter how much pain he felt.

For Noah, his love was a constellation of singular moments like this one. He navigated from stellar experience to stellar experience to keep on course with the next brilliant moment of love because he feared that no single moment was enough. Noah was bound by the imperfections and desires of his flesh, the flesh that lied: *perhaps there will never be another moment like this one.* On this navigational path, he was fast approaching the doldrums, and, unlike the casual expression of boredom, Noah understood that the *doldrums* meant that he was approaching the tremendous heat of the equator, that line in which everything is held in balance and accountable. At the very line of heat, the planetary breath rises and exhales. The doldrums is that exact moment when the planet chooses to inhale again—or not. He hoped he could finish his mission before they were both out of breath. Even now, the heat from his love, his passion was quickly rising. Even now, Noah labored for breath. Even now, he could hear Charlie fill his ear with all too believable suspicions.

Andburg touching her. Noah cried inside again, for it was his love that crippled him now. Even as he was aware of his irrationality, he could not control the impulse. A life of belief grew inside of him like a fingered tumor. He wanted to tear the clothes from her body and cry *whore*. He wanted to tear at her so she would not betray him. He had the power within to kill every living thing, and that thought both surprised and frightened him. He would not. He would not. But the decision to be above that impulse despite the pain was an effort known only by a few.

"What do you think?" Bambi grinned.

Noah turned from her. "You look nice."

"I look nice?"

He could hear in her voice that she was crestfallen.

"I have another dress. It's pink. Do you think that one would be better?"

He looked back at her shyly. "That one looks pretty good to me."

"Are you sure? Because the other one would be easy to step into. Andburg's girl—"

"What do you know about Andburg?" Noah snapped, the power and anger in his voice catching him off guard.

She looked at him, frozen in mid-sentence, stunned, angered, and hurt.

The heat flashed over his cheeks and he was ashamed. He had betrayed too much of his interior world to her: his jealousy.

"Ahhh," she stammered, "is there something you want to tell me?"

"Is there something *you* want to tell *me*? Did you see Andburg?"

"No!" Her face flushed with anger. "I saw his girlfriend, Tracy, this morning, which if you hadn't been so distant toward me lately, I would have told you about."

"Tracy, huh?"

"Yes, Tracy. We were buying dresses at the same place."

"Sorry," Noah mumbled. "I think the ark is getting to me."

"Well, I wish you'd deal already. You're impossible to live with."

"What did you think of her?" Noah was desperate to change the subject.

"I didn't think much of her. When she found out that I wanted this pretty Russian designer dress, she bought it out of spite. I saw it in her eyes, and I'll bet you that she doesn't even wear it. She wanted me to wear the pink dress, and at first I thought why not, because it is truly lovely. Then I got to thinking that it would serve me better to pick out my own dress, so I went back and got this one, but you don't even like it."

Noah let out a tiny breath. She had no clue as to the effect she had on him. He stepped up to her and gently kissed her on the shoulder. "You are so beautiful, I don't even want to see my unworthy hands touch you."

Bambi smiled and blushed. "Thank you," she said, looking up at him wide-eyed and happy. "I'm looking forward to this event, and I don't want us to fight." She retrieved a faux-fur beaver coat draped across a chair. "I want you to say sweet things to me."

"I've never seen that coat before. Where did you get it?" Noah missed his cue.

Bambi was tentative. "Ione lent it to me."

"Ione?"

"Yes." She smiled. "Ione lent me the coat, but I'm not sure how I feel about it even if it isn't real fur. I needed a coat to go with this dress, and it looks good."

He helped her on with the coat.

She rubbed her hand against the length of the sleeve. "It's very warm. I am glad it's not real beaver."

"It looks warm," Noah said, but he was distracted. He knew that they had to leave sooner than later.

"I'm ready now." Bambi patted him on the arm. "Shall we?"

Noah agreed, looked over at the dogs curled up by the heating vent, and with heaviness in his heart opened the door and followed her out. There was a soft drizzle. The rain had been intermittent for over a week. It was something to see the desert swelling with abundance. When the desert was satisfied with water, it teemed with life. Amidst the brown and the red, tiny flowers popped in purple, white and yellow. The sage itself shimmered with its silvery green even under the moonlight. For outsiders who looked across a plateau and saw nothing but brown space, dry sage, and sky, they saw nothing but dry. "It's so dry here. How can you stand it?" But for the person with high desert in his veins, the delicate beauty of the soft color and intense light was like first sight to a blind man. There was intensity beyond the pale for those patient and willing to see beyond surface. Everyone loved the rain, but they were nervous, too. Nobody had a reference to this kind of a monsoon except perhaps the oldest of the natives, who always had a reference for everything. For the rest, the thing that they prayed for most—the rain— was becoming a hindrance, and there was a little less joy and a whole lot more cursing.

Noah helped Bambi through the puddles as she tip-toed to the truck so that her golden slings wouldn't become ruined by mud. Even so, Noah saw that her hemline was dirty. As they approached the pickup, he had a sinking feeling that he was leading them both to their deaths. He couldn't shake the feeling that he was about to betray her with this test, as he believed that she was about to betray him. She seemed so happy. Noah tried to remain steady and stoic. To his dismay, the truck started right up, they didn't get stuck in the mud; they traveled the entire way past dead man's curves, hills, and spontaneous streams cutting across the roadways. To Noah's greater dismay, they made it to Andburg's party without a hitch. He remained very aware of the pain in his chest generated by the lewd scenarios in his mind. Noah, unable to rise above his mental chatter, braced himself for the worst.

Chapter 36

"I think that's a good spot." Panda Girl pointed to a mound between two misshapen fruit trees near the ark. "It's on slightly higher ground." She was completely swallowed up in a man-sized Gore-Tex slicker. There had been a slight break in the heavier rain pattern, and so the drizzle was tolerable, though it was cold and muddy. The clean-cut college suburbia kids had begun to cake with mud, even with the high-tech gear, so that they looked oddly like autochthonous aborigines newly sprung from the earth. They took to their neo-tribal duties like ducks to water; they intuitively knew what to do.

Heart-Song and the Dreamer held up a heavy tarp between them. Because of the discomfort, speech was limited. Everyone seemed to be in survival mode, and so they set into action without a word, securing the tarp between the two trees at a slight angle so it wouldn't collapse with the weight of the water. The prep work created a reasonably dry shelter from which to set up the tent. Panda Girl began to scratch out a trench with a sharp rock. She struggled with her task, so Ione found a stick and joined in, digging out a shallow base where the tent would be. Before long, the Dreamer was laying out the tent poles.

They had chosen the perfect spot where the water naturally drained off. The trench would help ensure that the tent floor remained dry. Ione wondered about the odd trees. They looked like nothing she had ever seen before, as if they didn't belong to this planet, and they were already dying. The darkish fruit had shriveled and the leaves were falling off. The crew worked slowly at erecting the shelter as they were still refining their outdoor finesse. With Tabani and Ma Shepard working alongside, however, and lending their expert skills, it didn't take long before all the tents were up. Ione noticed that there was a tent surplus, and wasn't sure from where they'd all come. It occurred to her that theirs was the beginning of a tent city, and that more would arrive.

Tabani and Ma Shepard removed their shelter from the ark and brought it in closer to *The Tribe,* as the kids were now referring to themselves. Ione watched the Prophet Twins work; they appeared even more ethereal after non-stop praying, their energy as radiant and clear as crystal sun-catchers. They seemed to move at a different pace from the others—a little out of step with time—a little slower, unconcerned, like the water itself. Still, everything got done with efficiency and speed.

Ione was relieved that things were running so smoothly. She was reassured that their intention was in alignment with the highest good. She'd been worried about the students when she first told them about the ark and suggested that they set up camp and help with its construction.

At first they were pleased with the idea, but became hesitant when the first box of gear was opened. *Camping in the rain with this? It's so old!* She'd reminded them that it was a real-life adventure, a right-now Noah's Ark, and that working in dire circumstances would only toughen them to any challenges that lay ahead. Gradually, they returned to acceptance as they dug through more boxes. Once set into motion, they became more excited and their exuberance became contagious as they continued to sort through gear. Some of the gear was new enough, they decided, to be helpful. The Gore-Tex slickers made them cheer despite the mismatched sizes.

Ione knew the equipment wasn't the latest and lightest, but it was sturdy and would work for their purposes. She'd run wilderness retreats, and so had plenty of gear. They'd stuffed equipment into stuff sacks and stuffed the stuff sacks into Hefty Bags. Ione was determined to maintain as much dryness as possible, which she found ironic, given they were in the desert. There was something unnatural and unpredictable about this rain. She didn't know how long it was going to last or if it would ever stop. The Rio Grande River was running fast and high for the first time in many years. The radio reported flash floods in the arroyos, a reminder that Mother Nature could be treacherous at best. Ione had worried about these inexperienced and youthful questers, although now that they were out here in the elements they didn't seem to mind that their adventure was rugged and wet. For Ione, however, for the first time in a long time she felt fear—caught between her training in non-attachment and an unexpected maternal instinct. It wasn't merely concern that the kids would get cold and wet; she was afraid that she would have to watch them die. Her fear was becoming intolerable. She worked on releasing it during her evening chants and compassionately commended herself for feeling what most mothers on the planet experienced daily. She admired all the feelings such attachment brought her, both the hope and the despair. She loved them. She wondered about their parents and what they might be feeling with these young adults gone missing. *They think that I'm on a school field project* was the only explanation that had been shared with her. Seeing them now, having fun, and yet being focused and capable did a lot to quell her concerns. Besides, Ma Shepherd and Tabani had seemed as if they'd been waiting for them all. Ione knew that fate was not under her control. She was not responsible for what happened next.

"Come, we're preparing for ceremony." Tabani approached without her sensing him even as she was thinking of him. "Finish setting up your tents, unpack your belongings, and put on these robes." Ma Shepard handed out dry tunics to everyone while Tabani continued to gently gather stragglers. Some of the tribe turned to Ione as if she had the answers to what was coming next. She didn't know what to tell them. She knew about as much as they did, perhaps less. They did what they were asked and then followed Tabani to other side of the ark where he had days before prepared a sweat lodge from bent willow saplings tied together and covered in heavy tarp. Ma Shepard had returned her attention from setting up camp to attending to the fire pit. It was warm near the blaze, where the stones were already hot under the embers. Ione couldn't imagine how the twins had managed to keep a fire pit going under such soggy conditions.

As if to answer her question, Ma Shepard took from her medicine bundle several deep blue pebble-sized rocks and threw them into the pit. The flames jumped into a brighter, green-based blaze. What wonderful magic, Ione thought. Everyone seemed to take a step forward to appreciate the warmth. They looked as if they were taking a vow of poverty in their shapeless tunics and bare feet. Tabani looked deeply into each of their eyes and smiled. "Welcome. Today has been difficult, but you have done well. This day marks your initiation into the global community, into global awareness, as you turn away from those limited beliefs based in materialism handed to you by your fathers and step forward into personal responsibility and commitment toward an unknown future. We are on the cusp of the purification time in which much of material matters will be destroyed so that a new pathway into spiritual oneness will be created. As prophesized by different masters in all nations, there will be one world, under one spirit. I wish I could say that we have much to teach you, but it is you who will teach us even as you lead through trial and error."

Nobody was sure how to respond to her sobering speech. A purification time didn't sound like much fun to any of them, and a somber pall fell through the group. Then Tabani continued. "We have ceremonies to teach you that will make you feel more whole and help assist you through the difficult passage. During lodge, you will access your own soul's code as you prepare to step into leadership roles for the others who will come. Before we step into lodge, we will unwind the old belief patterns of our families' programming, which will no longer serve you in this next millennium, and symbolically leave them in the fire. Then we will bring into our bellies the unlimited knowing of the natural world. It is important to be able to establish a direct communication with your higher self and your intuition in order to be guided, for you will face many situations that have no correlation to the past. You will only have this fire in your belly to guide you. Let it be so!"

Tabani took from his pocket herbs and cast them into the fire. The sweet aroma of rose-musk and almonds filled the smoke. Ione's spirits were immediately lifted, and she noticed that everyone else began to smile. Tabani began to play a tiny tin whistle to call in the spirits while Ma Shepard stepped up to the flame and, with the rotation of her hand, began to unwind the energy around her solar plexus. With an elegant motion, she cast the unwanted energy into the flames and gathered toward her belly all the warmth of the fire that she could. Then she stepped back into the circle and beckoned for the next person to do so the same. One by one, the Tribe members stepped up and did a variation of what Ma Shepard had shown them. When it was Ione's turn, she had the greatest urge to dance, and though this was a reverent ceremony, she did just that. She followed the deep internal rhythms of her own spirit. She enjoyed the laughter—hers and theirs—as she unwound all the negative programs that she had received on being an older woman in a culture that prized youth and beauty. She brought into herself the sacred heart of the mountain and claimed her power there. She felt larger than life and very present.

After the fire ceremony, one by one, they entered into the lodge by crawling through the opened flap door. Tabani and Ma Shepard welcomed and gifted each with sprigs of sage and cedar as they entered the lodge. As Ione looked around the cramped space, she saw how they were already beginning to transform into children of the earth rather than children of the world as the polish of civilization rubbed away.

"Lodge is a return to the mother and an honoring of her through prayers in four directions, also known as the medicine wheel," Tabani said. "My sister will be the fire keeper and bring to us the stones. Each stone is to be greeted, *Welcome, my sister,* and anointed with the sacred tree resin, copal. Each person here will say a prayer, and to honor that prayer we will pour water onto the rock. The heat will help us free ourselves from thoughts so that our true essence can fully emerge."

It was very dark in lodge, and there was a quiet anticipation. Tabani began to sing a soft soulful tune, and some of the others joined in though the words were in a native tongue and the song resembled a mournful humming. Ma Shepard opened the flap and lowered the first glowing hot stone into the fire pit with a pitchfork. "Welcome, my sister," they stated as instructed, and Tabani struck the copal against the hot lava rock. The lodge was filled with a wonderful scent. It smelled to Ione like high church, though earthier and in many ways sweeter.

"It's raining, again." Ione couldn't determine who had spoken. It was a male voice, huskier voice than that of the Dreamer, and carried to be an undercurrent of passive complaint. She was still trying to learn who they all were. No one felt the need to reply.

In the dark she heard Tabani clear his throat and begin his prayer by addressing the grandmothers and grandfathers of the East as he called in the animal spirits and the guides. "We give thanks for the passion of all things and the courage to begin anew. We give thanks to eagle and to fox who show us the enlightened path and the cunning path." Tabani lifted up the hand-dug gourd bowl and took a long drink of water before offering the rest to the stones. The steam that arose was shocking, and Ione felt sweat move uncomfortably down her neck even as that on her face stung her eyes. She instinctively began to rock back and forth so as not to focus on the rising heat. As more time went by, more prayers and more rising heat, Ione began to feel the panic and stiffness in her body release; she grew drowsy, or was it faint? She couldn't quite tell.

The *Talking Bowl*, as Tabani had referred to the gourd bowl, came around to her again, and he said, "I give thanks to the mother earth and ask mercy and compassion in assisting us through earthly changes. I ask for courage as we prepare to embark on our destiny and walk through the shadowed valley of death. I give gratitude to bear who teaches us resourcefulness after the hibernation and all the ancestors who are here tonight to remind us that death is a natural counterpart of life and to not fear that with which we are gifted—our immutable light." Ione drank some of the water, and emptied the bowl onto the fire. Steam rose up and filled the tiny space with wet heat. The sound of the rain on the lodge was methodical and soothing, and a part of her wanted to sleep and wake up when it was all over. Then there was a catalyst of bouncing of energy—tiny white lights seemed to shoot through the piles of rocks— and she snapped awake. As she felt the energy in the lodge change, she knew that what they had invited in had been invoked into their dimensional space. She entered her mind's eye and saw a vision of a young man returning to new earth after the storm. *The Global Child returns*. This phrase popped into her knowing, which also told her he was a return of the un-manifest creation back to form from the land of star people. Was this the Christ return? A Buddha, or some other unnamed deity? She couldn't tell. She knew him to be a holy incarnation whose presence would feed the world. He was beautiful, and Ione was moved by hope that the planet was unfolding in timely destiny. Then there was a rushing forward of animal spirits, and she could feel their urgency to have their voices heard by human beings who believed beyond the veil. As she came out of her vision and returned to the altered space of lodge, she looked into the red glow of the pit. Ione continued to stare, and it seemed as if the rocks each had a unique face. She could feel them as separate personalities and as she continued to feed them with her attention they seemed to heat up and deepen their glowing red flush. She put the fresh sage up to her nose to keep from passing out. She had lost track of the number of rounds, or how long they had been praying and singing, but it seemed as if they had been there for hours. It was now so hot she didn't think she would survive the initiation. Her heart rapidly beat, and she hoped that she would not have a heart attack.

Ione closed her eyes and even as she swayed seemed to drift off to sleep. A very soft voice spoke, and when she realized that she was hearing Ma Shepard for the first time, Ione's eyes flashed open. Who knew that Ma Shepard could speak? Ione had missed the question, but Ma Shepard was retelling a native flood myth. To hear her voice was a little like hearing a rock talk; it was nearly unbelievable and yet it evoked a trance. She spoke each word slowly as if it held importance in every syllable. Her cadence was as methodical as the rain.

"Nanabozho is one of the most powerful deities in ancient lore and explains the reasons for the first flood. Nanabozho is a shape shifter and is a trickster, often taking on the form of coyote. Many mistake him for a clown, but that is only to disarm those who can see no further than the outer skin. In actuality, he is a powerful magician."

As her story unfolded, it was clear that it would last the night. Stories like this were meant to be didactic, Ione knew, not only to teach through the telling but also to teach through the sitting. She wasn't sure she'd be able to remain awake for the whole narration, but as an elder she believed she'd earned the privilege to drift. She did enjoy what she was hearing—she loved stories—and there was nothing immediately left to do but to listen and to sleep.

"Nanabozho trusted few," Ma Shepard continued, "but he was very close to his cousin. They hunted together and liked to drink sometimes. He went to his cousin's house one afternoon, but the house was empty and the only things that remained were a few drops of blood and the serpentine trail of a demon snake. Nanabozho was furious. He picked up his rifle, sheathed his knife, and tracked the serpent. He passed great rivers, trudged through forests, climbed mountains until he found a spirit lake near a dying ocean that was as green as seaweed, putrid, thick and primordial. This was the *Lake of Devils*. Nanabozho was very brave and he jumped into the darkness and became an otter...."

When Ione woke up again, she had a vague recollection that there had been a mighty battle. Nanabozho had set the lake to boil, and the demons had been driven to the shore where he had disguised himself as a shade tree. The Great Serpent was dying of a fatal knife blow to the heart and called upon his monstrous father for revenge on all life; the father who lived in a cavern in the deep sea sent forth a wave that would cleanse all the evil. Those were the basic parts Ione could recall as she listened to the prophetess continue to weave her intricate lore. Ione quickly picked up the part that the floodwaters were fast approaching, and she imagined what that was going to be like. A big flood's coming, a hero's journey for those who survive by miraculous means and witness the reshaping of the earth. The teaching was that there had always been a reshaping and there always would be. It was the cyclic nature of all life.

***

Tabani lowered his voice. "For my sister to share her voice with us is a great honor."

"I liked it," said Heart-Song. "I've never heard it told that way. For us, the flood myth was always about a patriarch named Noah who was chosen by God because he was the only decent one around, though if I remember my Bible stories he had some inappropriate relationships with his children."

"That was only because we are supposed to remember that Noah was human, too—fallible, you know," said the Panda Girl with great conviction.

"These stories are real," said Tabani. "Only the names have changed according to the culture. The story itself—." He stopped to listen to the rain.

"Do you think this is another flood?" someone asked.

"It might be the same flood."

"What do you mean the same flood?"

"How do we know time is linear? Our way has always recognized the circular patters so we have been careful not to disturb the force too much, but something very drastic has happened, and I think there has been a time shift."

"What could cause that?"

"A planetary trauma. A great fire under the polar ice caps." Tabani spoke and the tent became quiet.

"Do you think that can really happen?" said Panda Girl.

"Anything is possible," said Tabani, and Ma Shepard mirrored this statement with a listless, sad smile that Ione could barely make out in the dying red glow of the rocks. "This is a major time shift. It is a time when all the tribes of the world will come together to share their knowledge so that the ethereal threads in the dream of life will be restored, and the web that sustains all creation will be repaired and strengthened. There will be a return to ecological harmony with the Mother that supports us. We will once again learn how to live with open heart. Even now, all over the planet, ceremonies are being shared so that the balance on the earth can be restored. We are one tribe among thousands that have joined in with sacred ceremony on this evening. We will soon be joining them by the tens of thousands. Those who did not turn a deaf ear to their dreams will become the survivors."

"That sounds overly idealistic," came the same icy voice that had earlier complained. This time the passivity had been stripped away. It took a moment for anyone to respond, so stunned was the group by the infiltrating negativity.

"Icepick!" Ione could hear Panda Girl trying to calm.

"Only through practice can the heart of man change." Ma Shepard spoke. Her voice was soft and compassionate. "For the earth to survive, there must be a return to equilibrium. For the planet to keep rotating, there must be a return to the divine feminine nature. Only through this return will the male dominance be held in check. That is…if it is not too late." She then turned her face away from the stones as if she could see too much.

Tabani looked at her. "It's late. My sister is tired and we all need sleep. We will be working hard in the morning on the ark."

It took a moment for the group to break the trance, disband, and crawl out into the rain where they were washed clean. Each found the tent and pallet they would call home, and began to settle in for the night. As Ione slowly made her way through the dark, Tabani accompanied her. She had hoped that he would, so they could have a private moment to speak.

"So do you really think we can finish this ship?"

Tabani remained silent for a long time. "Yes."

"Has he been here?"

"No."

"Do you know of whom I speak?"

Tabani stopped walking and turned to Ione. "Yes. The ship was not constructed with human hands. That is why we were summoned by spirit, so we could begin the necessary cleansing ceremonies. Of course, we can't finish the ship in the nature that it was made, but we can finish it in the nature that it was intended. With the help of the ancestors, the ship will sail and survive the changing winds." Tabani put his hand on Ione's shoulder. "In our culture, demons are part of the human existence. They only take on power when they are lain in opposition to tribal morality. That is why we include demons in our prayers—they are masterful magicians that must be respected. The one thing a demon cannot stand is to be included in love. That is why he has not been here. As long as we continue, he won't be back. But if he should return, that will be fine as well."

Ione nodded her understanding. She felt some relief in her body, and realized how deeply she had been holding on to anxiety. How odd, she thought, and smiled. It had been a long time since she'd been challenged with an unruly emotion. She knew that she was reaching her own growing edge. The one constant of being alive is that there's always an opportunity for growth. The internal steering mechanism was the intensity of human emotion. Ione, in that moment, had substituted her feeling for God for the sudden and odd experience of family. That they all survive was important to her. She desired outcome. If singing love songs to Charlie was what it took, then so be it.

"Thank you, Tabani. I can only imagine the dedication you and your sister have put into preparing the way. Thank you."

Tabani bowed his head, accepting the praise.

"Ione! Tabani!" Panda Girl came running up, out of breath and nearly in tears again. She held a tiny flashlight in her shaking hand. Her black hair was pasted to her pale skin. "Icepick is gone."

What do you mean Icepick is gone?" Ione was suddenly able to put a face with the voice, and that knowing chilled her. Icepick. They had given him that nickname because he had a habit of being a loner and was sometimes cold, but he had been their friend, and he was a survivalist, so the group had valued his abilities.

"Yeah. I don't think he could handle any of this. He called that story Ma Shepard told us witchcraft and bullshit. He said he didn't want any part of this cult stuff, and he packed up the few things he had and he's gone."

Tabani and Ione looked at each other. "Hmm. Interesting turn of events," said Ione.

"Yes," echoed Tabani softly, "but don't worry. Go back to your tent. Get out of the rain and put your mind to rest. All is well and your friends are safe."

"I just thought you'd like to know."

"Okay, then, good night."

Tabani and Ione continued to walk. "Likely more will come."

"I know," said Ione.

"Ma Shepard already prophesied this unfolding. Time for us to get some sleep before morning. Every hand will be needed to finish this project. Take care of yourself. The Global Child draws near."

"Thank you," she said just before she and Tabani parted ways, each entering their own tent. The little tent village passed through its first night in peace and gentle rain. Ione was glad there was enough equipment to keep everyone dry, warm, and rustically comfortable. As she fell asleep, she wondered about the Global Child. Was Bambi going to have a baby? She chuckled once before she sank into exhausted, dreamless sleep. *I wonder what made me think of that.*

Chapter 37

Tiny silver lights sparkled on every branch in every tree. The junipers and piñons glowed from their trunks. The sage bushes, stunted and tough as they were, were ornamentally lit so they, too, looked as if they were out of a fairy tale. The drops of moisture refracted light into miniature rainbows. Tents faced a plaza whose centerpiece was a fountain frozen into an ice sculpture. An embracing mermaid and merman floated in melting ice. The tents had been sprayed with a white compound to make them appear dusted with snow. The ground was frosted, and synthetic icicles hung conspicuously from the ironwork. Bambi pulled the collar of her coat tighter as she held on to Noah's arm.

In the midst of this winter wonderland, flowers bloomed everywhere, delicate and perfumed. The fragile beauty of roses and orchids was emphasized by the frost. The words *dazzle* and *shimmer* came to Bambi's mind. It must have taken weeks to set this up, she thought, and cost a queen's ransom. Fantasy blended seamlessly into reality in the way a child always suspects is possible. She knew she would never see anything so wondrous again.

"Noah, it looks so real," her near gasp ended in a whisper. She leaned into the warmth of his closeness, but he seemed to pull away.

He could have whispered, *I love you beyond all compare.* Instead, he mumbled, "Which tent?" His voice preoccupied and strained.

"I don't know. How do we pick?"

"Each tent has a flag." He pointed them out to her. "A picture icon is on every flag. See, fork crosses knife—that's food. A fiddle and drum—the band. And that one." Noah grimaced. "Lips."

That tent was darkened. From where she stood, she could barely make out royal crimson couches and soft candlelight. It looked Roman. Bambi pulled on his arm. "You want to go there first?" She felt him stiffen.

"Maybe later."

A slight charge of anger in his voice shivered down her spine. She no longer understood who Noah was. He'd never before been this hot and cold with her. Sometimes she wondered what had happened to the man she'd fallen in love with. This Noah was closed, obtuse. It was as if she was out of paradise and into the wilderness, and she couldn't bear one more single moment of not being seen by him. She wasn't even sure she liked Noah anymore—not this Noah, at least—and she couldn't imagine being stuck on a ship with him for no telling how long. She'd told him that she'd been transformed in the desert monastery, surely he could see that, but he had been distracted, focused inward, often erupting into unexplainable fits of anger. He hadn't even asked her the details of her vision. If he had asked, she might have told him that her body felt different, perhaps pregnant. Of late, he had been staying away. She felt abandoned, and a part of her wished she'd stayed in the monastery, come hell or high water.

Noah looked around, distracted by the tents. "Tracy must have *gotten* her way."

There was something in the way he'd said, *gotten* her way. "I think it's beautiful and probably to our advantage that she got her way. After all, it's been raining for weeks." Bambi was cross, but she answered him despite her resistance to small talk.

"Yes, they're nice, but I know that Andburg does have a practical side. He never wanted to have this kind of hype. Beer and Band. You know, like that."

"I don't believe that about Andburg, but even if it's true, what good is practicality now? This may very well be the last big event in our lives. After all, Noah, it's still raining. And there is nothing wrong with tents!"

"I never said there was anything wrong with tents, but this is over the top. Stop being so difficult!"

Bambi had the urge to break away from his arm. She shut down, made up her mind not to speak to him further. He seemed sad, but he gave her an *I'm sorry* hug. Now it was her turn to stiffen. She felt as if he were obliging her. Even worse, her enchanted moment was ruined, and she wasn't sure it could be salvaged. She didn't want to have a fight. She didn't want to be so angry with him. She wanted to feel close and in love. *Why was he being so difficult? Does he not understand how much I love him?* For Bambi, there was no greater gift in this world than the gift of true love—for self and others. Those who passed it up as unimportant, or unable to see it, or were numb to it were cursed to collapse into the black hole of selfishness and continual wounding. It was this wounded ugliness that had been projected into the world, and that corruption had led humankind to the eve of planetary destruction. She had thought Noah was different. She wanted *her* Noah back. The one who spoke to her through the openness of his heart, the one who was capable of great love and compassion? What did it matter if God needed him? She needed him, too, and she was no less divine then creation itself. Perhaps it was too much to ask of one man to save her, much less the entire planet. Bambi knew she had her own set of expectations to let go of. Whatever was unfolding was not about their personal drama. She just needed a little more attention, and she would have to figure out some way to get that.

"Should we go in and meet our host?"

"Yes. Let's go in." She bravely returned his smile, though she was hurt and frightened. She was suddenly aware of how high the stakes were. Together, they stepped across the plaza to the edge of the bright white light that came from the fiddle and drum tent. There, the band was already playing more blues than bluegrass. It was still early in the night, and the dancers hadn't yet warmed up and let their hair down in their alcohol-induced haze. Although the dance floor was empty, there was a milling crowd around the champagne fountain. Somehow, Noah knew to pick the right tent, the one they would find Andburg in.

Bambi saw the dark haired femme fatale gracing the presences of everyone in sight, especially the men. Tracy held court while Andburg quietly got drunk. She looked fabulous in her Valentino haute couture— pure white like a fallen angel that offset the blackness of her hair teased high and wild. From where Bambi stood, she could see the dress was striated by stiff raw silk banded by mesh slits that clearly showed a peek-a-boo of olive skin. Her sleeves were capped in white fur. Bambi took a deep breath of compassion, removed her coat and handed it to Noah. She held his arm as they flowed forward into the sea of socialization, into the bustle of what might become the last great party of her life. She looked squarely over at Tracy, and didn't even care if there were competition. What did it matter whose fur was real? That kind of competition was a social illness, and Bambi was willing to buy into it just so far—just enough so that she would experience herself as desired, but not enough to trade her soul. Her authenticity was non-negotiable. With glitter and excitement everywhere, Bambi caught the energy and tried to absorb everything, just in case she would never see anything like it again. In her heart of hearts she knew that she would not, but she also believed that there was something better coming.

Chapter 38

When Bambi stepped into the tent, all eyes turned to her. Dan had a bird's eye view from an upper support. The tent was huge, a circus tent without the stripes. Nobody could see him, but he could see everyone quite clearly. He was keeping his eyes out for Charlie. Charlie was loose somewhere, but where? Dan was beginning to suspect that Charlie had taken on a new disguise. It was important to find him since Noah's second test was fast approaching. Noah would have to transcend his personal pain and suffering in order to maintain his heart-centered alignment with the cosmic forces and bring divine plan forward into physical manifestation.

Dan would have liked to say that it had taken the Devil to get him out of the Arctic, but he couldn't. It had taken him a while to figure out how to get back. He had followed the faint smell of sulfur through the in-between spaces of time. He materialized at the party just in time to see the humans show up and begin their usual song and dance—jockeying for power, propelled by insecurity and fear.

Although Bambi seemed oblivious to her effect on the room, Dan saw Tracy stop in mid-sentence, something he'd never seen before. She quickly recovered, placing her hand on the arm of her male companion to regain his wandered attention. She laughed a little louder and strategically turned her bronzed body so that there was more than one man following her form as the golden Bambi made her way through the room. Tracy, despite her efforts, could not control the attention of everyone. The crowd parted and murmured in Bambi's wake. Tracy's body stiffened almost imperceptibly as she approached.

"Darling, very good of you to be here," Tracy spoke first. "This is a nice dress. I guess the Chanel didn't fit."

Bambi grinned. "It was too big."

Dan closed his eyes. He hoped that Bambi wouldn't get sucked in. She didn't seem rattled, but Tracy was a master at destroying confidence.

"You look lovely, too." Bambi lifted her hand to the fur sleeve. "Is this mink? I thought it might be mink. You know there are faux furs that look like the real thing."

"I see that you know that well." Tracy looked down at the coat Noah was carrying. "Actually, my dear, this is polar bear." She smiled when Bambi lowered her hand, stunned.

"Polar bear. Aren't they endangered?"

"Yes, but it doesn't really matter to me. I chose this fur as a political statement. Fur is fur. We shouldn't distinguish on the bases of some merit scale. Whose right is it to say which animal is worth more? We either value the life of an animal, any and all animals, or we don't. Humans kill animals. It's a fact of life that I don't see changing anytime soon. Why is the life of a cat, or a mouse, or a lama worth less just because they're common? If humans really cared about *animals* there would be no Endangered Species Act. We wouldn't even have zoos; there'd be no need for them. Besides, there are enough polar bears right now so that their numbers are being thinned legally with the right permits. This one so happened to be shot with the right permit. He looks good on my dress, don't you think?"

Bambi stared at the sleeve, still speechless.

"I love the shock effect, especially with this room of scientists and environmentalists who really do need a reality check from time to time. Don't get me wrong. I want them to save the world just as much as anyone, but they sometimes carry the moral high ground as long as it is convenient for them. I know I've been with Andburg long enough. Anyway, it's only a polar bear."

"Polar bear," was all Bambi could say.

"Did someone say my name?" Andburg joined the conversation. He looked aristocratic in his tailored suit and polished Armani wingtips. He was a nice looking fellow who seemed completely at ease in his body. He had a precisely trimmed beard that had a hint of red—just enough for those who were admiring him to see his Scottish roots. Andburg had the charismatic ability to disarm any crowd because he was so outgoing and friendly. He was a genuine guy who didn't try to put on airs. Andburg would have appeared just as comfortable and unaffected standing on a beach in his wet boxers. Andburg held a beer, but that didn't stop him from hugging and making sure everyone had what he or she needed.

"Pretty cool, huh?" Andburg turned around and looked at the eager group filling their glasses in the champagne fountain. "It looks like a goddamn convention."

Noah laughed despite his hyper-vigilance.

"She did a good job, though." He turned to Tracy and tipped his beer to her. "Kudos, my dove. I know I was a little resistant."

"Bastard." She turned a cold shoulder to him. "He always does this to me," she whispered to Bambi and anyone else who could hear. "He treats me like a queen when we're around others, but behind closed doors, well, that's another story altogether. He's never happy with anything I do. Resistant, yes, but then when all is said and done, and he sees how happy I've made people, then he likes it. At least, publicly. You have no idea who this man is. He's a regular Dr. Jekyll and Mr. Hyde. I know you don't believe me; why should you?" She implored Bambi with her eyes. "Is Noah like that?"

Bambi didn't answer. She didn't know how because only recently had his behavior defied reason. She smiled and her heart softened some for Tracy. She did feel for her, though she was embarrassed for Andburg. This public airing was embarrassing. They were one of the wealthiest and most successful couples she'd ever met, and their problems were so common. All that privilege, and they were still ordinary.

"I apologize for her. She is a little high-strung, but she does help me throw an excellent party, and she's an excellent corporate lawyer. She defends the basic rights and freedoms of money."

Tracy turned to him and Bambi took a step back to avoid verbal shrapnel. To everyone's surprise, Tracy didn't say a word before storming off.

"You got a live wire, my friend," Noah said.

"Yeah. Well, she'll be back. She always comes back."

"This is a beautiful party, and I'm enjoying it so much. I've never seen anything like it." Bambi smiled, and when she smiled Andburg smiled, too.

Noah's heart ran deadly cold.

"Come with me, I'd like to show you around some." Andburg gently took Bambi by the elbow and escorted her over to the champagne fountain. Noah followed closely. Andburg picked up two glasses and filled them, handing one to Noah and one to Bambi. Noah refused and so Andburg drank it himself. He then relieved Noah of Bambi's coat and called to an attendant in a white jacket, "Make sure this gets hung in the coat room."

"Very good, sir."

"When you're ready to go, all you have to do is ask for your coat from one of these white jackets."

Andburg patted Noah on the back while he continued to banter with Bambi. "You know, Noah is a good dude friend. He knows where the bodies are buried, so to speak."

"Yes, he is a good man."

"Do you think you two'll get married?"

"I don't know. The way the world's going, I'm not sure it's worth it," she said, quickly glancing at Noah.

"I don't think things are as bad as you might imagine."

Bambi continued to look at Noah for clues as to how much she should say, or how much she was supposed to know. Was she supposed to tell Andburg that she knew how his project had destroyed the world, and it was only a matter of time before CNN would be on top of that story with around-the-clock coverage? Noah really didn't look at her, so she launched into the truth. "Noah tells me you're working on a secret government project on the earth's poles."

Andburg looked over at Noah and scowled. "Not so secret, perhaps. Yes, my team and I are working with a renewable energy source that will change the face of the planet as we know it."

No doubt, Bambi thought. "But you ran into some trouble."

Andburg shot Noah a dirty look then a softer look at Bambi. "Okay, we did run into a tense situation not too long ago, and I was a bit worried, but that situation has been resolved. I received a satellite transmission from my project manager, and he assured me that all is well."

"And you believe him?"

"Implicitly. Besides, I'm flying to the Arctic the day after next. Believe me, everything is under control."

"So why do you think it's raining so much?"

"Bambi, don't worry about the rain. This is an old weather pattern. One hundred years ago, there was a monsoon season. This rain is nothing to worry about. It's good weather to read or to make love." Andburg winked at Noah, who was mute in his stiffness. "Come, Bambi, don't worry. Let's dance."

He began to lead her to the dance floor. She turned to Noah to rescue her. He didn't look at her. Dan saw her fear and confusion, quickly masked. She shot Noah one more look before following Andburg onto the dance floor where *Jamaican Snow* was strumming a happy little number on the banjo and base. Dan watched the whole thing. He saw the unhappy Bambi dancing, trying to have a good time despite her anger. He saw Noah, who hadn't had a drink in years, reach for a glass of champagne. The way things were unfolding, drinking wasn't going to help. When Dan saw Noah fill his second glass, he knew that, as his Daemon, he had to do something. With one swoop he glided close to Noah's head. Noah startled and dropped the glass. There was a broken splatter at his feet. Only one or two people turned to look, but seemed unconcerned. However, when he began to yell, "You fucking bird," there was a wide circle of people who stopped what they were doing to stare at him. Noah abruptly stopped, wildly looked around, and then stormed from the tent.

Chapter 39

Dan flew from the tent. He knew Andrea was somewhere nearby. He'd seen her arrive in the dump truck. She was the only one he could really talk to. She had fully awakened to her ability to communicate with animals. He was certain she'd be better equipped to listen to him, and he didn't have to enter her dream state. He found her at the food tent. She was just about to pop a Vienna sausage into her mouth when he landed on the white tablecloth just next to the Brie.

"You know that's not so sanitary," she said as she licked her fingers.

"I really don't think it matters at this time of complete urgency. I need your help."

She grinned and went to stabbing at the ham cubes. She was the only one in the tent not dressed in evening clothes. She remained defiantly comfortable in her jeans and sweatshirt with two embroidered kitties and the message *will work for tuna*. Dan admired her eccentricity. "Charlie's here. Noah's beginning to drink. We need to find them both before it's too late."

"You know that in England the difference between an eccentric and someone crazy is about two hundred and fifty thousand pounds?"

"Andrea, aren't you concerned?"

Andrea grinned and stabbed another cube. "Yes, but I'm eating, and I've never been to a party like this before. I want to enjoy, so I can die without regret."

"Not many can say that, so get another ham cube and let's go."

Andrea thought about it a moment. "I do have one regret."

"What's that?"

"That I went to Vassar and didn't become a professor. A private college like that was less of an opportunity and more of a social weight, labeled as unlived potential."

"Is that how you feel? Now?" Dan was becoming a little desperate.

"Not since menopause." Andrea laughed, and didn't seem to care that her mouth was full. "Besides, I know who I am and the service I've provided for my little corner of the planet. It's amazing what people throw away. I once found a bike for a kid who had no bike. He was the happiest little person that I've ever seen in my whole life—no more running alongside his friends." Andrea fell silent. She picked at the black olives, put a couple on her fingertips and pretended they were jitterbugging. The motion of her fingers slowed to a waltz.

"Come with me now, Andrea! Bambi and Noah must be given a fair chance to succeed."

"Why should any of us be given a chance?"

"This doesn't sound like you, Andrea. What's—"

"Hey, there, do you mind passing me that knife. I'd like to try this Brie. Is it good?" Dan and Andrea stopped in mid-sentence. Before them stood a burly redheaded young man with a beard wearing blue jeans and a T-shirt with a turtle on it.

"Like your shirt," Andrea said as she handed him the knife and ate the olives from off her fingers.

"Thanks," he said, pointing at the turtle on his T-shirt. "This is Alfredo."

"Alfredo?"

"Yes. He's a rare Batagur Baka from Malaysia. Girls think he's sexy. I'm one of the founders of TSA." He extended his hand. "My name is Brian."

"What's TSA?"

"Turtle Survival Alliance." He smiled and swallowed. He was already scanning the table for the next bite. Andrea liked him immediately. He stopped for a moment to retrieve a bit of ham from under the serving plate rim. "Easy to find us; just Google."

"What do you do for this TSA?"

"I'm an Ecological Evolutionary Developmental Herpetologist." He grinned. "That's my official title, anyway. I like to think of myself as biological engineer, helping turtles hatch one egg at a time."

"You're kind of like the family pediatrician."

"More like a sex specialist. We've been able to release ten thousand of these guys back into the wild. People don't really get how cool turtles are, but they're remarkable. Here, look at this." He pulled from his wallet a lovingly worn image of himself crouching before a giant tortoise, scratching under her out-stretched chin. Both Brian and the tortoise were smiling. It was an odd family photo, but a family photo nonetheless. "Kind of looks like you. Sweet."

"Thanks. That's Harriet. She's one of the oldest known land tortoises, a hundred and seventy-two years old. We know because Darwin found her when she was only five years old and the size of a dinner plate. She was born sometime in November 1830, and she is amazing. She lives in a zoo in Australia and responds to a half a dozen human words. She really liked me. Followed me around most of that day, gracing me with her presence. I think she had a lot to tell me. Sure wish I could speak turtle."

Andrea returned the photo. She was touched by the passion this young man showed for such a fragile species. The turtle looked so happy. And what was that expression on her face? Love? She wished she had just fifteen minutes with Harriet. She had some questions she wanted to ask the old girl.

"You know the tribes here believe the turtle represents the planet itself, and the totem often represents healers."

"I know." Brian suddenly looked crestfallen and tired. "So many good people are out there doing what they can to save species. We're all working so hard." He carefully put the photo back into his wallet. "The most exciting moment of my life was sitting on a beach in North Carolina the exact moment a mass hatching began. Mounds—like miniature volcanoes—suddenly busted open, like the entire earth gave birth. Out came ten thousand forms of new life all with a single focus: to survive. So many of them don't, but they never give up. Life often pushes through insurmountable odds to choose itself." He looked at Andrea and blushed. "I've been rambling."

"No, thank you."

"Is this owl yours?"

"Let's just say he's an old friend."

"I understand. I swear, sometimes it's as if I can talk to them, too." Brian took another couple of crackers and began to move along the table. "See you both around."

Andrea waved once, and then turned to Dan. "Okay, I lied. It's not that I don't care. It's that I care too much. I'll talk to Noah, but I wouldn't count on it helping much, if he's got his mind made up about something."

"I'll be there to help you. Together, we should have some kind of influence."

"Okay. But, well…did Bambi cheat?"

"No," Dan said, though he wasn't sure what kind of tricks Charlie still planned to pull. "This is the second test Noah must pass. But we can only help him so far. It will be his choice, his experience to transcend. He must practice the true nature of love, not one ego-driven by possession."

"Okay. I just speak better if I speak from a place of truth."

"That's all any of us have. If we wish to cultivate authentic power, we must speak from our core of truth. That's our ace, as it were. An ace Charlie will never be fully able to understand." Dan reached out and tore a piece of fruit with his beak. He knew the form he had chosen was powerful and that he hadn't even begun to scratch the surface of his capabilities. If Dan could have smiled, he would have. There didn't need to be more light than shadow, there just needed to be enough light.

***

They found Noah sitting on a bench. His hair was down, and the rain streamed ringlets in its tangled length. He looked like a wild man. He had a drink. What was that, Scotch? Andrea couldn't tell. She looked hard at his lap. What was there? A revolver? What she could tell was that he was not doing well, and her heart went out to him. She had no idea what to say to make him feel better. She decided not to try. "May I sit?"

"Suit yourself."

Andrea sat. The wet was uncomfortable. "A gun?"

Noah stirred, as if he wanted to touch the nickel plate. "Semi-automatic."

"Why do you have a gun, Noah? Absurd that a peaceful man has denigrated to such brutal measures."

"I'm not responding to that."

"No matter what you think Bambi's done, killing will never end your suffering. That gun will make a victim out of you."

"Not me."

Dan fluttered down.

"Oh, it's him. Well, I'm not listening anymore. He can talk or hoot or screech as much as he likes. I'm through!"

"Noah, why are you so upset at Dan?"

"There's never a warning with him. Besides, what has he ever really done? He never warned me about Bambi and Andburg. I'd shoot him if I thought I had enough bullets."

"I'm your Daemon," Dan said to Noah, but, as promised, Noah refused to listen. "Tell him that I'm here to keep him on the right track. Tell him that I might not be an ideal Daemon. I may not have picked the best animus disguise, but owls are pretty symbolic of what I need to teach him. Tell him. Tell him that I'm doing the best I can and I need him to cooperate. I'm the best Daemon he has."

"You want me to tell him all that?" Andrea turned to Noah. "Stop being stupid."

Noah didn't say much at first. Then he smiled just enough to ease the tension of the moment. "I realize that I'm focusing my anxiety on him, easy target. Unfair, displaced anger, perhaps. I'm sorry."

Dan rippled a high-five motion with his wing.

"Okay." Andrea became serious again. "How do you know Bambi has been unfaithful?"

"I feel it."

"But you don't have proof."

"Charlie told me."

"Charlie's a demon. I don't know about you, but last time I checked demons weren't credible sources."

"I don't know that for sure. I mean about Charlie. He's taught me so much—built so much. He's become a father to me."

"He growls."

"So he growls."

"Okay, love Charlie. Remember this at the very least: you're basing feelings on what someone said and not direct knowledge."

"That's true. That's why I'm waiting."

"You're setting a trap?"

"Yep." Noah took another sip from his glass.

"And you call Dan creepy?" Andrea reached into her pocket and pulled out a pocketknife. She opened the blade. "You're right here, Noah." She put her finger on the blade. "On the edge. One false move." She cut her finger just enough to bead a drop of blood to make her point. "You're like a slug cozening up to a salt shaker saying, 'I can handle this.' Haven't you been told that folks that go out looking for trouble find it? Those who set the trap often step in it. This is dangerous territory you're in. You're taking your gospel from Charlie who *might not be a demon*? I thought your love for Bambi was bigger than that."

"I know you're trying to help, Andrea. You're a good friend. You just don't understand. It's like I'm infected."

"You'd better find a way to get disinfected because you're likely to pull a lot of people down with you if you're wrong." She snapped the blade closed.

"Tell him that he must stand in the light of his heart in order to discern truth. If he is in his loving, he will know the difference."

"Dan says 'be true to your heart'."

"I am."

"Seems to me you're being selfish. Why don't you go in there? Get Bambi. Tell her your fears. Go home. Sleep on it. You'll feel better in the morning."

Noah drained the glass and threw it against a nearby rock. They all heard the crystal shatter.

Andrea stood up. "This isn't love. This is boyish immaturity. Little boys stomp their feet when their toys don't work right. Dare I say grow up, Noah? You're not the only one who's ever been in love."

Noah's shoulders slumped. One side of him had softened in her truth. The other was bowed up and ready for a fight. Noah couldn't decide what to do, so he folded in on himself.

"It's your turn, bird. I can't reach him."

"He will have to choose," said Dan. "That's his test."

"Dan says 'good luck'. Remember, the real truth comes from your heart. I have seen nothing less than loving support from your woman. You're lucky to have her. I hope you can get past this test." Andrea looked up at the rain and squinted. "This definitely is not all about you. Hope you get that." She turned her face to him. "Noah, you're a good man. I have faith that you'll make the right decision, a decision that won't be based on your ego's needs."

"Thanks," Noah said. "I know you're only trying to help. I'll call you in the morning. I'm not going to wait here much longer. Just want to think some about what you said to me."

"Please give me the gun, Noah."

"No! I need it, just in case."

She nodded. "Call me. I'm going home. It's wet, and I don't want to get sick. You should take care of your health, as well."

"This isn't bad. It's not too cold. And I'm tough."

"Don't be too tough, cowboy." Andrea patted him on the back, turned, and walked away in the dark. She had a half mind to go find Bambi and give her a head's up. Dan fluttered above her. "Thank you," he hooted.

"I hope it was enough."

"You did your part. Time will tell the rest."

"What next?"

"I'll keep an eye on things here. Try to keep him safe. Charlie is loose somewhere. I can smell him."

Andrea wrinkled her nose. "Well, I'm done with him. Hope I never have to be in the same boat with him again."

"I hope you won't have to be. Go home and be safe. I'll contact you soon." Dan took off into the night sky.

Andrea walked on in the insulated silence of manufactured ice, something from out of the future—artificial and alarming. Weird. The sounds of the party fell into muted echoes. It was comforting to be on the outside of it. It was comforting to hear the sounds of human life. Her intention was to go home. She was tired, but she decided to take one pass through the dance floor in search of Bambi to at least say goodnight.

Chapter 40

"Your body is sublime and these admirers are not doing you justice. They are mere hacks. Not connoisseurs." Charlie stepped up behind Tracy and breathed the words into her ear. He saw the fine hair that ran along the back of her neck stand up. "I can tell that a woman like you needs a good man." He put his hand boldly on her buttock and spoke more, so low that no other human could possibly hear. Her entire body stiffened, and she spun around and slapped him hard against the ear. The two men who had been attentively in her company scurried off.

"What bloody nerve." She began to call out for an attendant to bounce this lewd pervert, but Charlie swallowed her words and would have taken the breath right out of her body if she hadn't stopped talking that very second.

"Good, that's better. I didn't mean to insult you. I was merely direct with my request."

It had been easy to find her. She'd been watching Andburg trying to dance with Bambi. Charlie turned to observe. Bambi tried to leave the dance floor, but Andburg swept her into another dance move. He was a little drunk, a little silly. He wasn't necessarily focused on Bambi. He wanted to feel a little less lonely, and he was having a good time. Charlie saw all this and more. Charlie could also tell that she felt just sorry enough for him to oblige. It was clearly pathetic pity dancing, but Tracy did not see it that way. She'd been fuming and awaiting her opportunity to pounce and shred. Charlie smiled. *Good.* His plan was going well with very little effort on his part. This scenario was so easy. Too easy, almost. If Charlie could have felt guilt he would have, but all he could feel was the animal heat and rage underneath Tracy's perfume.

"Who are you?"

"Don't you remember me? I'm the guy who built that stage. Charlie." Charlie pointed to where the band was lifting the energy of the crowd with the energy of their notes.

"Oh," she said flatly. "There was nothing memorable in that meeting."

"That's because my focus was not on you, but on the job at hand. You are now my job at hand."

"I don't really see where that has a bearing on the current situation."

"Of course you don't *see.* I haven't begun to show you." Underneath Charlie's words there was an animal snarl that signaled the beginning of a mating ritual. Tracy wasn't aware she heard it, but her body unexpectedly responded. She was surprised by her reaction. She took a second glance at Charlie. He was so unappealing, nearly brutish, but she'd grown accustomed to indulging her sexual impulses. For Tracy, however, sex was about control.

"If you are implying Mr. — what is *your* name anyhow? Charlie?"

"You can call me Mr. Baal."

"Mr. Bowl. I'm not going to sleep with someone *Andburg* hired, if that's what you are implying."

"Se'irim, you are already known to me."

"Who is Se'irim?" Tracy suddenly felt exposed, seen, and laid bare in some barren truth. The desert flashed before her eyes — not the desert of New Mexico but some vast desert of white endless sand dunes like the curves of a virgin goddess where the minds of men were devoured by the heat. She saw in a flash that there had been giant pyres erected, flames, blood sacrifices all in her honor. It was exciting, not just exciting but thrilling, a thrill Tracy realized she had been seeking in her too-ordinary life. As soon as the epiphany hit it was gone like an evaporating mirage.

"This is not about me and you, although that is part of the plan." Charlie leaned in so close now that his breath caught the fine hairs of the polar bear fur and teased them into movement. "It's about him." Charlie cut his eyes again toward Andburg. "He has made your life so unhappy. Miserable. Tortured. Never truly appreciating you, never fully understanding anything about you. He was never able to serve you properly, and for an ancient soul like you that's a frustration so deep and lonely few can imagine the punishment. He never respected you with proper homage and that, my dear, has left you very, very hungry." Charlie bowed his head, took Tracy's hand in his, brought it to his lips, and kissed her fingertips with great tenderness — a strain for someone so truly savage. "This is your night to free every ounce of frustration you ever had in one long ...." Charlie saved the word for the image. He sent the image directly to her head, sharp in its focus, the way a needle begins to pierce the skin. He left the addict in her wanting more.

Tracy inhaled the images. She took back her fingers and placed them in her own mouth. She got the full picture of the two of them in carnal position and stood weak and ready.

Charlie moved back, cold now that he knew his prey was primed. Se'irim or not, she was no Kali. Charlie looked at Bambi, and found he was still disappointed that he wasn't able to have her. But that would ruin his plan. The Universe was governed by laws, no matter how random they sometimes seemed. Charlie knew, however, that even for demons there needed to be at least tacit consent. Charlie looked at Tracy who was in a near swoon. She was no Bambi, no Kali either, but he'd make the most of it. She wasn't bad looking and would look even better in her disguise. He might even impregnate her for her efforts. That'd settle her down some. He could if he wanted. He was interested in her enough that he would give her life doomed for damnation.

"I haven't even told you the best part."

"What's that?"

"He gets to watch."

Of course, she assumed he meant Andburg. "Good, he has it coming after everything he's put me through. But knowing him, he won't even care." She laughed callously. She tried to cover up the hurt.

Oh, she does love him, Charlie thought, poor bastard. "Shall we?" Charlie took her by the arm, and he led her to the dance floor where they shadowed Bambi and Andburg step for step.

"Hello, Bambi," Charlie purred when he dipped Tracy directly in their path. "Where's Noah this evening?"

Bambi looked startled and trapped. "He's around somewhere."

"Are you sure?"

She hesitated, but quickly recovered. "Yes. I'm sure. He wouldn't leave me."

"Bambi, such certainty."

"Hey, babe." Andburg blew Tracy a kiss. "The band is good tonight."

She ignored him and held on more tightly to Charlie as he swept her off her feet. They continued to dance, circling the other couple.

"How is the ark?" Charlie casually asked Bambi.

"I don't know," Bambi said. "I haven't been there lately."

"Neither have I," said Charlie. "I really should drop in. I hate leaving a project unfinished." He winked at her.

She quickly turned her gaze away. "Honestly, I don't think you've been missed." She scouted the room for Noah.

"That's okay, Bambi. You could never hurt my feelings no matter how hard you try." As Charlie said the words, he could feel Tracy's freshly sprung passion turn into a slow deadly simmer. Charlie had to be careful that she would not change her mind. He swung her in close and kissed her, an appeasement. Andburg saw the kiss. He didn't react. He didn't seem to care, which fueled her to a fever pitch. She was like a wild cat now, and Charlie could see the Desert Jinn begin to flash. He knew her to be like him—a fallen angel. Having mated with the sons of man, she was stranded on the planet for eternity.

"Andburg, you do remember—" Tracy said.

"Charlie? Yeah, he's the guy who built this stage. You did a great job, buddy. I imagined this to be a simple event, but it all turned out all right. The tents were a good idea. Now with the rain, I would say it turned out for the beer and the better."

"Andburg, I don't really care what you have to say," Tracy said with an edge. "Mr. Baal, or Charlie, or whatever you wish to call him will be *talking* to me this evening, if you understand my drift. Not that it's any of your business, but there you have it. If I were you, I'd find somewhere to sleep tonight. But for now we're going to talk on one of those pretty red divans that's been charged to your account." She stopped dancing and drew close to Andburg, forcing him to stop in his staggered step. "If you think you can get into Bambi's panties, good luck. I know women like that: uptight teases. If I'm wrong, then bring her by. I wouldn't mind. What I do mind is how you consistently manage to go for inferior women, Andburg. You must have the bloodline of the lowborn to be constantly attracted to one *generation removed from white trash*. Fuck her, get it over with, but remember we're in it together for better and for worse." She kissed him lightly and with fire on her lips. "Just want you to remember what another man is about to receive."

Andburg pushed Tracy from him. "I give her to you," he addressed Charlie. "A gift from the host for a job well done. Consider it gratuity."

Tracy spun around and stormed off. Charlie barely had time to grab Bambi's essence before they left the tent. Once Charlie caught up with this Desert Jinn, he transferred Bambi's essence onto her. Bambi would never notice. She would be depressed, but she wouldn't know why. In an infusion of gold, Tracy transformed into Bambi's double. If he closed his eyes, even Charlie could pretend that he was escorting Bambi to the orgy. Tracy didn't know what was about to happen, but she hadn't asked. All Charlie cared about was that she'd given enough of her consent. Tracy believed that they would make it to Andburg's bed, but she would never leave the tent tonight. He hadn't decided if he'd kill her, but he had plenty of time. He'd know, when the moment came.

Tracy led him into the exotic tent: Moroccan influence layered over Roman decadence. The couches and divans were sectioned off by carved wood screens, which provided the illusion of privacy. It was cozy. A sitar played kirtans from somewhere in the haze. Tracy slid down on an unoccupied divan and rubbed the velvet with her hand indicating where Charlie should sit. He rolled his eyes. He wasn't accustomed to this role, but if he didn't oblige her the evening would end too quickly. Timing was everything. He sat, closed his eyes, and became aware of murmuring. He estimated that there were twenty, maybe twenty-eight souls in the tent. Whatever the number, it would be enough to work with. There would be a harvesting tonight. He inhaled the pheromones and the emotions. They were all seeking attention and love. None of them realized it, but they were all trying to get back to God. Charlie understood that. It was the one big love that he could never get back, not now. Things had gone too far. Charlie consoled himself with the thought that he much preferred having his freedom. Still, he understood the hidden fears behind the human condition. Not too difficult to figure out that all human tragedy spun from that separation leaving a big, gaping hole, an empty space lined with fear and loathing. Not an easy thing to know one was kicked out of divine union more than once. Reincarnation. Karma. They sought to stuff the ugly dark spaces with distraction, easy gratification, and self-glorification, *What have you done for me lately*? Such distraction was an easy fix, but it always wore off because, by its very definition, the desire could never be filled. Wait an hour and the hunger returned. It was easy to attract these hungry moths to a dim and an inferior light. All he had to do was dangle the illusion of something better—more wealth, more prestige, better odds on the game of life—and they cashed in their blue chip stocks. They all believed that happiness was external and, therefore, obtainable. It was right around the next corner. It was the next drink, the next fling, the next experience. It was the promise of a good time, a new thrill, something better. For Charlie, harvesting these hungry ones had become so simple that it was boring.

Tonight he'd offered illusion on a grand scale. Tonight sex was on the menu. It would fill the craving and satisfy the hunger for belonging, at least until the illusion wore off, which would be before dawn. Once they woke up, their loneliness would return. Once they remembered the night before, the various positions they'd been in, the compromises they'd made, the full light of reality would burn just a little, and for some the shame would burn a lot, enough to remind them that they were still human and, therefore, suffered. Some would cry, some would rationalize, others would want *more*. All of them would remember the pain and the struggle of being human. It was messy to be human, tragic to be divorced from the animal nature, because when it did sneak up on them, they never knew how to handle it, so starved were they for that which they denied. They would all turn to the next thing to soothe their souls.

"Are you just going to sit there and let me cool off? Do you know how lucky you are to be here with me?"

Charlie looked over at Tracy. He was annoyed. Anytime she spoke it was annoying. He didn't want her to talk, so he muttered a quick and easy spell. Tracy's head became that of a goat with a human smile, not enough of a transformation for her to even notice, but enough to limit her ability to speak without braying. Other than that, she wore Bambi's essence well. He patted her on the knee. She kicked at him just a little. "I like you, Charlie. You make me feel funny."

He knew that Noah would have to get there soon for the illusion to take hold. Once she started sweating, it would melt into sticky exhaustion. Tracy stretched out on the divan and began to caress his thigh with her foot. "Not yet, dove." He pulled her toes up to his mouth and kissed them.

She pulled her foot back. "Don't be a dud. Let's see if you perform like you promised. I want to see it." She brayed softly. She reached for him and he grabbed her wrist with his claw, no longer interested in maintaining his disguise.

"Ouch, you're hurting me." Blood trickled from the cut.

Charlie ignored her. She was a big girl. She could handle it. He felt Noah's panic enter the tent. Charlie's thoughts and attention were diverted like a beacon to that resonance of confusion and desperation. There is a delicate balance between little boy grief and potential killer. Charlie knew exactly where the man stood—dripping in rainwater and self-righteousness—it got the *good* men every time—by the acrid smell. Noah was searching, possessed by irrational indignation and pride. He was here to prove that he was unworthy of true love. Good, Charlie thought, now I don't have to kill her. He looked over at Tracy with disgust. Nothing worse than a demon-goddess crippled by love.

Charlie stood up and began to recite a mantra, an incantation to the Holy Spirit, but the words were in reverse: *Irs aynatacha. A Tivatirach. Irna. Irna Irna.* As he chanted, he commanded control over the physical reality, both flesh and mind. Thunderclouds rolled in, and a lightning bolt ripped open a hole in the tent, exposing the room to the elements. Charlie imagined an altar in the center. An altar with harness and straps sprung up. Necessary restraints, because once he unzipped that Desert Jinn, she was going to be a volatile mass. Spontaneous fires cropped up wherever Charlie focused his gaze. Thus, he created the illusion of light with dramatic flair. It was a trick that had never failed him.

The strong souls in the tent became frightened and ran off. The weaker souls were drawn to the creation with curiosity. More than one thought they were seeing a cool light show and were probing the scientific possibilities of how their host had managed to pull it off. The inner light of many who remained was dim. They were looking for a new type of thrill, anything not to feel numb and lost. Not wanting to disappoint them, Charlie pointed to a spot just above the altar. A neon sign appeared. It flashed: *This is the place.* The crowd gasped and clapped. Charlie looked to where the sitar player had been. He had abandoned his instrument. Good thing. This crowd was not into love songs for God. Charlie pointed and a band of shades materialized. They brought with them exotic instruments, carved and polished black, from the most ancient Mesopotamian shrines long ago sealed, cursed, and forgotten. Charlie struck up the band like a flame, and they produced primal sounds meant to stimulate the lower charka and produce electrically charged erections. There would be no relief. Once the dancing began— and an eager few had already begun—it would release the Kundalini. Like a snake, it would enter the gyrations and create a destructive force in the procreation urges. There would be enough distortions to keep the party rocking all night, and Tracy was going to be the centerpiece. He hoped she could handle it.

Charlie set up three stripper poles and three dancers of his choice. They were cheerleaders in go-go boots, and they generated excitement when they began their low grinding moves. The crowd was riveted and cheered in unison when each girl popped open the front snap of her tight vest.

Charlie, out of a twisted compassion's sake, gave the onlookers one warning. One warning only. After that, it rested on them. "Good evening ladies and gentlemen. I welcome you to the surprise event of the evening, compliments of your host and hostess. This is an adult dance party and anyone not of the age of consent must leave now." The crowd began to dance, free form pelvic thrusts and air guitar humping. Not one person left. In fact, their number had grown significantly. Charlie estimated there were now sixty people present, drawn in by the music and the half naked girls. "Now, ladies and gentlemen, things might get out of hand here tonight—the band's going to be lickin' and the whisky is flowin'. In other words, it's about to become very carnal." Charlie surveyed the crowd and his dance party creation. Again he noticed that no one left. "A word of warning, once you begin to drop your inhibitions, you won't be able to leave." More couples began to dirty dance. Again, nobody left. "Have a good time folks." That was the last thing Charlie would say to any of them.

As he turned, there was only one human not dancing. Noah stood nearly hidden in the shadows and stared at the woman he believed to be Bambi. His mouth was drawn tight and his face drained of color. If Charlie could have, he'd have felt true pity for the man and the corruption of purity. Oh, well, he thought, this has to be done.

Charlie took on the mantle of Andburg long enough that Noah got a full and painful look as he stepped over to Tracy and began a close and tender dance, kissing her, stroking her. Tracy, as Bambi, responded and things quickly heated up between them. Noah stood like a soldier, a man prepared to handle any level of truth, a man prepared to die with nobility. Charlie made sure Noah could not see Tracy's face because he knew the illusion wouldn't hold. He just hoped it held long enough. Charlie could tell by Noah's expression that what he saw was his best friend holding his beloved in a compromising position, his hands roving the length of her body. Noah watched until his entire soul was completely consumed. Good job, Charlie congratulated himself. The planet was doomed for the ark could not set sail with its captain consumed in his own personal hell. Charlie was positive the rest of his plan, that Noah would kill himself that very night, would come to fruition. There was even the delightful possibility that he'd take both Bambi and Andburg with him. It tickled him to know that at least one someone would die before dawn. Charlie gave Noah a short nod. It was more than Noah could bear. He turned and ran.

With Noah gone, Charlie no longer had need for his disguise. He removed the thin illusion of Andburg and stood in his full demonic glory. He was a god. He stripped the gold from Tracy, leaving her naked and in awe, looking up at him with slight flickers of horror and recognition. She screamed and tried to pull away, but it was too late. She would not be able to undo what she'd done. He roughly pulled her up and dragged her to the center of the room to where the altar stood. She cursed him in her native demonic tongue, but to no avail. Charlie strapped her in. He turned to the crowd and spoke his demonic spell, putting them as one under his control, removing any lingering inhibitions. He laughed at the mass of naked flesh as the revelers began to indulge indiscriminately, in every position imaginable and in every combination possible. Charlie returned his attention to Tracy, who began to cry. She was no longer bound by illusion, only restraints.

"You said you wanted to see it."

Charlie showed her what he was.

"Oh, God," she cried.

It was Charlie's night. He ruled, commanded, and offered to the hellish realms every ounce of human lust, greed, and pain as his captives were driven relentlessly toward relief that never came. The room became one pulsating, throbbing organism that shuddered into dawn. Tracy, as promised, was the center for all, until she broke and became pure fire once again. Before the dawn, she was seeded with twins, both demonic and human. She had become the fertile sacrifice for the vice of men, but her rage ran so deep that she became a firestorm in the center of hurricane-force winds that shot into the atmosphere like an apocalyptic cloud.

Chapter 41

The sound of the key in the lock woke Bambi. Once she realized it was Noah, she was relieved. He was home. He was alive. That's what mattered. She was angry and hurt, but when she exhaled she knew those feelings were secondary to the relief. She got up from the couch to greet him, but paused. Something wasn't right. He was completely covered in mud, and Bambi instinctively knew that he had walked the entire way home through the storms. He was a man she no longer recognized, hardened and hateful. She was frightened, grateful that Andrea had insisted on staying the night, still asleep in the bed. Bambi had willingly taken the couch; she feared the dark.

She'd found herself abandoned at the party. She'd stopped dancing with Andburg when he had stumbled forwards toward a chair and returned to where she'd last seen Noah. He wasn't there. She'd searched everywhere, scanning the small groups. Some had tried to engage her in conversation, but she bushed them off with the explanation that she was looking for a man. "Who isn't?" chimed a lady whose silver blue hair matched her nail polish. Bambi smiled, and said that she'd *had one, but she'd managed to misplace him.* The group laughed. She described Noah to everyone she approached, but none had seen him. She finally called for her coat and took her search from tent to tent. Everyone she knew seemed to have vanished. No Tracy, no Charlie, no Andrea, and still no Noah. She hadn't even seen Andburg. She searched everywhere except the Romanesque tent. She'd tried to approach it, but there was something going on inside that made her uncomfortable, sick to her stomach. She knew was that if Noah *was* inside, she wasn't going to find him because she wasn't going in.

She had given up her search and was trying to find a phone to call a cab when Andrea suddenly appeared.

"Where's Noah?" Bambi could feel her panic turn into anger. "He left me!"

Andrea tried to explain the best she could about Charlie and Dan and Andburg, but she got confused. The more Bambi fired off questions, the more Andrea seemed to get the facts tangled. Something absurd about a triangle and a trap. Andrea had finally convinced her to get into the dump truck and wait at home until Noah resurfaced. Now he was here, out of his mind, insane. His arm was slack at his side, but he held something in his hand. What was it? A handgun? Bambi had difficulty breathing.

He turned to look at her once and then passed through the room like a ghost. She didn't even dare whisper his name. He went to the closet and tried to pull a backpack down from the upper shelf. When it got stuck, he paused for a moment and then punched a hole through the door. The loud sound brought Andrea, who positioned herself protectively next to Bambi. They watched as he finally yanked down the pack and filled it with a few clothes, food and water from the fridge, a pocketknife, a mirror, and a flashlight. He had his canteen. Andrea put her hand reassuringly on Bambi's shoulder.

Noah turned again to look at her. When their eyes met, some of the hardness left his, replaced by a look that was sweet, tender, and familiar. "You are so beautiful to me. Haven't you known all along how much I love you?"

"Noah, what's going on? Please talk to me."

"I don't trust myself to stay here with you." He turned toward the door. "Don't follow me, Bambi, or I'll kill us both."

He said it so matter-of-factly, without hesitation, she knew he meant the words. Her whole world had turned upside down and crazy. Only Andrea's hand on her shoulder made her feel safe. Andrea, whose constant and loyal presence assured her everything was going to be all right.

"Let him go," Andrea whispered.

Noah flashed her an angry glare. "You probably knew about them all along."

Bambi felt Andrea's grip tighten. Andrea didn't respond or defend herself. Bambi thought she heard him pull back the hammer as he stepped forward. "I love you," she said, almost involuntarily. He stopped. She knew that her voice had cut through. His eyes softened once again. "I love you, too. Even now. Until the end of the world." He fled out the door.

Andrea leapt into action. She locked the door and barricaded it with a chair. "Let's go. He might come back."

Bambi was numb, but followed instructions. Andrea told her what to gather. Together they packed. She whistled for the dogs, and they all jumped up into the crowded dump truck cab. Andrea cranked the ignition, and they lurched forward. Bambi felt like a battered wife, leaving on a dime with only the few things she could carry. Such a strange sensation to meet up with a future self that she'd believed circumstantially impossible. She had never expected this flight would be her life story, her fate. Noah with a gun?

Bambi looked out the window. A tremendous thundercloud rolled in, thick and black. The more she looked at it the more she realized that it didn't so much as roll in as it boiled in. Lightning strikes inside the cloud illuminated the charcoal dark. What an odd cloud, Bambi thought. *Is this Armageddon?*

"Where are we going?" she finally asked Andrea. Wherever it was, they weren't going to get there in time.

"We're going to the ark. That's the only safe place for us now."

"Aren't you worried about that storm?"

"Yep. I'm worried about that cloud. Reckon it's not natural, so it doesn't matter where we try to hide. If that cloud's out to get us, it'll have to come on in and get us. But we're going to be at the ark. Strength in numbers."

Bambi felt immobilized and insecure. She chided herself that it was probably absurd to feel that way, but, life-threatening situation or no, it was her reality. "Do you think he loves me?"

"I think he loves you as much as he's capable of right now. If he could do better, he would. I mean, he didn't kill you."

"My man loves me enough not to kill me. What kind of love is that?" She suddenly began to laugh.

"Why are you laughing? I don't think this is so funny."

"Maybe not. But how would you feel if someone wanted you dead before the end of the world happened? Pretty nuts."

"I see your point." Andrea grinned, then chuckled, then laughed. All at once, everything seemed to be a lot less serious. For a while, they managed to remain in a space suspended from worry even as they drove through the shadow of the approaching cloud.

Chapter 42

Dan flew hard against the storm, determined not to lose sight of Noah. Things were reaching a critical mass. The only thing in his favor was that Charlie was detained in a battle in the center of this storm with a fireball that had once been Tracy. Dan had been horrified to witness her sacrifice. He'd heard stories of Charlie's atrocities, but to see it was beyond measure. But he guessed that not even Charlie had reckoned on Tracy being capable of manifesting such a natural destructive force. Her anger towards Charlie imploded during her rape. Her fire was the center of the storm and she was bent on revenge. Charlie was trapped in the storm cloud with her. Dan wondered if she wasn't a little more than Charlie had bargained for. Not my problem. His problem was making sure Noah wouldn't turn his own rage inward, making sure Noah was able to navigate the internal storm else he be incapable of fulfilling his destiny. As far as Dan was concerned, Noah had successfully passed the second test. His loving heart had transcended his personal demon and his ego. He was very close. A lightning bolt struck near to Dan's left wing, and he felt himself sinking. In a moment of despair, he called out to God. Then his world went black. All that was left for him was to fall, and hope for the best.

Chapter 43

Ma Shepard saw a different reality; she saw things that no one else saw such as possible scenes from possible futures, pieces of an unfinished puzzle. She walked parallel universes through portholes of time. There, she saw the future's fluid nature. It was difficult to predict because it was always changing, yet it was fixed. The universe itself was a paradox. However, if she saw enough of the pattern, then she could prophesize an outcome. For many years, her vision had remained consistent. More often than not, she found herself in a fifth dimension, an internal time-space continuum that was being created even as the Mayan calendar ended. The demise of one age was the birth of another. It was important that Bambi, Noah, and the ark enter this dimension. They carried life's blueprint, a blueprint that would be reintroduced into the world upon the return of the Celestial Child, the embryo that Bambi carried.

She smiled. Bambi had arrived, just as she'd seen. Before the ship set sail, there would be more arrivals, a significant return of the tribe. She knew there'd be a melding point between the contemporary and the indigenous cultures, a coming together so that the necessary repairs to the web of life could take place. Through ceremony, they could reweave the rips in the dream fabric of space and time. Ma Shepard turned her razor sharp vision deeper and followed the sound of the snake's rattle. She could see that Noah didn't *kill* Bambi. He had wanted to, but had resisted the temptation for revenge. However, she knew that Bambi was frightened and apt to act irrationally. She'd have a talk with her, settle her down.

She smiled. Bambi had arrived just as she'd seen. She would soon be followed by more to come. These small bands of light bearers would be led to high ground and prepare the way for the return. They would prepare the way by reweaving life's dream fabric through ceremony the way the old ones had always done. They would meld technology and indigenous wisdom to create a balanced future, one that could better support all life.

All in all, Ma Shepard was pleased. Noah had passed the second and most passionate level of his test. Now he was out there in the desert battling his personal demons, the ones Charlie had seeded. Ma Shepard knew that Noah had had a part in creating Charlie. He'd fed Charlie with his fear and insecurity; the demon would starve without that energy feed. Now Noah would have to learn to embrace his shadow before he could pass on to the next level. He'd have to be able to recognize what he was capable of projecting into the world and consciously not choose that.

He'd have to become the compassionate custodian of his own base nature before he entered his newly created dimensional reality.

Ma Shepard continued to rely on focus, a deep and penetrating inner stare, to explore current and possible future events. Noah had returned to the broken TV in the desert. It was silent, and Noah believed himself to be alone. Good thing he wasn't. She could see that he had a lot of celestial guardianship, including a galaxy of star children, those who were mostly responsible for the impending change, as they always, past, present, and future, carried the frequency of hope and renewed possibility. They had for a millennium been singing a celestial lullaby that raised the vibratory frequency, and woke up inner divinity, of those who listened. That frequency was inside Noah, as it always had been. It had never been on the TV screen, although he had perceived it to be. She knew that Noah's challenge was to tap into those inner resources and be willing to surrender to them. Noah would have to petition for help; spirit frequency had to be invited in—it didn't just randomly meddle. Noah's initial vision had been a necessary intervention. Noah was at a critical crossroads.

This wasn't just Noah's unfair fight with Charlie; this was Noah's internal fight with himself. Ma Shepard could see that he'd eventually exhaust his energy. Only then, when he completely surrendered, would he be able to choose something else. There was likelihood that the ark would set sail, but there were wildcards not completely revealed. She looked inward again. A circle of vultures, a good sign. Vultures were the only birds that could eat death. That there would be a death, she had no doubt. But what kind of death? She took three tiny sparrow bones from the medicine bag that hung in a leather pouch close to her heart. She took a moment to steady her focus, and then a quick throw. A broken pattern. A face she knew well. A possible outcome.

She closed her eyes and sat very still under the heaviness of it all. Noah had his work cut out for him. He would have to be a man of incredible strength with an inordinate reserve of inner character, especially now that Bambi was pregnant. She picked up the bones and began her own petitions to the Ancestors. Noah would need all the help he could get.

Chapter 44

Andrea had little to do. Bambi was in council with Ione somewhere in one of the tents. Poor girl, she hadn't slept, and Andrea knew she would likely collapse into exhaustion that afternoon. She was tired herself—it had been a long night—but she was feeling energetic, riding on the fumes of nervous energy. She wanted to do *something,* but she wasn't sure how to help.

They had arrived in a panic the night before, startled to see so many new faces and the fires magically blazing despite the rain. Most of the newcomers were young, but not all, and more continued to stream into camp through the night. Each person had what Andrea would later describe as the vacant expression of someone sleepwalking, following a dream vision. She had been pleased, however, to meet the self-named Tribe. They were exuberant in their idealism, and they didn't seem to notice the rain. It hadn't stopped them from nearly completing the ark. They'd strung up so many tarps that parts of the ship were actually dry enough that they could work on large sections at a time. Their work was crude but competent—not at all like Charlie's otherworldly master carpentry with its elaborate carving like celestial bookplates. Those carvings were beautiful but they unnerved her. They were penetrating in their realism. Andrea half expected that if she stared too long they'd move. In contrast, what the kids had added to the ship was sweet, like children's artwork.

The tent city was haphazard, expanding as they furthered their attempts to keep comfortable and dry. Trenches were continually being dug to help drain the high ground. The Tribe had done something remarkable. They weren't afraid to try. They also had fun in spite of the rain and the heavy circumstances. Andrea felt she fit right in. It was the first time that she'd had that feeling in a long time—if ever.

Andrea thought about the storm at the party, and wondered where it had gone. The storm had erupted abruptly, breaking over the tent. She'd seen Tracy rise like a fireball of fury, taking Charlie with her. That storm cloud had seemed laden with intention, and she couldn't shake the feeling that it had something to do with Dan and Charlie, and likely Noah, too. Andrea was relieved that it hadn't lingered near. She worried about Noah, and hoped he was all right.

Andrea walked over a large kettle where a thick, dark amber, viscous compound slowly bubbled and belched. She saw a stack of pails nearby. Pitch! Andrea picked up a pail and carefully ladled in the hot, sticky substance that would make the ark waterproof.

When she stood underneath the ark, she fastened her pail to a pulley, and then climbed up the knotted rope. There they were, the Tribal crew, slapping down pitch on the deck. The half dozen or so college-aged kids were covered in mud, reminding her of Aborigines with good dental work. The thought made her smile. They were laughing and working hard, two things Andrea knew how to do. Laugh and labor. She pulled up her pail and found a brush. As soon as she dropped into the rhythm of the work, she was immersed into the same goal. The ark had to be seaworthy.

"How do you know how to do all this?" She turned to a thin girl with the biggest brown eyes she'd ever seen.

"We searched the Internet. Everything we learned, we learned from a Google search."

"How do you do that without electricity?"

"Oh, power packs." The girl smiled.

"What are you going to do when all this technology washes away?"

Her eyes deepened in color, and she looked pensive. "The future is not yet here. In the meantime, we have the Internet, so why not take advantage of it?"

"That's a good point," Andrea said. "Maybe you can show me how to use it."

"You don't know how?"

"It wasn't really around when I was coming up."

"Huh." The look on her face clearly told Andrea the girl had no frame of reference for not being Internet savvy. "Okay."

Andrea wasn't sure if the okay meant the girl was willing to show her how to use the Internet, or if it was okay that she didn't know how. She shrugged, and then threw herself into the task at hand, sealing the deck with homemade pitch. As the hours ticked by, Andrea lost track of time and then of thought, as if they had already set sail and were floating away from planetary reality.

***

Andrea wasn't sure how long she'd been working, so lost was she in the rhythm of the brush—back and forth—and the gentle sound of the rain. It took her a moment to register that the voices that she suddenly heard were chanting. Political slogans? Gospels? She wasn't sure. She stopped and sat back on her heels. She lifted her eyes and saw a small crowd of people in rain gear descending upon the tent city.

"What's that?" She asked the drummer still weaving rhythmic sounds to paint to.

"We don't know."

As the crowd drew closer, the crew stopped what they were doing and gathered around the deck rails.

"Are those protesters?"

"They have signs."

"What do they say?"

"Down with Satanists!"

"Who are the Satanists? And why are they here?"

"I don't know."

"I guess they're protestors."

"Why are they *here?*"

The people stood a respectful distance in front of the ark, carrying picket signs with crude slogans with obscure biblical references protesting the blasphemy of the Lord. Andrea didn't understand many of them. Her favorite read: *Go Home. God Made Only One Ark And You Weren't On It.*

"Good grief, that's Icepick!" The drummer pointed down at the crowd. "Is it? Yep, that's Icepick. How'd he get mixed up with those protestors?"

"So you used to know that clean cut kid down there with the Oxford shirt and khakis — and rubber duck boots?"

"He disappeared last night." Panda Girl pointed to a tow headed boy who gingerly waved, but didn't smile. "He got scared when Ma Shepard told that flood story. It's not what he studied in Bible class. He told me that. He said that it wasn't right that they were scaring us like that, and he thought we were a cult. He thought it was crazy to camp out in the rain, and he wanted us all to go home with him. He said that this ship and everything we were doing was a plot to mock good Christians. We just never realized he'd betray us this way."

"It seems that he's brought friends. What are we going to do with them?"

"Talk?"

"These people don't want to talk. They want to preach."

"They might like to talk."

"You think so?" Andrea beckoned the girl to climb down the ropes. "Let's go talk."

Panda Girl was reluctant, but followed.

"We'd like to talk with you," Andrea called out. The chanting became louder. She tried again, a little frightened by their mindless attention to their own agenda. There was no warmth in their eyes, only hatred and fear. They wanted the ship gone. She didn't stray far from the rope ladder lest she should have to scramble up. Panda Girl focused on the boy she'd once trusted. She gestured for him to draw closer, but he never looked at her. She left the safety of the rope ladder and drew closer to him. Andrea was apprehensive.

"What are you doing?" the girl repeated.

He finally responded. "Listen, Hope, I like you. I wish you weren't around these weirdoes. They're telling you a lie, and it needs to end before it infects everyone. I mean, what kind of crazy person builds an ark out in New Mexico and in the Twenty-first Century? We already had an ark. God isn't stupid enough to make us build a second one. He promised us there wouldn't be another flood. By staying here, you're calling God a liar. Hope, I just don't think that's right."

"It's fine not to believe it. It's fine to leave if you want to. But to bring protestors back here? What kind of crazy thinking is that? Where did you get these people?"

"It's just my Sunday school class. Besides, it's for your own good. We love you and don't want to see you do wrong. Love the sinner not the sin, Hope."

"What do you think you'll accomplish?"

"Enough attention so that you will all go home."

"Why don't you let us be?"

A large woman turned toward the pair. "She one of the little devil bitches. Down with false prophets. Down with Satan."

A tall thin woman with streetwise eyes approached. She didn't look like a protestor, and she wasn't carrying a sign. She was smoking.

"Who are you?"

"One of the neighbors. I wanted to see the tree huggers and the right-wingers get into it. I was hoping for a little reality TV, if you know what I mean."

Andrea rolled her eyes.

"Hey, I want to know what you people are about. I mean, what is this Green Movement? Would you have us living in the woods again? What kind of life would that be? Do you eat meat?"

"Sometimes," Andrea admitted.

"You're wearing a poly chemical blend. Do you see my point?" She blew a smoke ring. "Hypocrites. The problem with you tree huggers is you all still want to live in America, land of conveniences. It's hypocrisy. And this flood rumor." She looked hard at Andrea. "It's a government plot to scare us into another war—take away our rights. You're probably working for the government. I mean, what is this ship anyway?"

Andrea didn't know how to answer. *Where's Charlie when you really need him?* "Come on, Hope, let's get back to the ship. Like I said, these kind of folks never want to talk."

"What are we going to do?"

"Drum louder."

They returned to the deck, where the rest of the crew waited anxiously.

"They want us to go home. We want them to go home. It's a stalemate." Andrea announced flatly.

"What if they attack us?"

"They won't."

The drummer drummed louder. They began to sing. Soon the crew became used to their new circumstances. Andrea worked in close proximity to the Panda Girl so they could continue their conversation.

"How come you don't go by your name, Hope?"

"In my world there would be elevated roadways so that the little animals didn't get crushed under wheels. In my world there might not even be cars at all. It's hard work to build a world of possibility like that. One person has the ability to collapse the entire structure with an ugly and judgmental word. They have no understanding of the damage they inflict with their carelessness. Sometime, I guess, I don't feel so hopeful."

"Seems to me you're getting stronger."

"How do you know?"

"You went down there and faced a crowd of angry protestors, and you're here believing in a truth, your truth, that some say is insane. That was a brave thing that you did today."

"Thank you."

Andrea didn't have to look to know that she was grinning from ear to ear.

"Hey, folks, you're not going to believe this, but I think CNN is here."

"What!"

"Yeah, TV crews. The whole nine yards."

Now it was Andrea's turn to feel her own inner strength crumble. The news media was more frightening to her than Charlie. This project didn't need to be turned into a bunch circus freaks on an insane mission.

"Don't worry. We'll figure out how to ditch them." Hope noticed Andrea's discomfort.

"How are we going to do that?"

"We have to convince everyone that there's no story here."

Andrea looked at her. "That's brilliant. How are we going to do that?"

"I don't know. We'll think of something."

Andrea began to feel a little better, although her fate and the fate of the ark were now in the hands of children.

"Come on everyone, let's gather around." Hope suggested. The drummer stopped playing, and they sat in a circle on the deck underneath the tarp and hatched a plan they were almost certain would work.

Chapter 45

When Dan came to, he was vaguely aware that he was in another dimension. There wasn't anything particularly substantial about him. It wasn't so much that he no longer had an owl body. He did; he could tell by his shape. It was more like he was essence of owl, spirit without blood and sinew. He looked at himself. Something was glowing. He realized with a start that he had feathers of light.

At first frightened, he eased into his new perception of beingness, recognizing he was in a place of non-duality, no life, no death, a place of immortality in that death itself was an illusion. Had his spirit once again separated from the physical like a pit from ripe fruit and passed through the great door of transformation? He knew that the humans had to endure a process such as this, an experience needed in order to understand that matter could neither be created nor destroyed, but rather was in constant flux and change. Dan was no longer separated from his total knowing, but he was still frightened. This place was new, a nothingness that he had never encountered. He wondered if time itself were dying. Or was it a birth?

Dan positioned himself on a virtual perch, tucked his head, and waited. More time went by as if time itself were a lazy river and then disappeared into nothingness, and still nothing happened. Endless grey space with no direction—no up, down, backwards or forwards, no focal point, no place toward which to take flight. Dan's job had always been to keep track of direction, and now there was no direction to keep track of. He felt lost.

Dan closed his eyes and tried to remember the events that had led to this, whatever *this* was. He saw himself flying hard into the chaos, trying to keep track of Noah's direction. It had been obvious from the moment he broke through the vertical strata that supernatural forces were driving the cumulonimbus. It was tumultuous thunderhead, spinning counter clockwise like a hurricane only smaller and faster, with no center, no calm eye, only more rain and bolts of lightning. The further he flew, the hotter the air had become. At first he thought it was another one of Charlie's tricks, but it didn't feel like Charlie. It felt like *feminine* fury. It had felt manic and angry. It didn't occur to him that he was trapped in what had become of Tracy's revenge until he had finally reached the eye, and there he saw twins feeding off kinetic energy like mother's milk. Charlie *had* impregnated her, but it had backfired. They fed hungrily and grew at a rapid rate—new life in the form of destruction. Then one peeled its hungry mouth away from and threw a lightning strike, and Dan was seared. The way his wings had flamed, leaving a fiery contrail as he plummeted, was a painful memory.

As Dan fell, it dawned on him that the storm wasn't personal. He'd just happened to get in the way. The storm did, however, have its own agenda: the destruction of Charlie. The last thing he'd remembered was Charlie being consumed by the hungry twins he'd created. He'd been so sure of himself taking Tracy that way, but now that she had returned to her natural state as a Desert Jinn, he'd met his hellish match. Between the three of them, Charlie was being torn apart, one fiery bolt at a time.

Dan didn't know who he'd be without Charlie, his dark foil. That was the last thought Dan remembered having before his world went black.

***

Time is dead. Dan was convinced that he had to maintain some type of reference if he was to maintain himself. Since he himself was neither dead nor alive then it must be time itself that had to be one way or the other. Dan couldn't even begin to track this timelessness. He was lost, perhaps forever, in this grey prison. His notion of self began to dissolve, and the more he surrendered the more pleasant the experience became. He had reached the no nothingness, a truly groundless nature. Dan existed because he was. It was a happy state—no worries, no fears, no nothing. Dan drifted. It could have been a forever drift, and it might have been, had he not re-discovered the power of pure manifestation. One last defiant piece of individuation struggled to maintain experience.

Dan was trying to remember food. He imagined a banquet table filled with earthly delights, mostly fruits and some raw meat like the last party he'd attended. Who was Andburg? Suddenly a spread worthy of a king appeared—a candelabra centerpiece, linen napkins, and silver platters filled with food. Dan looked around, startled as he regained a sense of self, accompanied by the painful realization that he was alone again. Just beyond the table the endless grey remained.

More time passed. Dan continued to stare at the offering as if it were a mirage. Finally, he decided it was time for a showdown. Dan wasn't convinced that the food was safe to eat. One tiny pomegranate kept Persephone down with the shades, he remembered. Dan decided that he had nothing to lose—literally. He took another quick glance around, exhaled, and fluttered to the head of the table and began to scratch around. He found a delightful platter piled high with roast beef cuts, rare. He began to pull and tear, stuffing his beak with food. The food tasted real and filled his bird belly. After he'd eaten his fill, he became drowsy. He fluttered to the top of the centerpiece.

He closed his eyes and saw grey, grey both on the inside and out. However, something solid under his feet broke up the monotony. Dan began to dream, if that's what he could call it. It was more like a journey and a conversation between himself and a deity he would later know as Aditi the Ancient: the feminine archetype of the beginning. The Greeks called her Chaos, but that word didn't quite fit Dan's experience. There was no chaos, but rather endless peacefulness interrupted by the possibility of form. She was imagination in its purest expression, but hers was a place of randomness. Scientists were calling it the E8 code, a mathematical equation that represented the most perfect symmetry ever known with two hundred forty-eight variables. This was the dimension of freedom. Dan realized then that here was not the end of time. It had not yet been created. He was in the land before time. He could drum up a lot in this environment if only he believed with purity of thought. That could be a drawback because even his imagination had limits. He didn't know what they were yet, but he knew with certainty that he'd had to believe in himself if he were to survive.

The knowledge Dan received seemed to come from her, soundlessly reflecting all the endless possibilities of creation and the creations of his own mind. She was the ultimate mirror. When Dan peered at himself with his internal mind, he saw himself as he had become: a return to light in form. He embodied all of the noble qualities of the daemon, but he'd transformed. He finally understood why he had chosen to incarnate as owl, but he was beyond that now as he cracked open his limited concepts of being. He had to understand this process of duality if he were going to encourage Noah to do the same and become something bigger and brighter. Dan clearly saw that he no longer needed Charlie's shadow to define himself. He was free.

Dan continued to journey within the dreamtime grey, and there he caught up with Noah who was sitting on a rock, weeping in front of the broken TV, imploring God to return and to tell him what to do. The TV had become a hollow shell. It did not speak. Noah doubted himself and believed that all he'd been through had been a trick. Angry and bent on self-destruction, he held on to his pistol, his ultimate solution. The only way he knew to rid himself of the demon voices in his head was to destroy the place where they lived.

Dan realized that Noah, too, would have to traverse this dream and pierce the fog by aligning with light before he could free himself from the belief that he was responsible for all those souls who had chosen to manifest into the material creation. If Noah learned the lesson, he would understand that there was no separation, only projection and mirroring. The light as Noah, not Noah the man, was making this miracle happen. If he could figure it out, lay his burden down, and wade out into this river of time being born, there would be no limitation. Noah did not need one thing outside of himself to define his being, not even God. God *was* Noah and all other living, breathing creations, all one and the same. The way Noah was rocking in despair, Dan could see that he had a long way to go. *Poor Noah, you can simply let down your burden and walk away, free.*

Dan looked again and saw yet another window, another exit into possibility. Andburg was sitting at his office desk working on calculations and checking GPS status. He checked his emails. A message from Dr. Smart said everything at the substation was smoothly running, no reason for him to worry. In fact, there had been surprising discoveries in the CVRT graphs that he knew Andburg would like to go over once he got there. The lab was looking forward to his visit. Andburg didn't know these messages weren't real. He had no way of knowing, unless he ran an analysis program of the satellite data to realize that it wasn't live, and there was no reason for him to do that. He trusted his team. Only a handful knew that Dr. Smart was dead, and most of them, except for Dan and Charlie, were in the government. Andburg was about to confront his greatest fear: that his life-long project would fail.

Dan saw the two men and knew with certainty that he would have to bring them together to collide, and they would work it out until homeostasis was once again achieved. This was the point at which he had to reenter and assist as needed. He poked his head into Andburg's study first. Andburg had no preconceived notions of who Dan was. Andburg also hadn't had a drink in over twelve hours, one of his periodic dry-outs in which he confirmed to himself that he was in control. Had Dan not suddenly appeared, he might have held out longer, but he took a shot of Maker's Mark before he slipped out the door and followed the bird, driven by a compulsion he could not understand or ignore, to the desert, where he saw Noah, his best friend, the only one he loved more than himself, slumped on a couch playing Russian roulette with his last bullet.

Chapter 46

Noah pulled the trigger. Click. He laughed. He opened the chamber again to make sure that there was indeed a bullet. There was. He closed the chamber and spun again. Noah's lament was a plea for God's return. Nothing was on the TV, no indication that the TV had ever spoken to him, not since he'd first discovered it. Noah looked up and saw a form approaching. He put the pistol down and grew hopeful. He stood to greet his answer. His heart seized when he saw who it was.

"Andburg! I've got a gun and I *will* kill you. Get lost."

"I think I am."

"No!" Noah turned his back. He didn't want to hurt anyone. He just wanted to be left alone. He re-holstered the pistol, and with swift strength lifted the TV over his head and threw it hard against a rock wall, unleashing his fury away from the man he'd once called friend.

"What did I do?"

Noah unsnapped the holster and once again removed the Ruger. It felt solid in his hand. "You took the one thing from me that was truly important, just because you could."

"I don't know what you're talking about."

"Bambi. You." Noah gripped the gun a bit tighter and turned to face the rock wall.

Seized from behind, Noah was launched forward, and landed hard against the sandstone. He lost his both breath and the gun.

"That's what you think, you dumb shit?"

Noah rolled over, picked up a rock, and slammed it into the side of Andburg's face. Blood splashed on his knuckles. The blood excited Noah and scared him, too. But the gash didn't slow Andburg down. The two men wrestled in the mud, blood, and sweat, fist against flesh, bruise on bone. Dan, now fully emerged from the endless river of time, let them have at it until he perceived them tiring. Then he glided over their heads and radiated a light so intense that it shocked open their heart chakras. They had to stop if only to shield their eyes or risk going blind.

There is choice. Peace or violence? Heart or Head?

They stopped in order to comprehend what they heard. Muscles cooled within that brief pause, and then cramped as adrenaline pooled in the tissue. They were exhausted. Noah could no longer raise his bloodied arm. Andburg shifted into a wrestling pose, caught Noah's arms and pulled them tight under the rib line in a basket hold.

Noah was helpless, which made him even crazier, irrational. "Traitor!"

"I'm going to hold you here until you hear me out. I love you. I didn't do what you think I did. I couldn't. I was passed out that night."

"I saw you. I saw you both." Noah managed to spit out a complete sentence though his jaw was clenched tight.

"I don't know what you saw, but I'm telling you the truth. That it wasn't me, even if it looked like me. I swear. I know I can't prove it to you. I came here to try. I may be a lot of things, but I'm not a traitor. I'd rip my own heart out before I'd break yours. Listen to me. Tracy disappeared that night. Charlie, too. You know Charlie. He did some work for me—built that stage in a matter of hours. I didn't say much because he was making it easy for me, and I needed that job done, but there is something about Charlie. He reminds me of my father, and my father had an evil presence that marked his life until the day he died. He never killed masses of people, but he was capable of it. He used to beat me without flinching or blinking an eye. You've got to believe me—so much rides on this. I don't know why, but it does. It matters that you hear my truth. I know that you know something about Charlie that I don't know. You have a missing piece of the puzzle. Who is Charlie?"

Andburg's words resonated and cleared the poison from Noah's mind. He could not deny the sound of truth. Andburg was telling him the truth. Noah went limp, and returned to that night. Somewhere in his mind, he was embraced by the horror, trapped in the trauma. He replayed the images and the pain returned to him fresh, a sharp, cold blade that ripped up through his guts and through his heart. He was doubled over, a fragile shell of a man. He couldn't leave the scene. He didn't know how to break the torturous stalemate. The light that had blinded began to chant: *Love.*

The vibrations in his head heightened with an ecstatic frequency. Guided by inner knowing, a phrase formed in his thoughts. Though he didn't believe what he was saying at first, he began to chant: *I love you and I'm sorry. I love you and I'm sorry.* His words swiftly moved into real feeling. Once Noah felt the experience of loving, the burning vice grip that held his heart fractured, light poured out, and that which was killing him transformed. The illusion blew apart into a shimmery sprinkle of reality. He no longer saw Bambi in the arms of Andburg, but recognized Tracy and Charlie. Noah began to laugh. The spell was broken. He was free. Once he realized that he was free, the doors to his perception swung closed with a bang.

"Who is Charlie?" Andburg continued to desperately repeat.

"He's my personal demon."

"What?" Andburg released Noah as he, too, went limp with a low, deep moan. "Shit. I'm sorry, but grateful he's not my father."

They looked at each other and began to laugh. They were back to being lifetime buddies.

"What now?"

"I guess I go back to Bambi and apologize."

"What if it's too late?"

"I can't afford to believe that. How about for you?"

"I'm leaving for the Arctic tonight. I should already be on the plane, but I came out here for you."

"How did you know how to come out here?"

"An owl brought me."

Noah thought about Dan and wondered what part he had played. He wanted to ask, but his mind went on to other, more pressing matters. Deep inside, he knew he would have to apologize to his daemon. Maybe he didn't need Dan to save him; maybe he just needed a nudge, a push in the right direction, or the occasional blinding light. If they all worked together against Charlie, what kind of power would he even pretend to have? *Ohh, I'm a demon. I can make you believe in lies.*

"What you laughing at, buddy?"

"Nothing much, just how absurd life is." Noah looked at Andburg, really looked at him. In some ways, he looked the same as he always had, all the way back to those simpler days when he went by the name of Andy. Just a boy filled with innocence and pot, geeky, with glasses and limp arms that hung from his sleeves. He was brilliant though, always had been. What he would have become if he hadn't needed to numb the horrors, Noah reflected. Perhaps he could have become his own best friend.

"It's been rough for you?"

There was a slight tremor in Andburg's hand. Noah could tell that he was willing the shake away as he tried to mask it. "Life is what a person makes of it. My life is great!"

"I see." Noah looked down.

There was a silence that passed. Finally, Andburg spoke very slowly and nearly under his breath. "I know what I am, Noah. I discovered long ago that I didn't need to be sober to be great. Besides, my mind gets sharper. I swear that's true. I feel like my real self." More silence. Andburg stood up. "Now that Tracy's gone, though, I think it's time to clean up my act some, dry out." He held his hand out and pulled Noah up. "I'm going to get some help when I get back. Couldn't hurt, right?"

"No, I think it's a good idea."

"Noah, I respect your opinion. Do you think I'm an alcoholic?"

Noah struggled with his answer. He wanted to say no to make his friend feel better. "I don't know. I think you're in dangerous territory, and have been for some time. You have to answer that yourself. What would you tell me?"

Andburg broke into a sad smile. "I'd tell you how much I loved you." He turned and began walking away.

"Where are you going?"

"I've got a planet to save. I'll be back in three days. I'll call you then. You can go to an AA meeting with me. I hear they have hot chicks."

"Andburg," Noah called after his friend.

Andburg paused, but did not turn around.

"I love you."

Noah thought he saw Andburg nod, and imagined a smile as he trudged back to the road. There was no telling how far he'd have to walk before he could catch a ride back. Noah saw a shimmer coming off his friend's back. It looked like wings. He recalled something he was told once. *All alcoholics go to heaven because they've already done their time in hell.*

Noah took a deep breath. He had a deep-down feeling that he'd never see his friend again. He wanted to save him, but he knew that he couldn't save another soul. He would savor every bruise that healed as a memory of Andburg. With this thought, something profound in his being shifted. He looked up again and saw Dan flying off, looking bigger and brighter than he'd ever seen.

"I'm sorry. I'm sorry." He ran after the streak. "You are greater than Charlie could ever be." He stopped abruptly. He shook his head and smiled. He wasn't far from the ark. He could walk home, the place where he'd find his heart. The rain was soft and gentle as it washed some of the blood from his face, but nothing would be more soothing than her hand on his check. He crossed new pathways of spontaneous rivers. It seemed that the whole world was flooded. It wouldn't be long now before they would embark. Noah lifted his face to the rain. For the first time in a long while, he felt cleansed.

Chapter 47

Ione felt liberated in a way she hadn't in many years, though she was hemmed in by protestors. What she lacked in the power of youth, she made up for in experience and intelligence. At first she was sore, long-unused muscles aching in protest, but by the end of the fourth day she was re-experiencing strength and vitality. She also learned how to conserve her strength. Where it took her younger counterparts unnecessary steps to get the job done because often they were unfocused, Ione discovered how to do the same job in half the time. She was quickly recognized as a leader. She looked the part, too. As a child, Ione had always been interested in female pirates and how they had been celebrated for their power and unconventionality. Many of her childhood games had been based on role-play. She had been a voracious reader, had discovered some choice role models from Queen Artemisia of Halicarnassus in Greece, Dido in 470 BC, also in Greece, to Grace O'Malley who had three galleys and commanded two-hundred men. Ione didn't tell anyone what she was doing, she just allowed a sub-personality of strength and irreverence to emerge, changed her clothing and let her uncombed hair go wild—only slightly tamed with a headscarf. The kids took to the image. They began referring to her as Buck, short for Buccaneer.

She knew that what people were responding to was her newly awakened power. Ione had always known she was destined to lead. She just didn't know what that would look like. She couldn't imagine herself heading the ark; that would mean something terribly wrong had happened to Noah and to Bambi. Noah was still missing, but standing in as the captain felt deeply counter-intuitive. Ione continued to check in with herself, and she got no feeling that she'd be the captain of this vessel. Ione sighed, resigned herself to not knowing. She knew more would be revealed and likely sooner than later since she was expected to go into private council with Ma Shepard within a day or two. Tabani had spoken to her and said Ma Shepard wanted to give her a reading. Ione was thrilled. Information from any source was always welcome.

Ione saw Andrea sitting on a cargo box staring at the lines in her hands. She must have felt Ione's gaze because her head swung up. She waved, and Ione put down her rag and took the few steps to join her.

"Hey, there. Join me?" Andrea slid over.

Ione sat down.

"I hear the kids calling you Captain Buck. I like it. It suits you."

"I like it, too. Fun." Ione held Andrea's gaze and noticed a blush steam from her checks to her neck as she looked away. Oh, thought Ione.

"Not much to do now that the ark is finished."

Ione startled some with the recognition of truth. "It is done, isn't it?"

"Yep."

The women looked out over the deck. The kids were busy with the rigging. At this point in the construction, just about everything *was* finished. The ship was waterproofed, by the end of the day it would be rigged. In the belly, there were cabins, stalls, and numerous shelves where the samples would be stored.

"Tell me something," Ione said. "If the ark is to carry genetic material, why do you suppose Noah has built stalls?"

"Fresh milk and eggs."

"Hmm," Ione's voice trailed off.

"Why do you ask?"

"There are a lot of stalls. Are you sure they're just for cows and chickens?"

Andrea seemed distracted. "I wrote the blueprints." She was smiling, but her face fell, and Ione saw right away that she was terribly sad and wanted to say more, but perhaps couldn't.

"That's okay," Ione said. "You don't have to tell me."

"No, I want to. I know you'll understand."

Ione became quiet and prepared to listen.

Andrea took a deep breath. "I believe Noah when he says God spoke to him. I believe God speaks to many of us, but so few of us actually act. Before all this started, animals talked to me, but I tuned them out if I could. Since this project got underway, they've begun to talk to me more, to a point where their voices can't be ignored, and I see them differently now. I can no longer pretend there's a giant gulf between us, and because I no longer stand on the other side of that divide. I see the animals as my friends, especially the ones I've met at the Albuquerque Zoo. I wouldn't expect Noah to leave behind any of us when the floods come, and I don't intend to leave behind my buddies of various species. I don't know which animals will come along on this ride, but I want more here than just animal poop. I want the individuals who are not ready to end their love songs—their hooting, tooting, and pooting. I revised the blueprints, and that's why there are more stalls. And...I have a plan."

"What is it?"

"I'm going to let them all out, so they can decide."

"What are you going to do if more animals show up than the ark will hold?"

"What are we going to do if more people show up?"

Ione was silent. "That's a good reminder. Thank you."

The two women sat there for a long time, enjoying the quiet. A question occurred to Ione. "How will you know when to let the animals out?"

"I don't know. Do you think that I should go now?"

"I can't answer that, but if it's bothering you, what's keeping you here?"

Andrea blushed again. "The timing isn't right yet. Don't know why, but thank you. I think you are one of the most noble ladies I've ever met and I hope that one day we can call each other *friends.*"

"We are friends, Andrea."

"Yes, we are friends but I mean, *friends.*"

Ione gently touched Andrea's shoulder. "My dear, I don't think I can offer you the kind of companionship that you might be looking for in a *friendship*, but that doesn't mean that we can't develop a strong bond. You may be needing more intimacy than I can provide, but fate does have a funny way of working."

"Didn't mean to be so forward. I hope you don't take offense." Andrea sounded shy, her most private thoughts suddenly made public.

"Thank you for communicating your feelings. I know it couldn't have been easy. Go free your animals. Don't worry about this."

"No. Not easy." Andrea's face looked drawn. "I did love once." She stood up. "Beg your pardon." She bowed low, and kissed Ione's hand. She walked to the railing. "Lately, there's been a miracle. I've found my heart again. She swung a leg over and disappeared over the edge. Ione could hear her descend. For a moment, she was flattered by the attention. It had been a long time since she'd been the object of anyone's desire. If she were still interested in coupling, she might have taken Andrea up on her subtle offer. Ione stood up and raised her arms. The beautiful mystery of life was something to enjoy. It was so filled with surprises.

Chapter 48

Bambi would never know how Noah managed to pick the right tent in the dark. She'd ask him later how he managed to get through the paparazzi and religious fanatics, but he'd shrug his shoulders and tell her that he just knew. After a while, she'd accept his answer.

When he first slipped into the tent, she was startled and her entire body tensed up. Although the dogs had never even growled, she half expected an attack. What if they'd been drugged? She was ready to fight back when she heard his soft whisper, "Bambi, it's me." She was no longer frightened; she was angry.

"Why didn't you tell me who you were?" She hit him hard on the shoulder, and heard him moan, which she thought was odd. "You scared me, Noah."

"I'm sorry, baby. I thought you heard me call your name. You responded."

"I did?"

"Yes." He softly touched her hair.

"Don't play nice. I'm not ready. You *scared* me, and I'm angry."

"I'm sorry. I never meant to frighten you."

"I'll calm down, I suppose. So … are you still acting weird?"

"It's out of my system. It won't happen again."

Bambi rolled over. "You didn't see your face. The distortion. The hardness. I mean, a totally different person. I had to ask myself if I really knew you at all. Really, Noah, you looked certifiable."

"Okay, Bambi, I hear you."

"Damn it, Noah, stop trying to handle me. Just go away."

It was Noah's turn to withdraw into silence. Even in the dark she could tell she'd hurt him. "It took me a long time to get here," he said matter-of-factly. "Please, just let me lie here. It's raining again and I'm so tired. Can't you settle next to me? I promise not to touch you. Just let me rest."

She *had* been worried about him. He was so pitiful, what else could she do? "Stay, Noah, but give me space."

He was already breathing low and heavy. She turned over, steaming. *You could have tried harder.* She was going to tell him that but he was already asleep, so she let it go. She eventually fell asleep, but she was agitated, uncomfortable, and wounded, too. Things had turned into such a mess. How could she trust him again? She'd rather spend her life alone, what was left of it. A small trade-off for peace and independence.

***

With the break of dawn, there was enough light to see clearly. Rolling over to take her first look at Noah, she was horrified. His face was completely swollen. "Oh, my God, Noah. What happened to you?"

She woke him up enough to respond to her, but his left eye was completely shut, puffed under a deep patch of purplish blue.

"It's okay, baby. Don't worry about me. The eye will heal. I'm sure that it looks worse than it is."

"What happened?"

"I'd rather not talk about it."

"You have to tell me *something*, Noah."

"Short version. Andburg and I settled some business, but it's all over now."

"Did you fight over me?" Bambi was horrified, even more so when she realized part of her that liked the idea. Nobody had ever fought for her. "You don't still believe that we slept together, do you?" That was the one thing she'd finally gotten out of Andrea, along with the claim that Charlie had ascended in some sort of hot fireball with Tracy. She'd dismissed that statement; it made no sense.

Noah reached out and touched her lip. "We got it settled. Nothing for you to worry about."

"Noah, you have to tell me. Do you really think I cheated on you?"

"No. I get that you didn't do anything to me. I take full responsibility."

"I don't want you to do that, either. I want to know what gave you cause to go off the deep end like that."

Noah moaned. "Don't ask me too many questions."

"Was it Charlie?"

"I was dumb to believe him."

"Noah, I really believe that Charlie infected you. I told you he was bad news."

"Honey, that's behind us now, thankfully. Can we put it to rest? I'm embarrassed that his tricks made me so sick and ready to kill myself."

"What tricks?"

"He tricked me into thinking that I saw you and Andburg together."

"He didn't."

"He did."

"That explains a lot." She was finally relieved and felt a hundred times better. "I hope that you're able to let go of taking on too much of the responsibility."

She snuggled in and began kissing him where he wasn't bruised: his ears and neck. At one point, he winced. "I'm going to get you to the hospital."

"I'm not going to the hospital. The time is coming when there might not be hospitals. Besides, I know my injuries aren't life threatening."

"Do you mind if I get Ma Shepard."

"Okay. That's fine, but no hospitals. I'm not leaving you again."

Bambi smiled. "Okay, Rambo. But there is something else."

"What's that? Besides that I love you, too."

"Which I do very much. Our camp site has grown."

"I noticed that. There seem to be more tents."

"Yes, more tents. Ione is here, along with Ma Shepard and Tabani and a group of college students who call themselves the Tribe. Along with these friends are a hundred or so protestors and TV crews."

"What!"

She sighed. "Seems our little project made the nightly news."

"Isn't there something more interesting for them to cover like the Smart Bomb up at the Los Alamos Lab? Why don't the protestors tackle that abomination?"

"That would be left wing. The right wing isn't so worried about controlled nuclear attacks since they're already prepared for the Rapture."

"What are we going to do about them?"

"I don't know. We've been ignoring them. Luckily, they're keeping their distance. It hasn't been too bad. You'll get used to them after the first day. Although, I do believe that a reporter is trying to get an exclusive with you. I'll figure out something to tell him."

"Go get Ma Shepard. Let me think about this for a while."

Bambi unzipped the tent. "I'm glad that you're back. I was really scared I'd never see you again."

"I'm glad to be back."

She radiated love for him and hoped he could feel it. For the first time in a long time, maybe the first time since all of this upheaval started, there was harmony. Just seeing him gave her comfort and a renewed sense of commitment. She had her Noah back. They had a great destiny to fulfill. Nothing could stop that now.

Chapter 49

Jonas was repulsed by the dark. He felt at home in the Antarctic, where day knew not night for five months out of the year. On McMurdo Base, three a.m. lost meaning under a noonday sun. The only way to keep track of time was by capturing it in the hands of a clock.

Jonas drew the two halves of his pocket watch together. Click. That mechanistic joining of the hinged metal cover and the face brought him an odd sense of peace, like closing a box lid where all the dead members of his family were stored, especially his mother; he could easily access them by simply opening the watch. Everything that he had accomplished was dedicated to her, and he could not wait for that day when he would once again see her in heaven and hand her his earthly life record, and she would know the reasons for the things he had done. What would she say? If there were anything that she would be disappointed in, she would have to take that up with the heavenly chain of command, the source of his directives. God the father had become God his father.

As a scientist, he never revealed his beliefs to anyone. He secretly held on to the view of heaven as a safety blanket. He'd been only nine when he saw his mother blow her head off, soaking her pillow with brain and blood. When he had removed his great-grandfather's pocket watch from the nightstand by his mother's bed, he could smell the fresh lavender on her pillow and the rose water from her hair. As he opened two halves of the watch, he saw some of his mother's blood inside. He stared, trying to find meaning. There was none. The blood dried and, over time, became rust-like spots of where his mother used to be.

"Hey, Jonas." There was a knock at his door. "An encrypted satellite communication came for you."

Jonas stirred. "Thank you. I'll be down in a minute."

Jonas, like all the scientists on McMurdo Base, lived in a private room the size of a corporate cubicle. Only a few permanent buildings supported the hundred or so staff and handful of scientists. It was an ugly place. It looked like an old Sierra Madre mining camp with odd metal equipment jutting up from the permanently icy ground, run by a defense contractor, operated like a corrections facility, so worried were they for safety. The frozen ice shelf was called Ross Ice Shelf, which was a pretty ordinary name for a sheet of ice the size of France. The shelf was named after James Clark Ross, who had headed the first expedition in 1842. The base was home to scientists of all disciplines: terrestrial and marine biologists, geologists, meteorologists, upper-atmospheric physicists, geo-chemists, the list went on, all doing their research independently of each other. Some shared their findings while others kept their research to themselves. Jonas was of the latter breed, but he was in a place where loners were respected as long as they drank beer and played darts at least once or twice a week. Jonas never drank, but he was pretty good at darts.

Jonas looked at the pocket watch again, an anti-magnetic watch with a broken bow so that it would never again hang from a chain. He was very careful with it, keeping it in a small, royal blue velvet bag inside a small wooden box next to his Bible. He had a matching Bible in the substation in the Arctic where he also worked with Andburg on the cold fusion team, but it was his intention that the watch never be separated from this *terra firma* as long as the ice mass existed. The watch had been here before.

Greatly influenced by Wagner's *The Ring*, his great-grandfather had brought the watch with him to the island in 1842. He had been the only German on the ship named *Terror*, and though he was not the first man in the expedition to die on the island of ice, nor the last, he'd died there nonetheless. He's received no plaques for his professional sacrifice because of his nationalistic ties to a socialist movement that would eventually be subsumed by the conservative agenda that the world would one day know as Fascism. Jonas was only completing a trajectory that his great great-grandfather had orchestrated, even if unknowingly. Grandfather's remains had been interred in an ice cavern, but the timepiece had been sent home to Germany, passed down to the son, then to a grandson, and then to a great-granddaughter who brought it with her to America where Jonas had retrieved it the moment she ended her life because of a terrible mistake she had made at the age of fourteen.

Jonas put the watch away. He stood up and looked at the map on the wall. This was the place on the planet where all the lines converged, and, like earlier explorers who believed the world was flat, this was the place where they all jumped off into the last unexplored land mass. Jonas supposed he'd jumped off a long time ago, and there was no going back now. That was true freedom—knowing that he could never return to his point of departure. The second Bible, the one he had hidden in the science station on the other side of the planet, on the opposing pole, was his point of departure. It had been rigged to detonate a series of seven nuclear bombs—the seven sisters. Three of the sisters were buried under where Jonas stood. The other four were under his bed at the Artic. Enough data had been drawn from test explosions throughout the years that he knew exactly how much megaton was needed to get the job done without compromising the core integrity of the planet. They were expecting a tilt that would cause a flood so great that the planet would be cleansed—all save the chosen ones who would be sustained in an underground system that had taken decades to build. It was truly the eighth wonder of the world. They had calculated just how many cumulative generations would need to live underground before the nuclear winter had cleared. An infrastructure of technology would be preserved; rebuilding the planet's surface would be efficient and finished in a relatively short time, probably within three generations. The part of Jonas that was an impassioned scientific mind trained in pure observation really wanted to see what would happen next.

Jonas left his cubicle room and headed toward the communications room that the permanent staff here called the Clubhouse. He passed several other sterile rooms filled with the scant reflections of personality that could fit in a duffle bag. Jonas hadn't gotten to know any of the other scientists more than superficially, but they often entertained him through overheard stories of great survival, discovery, failure, and the continued battles with governments for funding of projects that weren't recognized as important in the short-term.

Jonas couldn't completely relate for he was hooked into the ultimate project—or was it that the ultimate project had hooked into him? He really believed the world wasn't the world it was supposed to be, and that with the right and controlled path of cleansing the balance could be restored. Jonas was uncomfortable with the word *genocide*. Those who had tried that approach before were really butchers, sloppy in the execution, and too myopic, singling out one race of people. What was needed was swift action, flawless design. This experiment had a scientific backbone and an architectural plan rooted in intelligent design. Jonas had seen things because of his affiliation with the *Protectors*. They were also known as the Protectors of the Apocalypse, but Jonas was uncomfortable with the common acronym POA. The Palestinians had ruined it for him. He used the term Protectors because there was a truth in how he felt about the mission and the sacrifices such restoration would take. Jonas was not a man without heart; he knew this was a radical social experiment.

Certain artifacts proved, however, that there was intelligent design in the universe, and these artifacts had been kept away from the public eye for a millennium. What Jonas knew, but could not say, had become the bridge between his theology and his scientific mind. If he ever had to explain why he had committed himself to something so radical, he would have to say that the perfect knowing of the universe was the point where science and religion came full circle. Jonas was merely one important player, a foot soldier, chosen, not asked, participating in a plan not designed by the sons and daughters of man. His job was simple: keep his eyes on Andburg for any deviation in schedule, make sure detonation points remained secure, and hide the master keypad in the Book of Revelation and keep it secure on the north side of operations. Thus far, both he and Andburg had done their jobs very, very well.

Jonas surveyed the clubhouse. Many of the terminals were open, and he found the one most secluded in the corner. He sat down and, by using an electronic key that fit into the USB port and a series of high-clearance security codes, he was able to open and read the encrypted document.

"Blowing in over the North Pacific Ocean—Hurricane toward Canada, over. Western Pacific Storm needs settling—unusual weather pattern, the likes never before seen. Threatens operation. Quick nuclear action needed—send joining code. Dropping *Alice* in the eye will dissipate storm. Please respond."

Jonas stared at the screen. He didn't like this deviation. He couldn't believe that they wanted to use one of the nuclear weapons—sacrifice one of the sisters—to break up a *storm*. Nothing was bad enough to warrant that type of action. It was sloppy, not part of the plan. He read the directive again. Wasn't Alice under the ice? Had someone removed her? Perhaps none of it had been true. For the first time since the age of nine, he did not know what to do.

"Jonas?"

Jonas snapped his head up. He caught himself from expressing surprise. "Andburg!"

"Jonas!" Andburg sounded relieved. The tenor of his voice revealed that he was coming unglued. Jonas saw the dark circles under his eyes, the puffiness of his skin, and the bruises. He looked as if he'd been in a brawl Jonas half stood. His heart raced, though he masked it with his flawlessly controlled countenance, reminding himself that Andburg would not read the message so publicly exposed.

"Jonas, may I talk with you?"

"What are you doing here?"

"I made an unscheduled stop."

"Little out of the way, Sir. Aren't you supposed to be heading to the opposite pole?"

"Yes."

"That's fifteen thousand miles off course."

"Yes, Jonas. I just needed to make sure you were really here."

"Well, I am."

"It seems some team members are missing. Are you aware?"

Jonas looked at him blankly. It was true. He had personally beheaded one himself, but the Protectors had worked hard to prevent detection. He wondered what Andburg really knew and wasn't saying. "What team members?"

"Mack. He hasn't sent the recalculation of the submersion patterns."

"Mack—Mack's on that. Don't worry. His wife's expecting, right? You'll see him when you land at the northern station."

"That's right." Andburg seemed to stare off into space as if he were checking his deep inner knowing. "He's not the only one."

"Operations are running as smoothly as possible, Sir. Everything's under control."

Andburg nodded. His gaze drifted toward the computer, and Jonas froze. He needed to say something to divert his attention. "I have so much respect for you. It has been an honor to work on the team with you—a growing experience. I value you…like…like a father figure. A mentor, if you know what I mean."

Andburg was staring at him hard. What was that feeling Jonas had in his solar plexus? *Love?* It was disconcerting, and Jonas wasn't sure what to do. The inconsolable child in Jonas wanted to reach out, claim Andburg as his father, but he remained resolutely steadfast. Andburg would never know his true identity.

Andburg unexpectedly gave Jonas a bear hug. "You're my man." He patted him. "I'm sorry that I popped in on you, but I really didn't know who to trust." Then he began to back up toward the door. "It was a great effort to get here, but some very strange things have happened recently. I'm trying to get a grip on reality. Sorry that this was so unexpected, but I had to do it. I just had to, but I can't stay long because I'm so delayed. Glad to know all is well on this pole. Expect the new plan in place next week; we'll be sending the recalculations. We'll talk about the next step before we go into full operations. Exciting stuff, man. Exciting stuff." He gave one last thumbs up before he half stumbled out the clubhouse door, and then out the heavy metal door that led back into the inhospitable environment and the plane that would carry him to the Arctic. Jonas still believed the team members there were alive and that the dream was viable.

Jonas breathed in hard. His forehead was damp and it took him a moment to realize that he was sweating. "God damn it!" One or two people turned to look. Jonas' internal control cracked—his rage slipped. It felt good; in fact, it was a relief. He returned his attention the computer screen and typed in his first defiant replay in over a decade—"Fuck You. NO! Over."

The reply was quick and left no doubt in Jonas' mind that he was truly on his own. "Termination of Member 368. Source protection denied."

Jonas stared at the screen. That would be the last email from them. He knew that they didn't really need his joining code; he had been important, but not irreplaceable. Jonas knew exactly what termination of source meant: that he would no longer have access to the powers that protected the chosen ones; he was an outcast, thrown into the wilderness and certain death. If there hadn't been a fixed outcome in this endgame, he would have radioed Andburg and confessed. But there was, and he had no power to change it, not that he was sure he wanted to. What he wanted was to reconnect with his mother; not the wounded mother, but the divine feminine who would make all wrongs right.

Jonas turned off the computer, took a quick look around and then headed back to his room. With very little thought concerning what he was about to do, he retrieved his grandfather's pocket watch, put on his snow boots, and insulated coat, grabbed his gear, and headed toward the dive base where he was meeting up with a team for a scheduled dive.

As he trudged the five hundred yards to the dive station, a lone penguin shuffled, nearly crashing into him. Jonas stood still. At the last second, it scooted past his boot and continued on its way. Jonas laughed out loud. He watched the chubby tuxedoed bird slip and slide, belly down, and then return to waddling as fast as it could. "Where you going in such a hurry?" he shouted. The penguin didn't break stride, heading across the tundra toward the distant mountains that jutted up from the ice plane. A solo penguin was a rare occurrence, but the scientists had noticed that on occasion one would not return to the rook or the feeding waters, but would rather begin a determined march alone into certain death in the mountains. As scientists, their job was not to attach human-behavioral theory to the phenomenon—no one was willing to say that the penguin had simply snapped. Their job was to observe. When Jonas saw the lone penguin shuffle past him, undaunted by his presence, he couldn't help but identify with its urgency. He, too, wanted to be free from the colony. He watched as it got smaller and smaller, until it was a tiny black dot against the snow. He admired the bird's unwavering dedication to its chosen course. He turned and continued on his way to the dive cabin.

"Hey, Jonas. Are you ready?"

The team stood inside the cabin built to keep the ice hole from refreezing. Equipment, tanks, and dry insulated gear were stored in metal lockers, along with emergency adrenaline shots in case a man went into shock. There were one or two bare wooden benches. Jonas smiled. "Yes, I am prepared."

His mates began to assist Jonas with a dive suit that would help protect him in the -2 degree Celsius water.

"Jonas, you can't take that watch down there, man."

"Why not?"

"What if it snags your suit, or your hand cramps? Dude, you know procedures."

Jonas grinned. "I'm breaking the rules, boys. Suit me up."

"Why don't you carry it in your dive belt?"

"I've got to feel it!" Jonas barked.

Team members shook their heads. "Okay, don't get your panties in a wad."

Getting the dive glove on over the watch was a struggle, but somehow they managed. The metal dug painfully into Jonas' palm. One team member strapped the tank on Jonas' back, another put on his headlamp, and the third hooked him into the safety cord. Once Jonas was suited up, he gave a gesture of readiness, and then plunged into the hole, instantly surrounded by the buoyancy of the deep space of ocean water. He gently fell, fell, fell into the dome of ice that they called the cathedral. Two other divers followed him.

The water below the ice was otherworldly, beautiful and surreal, a place of cold clarity within a blue spectrum of incandescing ice. Even in the suit, Jonas was aware of the angelic sounds of clicking booms and whistles of whales and sea lions. Magical. He landed on a shelf and began to slowly make his way along an oceanic ridge. He was aware of other life forms down here. It was a violent world in miniature and though the strange and bizarre creatures with long tendrils looked benign enough, they were capable of ensnaring and sucking the life force from their prey in order to survive in one of the most hostile places on the planet. Jonas intimately understood those needs.

Aware of the pressure he held in his palm, he reached for his safety line, and, with some difficulty, he managed to unhook himself. He muted his earphone and ignored the urgent gestures of the men who were diving with him. He no longer needed them. He began to drift. He was in no hurry. This journey in the endless void of violet and fading light was like none other. Jonas removed his glove and let go of the watch. He had no more need for control. He could not feel his hand anyway. It had turned blue. He was already becoming part of the Antarctic Ocean. He took in one last inhalation of luminous nano-particles—the Higgs boson. Then, with his other hand, he turned off the valve to his air supply. His body fought, but it, too, had to let go of the life force and drift. There was nothing for him but to exhale the breath of God.

Chapter 50

Ma Shepard's medicinal salve smelled rotten. Bananas? Something burned, something else wiggled. Noah wasn't certain if it was a trick of his mind, but he felt like he wore fruit salad with maggots. He couldn't imagine where she'd gotten the ingredients, or what they were—and he didn't want to know—but they worked. Three days later, he emerged from the tent nearly healed. It was a beautiful day, even with the rain clouds hanging low overhead. Noah looked around and saw more plainly the tent city that had sprung up. The ship was just ahead of him. He was startled to see it, carved wood against the blue. To his absolute amazement, and near bewilderment, the ark was complete. It was impressive. Even now, if nothing more were to be done, it would be viable in the wild and raging water. *Oh, my God. This is going to happen.*

He set his gaze a bit beyond the curve of the ship. There, above it on a ridge, was a makeshift parking lot of trailers marked CNN, Fox, ABC, DISH Network. Already telephoto lenses were aimed and ready with a near silent whirr of clicking shutters. Noah wasn't sure how he was going to get used to *this*. Below the camera crews, the line of protestors stood. He had already begun to tune out their absurdities while he'd drifted in and out of sleep. Noah sighed, turned around, and saw another crowd altogether quite different. They were scattered Dead Heads, lost since Jerry's death, looking for someone new to follow. They'd set up their camp uncomfortably close to the ark. They looked like they were having a good time, though, playing hacky-sack. Noah was impressed with the coordination of the two fire dancers as the balls of flame streaked very close to their skin. Other people were dancing around a bonfire. Some of the girls were half clothed, bare breasted, bodies draped with crocheted wrap-around skirts. He wondered how they could stand the chill. The boys all had dreads—even the white boys, whose dreads looked very matted. The entire spectacle from dancers to protestors to camera crews struck Noah as absurd. Then Noah saw Bambi on the ship. She peered down, waved, and gestured for him to join her. He was suddenly reminded *why he was here.*

He climbed the ropes and stepped aboard for the first time since he'd returned. The Tribe was finishing up the final touches. A drummer beat time. Everyone was focused on the job in front of him or her, and the general mood seemed elevated. Bambi looked confident and in charge. "Hey, baby." She gave him a big hug. "Welcome aboard, Captain."

"Thank you." He held her tight and gave her a kiss before stepping back to survey the work.

"This is the Tribe. Tribe, this is Noah."

They all stopped. "We've been waiting for you," said a girl with warm, brown eyes. "What do you think?" Her dark eyes darted around.

"I can't believe it. She looks ready to sail."

"I'd say she was unsinkable if I didn't think that would jinx us," said the boy with the drum.

"I guess it's a leap of faith," Noah replied.

"Is it true we're going to haul poop?" said the dark-eyed girl.

Noah nodded. "Yes, it's true."

"Well, I think we should take some of the animals."

Noah crouched down beside her. "What do you want to take?"

"I don't know. I'm kind of partial to the giraffe. It has the largest heart of all the land mammals."

"I think that's a very good animal to take. Perhaps when the time comes, we'll have a giraffe on board. I don't have much control over this, you understand?"

She smiled and touched him on the arm. "I know you don't."

The Tribe returned to the task at hand. They were soon engrossed in the busy harmony of their work. Bambi took Noah's hand and led him down below deck. He looked at the cabins and the empty stalls. "This looks good," Noah whispered. "Is there anything left to do?"

"Get more poop, and then pilot this ship."

"Thank you."

"For what?"

"For being you." He grinned. "Will you go to the zoo with me?"

"I'd love to go to the zoo with you," she announced. "We might have to sneak out."

"Maybe something will scare them off. Has he returned?"

"You mean Charlie?"

Noah nodded.

"Haven't seen hide nor hair of him. Ma Shepard has us incanting special prayers. She says that binding the ark with love will keep all dark energy away. Seems to be working so far."

"I guess it works until it doesn't." They climbed on deck. Noah looked over at a bucket. "Is that the sealant?"

Bambi held up a brush and handed it to Noah. "Why, yes, it is."

He took the brush, gave her a kiss. "You're a perfect woman."

"Tell me that again in an hour. This stuff stinks."

"I don't care as long as it works." He playfully brushed the soft bristles against her nose. Somewhere on the hill, a camera just recorded the intimate moment. His love play with Bambi would be on the nightly news. Noah suddenly felt like he was swimming in a fish bowl. The planet itself was spinning and spinning; it, too, had become very small.

Chapter 51

"Rock the boat. Don't rock the boat, baby. Rock the boat, don't tip the boat over...." Dan was singing. He was happy. He was really happy — wing and beak over talon happy. It seemed that everything was going his way. Charlie's plan had backfired. Bambi and Noah were back together. The ship had a crew and was floodworthy. The rain had stopped for the moment. Dan felt liberated, a yoke of responsibility off his winged back He was flying high, falling in love with the things he could do, with the bird he could be. He'd suffered being under Charlie's thumb, and now he was making up for it. Dan was doing a sashay dance step, sliding to the beat of his fluttering wing. He made a 360-degree spin and a side step right into the electric slide.

He wasn't paying much attention when he slid over what looked like a mere oil slick. His feet burned immediately. "Ouch, ouch, ouch." He had to stomp hard in the sand to sooth the singe. The slick laughed. Dan thought he recognized that evil laugh.

Dan hopped closer and peered into the pit. It was devoid of light. "What is it?" Dan said out loud.

"You don't recognize me? Call yourself a friend?"

It was Charlie, reduced to voice and shadow. "Charlie?"

"Who do you think it is, nit-wit?"

Dan peered back into the depths of Charlie. "What happened to you?"

"Nothing. Family life, I suppose. Little bastards took all of the singe out of me. Greedy little shits."

Dan hooted. "You should have been more careful. I would think someone of your caliber, your intelligence, has certainly heard of family planning."

"Could have, should have, would have. Thanks for your advice, little birdman. It so happens that *it* was planned...sort of. I haven't sowed seeds in centuries. She was so fertile. I couldn't resist. What have you been up to? Being ineffectual as usual? I guess you watched the whole miserable fiasco, you little pervert."

Dan checked in with himself. *It didn't hurt this time.* He felt his inner glow. Charlie's insults seemed to glance off without affect. Hmm, he thought, losing an ego, giving up attachment to outcome, certainly has its advantages. There's nothing to stick to. "I've been observing a lot of things. Thank you for asking."

"I have more things I want you to see."

"I'm not sure you have enough power to show me much of anything."

The slimy darkness wriggled. "It's in your best interest to see this."

The landscape suddenly changed. One of Charlie's parlor tricks? Dan wondered. A trap? Maybe he wasn't as disabled as he seemed. However, Charlie didn't move, and Dan didn't feel trapped. He looked around at the stark rock formations. They all looked like early life forms, frozen in rock, climbing out of primordial ocean.

"Where are we?"

"This is the Bisti. It's the oldest outcropping of rock on the planet."

"Why are you showing me this?"

"Just watch."

Dan waited. He liked this unusual place. Some of the formations were black and soft, carved from a sedimentary mixture of coal, shale, silt, and mudstone. Scattered around were large chunks of petrified wood. On closer inspection, some of the larger pieces seemed to still have preserved bark.

"How come this is still here relatively undisturbed?"

"The BLM never puts up road signs, and this is hard to find. They go by the old adage: If you don't know where you are, you ain't supposed to be there."

"They've done a good job. It looks as if nobody has ever been out here."

"I wouldn't go that far."

Dan felt a chill. What could Charlie-the-puddle possibly do?

Dan pushed off and sailed in a circular motion over the area. The formations were truly amazing. Earth recorded her history in geological patterns, especially if there had been a sudden cataclysmic event or a high concentration of a particular thought. These formations looked like forms from a Jurassic ocean: a giant sea turtle to the left, and a lizard with sharp teeth to the right. Some looked too primal to ever see the planet's sun again. Dan landed and hopped around. The sandy silt felt very primordial, and he could still sense the soup that this primitive ocean had once been—dark, thick, deadly—as creatures brutally carved out existence through competition and survival. Dan had an appreciation for how volatile changes on the planet could be. Some spanned millions of years, others the blink of an eye. He wondered how the memory of humans would imprint into the soil.

"I wouldn't go too far, Dan. Not before you see what I have to show you."

"What are we waiting for, Charlie?"

"The Cliff notes."

Charlie hadn't lost his obscure, sometimes cruel, humor. As if on cue, the familiar sound of Harley engines rocked his ears. In the silence, the reverberation was amplified. The sound struck a chord of fear. Maybe because Charlie was still potent. Maybe because, while one battle had been won, it was far too soon for the next. Dan wasn't sure, but he knew whatever Charlie had hatched, it was likely more brutal than his former plan. Dan reminded himself to trust. He was an angel of light. He wasn't the same being that he once was—nor was Charlie. And Charlie's last attempt had failed. Love was the stronger power. As the engines gunned, that memory was more difficult. Dan lit lightly down on the head of boulder to wait and watch.

A band of banditos rounded the bend in tight formation and parked close to the black stain called Charlie. The head rider dismounted, with the eleven others doing the same a second later. The leader stood a full towering foot above the others. Thick chested, he was tanned and leathery, heavily tattooed. His age and race was indeterminate. He sported a braided ponytail of graying reddish hair under his black bandana. Dan was reminded of the animal kingdom, survival of the fittest. There was nothing unique or unusual about them, nothing subtle in their mannerisms or dress. As far as bandits went, they took their image and subsequent posturing right out of the *Banditos Through the Ages: We Are Really Nice Guys* handbook. The two distinctions about this guy were his eyes and his intelligence—eyes flat, black like a shark's, with a total absence of light. His brawn was intimidating; his lack of compassion was frightening. He was all instinct and his energy spoke to Dan—*it's nothing personal if I eat you*—and it screamed, *born killer*. Adding to the fear, he was obviously intelligent. He began to address the stain in an ancient language.

"Ahiia. Yasa. Nemanha. Maniniieus. Mazda paouruuim vanheus. Xratum."

Dan understood enough to recognize the language: Avestan, a sacred liturgical text of the Yasna, an obscure Egyptian dialect that would have only been known by a very few scholars and/or ancient Egyptian priests. *Good, God. Who is this dude?* Dan's rudimentary translation gave him a portion of the greeting. *Hands stretched out in reverence.* He couldn't get more than that, but that was enough when coupled with the dramatic image of every one of the riders dropping to their knees in submission, the leader receiving a rolled up parchment from Charlie. *They must be his orders.*

The leader unrolled the parchment, quickly surveyed it, and nodded once to the black stain, indicating that he understood and was willing. He turned around, made a hand signal at which the others rose in formation and mounted their bikes. Another hand signal and they fired the engines with an impressive roar and followed their leader from the canyon out toward the badlands beyond.

The silence that ensued was deep, though Dan thought he could hear the drone of those engines still buzzing off in the far distance. More time went by. Finally, Charlie spoke. "That was Quigley."

"Who's Quigley?"

"My most loyal henchman."

"Why do you need a henchman if you're so powerful?"

"Every demon needs a henchman, Dan. It's sort of a status symbol. Besides, you didn't think you were the only one who worshiped me, did you?"

"I never worshiped you, Charlie. I tried to be your friend."

"I don't have friends, Dan. I thought you knew that."

"Everyone has friends, Charlie, even you. I love you in a way."

"That's kind of sick, Dan. On many levels."

"What's going to happen next?"

"I can't tell you that. However, everything you need to know I've already told you. You'll have to search your memory for the real clues. I'm not sure I'll ever see you again. You might say that I'm a family guy now. Tracy and I have settled our differences, so I guess I did get that unconditional love after all. I just wanted to say goodbye. I'll always remember our chess games."

"Where are you going, Charlie?"

"I can't tell you that, either. Wish me well." And with that, the stain vanished.

Dan took a deep breath, lifting his beak up toward the thinning light of late afternoon sky. He sat a long time thinking. What was on that parchment? Would it be murder? Dan vaguely remembered something Charlie had said. Bambi would die, perhaps? Since Charlie had failed at something, he was likely more dangerous now. He had more to prove. Obviously Charlie's plan was to harm the blessed couple. Dan began to feel pressured. He had to figure it out. Then he reminded himself that there really was nothing to figure out. That was one thing that the void had taught him. Until the next thing presented itself, all Dan had to do was be patient and to wait. Still, he had to resist the urge to rescue Noah and Bambi. Dan had to go against his nature. Dan had to be still.

Dusk gave away to night and the entire galaxy showed up for its starry performance. The elliptical dish of the Milky Way appeared from deep space, easily visible in the absence of light pollution and with no clouds in the cold, desert sky. The stars looked so close; Dan saw the possibility of flying among them. He, too, was a light being and could break free anytime from the time limitations of his material boundary. Even as he thought it, he began to glow, pushing back the solid darkness that held support for the cosmic sky. A meteor slipped and burned a red tail on its way down. Dan was holding off the darkness, but it took work.

Few, dazzled by the power of light, ever thought of the light's perspective. What the light feared was burning out and being swallowed by the dark; a lonely, lonely feeling. Dan didn't like it. He felt too alone perched at a high point at the bottom of a dead ocean. He concentrated his thought in pure being and intention. When he opened his eyes, he was up there in the center of the Milky Way. He was filled with heartsong. He'd done it! He'd broken free from the belief of can't. Here the entire chorus of light beings—all the star people who made up the Milky Way—surrounded him. Dan resonated with gratitude and joy. He resumed his song: "Rock the boat. Don't tip the boat over." This time, he was joined by a few million wispy voices. The light itself sang. The Milky Way itself was humming. From the Earth this appeared as phenomenon, a strange, unexplained iridescent shimmer never seen in human recollection. The scientists were busy with their calculations.

Dan did a dance step, and the star people followed his lead. He waved once to Charlie, who he was almost certain hadn't gone far. He double winked at the fair couple, now sleeping entwined in a tent near the ark, entranced by the miracle of their story: that they'd actually listened to their inner voices and moved toward manifesting a dream despite the odds. A million star people winked in unison, an awesome sight. Far below, Ma Shepard peered up into the night sky and whispered *Aho* to the ancestors.

Chapter 52

One God. One Ark. One Flood. One God. One Ark. One Flood. God wouldn't lie! That's not how we're supposed to die!

When Noah woke up, Bambi was cuddled under his arm and the two dogs at his feet. The protestors sounded closer than usual.

"Good morning, sweetheart," she cooed in his ear, responding to the movement of his body. "What would you like for breakfast? I think there are some dried blueberries and pancake mix left. Would you like blueberry pancakes? Or were those raisins I saw in the stuff sack?"

"That's a kind offer, but I really think that we need to take care of those protestors."

"What protestors?"

One God. One Ark. One Flood. One God. One Ark. One Flood. God wouldn't lie! That's not how we are supposed to die!

"You don't hear that?"

"Oh, those protesters. I barely hear them anymore."

"They're really getting on my nerves. Maybe I should do more to convince them to move on."

"Baby, I don't think they're the type of people who take to reasoning well. They do have a right to their opinion. Besides, the cameras are more annoying."

"Yes, but they're not waking us up."

"Not yet."

Noah kissed Bambi again, rolled over, slid into his long johns and pulled a shirt over his head. "Tell you what. Why don't I bring you breakfast?"

She smiled and stretched. "You are a prince. Just a cup of coffee will be fine."

"You got it." Noah unzipped the tent and squeezed out. He barely managed to stand before a skinny photographer approached, snapping close-ups. Noah put his hand up to his face. "Stop that. You're stealing my soul."

"That's a good line. Can I quote you?"

"Who are you?"

"Trenton Styler, managing editor of *Near Times*." The man lowered his camera and held out his hand.

"Really? Has the story gotten that big?" Noah ignored convention and the man lowered his hand back to the camera's body.

"I want a story on you and the desert ark. Would you be willing to grant me a ten minute interview?"

"Why should I?"

"Because I want to tell your story, your way. Because I believe you."

"Okay, then. I suppose. I mean, what's ten minutes in relative terms to the end of the world?" Noah paused, thought a moment, and then recanted. "How about eight?"

The man pulled a pen from the inside pocket of his photographer's vest. "I'll scribble fast. Your name is Noah?"

"That's right."

"Given name?"

"Yes."

"Last name?"

"Noland."

"Spell it."

"N-o-l-a-n-d."

"Kind of like *no land*, right?"

Noah said nothing.

Trenton licked his lips, glanced at his wristwatch, and shook his hand to free a hand cramp. "Let's move on. Siblings?"

"Twin. Died at birth."

"Twin. Died at birth." He scribbled as fast as he could. "Like Elvis Presley."

"No, no. I didn't say that. I don't think I have anything in common with Elvis Presley."

"Just editorial ideas to develop later. It's always good for our magazine if we can figure out an Elvis angle. Can we stick to the main point?"

"That's what I want you to do."

"We are, we are." Trenton glanced at his watch again.

"Please stop doing that. You're making me nervous."

"What, sir?"

"Looking at your wristwatch. It makes me nervous."

"You're the one who said eight minutes. I take time literally."

Noah shook his head. "Go on."

"Born?"

"Yes."

"Where?"

"Athens, Ohio."

"Then you just look Native American?"

"Do I?"

"Married?"

"In a relationship."

"With a female?"

"Yes," Noah said with exasperation.

"What's her name?"

"Leave her out of the article."

He nodded, but saw that Trenton scribbled initials that began with the letter x. "Her name is Bambi."

Trenton crossed out the previous notation and wrote in Bambi's name in the margin. "Has she ever been a stripper?"

"One more comment like that and this interview is over."

"Sorry, reporter's hunch. Now, you're building an ark."

"Yes."

"Plan to sail it?"

"I believe so."

"Publicity."

"Rather not."

"No, what I mean is are you seeking publicity? Do you have an agenda or a cause?" He paused and then whispered, "Is Green Peace funding you?"

"Not at this moment."

"Why did you build it?"

Noah didn't know what to say. He was suddenly feeling very silly, embarrassed. He wasn't sure he could claim his vision, especially if it was going to be written about in print and likely distorted. However, if everything were to be washed, away what did it matter what was said? "Um, I built the boat because I always wanted to know what it was like to build my own ship. I chose a common design." Noah glanced over his shoulder as if to prove his point.

"So God didn't speak to you?"

Noah was silent, thoughtful. Then he decided to safely say, "God speaks through us all if we listen."

Trenton furiously wrote notes, then paused and looked straight into Noah's eyes. "Mr. Noland, do you think you are crazy?"

Noah starred at him directly in his eyes. "Not for me to decide."

"Off the record. Did God speak to you?"

Noah nodded and looked down. He was surprised that he felt so vulnerable and anxious. Here he was standing outside a tent in his long johns. Noah realized that he wasn't making such a good impression, but he hadn't planned on being persuasive. He was just doing his thing. What he wouldn't give for the authority of a suit and tie, an office, and a large desk to feel powerful and protected behind. *I'm not crazy.* He had the urge to defend, but he knew protest was futile. There was more power in silence.

"How?"

"On an abandoned TV."

"On a TV? Listening to the 900 Club, were you? "

"No, I was not." Noah said a little more firmly then he had intended. He decided he wanted the reporter gone. "Listen, this is the last thing I'm going to say, and do with it what you like. I heard a voice on an abandoned TV out in the desert I was instructed to build an ark. I don't know who spoke to me, but it felt like the Divine. I might be crazy, but my girlfriend who's about to be a psychotherapist doesn't think so. She thinks I'm manic at times, but not crazy. I think there's another flood coming, but I don't know that for sure, either. I do believe that the planet is out of balance, and, because she is a sentient being, a consciousness of life, I'm pretty certain balance has to be restored. I mean even science supports that. I'm not the one creating monster storms and weeks of rain out here in the desert. I'm just the guy who responded to an inner call and built a boat. I don't know if it will ever sail, or just become my home."

"Thank you, Mr. Noland. That was very well spoken." Trenton finished his quote, offered his hand again with a smile; this time Noah shook it. He was still flushed with sentiment. Trenton opened his mouth, paused, about to ask one more question when they were interrupted by two men wearing black suits and dark glasses. Noah thought for sure they were CIA or at least FBI. Anyone who steps over the invisible social line wonders what kind of government report they've ended up on. Noah was no exception. He'd been half expecting a visit from officials of some ilk. He didn't have a permit to build on this public land, and there must be a number of violations. It was just a matter of time.

Trenton raised his camera. Noah looked down at his feet and wondered how he was going to play this circus. He couldn't pretend ignorance, not with the massive ship behind him.

"Are you Mr. Noah Noland?"

"Yep."

"Are you the responsible party for the ark?"

"I don't know. Maybe."

"Mr. Noland. We are representatives from a corporate interest, Palero Energy, chosen last year as one of the top leading energy sales companies in the world market. We got wind of your project, and we'd like to sponsor your endeavor."

"What would that entail and why me?"

"In our market analysis your little stunt—I mean project—is already reaching approximately 200,000 homes nightly, and those numbers double when we factor in Internet usage. There's a trend for companies to attach logos to current world events. The public associates the news with the logos, and the logos with companies that care. That translates into buying power and corporate profits. It's a win/win situation for all involved. We believe that if we attach our product name to your cause, we can benefit each other. What do you say?" The executively trimmed corporate representative removed his glasses and guilelessly smiled boardroom charm.

Noah was stunned. He didn't know what to say.

The man turned to his partner and made hurry up gestures with his finger. The man, dressed identically but with a different colored tie, a subordinate color blue, knelt down in the mud and opened the briefcase he'd been carrying. He carefully pulled out rolled up graph paper and an envelope. He stood up, ignoring the mud on his knee. Noah was shocked that a man in an expensive suit was willing to do that. It seemed extreme. Together, they unrolled the graphic design of their logo. Noah found himself staring at a wave, a crescent moon, and an oil drill surrounded by arctic wildlife.

"What do you want me to do with this?"

"For two hundred and fifty thousand dollars, and we do have the cashier's check right now, we will have our artisans paint this image visibly on the side of your ship and then take a couple of photographs."

"You can't paint that on the ark."

"Why not, Mr. Noland?"

"Oil drills are very disturbing."

"We want our consumers to understand that the core of our energy extraction company is not antithetical to environmental issues. Our track record speaks for itself."

"What's your track record?"

"We're a responsible corporation. We give back to right our wrongs. For example, we have an education endowment of which we're very proud. We have an unparalleled safety record, and we're investing in green, renewable fuel sources. We do see the wave of the future."

"Well, maybe so, but I don't want an oil drill painted on the side of the ark. It's disturbing."

"Is your only objection the oil drill? We can modify the image some."

"That's a starter, but I think I'm going to have to say no. I'm not comfortable with any logo on the ark. I don't really have a need for money and—"

"Mr. Noland," blue tie cut him off, "everyone is in need of money. Especially now, just before you launch. You might need a corporation on your side. Let's say the government comes to investigate you for homeland terrorism. You'd want to be legitimate."

"Sounds like you're threatening me."

"Not at all. However, if you change your mind, give me a call. We'll make the transaction as painless as possible, and the logo will be striking. I'm sure you'll like it." When he extended his hand, there was a business card between his fingers. Noah took it to be polite. He smiled. They smiled. The corporate representative nodded, his companion packed up his briefcase and they headed back down the hill to their black Mercedes.

"Maybe you should have taken the deal, Mr. Noland, if I might say so," said the reporter. "Those corporations are in bed with the government—not that I'm a conspiracy theorist. They might even be part of the POA."

"Who's the POA?"

"Rumors have been circulating for nearly fifty years about a world organization comprised of government insiders, global, and it's exclusive. I've heard they've been digging tunnels and underground chambers to maintain power in case of a planetary crisis. There's one underneath Taos Mountain. Scary guys if they exist, and nobody I'd want to mess with."

Noah shrugged. "Not much I can do about any of it. I just know that no corporate logo's going on the ark. I have their card." Noah held it up. "If I change my mind." He flicked it into the mud and laughed. "Not likely now."

"I'll put that in the article. Conviction and virtue."

"I hope that I can live up to my legend. I have to go now. I need to fetch a cup of coffee." Noah walked off, then turned around and called, "By the way, how do I get rid of that press corps up there?"

"Give them all an exclusive interview and then wait."

"Wait for what?"

"There'll always be a bigger story—somewhere. News demands freshness or it dries up. Wait."

Noah firmly nodded, accepting the man's answer.

"Okay, an interview and then wait." Noah got to the fire pit, found the camp stove, the potable water, the steel pan and set to work making Bambi's coffee. He prepared her cup with as much as love as possible. No telling when a freshly brewed cup of coffee would become a luxury. He was grateful. He balanced the cups and some fruit and strolled back to their tent, calling out to her to let him in.

"Come on in, sailor boy."

Noah grinned, handed her a cup, then the other, and then the fruit. He crawled in and re-zipped the door. If anyone had been eavesdropping, they would have heard giggles. There was a lot of movement and bustle and then, in a sudden shout of ecstasy, Bambi cried out, "God, I love a good cup of camp coffee."

Chapter 53

Andburg wasn't thinking about the three days of what felt like an endless flight from pole to pole, nor was he thinking about Tracy and how she disappeared on the night of his send-off. He was thinking about annelids. Ice worms to be exact. Ice worms were first discovered in 1887 on the Muir Glacier in Alaska in the blue slush pools of melted ice, a contrasting black—sometime a reddish rubber—string to the stark white of their environment. For a long time they remained mythological as their existence was questioned. However, they were real, worms just like the earthworms Andburg had cut in half during his third grade science class as his teacher assured the curious and squeamish children that the worm would not die.

As Andburg looked out the window of his chartered DHC-3 Turbo Otter six-seater floatplane, the mercury blue of the ice mesmerized him. From the air, seemed as though he were floating blue into blue. He trusted the captain as much as he could trust anyone and he felt free as the twin-engine plane methodically approached Baffin Bay. That feeling of freedom never failed him when he was in the air approaching the science station. Andburg decided this was as close to experiencing perfect union between space and timelessness as possible. If only if he could find a way to extend the experience of floating in air, weightlessness, he could find a way to transcend the depth of suffering just below the surface of his calcified heart.

Are you sure he can't feel the pain?

No silly boy, they are simple creatures.

But they have five hearts.

That is only so they can process the high concentration of calcium deposits in the earth. Now go on, cut. Mucus rings, slim tubes, heads or tails? Permeable skin. The whole damn thing breathes. Plow soil; plow soil so that the air and water can circulate below ground; plow soil so that root systems can breathe. What would it be like if every cell of my skin could breathe? What would it be like if I could do that for the planet?

In Andburg's emotional state of weightlessness, he was casually aware that a contributing factor to his feeling of freedom was that Tracy hadn't called. For the first time in a decade, she was silent. He couldn't even feel her presence in his mind. It was as if she no longer existed. Andburg couldn't decide if he cared or not, and this indecision startled him. He didn't have to solve it. It just *was*, and was a paradox: two binaries existing simultaneously; caring, not caring until that moment when he simply stopped the struggle. Up to that moment, she was the only one who understood what pain meant to him. Despite all of her flaws, she was the only one who valued it.

His newfound freedom from worry was as miraculous as the ice worm, a biological creature that lived in the most inhospitable environments on the planet, found not only on the top of glaciers, but also rimming oceanic volcanic fissures. It survived both fire and ice. In many ways, Andburg related to the humble creature. Unlike the more common earthworm, an ice worm had only two hearts. Andburg decided that was two hearts too many, though secretly he envied the five hearts. He couldn't imagine how much more calcification his own single one could bear.

The more Andburg understood the ice worm, the more he believed he was falling in love the way that Darwin had fallen in love with the biological studies he recorded. Like Darwin, Andburg had an appreciation for the individual. Diversification was more than the bottom line of numbers that many science teachers proclaimed. It was pure passion. Darwin had once serenaded an earthworm with a tin whistle because he wanted to know if the worm could hear. What scientists now knew was that the worm could hear high frequencies. They heard more than a human being could ever hope to hear. They could hear the Aurora Borealis flower nightly in the northern sky—psychedelic violets, ambers, and iridescent greens, each color with its own signature frequency—as they streaked and mushroomed into full bloom. Delicate. Life was so delicate, so fragile.

"We've reached a cruising altitude of 9600 meters." The pilot's voice from the cockpit startled Andburg. "Everything looks smooth. Our estimated time of arrival is approximately three hours and twenty minutes. We have a tail wind at about twenty kilometers and so we are expected to arrive early. I have the flight plan if you'd like to read it." They had just taken off from a refueling stop, and the pilot had picked up some supplies.

"No. I'm okay." Despite his broken nose and bruised cheek, which was already healing, he was all right.

"There's a cooler behind the fourth seat. Snacks and beverages. I believe you requested Maker's Mark, and I took the liberty of ordering some specialty beers from Coyote Springs, a beer pub outside Phoenix. Help yourself. There are some crackers and Almas caviar." The captain turned around and grinned at Andburg. "$700 an ounce."

Andburg grinned back. "Thank you. I appreciate your attention to detail."

"No problem, sir. You've been such a loyal patron to our company. We sure appreciate your business. Anything I can do to make you more comfortable, let me know."

"I will." Andburg turned around and focused his attention on the fourth seat. His automatic response was to give in to his impulse to drink. After all, he did deserve it. His life was so stressful, and he never drank to the point of being impaired. He was rarely out of control. Drinking simply took the edge off. Andburg knew that it was a maladaptive coping mechanism, but he'd done it for so long that he didn't know who he'd be without it. Hops, for Andburg, were a religious experience. Andburg had also dried out enough times to know that if he had to he could live without the substance, but then, why should he have to? He recalled his conversation with Noah, how he promised to seek professional help upon his return. That promise seemed an eternity away, and Andburg was going back and forth in his mind whether he needed help or not. He could not decide, so he chose not to have a beer so that he could prove to himself that he didn't need it.

Andburg fixed his gaze at the fourth seat and, like a bulldog, stared down the orange vinyl. Secondary function: flotation device. Andburg was resolved, but he could also appreciate the effort it took to curb his compulsion. He decided once he got to the science station he was going to find a batch of ice worms. He was going to find a tin whistle in Baffin Bay the final point of civilization before the snow bus picked him up and drove the continuous hundred and fifty miles to the substation. Andburg was tickled by the thought that he was going to find a worm, not just any worm, but his special worm. He was going to serenade that worm and be stone cold sober while he did it, even if it was the last thing he did. They both deserved it. Andburg chuckled, amazed at his ability to take himself less seriously. How long had it been? Andburg decided he'd contact his team, relay his plan to Dr. Smart. He'd want to go out to the glaciers as soon as possible. Andburg found his mobile satellite phone and put in a call. Surprisingly, his call would not connect. He tried it again. Hmm, that's odd, he thought. I just spoke to the man this morning. Dr. Smart had been sending daily updates via satellite. He was prompt and thorough; Andburg had not been concerned as to the status of operations. He tried again.

"Excuse me. I'm trying to patch in a call to my substation, and there's no response. Is there a reason the GPS should be down?"

The pilot checked his readings. "No, sir. Navigational reports are good. There's no report of solar flares. The satellites are tracking just fine, sir. Perhaps your contact simply stepped out."

"It's not like there's a Quickie Mart down the street."

"I wouldn't worry about it, sir. You know how temperamental technology can be. It's of the devil, I say."

Andburg nodded, but deep down he felt something was wrong. He stared out the window for a long moment, tried to get back the feeling of weightlessness. He couldn't. He sighed, unbuckled himself, and slid over to fourth seat and the cooler. He stared at the hard plastic lid and then lifted it up as easily as opening a familiar door. It was a pretty sight, those long necks poking up from the ice. He reached in and pulled out a deep golden brown bottle of Coyote Springs Amber. He reached into his pocket, fished for the Swiss Army that he bought for the bottle opener.

His first sip: *Yep, that is good.* Andburg went back to his seat and belted in. What could he do? He wasn't going to beat himself up about it, not now. He took in a few more sips. He felt calm. Even his own mother had never been able to give him that feeling of comfort, and he stopped asking for her nurturing hugs after his father did what he did to all of them. Andburg had decided long ago that he didn't need anything that he couldn't give himself. For now it was beer. He didn't care. He'd talk to someone about it when he returned to Santa Fe if it was still bothering him. Good Lord, there were enough counselors there. It wouldn't be difficult. For now, it was all he had to get him through. There were no ice worms up here to make him feel all warm and fuzzy, to make him feel connected to the universal order. Andburg relaxed some and settled into the enjoyment of the brew. The captain knew what he was doing. The beer was delicious.

"Sir, I'm getting in a report that there may have been a sizable tsunami off the coast of Greenland. Perhaps that's why you can't reach your substation."

"Christ! Off Greenland? That's unheard of."

"Yes, sir. They say that there was 7.2 sub-oceanic earthquake off of Greenland's northeast coast."

"Odd place for an earthquake. That's a stable region with low seismic activity."

"Yes, sir, but there is a strike slip in the Continental crust in the Wardle Sea. So I've been told."

"That's relatively a kingdom away. I can't imagine that affecting communication at the substation."

"Yes, sir. Just thought I'd mention it. Might be related, never know."

Andburg finished his beer. The world was so crazy now. He could barely recognize it. A tsunami in Greenland? "Hey, how's this going to affect our landing in the bay?"

"Don't know. Won't know until we get there. Odds are the bay was unaffected. That wave came in from the North Atlantic much further south than the bay. If it did come up that far north, we'd mostly have to worry about floating debris. The water itself should have subsided by the time we land. I'll let you know as soon as I get the reports in."

"Okay, let me know." Andburg stood up and got one more beer and a shot of Maker's Mark for the ride. He settled back into his seat and closed his eyes. He allowed himself to drift. He didn't know when he'd be able to sleep again, even if the Arctic Circle was in permanent twilight this time of year. The further north they flew, the further away from the sun they went, as if they were fleeing. Andburg welcomed the approaching darkness, a comfort after the glare of harsh reality. He *wanted* to flee from the sun.

Somewhere on a glacier, a batch of ice worms were undulating, secreting a chemical that acted on the ice like anti-freeze. Scientists studying the compound were excited. Someday in the near future, they'd be able to extend the life of transplantable organs. These worms were the secret to saving lives. For now, the life of the worm was precarious. There was a thin span of temperature that they could live in. Dropping below 6.8 Celsius meant the worms froze. Continued exposure at around 5 Celsius and the worms self-destruct, literally melting. Their name, *Mesenchytraceus Solifugus,* translated from the Latin as *fleeing away from the sun.*

There would be no sun for another one hundred and fifty-seven days where they were going. One hundred and fifty-seven days before there would be a return to balance. Andburg wondered what the rest of the planet would be like before that balance was restored—how many ice worms would have melted in the meantime? Andburg counted many numbers in his head—like counting sheep—until he could no longer keep sleep at bay. He fell asleep like a baby, cradled by the clouds in the darkening blue sky as the plane fled the setting sun.

Chapter 54

Noah and Bambi had barely made it to the last foothold of the knotted net—they were escaping to the zoo—when news crews mobbed them, tipped off by *Near Times* reporter.

"Noah, Noah. Do you really believe a flood is coming?"

"What do you think of global warming?"

"What do you say to reports that you're running an anarchist cult?"

The questions were fired off so fast Noah couldn't address them. The crowd pressed in closer, making him feel trapped. He looked up and saw Ione. Her mass of curls hung down around her face. She wore a headscarf to keep them out of her eyes. From this angle she looked a little like Mary Read, one of the most notorious female pirates in history. She spoke in a firm, reasonable voice. "You have all been fed false information. You are creating mass media hysteria."

Bambi, mouth agape, listened to Ione and then quickly began to scramble up the rope again. Noah couldn't figure out where she was going. She climbed a half a foot or so and hung slightly above Noah's shoulder and the crowd competing for the best view. She ran her hand through her hair, licked her lips, and transform into a theatrical movie star persona, something Noah had never seen her do before. She reminded him of a 1940's starlet as she played to the cameras with grace and innocence, all the while showing off the length of her long leg. "My friend is right," she announced in a voice loud enough to be heard by all, gesturing toward Ione, who was grinning from ear to ear, already aware of Bambi's ploy. "You have been fed false information. We are grateful that you're here, and there was really no other way to get you here. If you had known that we are filming a movie you would not have come. Now that you're here, let me thank you. We couldn't have hoped for better publicity."

Noah was spellbound. What would she say next? She continued to address the media very naturally and without hesitation. "We're launching a film called *Noah*. We're a small independent film company, and we need backers. We won't turn away Hollywood, and I know someone here must know Spielberg or Soderbergh. Our pitch is that an ordinary Joe suddenly turns into Noah. It should be fun—a family type film, you know—something very saleable." She gestured quotes around the word *saleable*. "Make sure you get that pun for your story." She scrambled up a little further. "I'll be the star, of course. My name is Bambi," she spoke slowly and with breathy punctuation, a little like Marilyn Monroe. "You don't know me now, but you will." It was all Noah could do to keep a straight face. "You're more than welcome to document the shooting. That would be great, free publicity for us. We hope to begin next week, so stay and watch. You are so very welcome. Oh, by the way," she flashed a vacant smile into the closest camera. "I'm looking for an agent." She looked directly at one of the reporters. "Please don't cut that out of your clip." She winked.

"So what you're saying is that there is no flood cult? You are not anarchists?"

"Look at us!" Ione corroborated Bambi's improv. "Do we *look* like anarchists?"

"No," a voice from deep in the media crew spoke up. "You look like a bunch of unemployed actors pulling a publicity stunt."

"It's a hoax!" someone else chimed in.

The news crews laughed, but Noah could feel their shame and disappointment at being duped. Suddenly all the cameras were lowered. Interest waned as they simultaneously deemed the situation no longer newsworthy.

"What are you saying?" said one of the protestors who had passed within earshot. "This is a commercial stunt?" He was red faced, flustered. "Are they making fun of us?"

"I don't know what they're doing, but I'm getting out of here. There's no story."

A cell phone rang. "Hey, everybody! There's been an unconfirmed report of a nuclear test explosion in some Atlantic storm, and a tsunami off the coast of Greenland, a possible connection between the two!"

"Hey, now that's *news,*" another voice drifted up from the crowd. "Who's ever heard of a tsunami off the coast of Greenland? Maybe that ice shelf is finally breaking apart and falling into the ocean. Maybe we're under nuclear attack by the Russians."

"Good thing you built a ship. You might need it after all, stunt or no stunt." Phones began to ring as callbacks were returned, and the story was confirmed.

"Let's go!"

The crews began to pack en masse.

"Hey, don't go," Bambi called after them. She was already waving goodbye.

The vans were loaded, the engines fired up. Almost at one time, they pulled out and like that, they were gone.

"Come on." Bambi tapped Noah on the shoulder. "This is a good time to get going." He nodded and helped her down. They glanced around— there were large empty spaces ahead of them; even the protestors had vacated, lost interest in the supposed theatrical stunt. When they realized there was no one around, the couple began to run in the direction of the pickup.

"Hey, where are you going?" Ione hollered after them.

"We'll be back soon."

"If you are going to the zoo, look for Andrea. She might need your help."

They didn't hear her, so excited were they to be free and on their way. Noah reached into the truck and handed Bambi a painter's suit. She quickly dressed herself in the protective covering, and he donned one, too. He danced a little jig as he helped Bambi in on the shotgun side. "This is serious," she chided him, but she was laughing at his celebration dance.

He shrugged his shoulders and then scrambled to the other side. He looked up at the bruised blue sky. More clouds were rolling in. The rain had not disappeared. He knew that they wouldn't have long before the rain returned. Noah only hoped that they would collect every sample that needed collecting. It would be a shame if any one animal species were left behind. He cranked the ignition and pulled out with a sudden lurch. Bambi screamed and braced herself, and they both began to laugh. It was warm moment. "Let's try that again," Noah said and he took his time with the clutch, effecting a much smoother exit. He pulled out on what used to be a dirt road. It was now mud. He knew he had to go through with some speed. If they got stuck, they'd have to walk back to camp, and the remaining samples would go uncollected.

"Baby, what if we get stuck? How are we going to get to Albuquerque?"

"Let's keep positive. We're going to make it. Let's keep focused on that."

"Okay, then. Let's scoop poop."

They were focused on moving forward as Noah carefully steered through the slick mud. Noah was grateful that Bambi was coming along this time. She was so good with details; he knew she'd make sure that no species were left behind. He smiled at their progress. Not once did they turn around and see that there was a tight line of motorcycle riders tracking them. In their innocence and determination they were easily followed all the way to the Albuquerque Zoo by banditos covered in mud like the bog men of Celtic lore. It was in their blood to kill. They knew no other way.

Chapter 55

Andburg was annoyed. He was cold. He was driving across the Arctic tundra alone. Nothing was going as planned. They had safely landed at Baffin Bay. The tsunami had not affected the bay, but everyone on the ground was talking about the anomaly. No one could explain it, at least not yet. Andburg was certain a team was out there working hard to solve the mystery. At least there was no loss of life. Greenland was sparsely populated.

All Andburg had to do was look out the window as he drove out into the tundra to confirm the sparseness and to know how desperate his situation could become. He was in a sudden and freak storm—a total white out, fierce and dangerous—and he had to rely on radar. He shouldn't be out in conditions like this alone, but he had no choice. There had been no snow bus waiting for him, a situation he found highly unusual. He still couldn't get a satellite connection with Dr. Smart, either, and had been in a low-grade panic since landing. Something was terribly wrong. The pilot had offered to go with Andburg to the substation, but after they secured another snow bus and Andburg had gotten a quick yet thorough tutorial, he was confident he could do it on his own. Besides, he wanted to make sure that he was in control of the situation. What if he had to cover up a disaster? He didn't want to have any witnesses. Besides, the snow bus was equipped with a state-of-the art navigational system. It was so self-sufficient it virtually drove itself and was built to withstand freezing temperatures and Arctic winds. Andburg opted to head out the hundred and fifty miles to the Arctic Circle alone. He knew the dangers, but was willing to take the risk.

Five hours into his nightmare, he was miserable and had to do everything in his power to manage his fear. Andburg was heading into an Arctic storm. Luckily, he had the radar. Without it, he'd be a dead man. As it was, he had to go much slower than he had planned, adding another six hours to his journey. Andburg gripped the wheel, took a deep breath, and exhaled a ball of fear and tension. He'd never been a smoker, but the pilot had left him a pack of Lucky Strikes. Andburg's hands shook when he licked the cigarette for luck, a trick learned from an old military friend of his father's, and lit it. It took every ounce of self-control not to stop driving, curl up in the back of the snow bus, and fall asleep into frozen, certain death.

Andburg pointed the vehicle into the vortex of white. He continued on and on, staring into a nothingness that could kill him. There appeared no up, no down, but rather pure white groundlessness. The bus shuddered each time an Arctic gust ripped in from the north. He'd had some close calls before, but had always felt fate was on his side. Andburg had grown accustomed to being golden. He'd never questioned it, or imagined that his luck might one day run out. But the further he drove into nothingness, the further he felt from luck. To make matters worse, from the corner of his eye he continued to see a harsh glint, which produced a deep and unshakable chill. He looked over at the seat next to him. Empty, as it had been each time he'd caught himself looking. Or was it? What was that? A blade, or more accurately the edge of a scythe occupied the seat. After three hours of experiencing such optical tricks, Andburg finally began to believe that death was his copilot.

He tried driving faster, but had to bring his speed down lest he roll the vehicle. He allowed himself another glance at the passenger seat. He was certain that if he looked just right, just quick enough, he'd catch the full image and not just the light and shadow of form. *Shit. I'm going to die. I can't believe that I'm going to die. This is so unfair. I have work to do. I have important work to do.*

The only thing keeping him going was his determination not to leave behind a legacy of folly and destruction. He refused to go down in history as a loser, a buffoon, a misguided, foolish man. What would his father say if he were still alive? That shouldn't matter, he knew, but somehow it still did. Andburg kept a tight grip on the wheel and drove at what seemed like an unbearably slow pace, inching forward, blind, but with unwavering trust in the equipment, determined to make it. *I've been in worse jams.*

He thought about that time in Rio during Carnival when he'd just turned twenty. He'd met a hot Brazilian woman on a brown sugar beach. He'd never seen a woman fully naked in full daylight out in public.

"But I'm not naked, boy. See, these are my panty under-bottoms." She towered above him like a goddess, and parted her legs just enough to show him.

He'd been too shy to look. "I believe you."

She was there to exploit his youthful embarrassment. He was there to forget the mistake he and Mona had made. She'd gained his trust; it hadn't taken much. He'd believed her about a great number of things, including *I mean you no harm*, and *everyone here does this—it's Carnival. Why are you being difficult, boy? Do you not like women? Do you not like me?*

The trap had been set. She'd plucked him from the beach, set him up for her drug lord cop to crack him open as easily as a fresh coconut. He was inexperienced, separated from his friends, and susceptible to exotic flesh. From the beach to a back alley door, a single room, a single bed. He fumbled forward. He was scared but determined. His hand felt like fire when he touched her. He only got that one good touch, but it was enough to create a lifetime craving.

"Do you mistake my wife for a whore!" The door slammed against the wall. Before he could sit up, he'd been clubbed and bound. A phone was brought into the room. His price had been set. It was the last time he'd ever call his father for anything.

You got yourself into that mess, son. You know my position on that. Tough love.

Andburg gripped the wheel just a little tighter.

"Can I make another call?" he'd asked his captors in a demure and exhausted voice.

There was silence.

Andburg understood enough about South American culture to understand what that silence had meant. No father worth his grain of salt would have handled the crisis in such a way. There should never have been a request for a second call. That silence was pity and disbelief. The father of a friend had stepped up to the plate, and for that reason he was set free for one-third the price, cut rate instead of cut throat. Andburg began his climb towards greatness with the undeniable understanding that his life was a bargain—worth less than cost.

He had returned to his hotel, back to the airport, back to the States, and never looked back. Andburg kept his focus on positive thoughts and that alone brought him a long way. For several years, however, he had tried to find a woman like that—an exotic death gem—to prove that he could survive anything. He never found her, not until he met Tracy.

As Andburg drove on, his mind's endless flicker turned to his life with Tracy, showing him a slideshow of love and hate. They'd begun benignly enough. She managed a bakery in Albuquerque while in law school. He managed a Los Alamos lab and was credentialed with security clearance. There were a whole lot of things he couldn't share and wouldn't even if he weren't a government secret. She liked that right away. Andburg wasn't sure why he was drawn to her. She made perfect pastries. He asked her what her secret was.

"Control."

There was something in the way she'd spoken, powerful with conviction, or perhaps it was the way she wore her hair that day, loose and wild, that made him fall. She was a paradox, and he was intrigued to know more. She felt just dangerous enough to be fun.

"So what do you do?" She'd finally spoken to him one day as if she suddenly decided to notice.

"I'm a Super Hero."

"Don't most men believe that?"

"They may, but they don't have the right clearance badge."

"Show it to me," she demanded.

She leaned across the counter, held the badge in her hand studying his photo, and then flipped it over.

"We have the same birthday." She stood up and looked at him. "Gemini. Cosmic twins."

"What does that mean to you?"

"Depends on which twin is out."

"I would like to ask you out."

"Not sure you want to do that."

"How come?"

"Because I like you."

She turned away from him as she loaded a cart. He admired her muscle definition. She reminded him of sculpture. A dish fell from the cart and shattered on the linoleum.

"Suit yourself." She looked at him dead on—didn't blink—and he saw that she *was* crazy. She scribbled her address down on the napkin tucked under his coffee cup. "I want you there at four o'clock. I want to see your tights."

"Dear Tracy," he addressed her like a post card that he wished he could write. "I really tried to please you, but I guess I never could. With us there is very little difference between kindness and abuse. I know that feels like freedom, but we always took it too far. I never meant to hurt you so badly."

They were both capable of something so much more, but couldn't sustain it. That made Andburg miserable. He knew his ultimate dream of deeper connection was there, but neither of them knew how to safely deal with the abuse that they had suffered as children. That's why he and Tracy continued to return to one another. The known reality was much safer than the unknown. Andburg had tried numerous times to have a healthy and loving relationship, but he got tired of failing and deep down he really never wanted to hurt any of those other women. There was no room in other relationships for his wounding and their helpless willingness to love him. At some point, no matter how hard he tried, he became mean.

"God!" Andburg looked over at the empty seat. "I promise that if I ever get out of this alive, I will get clean for good. I promise to leave Tracy alone so that we can both be free."

As Andburg drove head on into the storm that never let up, diligently following the little red blip of a blinking dot—the honing beacon—he began to hallucinate. He saw before him not the flat whiteout of the storm but rather a moving tunnel of nightmare images, flashes of his life. Not the good bits, but the shadowy, painful parts, the ones he worked on his entire life to bury, to hide, to forget. His mind began to shatter. There was absolutely no hope for perfection. He saw the little boy who'd been locked in the bathroom for several hours: punishment for wetting his pants. He saw that little boy curled up in the bathtub willing every tear away. He saw that same little boy—a little older—pushing a kid down the school steps for the same crime: crying. *They say you're a bully.* His father had hung up the phone, undid the buckle of his pants. Andburg was again in the family garage, bench-pressing away the pain. His first Miller, a brown bottle on the shelf within reach. *Good job, Son. You made State.*

Andburg heard his father in an endless loop. At the time, Andburg was already winning awards for math and science. While others praised him for his fine mind, his father continued to belittle him. Those words were hollow. Andburg had learned that praise was always chased with an impressive dose of verbal abuse. Andburg bench-pressed and was numb. Numbness was an effective strategy of strength.

Andburg, I'm pregnant.

How do you know it's mine?

Andburg, please.

She had been so beautiful with her red hair and shame. She had been young, too. Underage? Mona had been a foreign exchange student who had lived with them for six months. She'd been fourteen, he remembered now, but she'd never protested—not really. And it had only happened once or twice. He hadn't even known what having a baby really meant, but he knew he had to keep her silent no matter the cost. He'd given her a thousand dollars—everything he'd saved up. She took the money. She promised. She sobbed. He had handed her a Kleenex. *It's going to be all right, don't cry.* Her older sister arrived the next morning. Neither girl had said a word. The tentative closing of the door boomed in his head. He had never heard from her again. She'd honored their bargain.

"God, I am such an asshole! I guess you know that already," Andburg spoke to the ever-present nothingness. "I wonder if she kept that kid? I'm going to find her. It's time. As soon as I get back, I will make it right."

The tunnel took a turn, and every boogieman Andburg had ever created in his imagination flashed by, but didn't scare him. He'd seen them too many times before. Down the tunnel he continued. Another rapid turn and he found all of his insecurities waiting for him. Out of all the images, these were the ones that frightened him the most. He had carefully stashed them away in the deep recesses of his mind, and now they were loose, sounding the alarm of his many failures. With nothing left hidden, he experienced a sudden flood of release.

The final horror was Andburg's greatest failure of all: the destruction of the landmass. He saw in vision all that lived, now drowned, dead and gone. They washed by with horrific clarity. Dogs, cats, donkeys, bloated cows and horses. There were people by the thousands with bloated faces and swollen bodies like balloons inside of their tight sheaths of clothing. Eyes wide open, they stared at him as they swooshed by. Andburg began to scream, and he didn't stop until the next visual turn where he was buried in the deep dirt—safe, warm, and dry, far removed from the bloodless faces—their death, his fault.

Andburg was just falling into the feeling of safety, enchanted by the love song of worms, when he realized they were burrowing into the depths of him, which meant he too must be dead. He turned to the seat next to him; the now familiar glint of light did not disappear. The light came from the blade edge of the grim reaper's scythe. This time, he finally grasped the entire form. Death grinned as if to say, *Oh, come on now, don't take yourself or so damned seriously.* Instead, he just said, "Whatcha think?"

I tried to be good. All I wanted in life was to be a good little boy. For the first time ever in forty years, Andburg did something that was surprising. He wept. He wept for himself and for his child who might or might not still be. He wept for the whole dammed mess. The tears against his check were hot and they reassured him that he was still alive. He whispered in a quiet and demure voice, as if God might still be listening. "May I please get a second call?"

Chapter 56

"Anteaters definitely have OCD," Bambi said and she and Noah leaned against the railing and watched one compulsively pace the length of the exhibit, sweeping its extended appendage along the cracks and crevices of its containment. The anteater had coarse fur, like a porcupine without quills. It had a long thin head and a bushy tail. It looked a bit like a stick broom with legs. It swept and paced, swept and paced. It was exhausting to watch. It was so exhausting, in fact, that the other anteater was fast asleep.

"It looks pretty zonked out." Noah said.

"Yeah, he looks zonked out to me, too"

"Why do you think it's male?"

"Because he's letting the female do all the worrying."

"Maybe she's just more neurotic, and he's tired of telling her it's going to be all right, more ants are coming."

Bambi pinched Noah on the arm. "Hey, now."

"Come here." Noah hugged Bambi. "I love you. "

"You know I was teasing you about that anteater being male. I can't really tell."

"I know. I can't, either."

She kissed him. He grinned back at her.

"I think that's the ugliest animal in the zoo!" A woman said as she caught up to her three boys. "I mean, there's something about its nose. Creeps me out. You are ugly," she called out to the pacing anteater. The boys giggled. One boy, the youngest, picked up a pebble and threw it at the anteater. "U-G-L-Y. You ain't got no alibi." The pebble harmlessly ticked off the wall. The anteater never looked and the sleeper didn't stir.

"You really shouldn't throw rocks into the cage," Bambi said. She tried to be as nice as possible.

The housewife gave her an angry look. "Come on, boys, let's keep moving. It's getting near lunch."

Bambi turned to the anteater. "I think you're cool. And I think you're beautiful and unique." She looked at Noah and sighed. There was so much sadness in her heart, along with unexpressed rage. "I should have yelled at that woman and her little brat. Why didn't I? We're such an arrogant species, and some of us are crueler, dirtier, and uglier than any animal could ever be."

"You're cute when you get angry, Bambi."

"Noah, I'm serious."

"I know you are. How could you not be? But it's not in your nature to yell at some misguided stranger. You don't even know her."

"It is my nature, Noah. It is very much in my nature."

"What would you say if that woman was your client?"

Bambi's face softened. "Tell me of your suffering." She paused and smiled shyly, a bit embarrassed.

Noah remained silent.

"I know, I know. She feels ugly on the inside, and has an unconscious anger toward men."

They both looked over to the anteater's long phallic nose, and began to giggle.

"Feel better?"

Bambi blushed.

"Where would you like to go next?"

She thought for a moment. "How about the butterfly pavilion?" She paused. "Do butterflies poop?"

"I don't know. Let's go to the BioPark and find out."

"Shouldn't we go back to the front office and see if they're ready to open the cages for us?"

"I think we have a bit more time. In forty minutes, we're supposed to meet the attendant at the large bird exhibit for the keys. We have plenty of time for butterflies."

"Okay, then, shall we?"

***

This is a perfect day, Bambi thought as she held Noah's hand. They strolled the zoo like they were on a date. He put his arm around her. She leaned into him. It reminded her that she was in love, a great and satisfying feeling. She felt full, and she was able to let go of her unexpected misanthropy. Her heart was open, and she felt herself radiate positive energy into the world. There was so much to be thankful for, especially if she and Noah were going to have a baby. She hadn't felt the same since she'd returned from Christ in the Desert. She hadn't told Noah, but she'd stopped menstruating, a sensitivity to smell had caused her to be ill in the morning more than once, she was tired, and her clothes were getting tight. She didn't need EPT to know the signs. There'd been plenty of opportunities to get pregnant, but Bambi kept thinking about that day in the monastery when she had been immersed in light beings and celestial dust. She'd felt the changes in her body soon after that experience. The notion of a divine conception was beyond her imagination, but something extraordinary was happening.

"What are you thinking about?"

"The sky."

The sky churned, dark and gray, no rain, the calm before the storm. Bambi looked around. Everything was in its place. Families everywhere, large and trailing, small and clustered. There were whisperers and loud ones. Others were coupled like Noah and her, some were same-sex, and, once in a while, she caught a glimpse of a serene and solitary face. So ordinary was the day, she imagined life was normal, free from fear of imminent disaster.

A young mother strolled by with a baby carriage. Bambi caught herself peering in at the swaddled child with pink lips and checks, eyes wide with wonder. She felt a pang in her heart as she caught herself peering into a second stroller and then a third. In each face, she saw a brand new miracle. Deep down, and very secretly, when she looked at Noah's face she tried to imagine the face of their own child. *I want a baby*. The thought startled her. If she was pregnant, it would be a welcome surprise. "What's wrong, sweetheart?"

"What will happen to the children?"

"Let's just do what we came here to do," Noah finally whispered after a long pause. "We have to trust. What else can we do?"

"This knowing is a curse. I feel so sad right now. Being around all these people and animals—and babies—I feel helpless and insignificant."

"Do you want to leave?"

Bambi shrugged. "Yes, but no. You're right; let's just do what we came here to do."

Bambi remained silent, trying to find the center of her loving again. It was there, but was floating suspended in unshed tears. She noticed that others were noticing them as the cute, but odd, couple in the matching white painter jumpsuits. She laughed out loud. When Noah asked her what she was laughing at she shook her head. She didn't know how to communicate any of it. Her emotions were unstable. "Just ignore me."

He squeezed her hand.

"Look, Noah. We made it. Here is the Butterfly Pavilion."

"Let's find out if butterflies poop."

She smiled as he opened the outside door. She read the warning: *Please, keep doors closed.* She opened the second door and they entered a netted space, warm, moist and filled with flowers and wonderful smells. It took some time for her eyes to adjust to the fluttering movement of the butterflies. When she saw the first one, her heart soared. The delicate being had such a mighty power to uplift her spirits.

A sacred place, she didn't wish to speak. Benches were tucked near flowering bushes. She pointed and they walked over and sat. They settled into the stillness, waited, and watched. She meditated on the butterflies' delicate movements: glide, flutter, for a split second land only to lift up again in an epiphany of breeze. These temporal creatures tickled air currents, made visible life's fragile threads, air as spirit. Every butterfly had gone through the same process, liquefaction within the chrysalis, the struggle to break free back into material form, and into flight. The entire process was amazing, the span so short lived; no wonder the ancient Chinese had crafted poems around the mystical creatures. She vaguely remembered one, something like *the life of men is like the dream in a butterfly's dream.* She was young when she first read it and hadn't understood the poem at the time; it stuck in her mind only because she wanted to figure it out. Now she understood it all too well. This life of man was as temporal as a dream. A butterfly lit on her shirt. She looked down and tried not to breathe.

"Have you ever heard of the butterfly effect?" She asked Noah once the butterfly danced away.

"Something to do with random synchronicity?"

"When a butterfly beats its wings…."

"It creates a tidal wave on the other side of the ocean." They finished the line in unison.

She nodded slowly. "Small changes drastically affect long-term behaviors of a system. Over time, even a butterfly can effect a change in the world. Can either cause a tornado across the world …."

"Or prevent one."

A butterfly landed in Noah's hair, and they both remained very still. Once it returned to flight, Noah stood up, reached his hand out for Bambi. She gracefully took it.

"I guess butterflies don't poop."

"I hope this won't be the last time I see one."

They left the pavilion. Both were somber. What would the world be without the butterfly? Bambi inhaled deeply, troubled. "The merry-go-round? That's what I need not to remember the pain. I want to live all the happiest memories of my childhood. Noah, can we ride the merry-go-round?" She sounded like a little girl.

"Anything you want, baby," he said knowing there was little he could do to comfort her. "Anything."

Chapter 57

It was beginning to rain when Ione slipped into Ma Shepard's good-sized tent, closely followed by Tabani. Ma Shepard sat cross-legged in one corner, still and shapeless. Ione could barely make her out so thick was the incense and sage. There was a fire pit in the center; the warmth was comforting. Ione found a spot on a deep red rug and sat. She reached her hands out toward the glowing rocks. Tabani sat close to his sister. Ma Shepard was reading the flat green pattern of sage leaves spread out on a brightly colored woven cloth called a mesa. She had literally created a tabletop for the gods, and in turn, because the gods felt welcomed, they spoke to her through the patterns in the leaves. The readings that Ma Shepard had given during counsel, translated through her brother, were intriguing in their accuracy. She didn't even look up at Ione, so focused was she on the pattern before her.

Ione took long observant looks around her. She had been inside numerous times; something was different. Perhaps because it was the first time the space had not been filled with youthful energy. Ione noticed symbols—almost celestial in their constellation—traced with pinpoint accuracy in white ink along the upper circumference. They were difficult to make out because the smoke was thick, but the last of the afternoon light cut through the approaching storm provided some illumination. Ione was well versed in ancient symbols. Some she recognized, but others were foreign. She was thrilled by the mystery and made a mental note to ask Tabani about them.

She looked over at him. He was beautiful the way ravens are beautiful when they come into the world in human skin. His nose was beaked, his hair was bluish black. Although he resembled his sister, who was hardy, less delicate, her complexion ruddier, he seemed to be a different species altogether, someone belonging to the air. The combination of the two was earth and sky. His eyes were closed, and he seemed to be resting. She was attracted to him, yes, but a lost song within her reminded her that the male gaze no longer saw her in youthful splendor, a flower to be desired. The secret for a woman to age gracefully, she had long ago discovered when the last of her hot flashes had fired her pure again, was to shift the locus of power from beauty to wisdom. Ione closed her eyes, too, and began to settle, a deepening into the warmth where the troubles of the world seemed light years away. She observed her desire until it became ephemeral like a memory. Then she let it go. Andrea's gray eyes flashed in front of her inner gaze. There had been *desire* there. Ione smiled, cherished the experience of being wanted, and then released that, too. The bird-like quality of Tabani's voice stopped her from drifting off to sleep.

"The rain has returned."

"Yes, I hear." Ione calmly said without opening her eyes.

"Ma Shepard and I have petitioned spirit through prayer. Through our prayers the rain was staved off so the ship could be completed. The ship is complete."

"I know."

"The rains return."

Ione nodded, eyes still closed as she enjoyed the soft ticking of drops on top of the tent.

"There is a quickening now."

Ione took a deep breath and centered. She opened her eyes and prepared herself.

Ma Shepard caught Tabani's gaze, and Ione could see that deep and profound communication was taking place. Ione knew Ma Shepard was capable of speaking but chose not to. Ione wanted to know why. Her curiosity slipped away as soon as Tabani turned to her and began translating.

"First, to answer your questions." He pointed to the symbols. "Two great cultures simultaneously created these images. Most of the symbols you recognize are common in Navajo and Tibetan mandalas. These are representations of the earth from the last millennium and were transmitted into the collective. The ones that you don't recognize have only come into consciousness within the last ten years and are to be guarded by the first peoples until the time of reckoning. These have been shared among the indigenous peoples within five centralized tribes, and only during ceremony. They are the symbols for the new millennium."

Ione glanced up and saw a circle with four lines in the center.

"That used to be the medicine wheel, separating the four directions. The lines no longer divide. They are parallel, as shall be the peoples brought together from the four directions. Some of these symbols also represent the star people who will now take a more active part in course of the earth. The earth has been awakened and is shedding her mantle. They will assist in healing the trauma of rebirth."

Ione listened intently.

"My sister also wants you to understand that she does not speak because the act of silence allows for a purer message."

Ione had done many silent retreats, and she knew this to be true.

"Now, she says you must be vigilant and strong. The ark is not your destiny."

Ione caught her breath. She was prepared to die, but there were parts of her mind whose sole function was to keep her strong and fast to her life no matter what. She had not imagined herself not on that ship.

"You will not die. You will be a vanguard. Many will be called. Some are already here; others will join you on the way. Those who make it will find you. You must leave in the morning to prepare the way."

"Where am I going?"

Tabani pointed to one of the constellations. Ione realized that what she had been seeing was a star chart.

"Memorize this. You will lead, but you won't be alone."

"Who's coming with me?"

Tabani looked over at Ma Shepard and they both stared at the tent's opening. Ione could hear the followers drumming in the rain. "They will join you like children. They will be strong and they will listen."

Ione could feel the truth in her body. They would take shelter in the mountains, just as the story Ma Shepard had read to them during the sweat lodge had foretold.

"Where's the ark going?" Ione suddenly thought to ask.

Ma Shepard smiled and spoke simultaneously with her brother. "The fifth dimension where the offspring of humans will marry into a league of angels, and time will no longer be bound to gravity. They will call their father Noah, and their mother Gaia."

"Have you told him that?"

The prophets were silent. Ione took their silence as meaning *no*. She also took it as the end of her reading, though she had a hundred logistical questions and concerns. But she knew they were merely the messengers, so she thanked them and she left the warmth of the tent with a heavy heart and trudged in the rain back to her tent to prepare herself for when she had to lead, following the star constellation that she had memorized. She could hear the Tribe playing music, singing, and celebrating. There was a lot to celebrate. The rigging was up. The ark, the cradle of the new millennium, born of the sweat of human determination and the shadow of the fallen divine, was ready to set sail, carrying the codes of the entire planet, into a whole new dimensional reality. Ione wished, just for a moment, that she would be able to travel with them.

Chapter 58

It's magic, was Bambi's first thought when she saw her very first merry-go-round in the Stockton, California, mall. She was six.

"You're going to love this," her grandmother had said.

Underneath the glass ceiling to sky, the restored vintage ride was the most beautiful enchantment Bambi had ever seen. The beautiful animals, brightly painted and trimmed in gold, were exotic—even the horses, who had carved flame-like manes. There were scenery panels—hand painted landscapes. The lights! The lights made the carousel appear as if it were floating. Bambi had stopped in her tracks.

"Look, honey. Each of those animals is hand carved. Pick out the one you want."

Bambi couldn't speak. She couldn't imagine picking out just one.

As they approached the head of the line, the carousel operator noticed the little girl staring at the muscular black horse with the red and gold saddle, its neck stretched up toward the blue, blue sky beyond. "That horse," he said, "is called Stargazer."

"Which one do you want?"

Bambi looked over the carved selection. This merry-go-round was much smaller, less dramatic, but no less enchanting. She found her black horse again and pointed.

"Okay, let's get in line," Noah said.

Bambi looked over the heads of children who were all under four feet. "Noah, I've changed my mind. We're too big to get on that ride, and we don't even have children as an excuse. Let's forget about it."

"Bambi, it's okay. Don't be embarrassed. Let's go."

She reluctantly stepped in line, but she didn't look at the carousel operator when he took their tickets. They rushed forward to claim their animals. As luck would have it, no one wanted the dark horse. Noah took the flying pig next to her. The carousel started to move, and Bambi's inner child came out and she began to have fun.

"Not so bad, huh?"

"Thank you," Bambi said. "You know, I think this would be a better world if more adults visited their childhood wonderments and didn't let embarrassment get in the way." Then she stretched her arms way up and felt the freedom of that reclaimed child-like joy. She giggled.

Noah smiled, enjoying her pleasure.

As the carousel turned, Bambi got a glimpse of a shadowy figure peering at her from the corner of the building where the snow cones and tickets were sold. She stopped laughing. She looked for the figure again as the carousel completed another rotation, but it was gone. She was worried. What kind of man would be staring at her that way—she felt such malice from him. Was he staring at the children? She wasn't even sure she saw a man— or wouldn't have been, if it weren't for the feeling of danger. She closed her eyes and tried to reconstruct what she'd seen. He was heavyset. Something red. A beard? She thought about telling Noah, but he was enjoying himself now. She smiled at him and kept the feeling to herself. All too soon, the ride was over.

"Noah, I'm glad we went on that ride. It was fun."

"We needed that," he said, but he was distracted. He seemed to be looking over her shoulder and her heart jumped. "We must have let one out."

She spun around and saw a beautiful butterfly gracefully fluttering over the turnstile and just above the heads of the children in line.

"I think it's coming over to us. I think it's going to land on you, honey."

"Noah, don't be silly."

"Stand still." He reached out and held her hand.

They watched as the Monarch—Bambi was sure that a butterfly with black veins and those deep orange wings and spots could be no other— fluttered closer. It was a large specimen. Bambi estimated its wingspan would cover her palm if it landed on her out-stretched hand. She held her breath as it approached and passed over the crown of her head. Then it landed on her shoulder and moved down to the front of her shirt where it rested for a brief moment before moving on. "Thank you," she whispered.

"Bambi, look. There's something there. Don't move."

"What is it?"

"Not sure." Noah was leaning in closely. "It's an amber colored dewdrop."

She looked down at an amber colored dewdrop hanging on the fabric of her painter's suit. She was as excited as if she had been pinned with the crown jewels. "Noah, do you have something to put it in?"

He'd already fished out a small plastic vial and was carefully lifting the fragile offering with the flat of his pocketknife.

"Do you know what this is?" Noah held up the sealed container.

Bambi nodded. "Of course, Noah. It's butterfly poop!"

They cheered in excitement and hugged each other. "We got it! We got it!"

Several children looked their way and laughed.

"Come on, babe, let's go find the rest of the samples that we need."

"This way." She pulled his arm. She was pleased they had the butterfly's DNA, and didn't care where they went next. Any direction was fine.

She turned her head and saw him clearly. She didn't know him, had never seen him before, but the sight of the man triggered a strong reaction. Like a field mouse sensing the approaching shadow of the barn owl, her instinct was to run and hide. She was about to tell Noah, but something told her not to or they would both be in danger. She drew on her courage and inner strength to pretend all was normal, all was well. She did commit the man's face to memory. He had vivid red hair worn in a braid, a square jaw, no beard, and a heavy build He wore a bandana and a black T-shirt. She thought he winked at her, but he was too far away for her to be sure. She blinked, and when she looked again he was gone, leaving her with an unshakable feeling of danger.

"Hey, Noah, let's go this way." She gently pulled his arm, hoping that if they remained near crowds they'd be safe, and led him in the direction of a large crowd of birders. "That attendant must be in the birds of prey pavilion by now. He has the keys, right?"

"Oh, yes. It's time. Funny, I was just thinking about Dan. I haven't seen that funny birdman in a while, and, you know, I'm kind of missing him." He seemed startled by his realization.

"Okay, honey. Let's get going." She led him away, looked over her shoulder only once or twice while Noah continued to be distracted by thoughts of Dan.

Chapter 59

When Andburg awoke, he saw the blue white crystal patterns of snow in front of him and feathered on both windows on either side, light starkly broke through the cracks. He thought he was resting under a shroud, and he wasn't sure if he were frozen. He didn't feel cold. He didn't, in fact, feel anything, except contentment, something he rarely felt.

Andburg's mind slowly focused. *Where am I?* He remembered driving all night, collapsing only when he got to the substation, but it had been too dark and he had been too tired to get out of the vehicle. He'd been worried that he would get lost from the safety of the snow bus to the door of the substation. Now that he was more alert, he calculated that it must be afternoon. There would only be light for a few precious hours.

Andburg had to body slam the door twice before it gave way and he tumbled from the seat, landing in soft snow pack. He stood up with some difficulty and plowed through knee deep snow to the door. The substation was a welcoming sight. He still thought it odd that no member of the team had come out to find him. He choked back a feeling of dread as he brushed off more snow from the keypad and punched in the secret code. The double steel door clicked open. Andburg entered, much to his dismay, onto frosted ice. He heard something else activate, but he wasn't familiar with that faint beeping sound from deep in the interior. An alarm went off in his head.

"Hello!" Andburg called into the foyer, surprised by the force of, and fear in, his voice.

There was no response. Andburg wasn't surprised, but he *had* hoped he was wrong. He *still* hoped he was wrong. But the closer he got to the command center, the less hope he had.

He opened the second airlock and saw right away that the blinking red light indicated that the shell had been breached. He could hear Dr. Smart's distorted voice on an endless loop. This was truly hell frozen over. Andburg looked around, trying to locate the source of yet another beeping alarm, then almost wished he hadn't.

Two bodies were slumped over the central command panel, each with clean bullet holes gaping in the base of their necks. From the size and shapes of the bodies, he surmised that two of his A-rated team members lay before him.

Apart from the two bodies, there was no sign of another physical presence. He wondered what had happened to the others.

Andburg tracked the unidentified beeping to the back wall and galley kitchen. His gaze dropped to a spot on the floor just under the kitchen table, and one more of his questions was horrifically answered. He'd found Dr. Smart. Andburg stared down at the man who had once cut such a towering figure, and felt oddly at peace. This was a captain who had gone down with his ship. Dr. Samuel Smart was curled in a fetal position with his visor up. *Strange,* Andburg thought as he stared at the distorted blue, frozen face. His eyes were open and his lips were slightly parted as if he were still problem solving. Andburg understood that it took great effort to record while he was freezing to death. He wondered when the man had expired and if those had been live satellite reports or part of the conspiracy to betray the team effort. Only later, when it was much too late, would Andburg discover the true depth of the betrayal. Right now, all he had on his mind was to fix the damage, but first he had to discover what the damage was.

Andburg walked back over to the central command where the wireless audio was set up and pushed the eject button. He slipped the audio stick inside his parka, planning to listen to it in the snow bus, where he could slow it down and make the message clearer. When the sound of Dr. Smart's voice stopped, the only remaining sound was the steady beeping, which reminded Andburg of a bomb timer. He dismissed the thought. No one in the Twenty-first Century would use anything as crude as *beeping* to count down a bomb; there'd be a silent detonator.

Andburg crunched his way back toward the entry door where he stopped and stared into the gaping hole that went from the fabric of the interior clean through to the unchecked wilderness beyond. How could he have missed it? The breech was so big that Andburg's mind had not been able to comprehend until now. There had been an explosion and a fire. Underneath the ice crystals, he could see the charred scars of fire and smoke. And if there had been one explosion, there could be more. Andburg felt a renewed sense of urgency to clear the station, but there were still team members unaccounted for.

He searched the back rooms where each person had been given some privacy in a space roughly the size of a train berth. The bunk beds were neatly made and personal items stored in their designated places. Everything was in order. He found no other bodies, and not a trace of the two men still missing. Andburg was reluctant to conclude conspiracy just yet. It didn't make sense. They were government men, yes, but so was he, or he had been. This was clearly an end game.

At that moment, something primal surfaced in his psyche, and he went into survival mode. He would need food and water for the long trek back to civilization. He found a duffle bag and threw anything that might be useful into it: energy bars, bottled water, an emergency thermo blanket, a flashlight, and maps. In the built-in closet cabinet, he discovered a bottle of the best of Russian distilled Vodka. He looked at it for a moment, and was comforted. "For my team," he said, and took a swig before sticking the bottle in the bag. He'd save it for when they met again. He pulled the top cord to close the bag and quickly made his way to the entrance and out into the snow where he trudged back to the bus. He needed to listen to that tape. He suspected there'd be a great many answers on it. In his heart of hearts, he knew that he, too, like Socrates, would pick annihilation over shame.

Andburg fumbled with the tape. He fought his addiction and the growing awareness of the clean white bottle of vodka in the bag behind him. He was determined to survive this. He had come too far. He took a moment to settle before he could play the tape. He rewound and adjusted the speed. Dr. Smart's unfaltering calm voice filled the cockpit. Andburg focused on the information as Dr. Smart listed the play-by-play, facts recorded just after the explosion. Like Andburg, he had discovered his friends already shot. Dr. Smart left a detailed account up to the moment he perished. Then his voice faded into frozen silence. The most important single detail to Andburg was not the how or why, but the full revelation that the beeping *was* a bomb, and had begun count down the moment he'd entered his code in the keypad, the ultimate *fuck you*. Andburg began to laugh.

By the time he got a hold of himself again, he had to rewind the part that he didn't hear. What was that Dr. Smart had said about nuclear weapons?

"Likely a portable nuclear weapon. Perhaps several."

Andburg rewound it again and again. He heard it the same way the second time and the third time. "Overkill, you fuckers!" He leaned back, breathed deeply, and took a moment to think. It was hard not to take this personally. "Okay, okay, think, Andburg, think." There were some clues. It wasn't a silent detonation so that meant whoever left it had given Andburg a chance to problem solve. He was meant to find them. If he could find it, perhaps he could deactivate it. All he had to do was to break the code.

Andburg got out of the bus and headed back into the interior of the substation. He still had a chance to prove he was a super hero after all.

Chapter 60

As they approached the predatory bird exhibit, Noah again pulled from his pocket the list that Andrea had helped compile. Many of the animals had been crossed off, especially the large land mammals. Noah was surprised at how thorough they'd already been. They were waiting for shipments from a marine center in California for the larger aquatic samples. Dr. Roach had been very supportive with that endeavor, which reminded Noah that he needed to check in with the zoo's director about that shipment. Noah crossed off butterfly. He wasn't sure what to do about the other nine hundred thousand species of insects. Noah hoped that there were enough DNA samples in the organic material that he and his cohorts had gathered to create a proper mix of creation. He sighed. It was too much for him. He decided to concentrate on gathering the poop of the big birds, which was the exact direction Bambi was pulling him. She pointed to the zoo map where an endangered Andean condor was showcased.

Bambi was jumpy. Something had spooked her during the carousel ride. Noah tried to pinpoint what she had been looking at, but couldn't. As they passed the orangutan's cage, Noah drifted over to the plaque that read: Vanishing Animal going, going, gone. He looked at the cage's occupant, who was standing on top of a manufactured tree, pooping. Now you poop, he thought. The last time he had seen her she hadn't cooperated, and her handler had to bring Noah and Andrea a bag of shit before they left. He turned toward Bambi, but she was looking over her shoulder again and seemed uncomfortable. "She wouldn't poop last time."

"That's nice, honey." Bambi wasn't really listening. "Noah, I think someone's following us."

Noah looked. "What makes you think so?"

She shook her head. "I'm sure it's nothing, just my imagination." She looked miserable.

"Are you sure that you are okay?"

"Um-hmm. Can we just go and get our bird poop? We've already lost our birders."

"What birders?"

She sighed. "Never mind, Noah. Let's go."

Noah was concerned. He didn't know why Bambi wouldn't tell him what had unnerved her, or why she thought someone was following them. He caught himself looking over his shoulder, scanning the crowds.

They soon reached the bird of prey pavilion. As soon as they entered and saw the netted cages—as generous a space as the zoo could provide—they felt the oppression. These large birds would never fly. Out of all of the miserable birds, the Andean condor appeared the most unhappy, perched on a fake limb, hunched like a little old man. The bird had eight by twenty feet of space with a fifteen foot netted overhang and plenty of fresh food on the ground none of which it had touched. Noah had the feeling that it was waiting to die.

Noah and Bambi looked around for the attendant.

"Maybe we should go and check on him."

"Let's wait here for a moment. I'm sure as soon as we leave, he'll show up."

"I don't know, Noah. This place seems really isolated right now."

"It will be okay, Bambi—whatever happens. Let's enjoy this moment and try to cheer up our friend."

She turned to face the condor. "I wonder what it's like for you." The condor didn't respond. "His sadness breaks my heart."

"He's not just a bird; he represents a sacred trilogy of the Inca. The condor represents the upper world to heaven and the ancients revered him as well as the snake and the puma. This bird should have a two hundred mile territory. These birds are running on some otherworldly frequency. Did you know that sometimes a bird like this in the wild will fly up to a tremendous height and then plummet down to the earth like a fireball? Scientists have never figured out why."

"You know animals are incapable of committing suicide."

"Westerners think that way, but not everyone else does. Tabani was telling me how, in Peru, the Quechua tribes believe these birds are sacred beings, and sometimes show up in half-human forms during the most sacred ceremonies."

"Noah, I have something I need to tell you." She was worried that she'd never have another chance to tell him about their baby. He wasn't listening to her; he was looking at the entrance. Bambi's pulse quickened.

"Oh, it's Andrea," said Noah, sounding surprised. He waved.

"Hope you don't mind." Andrea was out of breath and seemed self-conscious when she walked up. "Didn't mean to crash the date, but I saw you back a ways and I've been trying to catch up with you. How's it going?"

"Fine," said Noah. "We've had a good day though we haven't gotten very far in gathering what we came here to do. We've been waiting to get into the cages. Bambi thought someone was following us. I guess it was just you."

Bambi shot him a hard glance.

"Wait no more." She held up the keys. "Apparently the director is gone and they're short staffed. It wasn't protocol, but I promised I knew what I was doing and wouldn't get attacked. I have this walkie-talkie if we should need an emergency staffer. They also told me there are some packages for us up front that we can pick up on our way out. It's our marine samples, but there are a lot of species missing. I'm sure of it."

"Thanks, Andrea. That's good work. I'm glad you joined us. I didn't realize that you wanted to come."

"Like I said, I had this feeling I needed to be here today. I didn't realize you guys wanted to come, either. I've been here since early morning."

"Well, I'm glad you are here. Do you know which key opens this cage?"

"Yep!"

They followed her to a side entrance. She unlocked the first of the double-gated door. The condor didn't respond, but Noah entered with reverence, as if he were standing before a great presence.

"You know, Noah," Bambi whispered as she followed him in, "I think all of the animals are sacred beings in their own way."

"Good point," he whispered back as he knelt down and carefully scraped off a sample from the side of the concrete cage—made to look like stone—and placed it in a small container and put it in his satchel.

"He likes you," said Andrea. She hadn't stopped staring at the statue-like bird. Noah thanked the condor and backed out of the cage.

"What else did he say to you?" Noah looked closely at Andrea whose face was transfixed.

"He says that all animals are grateful for our service to them."

"Aren't you going to relock to cage?" Noah said innocently.

Andrea grinned. "Best not ask too many questions."

"We can't leave it this way."

"Noah, let's just go," said Bambi, who was still jumpy.

Together, they focused on their work and soon had samples of all the predatory birds, including a Great Gray. Once again Noah wondered why he hadn't seen Dan. In an unsentimental way, he felt a little abandoned by his daemon.

They worked the rest of the day, making a final push to get the job done and managed to gather nearly all the zoo samples.

Still, so many species were absent. Noah felt responsible. He grieved for the ones he had not time or resources to collect. He knew, however, he was doing his best.

The last exhibit to visit was the aquarium. Andrea had insisted because there were some names not labeled on the aquatic shipment. She was certain there was no jellyfish listed though no one knew for sure if jellies even pooped. Andrea wanted to know, and she wanted to see the seals one last time.

Noah stood before the shark tank watching a very brave diver scrape the tank clean while sharks and sea turtles swam by her. *Now, that's trust,* Noah thought. With her back to the sharks, their eyes black as buttons, she showed no fear as she waved to the children. They seemed to love her as much as they loved the seals. Soon, a sizeable crowd had gathered and half dozen noses were pressed up against the glass.

Noah turned and smiled. Andrea, eyes closed, lightly touched an illuminated cylinder tank in the center of the room. Bambi was very still as if she held her breath. The jellies were beautiful: glowing specters of the deep. They had a lazy drape that was otherworldly—hard to believe that they carried an electrical charge so painful many swimmers had drowned.

"Look, Noah," Bambi waved Noah over, and whispered. "She's using Reikî!"

"It appears to be working," Noah whispered back. The jellies responded by slowly clustering near Andrea's hands.

"Wow," Noah said and Bambi began to giggle. "It's really working."

Before long, every jelly in the tank hovered close. Andrea looked over. "Good thing I'm not in the tank now."

"Do they poop?"

"It doesn't matter." Andrea grinned. "They don't need us. They'll slide right on out with the first wave."

"They're not worried about getting hung up on a door or something?"

She turned her face to the glass. "This feels good to them." She closed her eyes again. "The jellies aren't worried."

"Okay, last chance." Andrea shook her head and disengaged from the tank. "It's getting late. We should head back to the ark."

"I thought I'd see Dan here." Noah said still wondering what had happened to his little birdman.

"Don't worry about it. I'm sure he's fine," Andrea told him.

Noah laughed. "You're right. Let's head back."

Andrea said she would catch up with them. She looked very mischievous, and Noah didn't want to ask too many questions. He hugged her and wished her luck. He and Bambi walked all the way past the BioPark and were heading in the direction of the gift shop when Bambi suddenly sharply inhaled and stopped short. She grabbed Noah's arm. "He's here."

"Where?"

"Standing by the entrance. We can't leave this way."

"Who is it that we're afraid of?"

"The red haired man."

"What red haired man?"

"The man I saw at the merry-go-round."

"What?"

"Let's go!"

"Wait a minute, there's Andrea."

Andrea came running up, giggling at whatever great prank she'd just pulled off. "We have to go right now!"

"What have you done?"

"Tell you later."

They'd nearly made it to their loaded trucks, when they saw not just the red haired man who had frightened Bambi, but an entire motorcycle gang barricading the vehicles.

"This can't be good," Noah said.

"Talk to him, Noah," Bambi pleaded.

"He's not here to talk."

"Noah, honey, I know this isn't a good time to tell you, but in case something really bad happens, I want you to know that I love you and I—"

"I love you, too."

"Noah, I'm pregnant, and you'd better say something really clever because I'm scared."

Bambi began to cry. Andrea hugged her, but Noah kept an eye on the approaching danger. It wasn't his fault she told him *now* in the middle of a crisis. "Honey, I love you. Why are you crying? I love us having a child together. It's great! What do you need me to say?" Noah hadn't gotten very far when he felt a punch to his leg, an explosion of pain, and realized he'd been shot. In one heartfelt plea, he cried out for divine intervention. To his amazement, a blinding light appeared. It was the last thing he saw before he blacked out.

Chapter 61

He had two rooms to choose from. Andburg headed to Jonas' room. He rummaged through the built-in cabinet and each drawer. He threw everything on the floor and closely inspected all boxes for a possible false bottom. He was angry that he hadn't yet found the detonation device. It continued to beep relentlessly. "Shut up!" he barked.

When the closet was completely empty, Andburg turned his focus onto the mounted night shelf by the lower bed. Nothing but Jonas' Bible. How many times had he seen *that*? He knew that Jonas was religious, but no one spoke about it. This was, after all, a science team and Jonas' *private* life had always been an uncomfortable topic, especially for Jonas himself. Jonas had a fine mind. Who cared what he read in bed. Now the flaked brown cover stuck out like...well, like a Bible in a science station. Andburg sat down on the edge of the bed and cradled his head in his hands. *You little psychopathic prick. This is such a nightmare.* Andburg ran his hands through his hair and then scrambled through the book. It fell open in his hand to *Revelation* where Jonas had marked the pages with the slender red ribbon. Stuffed inside the pages were also photographs and a letter.

Andburg dumped the contents out on the bed. There were several photographs of a very beautiful woman. She had red hair, was vaguely familiar, though in three of the photographs her long hair fell into her face and her features were obscured. She sort of looked like that exchange student that he had remembered from his youth. Andburg sucked in his breath, so great was the shock. This had to be coincidence. No way could he be rediscovering his past here. In one photograph, she was holding a baby. A baby! He stared at the image for a long time. He flipped the photograph and in the corner there was her name, *Mona*, penciled in. Something very deep and uncomfortable stirred in the recesses of his memory. She'd kept the baby? Did that baby grow up to be Jonas?

Andburg opened the letter. There was not much there to indicate who she'd become, or where she'd gone that day she had left his house for the last time. In fact, Andburg had to read it a second time to realize that it was a suicide letter and this Bible had been left for her son who was ... Jonas! Jonas-the-betrayer — the man now responsible for global homicide.

Okay, you little bastard. Andburg pulled out the pocket knife that he had carried since adolescence and carefully cut away the Bible's backing. There, as he'd suspected, was an electronic coding panel, red digital numbers flashing a countdown. Seven of them. *Seven. Like the seven seals? Why would you do this?* Andburg knew that Jonas was smart, but he wasn't that smart, and there was no way in hell that he could have pulled this off alone. *Who are you working with?*

He turned his attention back to the highlighted passages of Revelation. *The Chosen.* This group *really* believed that they would inherit the earth, but why would they want an earth devoid of life unless they knew they could repopulate species after the destruction, after the flood. *Noah!* Noah was building an ark, a virtual storehouse filled with genetic material. Andburg had read about it on the Internet. He knew that his friend wasn't psychologically built for such religious fanaticism, but he was just stupid enough to fall for some smoke and mirrors by very crafty individuals who were. Andburg wasn't sure how they'd pull it off, but he now realized that no matter how close he was to creating an endless power supply for the entire planet, these guys had no intention of opening their club to the masses. Seven small nuclear bombs strategically placed along the polar shelves would raise ocean levels within twenty-four hours. Andburg saw the game plan in one horrifying crescendo, and he knew it was true.

Andburg took a pen from his inside pocket and began to read, looking for codes. He circled possible number sequences. He wasn't sure he was capable of cracking this—it felt beyond him—but he'd die knowing he'd given it his best. While he worked, his hand trembled slightly. He had to do something about that. He leaned over, pulled the bottle from the bag and took a sip, just enough to steady himself, then returned his attention to cracking the code. He was quick. He had to be. He cracked the first code and was on to the second when the first code spontaneously rotated, and scrambled again like a mutating virus. He went back to it, made one minor adjustment, and cracked the code again, but as soon as his attention was diverted, the code once again shifted. Andburg realized with a gulp of panic that these numbers weren't fixed and that they rotated in integer rounds. Okay, if he could solve them all in links of three, and if he was just fast enough, he could crack them and adjust them. He took one more sip from the bottle to steady his hand, determined not to slip, determined not to fail.

Chapter 62

"Chakati, Chakati." Ione heard the desperate cries to hurry. What was that language? Not Spanish. Tribal Quechua? Ione didn't know, but she knew they meant for everyone to make haste. She was just pulling tight the last strap across the watertight supply duffle. The horses were nearly loaded. She and the rest of the Tribe, which included an ever-increasing mass of people ready to flee to the mountains, would be gone within the hour. It would take them thirty-six hours at a swift pace to reach the place where they would be safe from the water. She had hoped to say goodbye to her friends, Noah, Bambi, and Andrea—especially Andrea.

Tabani had whistled shrilly earlier that morning, and hundreds of horses had come down from the mesa, everywhere there was the sound of … *hoofbeats*.

"Where did all these horses come from?" She had turned and spoken to one of the matted-haired boys. He grinned, and then ran toward Tabani, who was splashing toward the lead horse as it approached camp.

Loading horses in the rain was not easy. Tabani was very useful in directing, but breaking down camp took a long time. Ione wished that Tabani would lead them out, but since that wasn't the plan, she paid close attention, knowing that it would all soon fall on her shoulders. Tabani reassured her several times that they'd be fine, that the flood wouldn't kill them, as far as his sister could read into the future, so they shouldn't worry about the rain, but they must remember to dry their feet out at night. She wondered what kind of people they would be without the technology to keep themselves dry. There would be a return to a simpler way of life, of that she was certain. A cry for help interrupted her thoughts. She saw Bambi, waving wildly, and pointing at the truck. Tabani was gathering planks to make a stretcher. Ione joined him, and hurried up to the truck. Noah's leg was bleeding, but Ma Shepard was already administering an herbal healing bundle to the wound. Andrea tried to drape a waterproof poncho over Bambi, who was still trying to explain what had happened at the zoo. Bambi waved her away.

"There were twelve of them. Bad, scary men. Cruel men. We wouldn't have made it if it weren't for Dan, Noah's birdman friend. He just appeared as a flash of bright light and all of the bikers just disappeared. Gone, poof. Except for the red headed leader. He escaped. He's still out there. Somewhere."

"We're all right. We're all safe now," Noah kept reassuring her even as Ione helped the others get Noah on the stretcher.

"Good grief. I can walk. I don't need that."

"Noah, get on," Bambi said with exasperation.

Noah allowed himself to be helped onto the planks and was carried to Ma Shepard's tent. She was already beginning her incantations as she followed close behind, singing.

They all trooped inside, laying Noah close to the fire. Ma Shepard removed the makeshift tourniquet, took out a rattle, and began a melodic whistle as she commenced her healing ceremony, inviting spirit to come in and assist.

Tabani began to sway and then spoke. "Noah is fine. This is a flesh wound. It will not stop the unfolding of events." He opened his eyes and looked directly at Ione. "You and your party must delay no longer."

Ione looked at Bambi and then Andrea. Bambi shook her head. "Where are you going?"

"I thought we might wait 'til morning. I haven't said good bye to my friends." Andrea addressed Tabani.

Tabani closed his eyes. "I am sorry, but goodbyes are sometimes like that. We have no more time. The group is ready. You are ready. You must go."

"Where are you going?" Bambi said.

Ione shrugged. "To the Taos Mountains. We're supposed to secure some secret tunnels. Tabani says the mountain has been awakened and is cleansing itself. A virus is killing off those who dwell there now, but we have to make sure they're all dead and burn anything they've secreted on."

"Gross!"

"Not a job I would have picked for myself." Ione lifted up a small stick that was cooling by the edge of the fire pit. She used the hot ember to burn through a lock of her hair and passed the strand to Bambi. "Make a rag doll, and sew my hair into its breast," she instructed. "When you give it to your child, let him know he has a grandmother who loves him very much."

"How did you know?"

Ione hugged her. "Don't be scared. Every baby brings with it blessings for the future."

Bambi smiled and thanked her, tears on her cheeks.

"Remember, we will join you," Tabani said to Ione. "Look for us."

Ione smiled at Andrea, then slipped out of the tent to join the waiting Tribe. She took one deep breath. She was going on an adventure. That was what she'd tell herself every night as she faced the journey toward Taos. *I'm going on an adventure.*

One of the boys held her horse steady as she mounted. She mounted with little dignity. It didn't matter. She was on his back. She rubbed his neck, sent him a mental "Thank you for your willingness to carry me through the night." The horse was fat and gentle with a back strong enough to support her girth. Ione felt an instant kinship, and as they began forward movement, she had the feeling that everything was going to be okay. She took a long last look at the ark, knowing that all the people that she loved, her chosen family, would be on that vessel. *Goodbye. I know we will see each other again.* Then she faced north, looked up at the star pattern hanging in the night sky as Tabani and Ma Shepard had shown her. Like a good map, it was reassuring. Ione kept her eyes on the stars, her memory on the star map, and did not look back as hundreds of hooves thudded across the rain soaked earth as they traveled toward the safety of the awakened mountains.

Chapter 63

$$E=\sqrt{(pc)2 + (mc2)2}$$

[Where m is the rest mass of the particle and c is the velocity of light in a vacuum].

Dan was radiant in light, surrounded by star children, which gave him a great bird's eye view of events as they unfolded but made him powerless to interfere. He continued to watch Andburg desperately struggle with the equation. He was on the right formulaic hunch with Einstein's proof for quantum electronics, plugging in integers from the polar equations of logarithmic spirals. Dan was impressed he'd gotten that far, given he was Andburg and not Einstein. Dan could see where he was making a miscalculation, but was unable to assist.

Dan had been able to step through the dimensional space and time barrier only once, to save Noah's life, and only because he was Noah's daemon and so had tacit permission from the universe to interfere. He had completely covered Noah in light the moment before the bullet reached him, and had been able to redirect it from aorta to femur. Noah would recover. Dan had tried to help Andburg, too, as he struggled with the equation, but had met with resistance, an invisible barrier. All he could do was witness Andburg wrestle with the impossible. Despite the unfolding horror, all was unfolding according to divine plan, all players carefully chosen for their appointed roles. Dan felt himself pleasantly fill with effervescent bubbles until he burst into laughter. He let go of the attachment to outcome.

Andburg continued to work at solving a paradox that light could be both particle and wave. He had figured out that much, and was plugging in numbers for the ultimate proof without words—the spiral code for black holes. Black holes were portholes into time, and could serve as pathways for time travel. With time travel, there could be a reversal of outcome. It was a long shot, but at least Andburg hadn't given up.

Whatever the equation was, the closer Andburg got to solve it, the faster the codes shifted. He would plug in one set of correct numbers and all the codes would change again. It was slippery.

Poor boy. He almost had it that time.

Dan turned his head. Floating beside him was a star being who looked very much like Einstein. He was studying Andburg's calculations. *Oops, he lost it again. Just out of reach. I think he's trying too hard.*

Dan smiled. *I'm not judging at the moment.*

Good answer. Einstein took out a pen from his breast pocket and fired off a quick proof on the air in front of them. To Dan's untrained eye it looked a little like a football team's playbook. *He would probably like this outcome better,* said Einstein.

Your genius is lost on me, Doctor.

Nothing to get lost about. If those bombs don't go off then this won't happen. Einstein pointed to a picture of possibility, the birth of another dimension. It looked like a crystal flowering at a great rate. Then another crystal flowered from the center, and then another crystal flowered from the center, and then another. *And if this doesn't happen then this doesn't happen.*

Dan again looked at the equation. He didn't understand it, but he recognized beauty when he saw it. The star children were happy because they were about to go *home.*

What Andburg is working with is the very origin of time. This is a birth, not a death. What we have here is planetary contractions. To end it now we would lose this new dimension. What would you choose? Destruction and creation is the same thing.

Good thing I don't have to choose, Dan thought-spoke.

Good thing I don't, either. At least, not at this moment. Then again, every moment is a choice. We can choose probable outcome. We always get a split second to settle on a reality when we look at stars from one side. Then Einstein began to laugh and Dan with him.

They stopped laughing when the first nuclear bomb exploded. From where they floated, it appeared as a tiny pinprick flash. Then there was another tiny flash.

Einstein sighed. *That explosion is the end result of probable outcome.* He floated far and away, following an ark of probability where light was both particle and wave. He stepped back, winked at Dan, and waved once. *We will all be joining in this time, but don't despair. See? The star children are containing the destruction in a web of light. It's bad, but not as bad as it could be.*

The star children sighed when they saw the planet Earth, the Mother, shudder in her pain. *It is such a beautiful experiment,* they all said in unison. They began to sing again. Dan heard sorrow in their song. Had their singing been a lament all along?

Einstein was floating further away now. He stopped for a split second and looked back at the spreading cloud. *We have much work to do now. The water has broken. The birth begins. The star children will be descending soon.*

To Dan, it felt like the beginning of an eternity.

Chapter 64

"Eureka," Andburg screamed and fell to his knees, careful not to drop the bottle of vodka. He regained his balance and dusted away a small circumference of frost from off the glacier. There they were. He could better see them, about two dozen or so ice worms. He hadn't dared hope he'd find any.

"I love you." He leaned in closer and began to serenade them. "I love you. I love you." He felt himself getting cold. He took another swig from the bottle and in the sweet letting go he wondered what would come first: the seventh and final nuclear bomb explosion or freezing? He had tried his best to stop that first bomb, then the second, and then the third. They had all slipped away from him. He hadn't meant to fail. "Oh, well," he whispered to the worms. "What can I do now? The genie is out of the bottle. I think I almost cracked the code, but it was like a virus; as soon as I cracked one number sequence the numbers would change again. I've never seen anything like it. It's a new weapon. A smart weapon. Smarter than you or me. But that's okay, we'll think of something. How about another song?" Andburg sang *Amazing Grace*. He looked around and, damn it to hell, it seemed that Death had followed him all the way out here.

"Stop grinning at me. I really don't know what's so funny. If you insist on hanging out with me, I insist that you sing. No, no, I mean it. The worms don't mind if you're a little off tune."

He began to sing again, changing the words up some. *She promised me; before she died she would set me free, lived so long 'til her head got bald, got out of the notion of dying at all.* "I suppose you don't appreciate those words. I mean, who gets out of dying, right?" Andburg addressed Death. Death did not address him. Andburg grinned. "You realize I'm charmed, right? I am the golden boy."

There was no response. Andburg waited for the next blast. From his calculations, each explosion was set twenty minutes apart, and three of them would likely take place at the Antarctic. Seeing each explosion from this distance was a captivating experience. He felt far enough away to feel safe, and, in Andburg's hazy brain, the explosions were nothing more than test bombs. He could make that reality so. He'd seen plenty of test bombs, although none of them had been nuclear. He was now part of a very exclusive club.

The color of the ice began to deepen to pink and sea foam green. He looked up to the Milky Way. He could see the thin edge of the disk. It looked like a frosted bowl of glory. It was humbling to see the edge of the solar system, a reminder that there was so much more out there beyond the limitations of the human mind. Then he saw the Aurora Borealis break open, the gasses streak pink and green glow-in-the-dark trails across the low horizon.

Right on schedule, a rumble. The horrifying reality was not the initial blast, but rather the mushroom that peaked like an orgasm. From where he stood, he saw it hang, frozen in air, in its own way beautiful as its center glowed blood red with its own life, a need to consume.

Andburg scooped up a handful of ice worms, turned his back on the blast, and began to walk out on the tundra. He could barely see, but the glow from the ice gave him the feeling that he was walking on the moon. He forged ahead. With the clear sky above, he imagined that he could see the star points. They began to slip from their positions. He rubbed his eyes and lifted the bottle to his lips, only to realize he'd left it behind. Another star slipped, and then another and another, streaking across the horizon. There was light all around him. He stopped, dropped to his knees, caught up in the ecstatic thrill. In that moment, he felt every ounce of pain lift away. He felt remarkably light. Gone was the self-hatred, the loathing. He was free.

He looked overhead, and saw ethereal beings floating far above him, his pain body between them, hanging down like an exhausted suit. In a flash they were gone. Andburg felt complete and perfectly at peace. He experienced remarkable mental clarity: transcendence, no thought whatsoever.

"Within the alignment of this light, I forgive myself." He said it, and then again, "I forgive myself," with full conviction.

Light zipped throughout his body. Stars rushed in, balance was restored, and in an instant he no longer hated his father. He knew that the stars had come to remove the planetary veil, and to restore balance to all things, not just him.

His thoughts were interrupted by the Siren's ocean song. He cried listening to the harmony of her perfect voice. He knew then the reason sailors jumped overboard.

In the distance, the sound of cracking shot along at a great speed Andburg could not out run. The Arctic shelf opened up beneath his feet and he fell, holding tightly to his handful of worms.

Chapter 65

"The best laid plans of mice, men, and stars," said Charlie, looking through the glass darkly of his video camera while spying on the goings on of the rebellion. Those star-beings were preparing the way for The Global Child. He didn't know yet who would play *that role*, but he knew that whatever *it* was it hadn't arrived yet. Something celestial had impregnated Bambi. The stars were singing praises. He couldn't believe that the stars wanted to send one of them through again. Nobody had asked him, but the definition of insanity was to do the same thing and expect a different outcome.

He returned his attention to his viewfinder. How quickly events could change. Remarkable. The star children were already pulling open the fabric of space, activating a porthole, an entry point into the fifth dimension that they had newly created. They had also encased the nuclear explosions in light, thus containing the destruction. Not enough, however, to stop the flood. Silly Andburg, he thought he could figure out how to reverse time, to control wormholes, to save his beloved earth? Charlie smiled. The earth would be fine without Andburg.

He knew why the star children were making their attempt. They were not ready to give up on their pet project: human beings. They were breaking the space-time barrier between material and substance by collapsing dualism. They wanted to create a place where consciousness had fewer distortions and increased fluidity. The higher frequency would rejuvenate the planet. With the eventual return of DNA blueprints, Earth would become a utopia.

This rebellion was naïve at best. He should know; he'd been the original anarchist. It was the nature of the shadow to separate itself out. They would find this out for themselves in time.

Charlie tried to peer into the tunnel that the stars had lined with their own light bodies. They were preparing the way for Noah and his ship, but he could see nothing further. Charlie shifted his view back toward the planet and watched the Earth tremble, her rotation tilted. The ocean drew back and raised its arm for a mighty counter blow. Then two separate tsunamis radiated from the poles and he watched as the construction of civilization washed away.

"Wow, wow," he kept repeating as he look at the terrible unfolding.

"Bye-bye, cruel world!" Charlie laughed with glee, anticipating seeing Noah's whole damned plan just…wash away. They'd never make it to the ark in time; the destructive wave was moving much too fast.

Charlie knew that Noah's third test was about to be set in motion. He had to transcend the illusion of death. How crippled would he become when he saw Bambi and his unborn child dead? No mortal man had been able to pass that one thus far.

Charlie saw Bambi in his close-up. She was glowing beyond the blush of pregnancy. For a moment, he questioned his motivations. Now that he had twins, he saw himself and Tracy creating an entire army of dark angels. There was nothing he could do about that questioning now. He was committed to his part, and unexpected sentimentality could not get in the way of the final outcome. The orders had already gone out. His most loyal henchman would find her. He always did.

Chapter 66

Noah woke to the sound of loud snorting He lifted his head, listened, and tried to identify the animal. Noah slid his arm from underneath Bambi's head, kicked the sleeping bag down, and crawled over to the tent flap, pleased that he was able to move. "Animals!"

"What, honey?" Bambi said, still groggy. "I let the dogs out earlier. They were barking something crazy last night. Didn't you hear them?"

"I guess I didn't." Noah pulled the liner around his waist for modesty and stepped out of the tent into a light drizzle. Zoo animals were everywhere.

If this hadn't been Noah's reality, he would have sat back and laughed at the lunacy of the remaining people running around in the mud, attempting to corral animals who scurried every which way.

Noah was shocked at the sheer numbers of life forms. He had no idea how much weight the ark could bear, or what they were going to do for food and water. A tapir, sensitive to Noah's glance, froze for a moment before returning to its frustrated rooting.

"Where did they come from and how did they get here?" Bambi poked her head out of the tent.

"I don't know, but I suspect Andrea had something to do with it."

"Where is she?"

"I don't know, but I'm going to find out."

"You might want these. That liner is pretty thin." Bambi held out a set of Noah's clothes wrapped in a plastic poncho. "Noah, I can't find that butterfly sample. I've looked everywhere for it. Do you have it?"

"No. I gave it to Andrea. She was supposed to get it aboard the ship. I'll ask her about it. I'm sure that it's on the ark." Noah dressed, kept as dry as he could, slipped on his sandals, and went toward the heart of the chaos. A chicken scrambled over his feet. The boy chasing it nearly collided into Noah. Noah caught him by the arm. "You'll never catch it that way." The boy flushed. "Let's find Andrea," Noah suggested. "She can probably talk the chicken on board. Have you seen her?"

The boy shook his head, but pointed to Tabani, who was yelling out orders. Noah marched over. "Tabani, wait, wait, wait. I have an idea." Tabani stopped in mid-sentence. He seemed distressed and perhaps a bit angry. "Listen, this seems to be Andrea's doing."

"Do you know where she is?"

Tabani caught his breath. "She left last night. She's not back yet."

"Did she say where she was going?"

"She had a friend to get. Looks as if she went back for her friend plus some at the zoo."

"It would appear that way. Let's just wait for her to get back and coax everyone on board."

Tabani took another deep breath. He looked hard at Noah. "We're running out of time."

"Yes, Tabani, I know, but what else can we do? I'm not even sure we have room for all these animals."

Tabani looked back at the ark. "Of course we have room. They aren't all going. The ones who do will help you survive. All we know is that the time is now. You should already be aboard."

Noah saw the concern in Tabani's eyes. It was true. Time was running out.

"Noah!" Tabani put his hand on his shoulder like a brother. "Be brave. This ship is the vanguard of something beyond imagination. You and your progeny will become something more than this in the marriage of scientific mind and indigenous knowing. Imagine a freedom never before known to life, no separation between thought, creativity, and materialization. This has been prophesied for thousands of years. You and Bambi are about to witness the birth of a new calendar, of a new age. You are a pilgrim heading into a world of new belief. Do you know how fortunate you are?"

"That's not helping!" Noah spun around and headed back down to his tent. He had a child on the way. Everything was different. He almost tripped over a piglet that was resting in the mud. "Damn pig," Noah muttered under his breath.

"You have to go. It's your duty! The baby can't survive this planet. If you stay you will lose everything." Tabani called after him. "The star people and the animals want to be free. Free them, Noah!"

Noah stopped in his tracks. How did everybody seem to know about the baby? There was a lot of responsibility on his shoulders. He looked over at the ark, a fully equipped ship—a miracle. It was ready to go, and, he realized, so was he. Noah couldn't see them from where he was standing, but he knew that those carvings were there: the human history, outcome lying in the balance. Tabani was right. He did have a duty, and he had agreed to complete it. The Tribe had already loaded and labeled the samples. They were kids, but they didn't seem afraid of the future. They were all ready for an adventure into a new world.

Someone had led a giraffe aboard. It was rubbing its fuzzy nubs on the edge of the upper deck. A dove, seemingly out of nowhere, suddenly landed on Noah's shoulder, cooed, and began grooming his hair. It tickled. He laughed and released the sound of hope into the air. Noah looked in wonder. They were wonderful. He couldn't communicate with them like Andrea could—at least not yet—but each of them had a personality, and had an important role on the planet.

A change was under way, a lying down of the lion with the lamb. Noah could feel it, and it was worth setting sail for. All he had to do was get on board, take the next right step.

He wanted to talk things over with Bambi. She was always so level headed, and he valued her perspective. He walked back to the tent, but she was gone. Where was she? He returned to the ark and boarded. He looked out over the deck. She wasn't chasing animals. Noah looked back at Tabani, who was still trying to direct animals toward the ship. "Have you seen Bambi?" Noah hollered, but Tabani couldn't hear him.

"Have you seen her?" Noah asked the piglet who had followed him. The piglet didn't respond, either. Noah turned his gaze to the sky. He saw the dove approach and land on the ark. What was the story of the original Ark? Forty days before land was seen again?

"Andrea!" He saw her duck behind rigging. Noah sighed in relief. Not only would loading the animals go much smoother, but she would likely know where Bambi was. However, it was unlike Andrea to hide from him; that she seemed to be doing so gravely concerned him. Noah shook his head. *Okay, the way to find out is the first step forward.* Noah squared his shoulders and fortified his heart with courage. He needed to find Bambi.

Chapter 67

"We can't leave without it!"

Andrea nodded and tried to remember if she'd even seen the butterfly poop.

"Andrea, you have to think faster. Everything else is loaded on the ark. Where is it?" Bambi sounded tired and exasperated.

Andrea refocused her thoughts and retraced her steps. She had gone to the zoo last night. It was dangerous and risky, but she had to make sure that she had let out all of her friends; she couldn't just let them sit in cages with an approaching flood. A very dramatic event, emptying out a zoo, and she'd secretly wished someone had been there to see her do it.

It had taken her hours. To her surprise, many of the animals already knew. *How did you know? It's in our memories to run to higher ground.* They each chose a destiny—some of them chose to make a run for the mountains, others chose the ship and followed Andrea home. Some arrived faster than she could drive. None of the marine life came, of course, but they assured her they would be fine. Just to be on the safe side, Andrea unlocked their tanks so that when the water came they wouldn't be trapped. Then she left.

Andrea would have preferred to reach camp before the animals so that she could have explained before the chaos hit in the form of quaking, snorting, and grunting. But she'd been delayed. She'd stopped at Noah's house, just to make sure that none of the samples had been left behind. Nothing seemed to have been overlooked.

"The vial. Surely you remember it, black with a blue stopper. Noah said you put it in your pocket just before he was shot. Do you think you left it in the truck?"

"That's it. It must be in the truck!"

"Let's go get it."

"Not that easy."

Bambi frowned. "What do you mean?"

"The truck's out of fuel. I left it at Noah's."

"What do you mean the truck's out of fuel?"

"You know, like when I turned the key in the ignition, nothing."

"Nothing?"

"Yeah, nothing."

"I have to go back."

"Don't. Time's running out."

"No. I have to get it."

"You can't. It's too late. Look. The animals are loading now. The supplies have been stocked. The hatch has been battened down. If you go and the flood waters come, then nobody can save you."

"What kind of world will it be without butterflies? I intend to get those butterflies on board."

"Please don't go, Bambi. Let me go." Andrea pleaded with her friend, but Bambi was already climbing down the rope ladder with amazing speed and agility. Then she was on the ground and pulling a donkey close.

"Let me go," Andrea called again. She was met with silent resistance. "At least take a horse, for God's sake."

"I don't have a horse. I have a donkey!" Bambi managed to mount the animal. She dug her heels in, the donkey turned around and, to Andrea's surprise, began *galloping?* They headed toward the muddy road that led to Noah's.

"Let me go with you?"

"Stay here, Andrea," Bambi yelled over her shoulder. "You need to make sure the animals are safely on board. Stay here and finish loading, and don't tell Noah. It will only upset him. Don't say a word. Promise!"

Andrea was at a loss. She could see Noah heading her way. *Upset him?* That was an understatement. Andrea whispered, "Good luck," as she watched her friend disappear over the bend, intent on bringing back the amber, dewy drop of butterfly droppings.

Andrea took one look at Noah, then scaled the ladder and ducked behind some rigging. She knew she couldn't lie to him, of all people.

Chapter 68

"A donkey? She left on a donkey. What was she thinking?"

"The butterflies."

Noah was already on a horse. "I have to go get her. If I don't return, you take charge of the ark."

***

Andrea's dump truck sat with the passenger's door wide open and a donkey tied to the door handle. No Bambi. *She must be inside.* Noah dismounted the horse, called her name, took a quick stride to the open door, and stopped short when he stepped into a puddle of water. If he hadn't been so worried about Bambi, he would have heard the sound of a motorcycle in the distance; he would have heard the continuing drip of water from the faucet, the drip that they'd never been able to fix. All Noah could think was *why isn't she right at the door?* He called out to her again and turned his gaze toward their bedroom. His heart stopped and his breathing quickened. He didn't want to go in. Something wasn't right. Water and mud were everywhere. It was silent, damp, and dark. "Bambi!" When she didn't answer him for a third time, panic seized him. He moved forward through the shallow water.

A strange glow filled the room. He saw her face down on the floor in about six inches of water. Surely not enough to drown. Noah stared at her as denial set in. Who was that woman? She had a red silk cord around her neck. Her face was pale. Her lips were blue and slightly parted. She looked beautiful and grotesque. In fact, she looked too beautiful to be dead; yet there was no life there, either. It was like staring upon the face of a mannequin, a Bambi mannequin. She couldn't be dead, but she was. And with her, their unborn child.

His body snapped into action and he hauled her up to the bed. He untied the cord. Her hand was closed. He pulled open her fingers and removed from her tight grip the vial of butterfly sample she had been so desperate to retrieve. A world without butterflies. Now a world without Bambi. He put the blue-topped vial in his own breast pocket. Then he got onto the bed with her, straddled her body, and pressed both hands down hard just under her sternum. He began to perform CPR, thrusting down in rhythmic beats. One, two, three, four, one, two, three, four. He stopped and checked for signs of breath, his ear against her cold, wax-like nose. No sound. His breath was met with chill. He wouldn't believe it. He couldn't afford to believe it. He continued to thrust his fists against her chest, again and again, blows in a fight with death. "Don't you leave me,

Bambi! I won't stand for it!" He only stopped when he realized that he was beating a corpse. She was not coming back to him, and that was not her fault. He collapsed, frightened. "Fine." He made up his mind. He was going to stay with her. He would wait for the great wall of water, or whatever was to come. His mind and heart turned coldly away from the divine. He suddenly had a newfound understanding of Charlie. "Go to hell," he yelled at the fading halo of light now receding to the corner of the room. He had a strong and distinct feeling that he was not alone. "I'm not playing."

"Noah, you must return to the ark." It sounded like children's voices.

"Why take everything from me?" he cried out in agony. "I want the whole universe to hear my suffering."

"Anything worth living for is worth dying for, and then living for again in deeper soul, so you know there never was a death. You must return to the ark."

"Bambi is dead. My child is dead. I have nothing, so fuck you! I will no longer be your human hand puppet!"

The voices echoed and deepened until Mother Earth herself spoke to him. "Have faith, my son."

He looked down at Bambi's face. "I'm not leaving her!"

There was a tap on Noah's forehead. There was a tingling explosion of rainbow light, and then a vision of the world's suffering: disease, death, hunger, murder, rape, pestilence, anger, fear, rage, jealousy, and slavery in all of its forms. Then he got a glimpse of Bambi's death. He saw the moment she gave up life and moved into Other.

"Noah, mine is one life among many. It's all our suffering, and all our compassion. You must trust that, despite appearances, all is well in the world."

"How can you ask me to trust?"

Noah saw a blue-robed woman with rosy checks and ruby lips. She cried. Her tears rolled along the contours of her checks, and sparkled as they slid down. Though she had been standing in the center of the darkness for a long time, a feeling of peace radiated from her. Hers were not tears of sorrow, but rather tears of compassion. Here was a profound and nearly overwhelming presence of love. The tears collected, pooled, and flooded the earth with mercy.

"You are not the only one to suffer. You have a duty, a purpose far greater and transcendent to the suffering you believe is currently heaped on you." Then in the gentlest voice he clearly heard, "It is time to heal."

Noah was too tired to fight. "I surrender. I will return to the ship, but I'm bringing her back with me."

There was a long silence. "Bambi is not in that shell. That shell will slow you down."

"I cannot leave her."

The voice and the vision were suddenly gone, but there was a vibration frequency that resonated in his chest cavity. The pain grew in intensity until Noah cried out in agony and grabbed his chest. He thought he would throw up. *I'm having a heart attack.* But he was wrong. His heart chakra had blown open. All the emotions he had ever tried to block flooded back, and he had no choice but to feel his world of pain. The emotions threatened to swallow him whole.

Noah glanced out the window at the gathering storm clouds. There seemed to be an edge of darkness encroaching, and he knew instinctively that he had to hurry. He rolled Bambi's body in the bed covers, lifted the weight in his arms, and carried her to the donkey. He laid her across the animal's back and remounted his horse. Horse and donkey set off across the wet terrain, back to the ark.

As they galloped forward, Noah looked down. Rivulets of water began to rise up over the animals' hooves. They splashed onward. In the distance, he could make out the ark. Quite unexpectedly, the wind kicked up and carried with it whirling clouds of paper that danced in the wind before dropping into the water. Flashes of white debris floated like tiny islands. One scrap became tangled in his horse's coarse mane. He grabbed it, flipped it over. It was a photograph, a snapshot. They were all snapshots, thousands upon thousands. He held between his fingers a fragment of ordinary life: A little girl before her birthday cake. A grandmother wearing a tailored dress. A couple picking flowers.

Another gust of wind ripped these fragments from Noah's hand, swirled them topsy-turvy just out of reach. More photographs stuck to him, and he collected as many as he could before each was eventually ripped away. Moments caught in time: a birth, a dance, a funeral—all impossible to hold onto.

Noah heard a loud sound somewhere in the distance. He looked, but couldn't tell where it was coming from. By the time he saw the surge, it was too late. It broke over him, knocking him off his horse. He saw Bambi's body tumble away. He inhaled the water. There was another gasp and then a flash of light. *Dead.* Death was much easier than he imagined it would be. All he had to do was surrender to the light, and the light was everywhere.

What happened next was dream-like, and Noah would never remember much of the fading details. What he would one day tell his grandchildren was that a celestial being, in the form of a condor, appeared to him, mighty and unveiled, half bird, half man, with powerful wings that churned up the water. Noah felt himself yanked upwards. Breaking through to the surface, he was greeted by light so intense he was blinded. But not before he saw Dan holding Bambi's limp body, no longer wrapped in the bedding. "Holding" was the only word he had for her levitating in light. He had never seen his daemon so beautiful, so transformed, and so magnificent. So reassured was he that she was not lost to him forever that he succumbed to the darkness of his mind shutting down.

Chapter 69

"He's back," Andrea said triumphantly as Noah came to, a little soggy, a little groggy.

"Bambi. Where is she?" Noah tried to move, but realized that he was wrapped tightly in a blanket. His dogs were licking his face. He was happy to see them, glad that they had made it on board. Andrea was crouched over him, grinning. She had just seen a miracle. She didn't answer him immediately. She couldn't. Noah had just enough mobility to turn his head, and he recognized Bambi's form similarly wrapped. It seemed that they were both prepared for burial at sea. Noah remembered, and a wave of vomit curled in his stomach. He turned his head away.

"No, no, no, Noah. That's not me." He heard her soft, sweet voice, but he thought his mind was playing tricks on him. Yet there she was on her knees, already working to unwrap him from his chrysalis.

"See, baby, I'm not dead. I'm not dead." She was crying, and her tears fell on his cheek, but still he had a difficult time believing. "I thought you were dead, too. But we're not. We are here, right where we're supposed to be." She held on tightly to his neck. "It's going to be okay. Dan broke some rules in getting you back on the ark, but it's going to be okay now. And we'll worry about all that stuff later."

Her heartbeat against his chest finally convinced him.

With her help, he stood up, shaky, and nearly fell; the ship was no longer on solid ground.

"Be careful, honey."

He held on to the rail and looked overboard. Water poured in from all directions, churned up, and muddy. It was a rough ride.

"Tabani says that the worst is not over." Bambi's brow was furrowed.

Noah looked around, dazed. He looked at the blanket that had been next to him. It was flat and empty against the wood deck. Only moments before, it had held Bambi's form. He couldn't tear his eyes from it.

Bambi smiled a knowing smile. "That wasn't me," she whispered again.

"What do you mean?" Noah found his voice, but it was weak and watery.

"Dan played a trick."

"I don't understand."

"I guess he learned a thing or two from Charlie. If Charlie could take my essence and fool you, then Dan could take my essence to fool that killer. As it turns out, air and stardust cannot be murdered."

"But it fooled me, too. Why did it have to be that way?"

Bambi didn't speak for a long time. She looked sad. "I guess if that hadn't happened to you, then this wouldn't have happened to you." She pressed her hand against his chest where he now had a transformed heart.

It was Noah's turn to be silent because deep down he knew she was right, but he didn't understand how she knew.

"Okay, you lovebirds. We need a captain. Looks like we're sailing into something that'll need navigational skills." Andrea held out a pair of old faded jeans for Noah. "You might want to get dressed."

Noah looked down, realized that he was naked, and quickly pulled on his jeans. "Let's get navigating."

"Aye, aye, Captain."

Noah stopped, realized that he didn't have the vial. The butterfly DNA had washed away. "Oh, no, Bambi … the butterfly."

She smiled broadly. "Don't worry, darling. I have it right here, compliments of a condor and an owl that we know."

Noah knew then that all was going to be well in the world. They were going to survive.

"Tabani says that we must brace ourselves because the wave that has drowned the world is approaching," Andrea said, obviously distressed.

"That wasn't the wave that knocked me off my horse?"

Andrea snorted. "That was the first surge. Tabani promises that the second surge will more powerful, a hundred foot wave or larger."

"How are we going to survive that?"

"I don't know."

Noah looked pensively out toward the horizon.

***

Several prairie dogs stood balanced on the ship's rail. Their job was to signal the first threatening vibration, and they took the responsibility seriously. One of them—the shortest, fattest one, snapped his head up when he heard the humans talking. With all due respect to Tabani and his sister, the coterie had been the first to warn about the second wave. Not that the dog minded all that much; he just hoped that in this new world order credit would be given where credit was due. That's why he, the other nineteen, and a litter on the way, were on the ship. Fifty had stayed behind; they could not imagine life beyond the zoo. Personally, he hadn't had much faith in the zoo since his second month, but he'd never had the freedom to choose until now. He still believed in this system's change, even if he was compelled to keep a sharp focus on that shining owl perched on the stern. He had to get used to this treaty of kindness. Could he trust it? That was yet to be seen.

There was a tingle in his toe. He froze. There it was again, a tremor, and it rocketed up his spine in a way that indicated speed and a fast approach. He barked and stomped his foot. He and the other prairie dogs scampered down and ran as fast as they could into the storage box that the colony had taken over as home. Inside staring out through the slats, what they saw would go into their nightly tales. Human feet began to run back and forth, back and forth, and several barked out orders. They could have sworn they were looking at big prairie dogs in action, and the colony was amused.

Chapter 70

In a moment of calm, the undertow receded. No one was sure who first saw the second surge, but when Noah caught sight of the fast moving crest, a white line across the vast horizon, he became aware of how still everything was. Tabani heard the animals down below deck press together.

The crest grew in size, a wall of water. The ship listed. Then the wall became a mountain, as though an entire ocean pouring out of a bowl. The sight was both terrifying and awe inspiring. Andrea put her hand on Noah's arm. It was surprisingly heavy. She was screaming, but he couldn't hear her. It was as if they were already submerged. She pointed to the cabin stairs, and, when he did not respond, slapped him hard on the face.

With that, time began to catch up to itself. Noah felt the shadow of the curled wave begin to collapse, and self preservation became paramount. He ran because he had to keep up with his legs. Andrea was right beside him. It was unlikely they would make it below deck—too late—but they dove. In the split second before he tumbled down the stairs, he caught sight of Bambi standing on the upper deck, her hair dripping with spray and her arms stretched upward, a priestess taming the wave. Her belly glowed. Then the glow intensified and, as it grew in brightness, a constellation of firefly-like lights suddenly appeared. A hundred at first, then thousands, millions, more than the mind could comprehend. On closer inspection, Noah saw that they were tiny stars. He thought about his vision in the desert when he'd seen his first light being. They were all like that one, but so many more, and they zipped about until they quite suddenly merged, forming a wall of light, a barrier to the wave. Seamlessly, the wall held back the water. Noah was reminded of an old film sequence he'd seen as a child: Moses parting the Red Sea. *Cool* was the most profound thing he could think to say. Once, such Hollywood tricks seemed implausible at best. Now, he knew nothing would ever be implausible again.

"Wow," Andrea said.

Noah said. "The wall held."

"Come see!" Bambi hollered.

Andrea and Noah climbed to the upper deck, and stood by her side. Noah finally saw what she was pointing at, the mouth of a gapping tunnel ahead, to which the ship was pulled by an invisible current.

"We are in the river of time." Tabani appeared out of nowhere, followed by his sister, Ma Shepard, and a dozen or so others. "It flows into a fortified wormhole that the star children have created for our transport."

"It's beautiful," said Panda Girl, the only original tribal member who had not followed Ione.

Ma Shepard walked up and gently flattened her hand against Bambi's belly, which still glowed, but was no longer as bright. She said three little words, which everyone heard. "Welcome, Global Child." Then she began to sing a soft tune, a lullaby. Soon everyone was singing. The storm had passed, and they were still alive. Some were crying, all were grateful; nobody cared where the current would take them next.

Chapter 71

"Reality. It's all about where we choose to put our focus. That's the great lesson you will bring with you when this ship sails off into the sunset. Good luck to you," Dan said as he lifted off the ark. Where they were going, he didn't need to go. He'd already been inside the timelessness. They were going to be fine. The star children would make sure of that. He, on the other hand, was going to become an anchor star in a brand new constellation. Someone had to fill in the gap, and he'd always wanted that honor. Perhaps he'd get a fancy Latin name like Agnitio, meaning recognition and knowledge. He believed that suited him well.

"Dan, Dan…I'm going to have a baby."

"I know," Dan hooted back. "You've done well. Love is the only real purpose in life."

She smiled and waved. Noah had his arm around her. They were a beautiful couple. Everyone seemed happy. Even Andrea had a new friend, a woman strong and lively, who had joined the crew late. They were laughing and exchanging stories about refuse and sustainable energy. A half-colony of prairie dogs, stiff on the rail, looked out over the currents of this golden time. They carried the bloodline of pioneers. They saluted Dan.

The higher up Dan flew, the more he could see. A pod of whales and some jellyfish moved alongside the ark. They were beautiful to watch. They were finally free. It was good to be free.

"Dan, we have a chess game to start." He could hear Charlie's faint voice, and knew that he'd have to face what he'd done—someday. Saving Noah's life wasn't really cheating, he told himself. After all, the man had already chosen life over personal suffering, thus passing his third a final test. Technically, that had been the deal. *That's what Charlie gets for being too certain that there is no more mystery.* There was always mystery, and that's what kept existence so interesting and worth living.

The Tribe would be successful. Dan had fast-forwarded Charlie's time-machine camcorder to that chapter. He couldn't help it. He saw just enough to know that they would create something new and interesting down in those caves, and they wouldn't be down under for long.

He could hear the elephants trumpeting below deck, keepers of the collective story. Then the giraffes joined in with song. Their hearts were the largest hearts of all land mammals, the planet's collective heart. They held in their consciousness the unfailing eternal mother love of Gaia. They were Gaia, as was the dolphin, the goat, the cougar, the wolverine, the snake, the bird, the monkey, the cat, the bear, the rabbit, the deer, the prairie dog, the turtle, and the lynx—all of them, including all that they ate and all that they excreted. Many of them had chosen to stay behind because they loved her so much, although there was no guarantee for their continued survival. They loved unconditionally, and that love was worth the risk. For, they were all the eyes, and breath, and feathers, and teeth of the divine expression of creation.

To give all life a chance of survival—wasn't *that* worth building an ark for? Noah, Bambi, Andrea, Ione, Tabani, Ma Shepard, the Tribe, Dan, and the star children all thought so ... and so it was.

And so it was.

About the Author

   Patricia L. Meek derives her inspiration from mysticism, archetypal imagery, and the life and death struggle within the natural world.
   She was one of the winners of AWP Intro for Fiction, American Writers Program for the introduction of emerging writers in fiction and poetry. After earning an M.F.A. in Creative Writing from Wichita State University, Wichita, Kansas, she taught English composition and creative writing in Kansas, California, Utah, Louisiana, and New Mexico.
   Meek also holds an M.A. in Counseling from Southwestern College in Santa Fe, New Mexico, where studied transpersonal psychology and holistic healing practices, including Reikî and Noetic Field Therapy. This interest in the subtler forms of human consciousness led her to the high Andes to learn the ceremonial and initiation practices of the Q'uero Paqos.
   She currently works as a therapist in Southern Colorado and frequently returns to her hometown of Baton Rouge, Louisiana.
   For additional information, please visit her website:
www.patricialmeek.com

ALL THINGS THAT MATTER PRESS ™

FOR MORE INFORMATION ON TITLES AVAILABLE FROM
ALL THINGS THAT MATTER PRESS, GO TO
http://allthingsthatmatterpress.com
or contact us at
allthingsthatmatterpress@gmail.com